THE DARK MAESTRO

THE DARK MAESTRO

A Novel

BRENDAN SLOCUMB

Doubleday
NEW YORK

FIRST DOUBLEDAY HARDCOVER EDITION 2025

Copyright © 2025 by BNS LLC

Published by Doubleday, a division of Penguin Random House LLC, 1745 Broadway, New York, NY 10019.

DOUBLEDAY and the portrayal of an anchor with a dolphin are registered trademarks of Penguin Random House LLC.

Library of Congress Cataloging-in-Publication Data
Names: Slocumb, Brendan, author.
Title: The dark maestro / Brendan Slocumb.
Description: First edition. | New York : Doubleday, 2025.
Identifiers: LCCN 2024032065 (print) | LCCN 2024032066 (ebook) |
ISBN 9780593687611 (hardcover) | ISBN 9780593687628 (ebook)
Subjects: LCGFT: Thrillers (Fiction) | Novels.
Classification: LCC PS3619.L645 D37 2025 (print) |
LCC PS3619.L645 (ebook) | DDC 813/.6—dc23/eng/20240712
LC record available at https://lccn.loc.gov/2024032065
LC ebook record available at https://lccn.loc.gov/2024032066

Book design by Nicholas Alguire

penguinrandomhouse.com | doubleday.com

PRINTED IN THE UNITED STATES OF AMERICA

1 3 5 7 9 10 8 6 4 2

First Edition

The authorized representative in the EU for product safety and compliance is Penguin Random House Ireland, Morrison Chambers, 32 Nassau Street, Dublin D02 YH68, Ireland, https://eu-contact.penguin.ie.

To Ian Hargis.
I can only begin to express how grateful I am to
have had you in my life for the past thirty-plus years.
Everything we've been through—from convocation, to
pulling all-nighters for Music History, to weddings,
to marching band, to SMOOTHIES, to a night in
the box . . . to, quite literally, saving my life.
I thank God for you, brother. Love you.

THE DARK MAESTRO

THE LAST CONCERT

THE FLASH of the FBI badge would wipe away, forever, his identity.

Until then, he'd been a musician, a cellist, a prodigy. Soon he'd be a fugitive, a faceless and nameless shadow.

But right now the musician known as "Curtis Wilson" focused on delivering—with all the passion and virtuosity he could muster—the infamous cadenza of Kabalevsky's Cello Concerto no. 2, op. 77. The Kabalevsky was all about passion: a sweet lament that builds, twists in on itself as the soloist breaks away from the orchestra, and explodes center stage to display his technical prowess and musicality. As much as Curtis loved the piece, it was a motherfucker, demanding flawless execution of complex fingerings and bowings, with rapid runs spanning multiple octaves. He'd spent months drilling each passage, day after day, before he could even manage to play it all the way through.

And now he would be onstage with the New York Philharmonic at Lincoln Center. *The New Yorker* promised that listeners would be "dazzled by this rising star's prodigious abilities."

Still, the audience had no idea what musical euphoria was in store. He had to make them *feel* it.

Which was why, twenty minutes before the performance, he wasn't in the greenroom—where the FBI had expected to find him. He later learned that agents searched for him while he sawed away in the bowels of Lincoln Center where the acoustics were better, going over the Kabalevsky's multiple octave leaps.

Once more and then I'll call it quits, he vowed, tightening his grip on the cello.

Ten minutes to go. Maybe he could run through the beginning of the third movement, right before the saxophone solo. Then again, he had to wind his way up through the labyrinth of stairways and corridors to get to the stage. And he should probably find a bathroom on the way. Pee and check his tie in the mirror.

A knock on the door, and it opened. "Mr. Wilson?" A tousled head with a microphone and a headset poked in. "Dude, you're impossible to find. You have like five minutes."

"I needed to go through this one more time," Curtis said, more defensively than he meant to.

"We need to get going." The stage manager pushed the door open, gestured with her head for Curtis to follow. "You need anything?"

"I think I'm okay." He followed her out into the corridor. "Although a pit stop would be a good idea."

"Okay, let's hustle then." She was wearing a Batman T-shirt. "There's a bathroom on the next level up. I'll take you the back way. It's shorter."

"You into superheroes?" Curtis asked as their footsteps rang in the stairwell. "Looks like you're more DC than Marvel."

She laughed. "I heard you were into comic books, but I didn't believe it. Yeah, you got me. DC all the way. But Marvel is cool." She hesitated like she wanted to say something further.

"Spiderman or Nightwing?"

"Nightwing," she said. "Better costume and not nearly the baggage."

"Check this out." Curtis paused on the steps and lifted a custom-made tuxedoed pant leg to reveal his Captain America socks. The red, white, and blue shield above his ankles would be front and center for the audience.

"Those," she said, looking back, "are seriously dope."

"You read the new issue of *Nightwing* yet?" he asked her. In minutes, he'd be center stage in front of a sold-out crowd, with the New York Phil, in Lincoln Center. This was an opportunity of a lifetime, and he should have been thinking about the intentions and emotions of Kabalevsky instead of Nightwing's costume. But there it was.

"No, haven't had time. I haven't checked my pull box. You?"

"Got it yesterday," Curtis said. "I ain't going to ruin it for you. It's good. I'm about halfway through." The latest issue of *Nightwing* slept half read on his hotel bedside table, a sheet torn from the hotel notepad marking his place. He was looking forward to finishing it tonight. Before Nightwing fought Blockbuster by the Bludhaven central library, Blockbuster had planted a bomb at the hospital. No way Nightwing could make it uptown before the bomb went off.

The next level up, she pushed open the door and gestured to a bathroom on the other side of the hall. He took the cello with him, laid it down next to the sink as he peed and checked his tie.

"What's your name?" he asked her when he shouldered open the door.

She was slouched against the wall, one hand cupping her ear. "Ellen," she said. "And we've really got to hurry."

He followed her up a narrow stairway, faintly lit, that wrapped irregularly up the wall. The higher he climbed, the more he could hear the music. The orchestra was in the final strains of Borodin's Overture to *Prince Igor*.

"Yo, so when I'm done we need to finish that Marvel/DC comparison," he said. The orchestra finished, and the applause began.

"Sure," Ellen said, opening a gray door marked "3." "Follow me, it's right around the corner." She shouldered open another door, and they were directly backstage. "You know," she was saying, "I heard you were cool, but dang. Yeah, I'm down. My roommate is a bigger dork than I am. She knows every character from DC, Marvel, and Image."

"I found my people," Curtis joked. It seemed unusually crowded with stagehands and other people, he thought vaguely.

From the shadows behind them, a man in a suit—looking more like a bureaucrat than a stagehand—was heading his way, eyes focused on Curtis. He had one hand in his lapel, and seemed like he wanted to speak to him, but right then Maestro Kastenmeier, hand outstretched, strode into the wings to escort Curtis to the stage.

Then the lights were dazzling, and new applause rose up.

He set up the cello, placed his calloused index finger on the string, and waited for the maestro's cue.

The orchestra thrummed to life.

Curtis would remember, with startling clarity, this last concert. There on center stage, with one of the great orchestras at his back, one of the greatest conductors cuing him in, and one of the most elite and extraordinary audiences on the planet at his feet, he burst the Kabalevsky open with a meaty pizzicato. He was in it.

He imagined a vast landscape, where rolling hills gave way to towering mountains. His cello painted the shadows circling behind the trees, a few faint beams of light glimmering in the twilight. Then the terrain turned treacherous. *All is not easy: there are obstacles to overcome, but we will do this together,* Curtis told the audience.

His bow played a long and sweeping open string. He milked every bit of the next note to give his trademark Curtis Wilson vibrato—the vibrato that the *New York Times* called an "eloquent tremor"—its full breath. He was in the zone.

When the allegro started, his head was down, shoulders raised, and he dug into the strings. The orchestra was right with him. He set the pace. He was in control, despite the music's borderline violence. He'd joked with someone during rehearsal that he devoured anarchy with his cereal every morning. After all, he was a product of Southeast D.C.

Then his cello's voice became an elegy, capturing the depths of human sorrow and yearning. It circled around the sound and taste of the word *loss.*

In the ache of unfulfilled dreams, the melody transformed again, burst forth with exuberance, and the orchestra swelled behind him as he led it to embrace his triumph.

All too soon, the music thundered to its glorious and terrible conclusion. In the final strains, he kicked one leg up, fully exposing his Captain America socks. The audience roared as they jumped to their feet.

Minutes passed as he bowed. A standing ovation. He took a breath—he didn't know how long it had been since he'd even breathed—and inhaled the audience's wild energy. They were feeding him oxygen, and life. He closed his eyes and bowed again.

Afterward, he searched his memory to try to find any indication of the FBI agents even then waiting for him. He remembered the man in the suit, eyes narrowed, coming toward him; and he mentally cataloged each aisle, hunting for some sign of a plainclothes policeman, arms crossed, staring malevolently down at him. As if this were *The Sound of Music*, and he were Captain von Trapp moments before the Nazis would descend on him and attempt to carry him off.

Out front he saw nothing. Just the glittering audience, hands raised in applause. A few ushers leaned against the back wall. Security guards manned the fire doors on both sides of the house.

Maestro Kastenmeier gestured for him to come forward and take a bow. The maestro clasped his hands warmly. "A triumph," he told Curtis. "Truly a triumph. I'm so glad they recorded this. I think it's going to go down in history as one of the best performances of the Kabalevsky. Ever. Daniil Shafran would be proud."

"Thank you," Curtis mumbled. No matter how many times people praised him, it still made him uncomfortable. He bowed again to the audience, thinking incongruously of the *Nightwing* comic book, half read by his bed. What quip would Nightwing spout off after a victory?

And then, finally, his final performance as Curtis Wilson drew to a close. The house lights came up. He shook hands with most of the orchestra.

He hugged the first oboist, a diminutive lady with still-flaming red hair. "You killed it, man," he told her. Elisabeth von Hohenberg was legendary, in her late seventies, and one of the greatest performers in the world. Curtis had watched her on YouTube hundreds of times, and had played with her three times before tonight. She'd told him after the last performance that they needed to have dinner sometime, but they hadn't set a date yet.

Now, still glowing with triumph, he threaded his way backstage. Ellen, the stage manager, clapped him on the back. Curtis meant to get her number so they could talk comic books, but didn't have a chance. He'd ask someone tomorrow, he figured. Meanwhile people milled around him, talking about his phrasing and the vibrato, and when the recording would release. At last he found himself at the door to his dressing room, opened it.

For an instant, he thought that the room was crowded with more fans in search of an autograph or a selfie.

But there were only two of them. A man and a woman. The man, in a dark business suit with a forgettable tie and polished shoes, was standing up, coming toward him. The woman, with Asian features, hung back in a gray suit, a string of pearls gleaming against her blouse.

"Mr. Wilson," said the man. It wasn't a question. He was tall, with old-fashioned seventies glasses perched on a fleshy face. The broken capillaries of a heavy drinker starred his nose and cheeks.

"Can I help you?" Curtis asked.

"I'm Agent Mitchell," the man said. "I'm with the Federal Bureau of Investigation." He flashed a badge that Curtis didn't read. Later, after those first blurred moments, he'd remember other details: The way the woman peered around Curtis to look down the hall. The shine of Mitchell's glasses, and how he'd said "Federal Bureau of Investigation," rather than "FBI."

"What—who—" Curtis began.

"You need to come with us. Right now. Please gather your—"

"What do you mean? I can't just walk out," Curtis said. "I've got a reception to go to. Who did you say you were again?"

"We're with the Federal Bureau of Investigation," the man repeated. And then, when Curtis must have just been staring stupidly at him, he said impatiently, "The FBI. Look, you're going to have to skip your reception. We're taking you into protective custody. Effective immediately."

"What—why did—"

"It's about your dad."

"What? What about my dad? Is he okay?"

"This is not up for discussion. You can't stay here. Grab your stuff. Let's go."

Part 1

IN THE TIME BEFORE

1

CURTIS

MISS JACKSON'S NOTE, folded into quarters, had been firmly attached with a safety pin to Curtis's navy-blue polo shirt. Five-year-old Curtis tapped it anxiously, peering down to make sure it had survived the trip.

His mama, who had picked up Curtis from school, leaned around him and pushed open the apartment door. Shouts poured out. Daddy's voice. Something shattered.

On the way out of kindergarten, Miss Jackson had tried to hand the note to Mama, but Mama put both her hands in the air like she was a bad guy surrendering to a policeman. She backed away from the note as if it had teeth. "Nuh-uh," she told Miss Jackson. "You need to talk to Curtis's daddy."

Miss Jackson had looked down at Curtis, and then at Mama, who was wearing a torn hoodie with her blue and purple gang necklaces. She was already edging down the block toward the bus.

"I'll pin it to you," Miss Jackson had told Curtis. "That way you won't lose it. You give it to your father and get his signature, okay?" Curtis didn't want to be pinned like a baby in a diaper. Miss Jackson didn't believe him when he told her he wouldn't lose it.

Now, as Mama let him into the apartment, the sounds of Daddy's and Larissa's latest fight battered at him. He just wanted to give the note to Larissa, so she could give it to Daddy, so Daddy could *get a signature*. Curtis wasn't sure what *signature* meant, except that nothing was as important as having one. Just thinking of the *signature* not happening made his heart hammer, and he thought he might cry.

Larissa and Daddy didn't notice that Curtis was back. Daddy was home early, and Daddy was mad and was walking around, yelling and throwing things—a fork, a Tupperware container, a dinner plate that exploded against the kitchen wall—and Daddy was saying to Larissa, "Dammit! I don't know what I'm gonna do!" and Larissa—who usually called Curtis and Daddy "baby" or "*papi*," smiling with those big white teeth of hers—was scowling right back at Daddy and saying, "Breaking everything in the house ain't gonna make it any better."

Daddy didn't usually act like this. Daddy was quiet and didn't talk that much. Usually, as soon as he saw Curtis, he'd do a big goofy grin and then they'd "thumbtouch": right thumb to their own forehead, and then tap thumbs with a "Hey man."

But today there was no thumbtouch, no "Hey man."

"He's gonna kill me," Daddy was saying. "That's it. That's gonna be it."

"You just have to explain it," Larissa told him.

Curtis turned to walk himself back into his mama's legs, hold on tight, but Mama pushed him forward. "Go on now," she said to him. "Go on." She patted his head and gave him a little shove. He was distracted, looking at Daddy, who had his head in his hands and didn't notice that Mama had shut the door without even giving him a goodbye kiss or a hug.

"Ain't no way of explaining that he'd understand," Daddy said.

Curtis checked the pinned note again, slipped off the backpack that Larissa had bought him special from the Dollar General, and went through the living room and down the hall without Daddy or Larissa noticing. He carefully closed the door to his room, to shut them out.

For a long time, Daddy and Larissa shouted and broke things.

He'd been hungry, but nobody came to check on him and ask him if he wanted vanilla wafers and a glass of milk, although that morning Larissa had promised them if he was good. His stomach rumbled. But the excitement of the day had worn him out, so despite the yelling and the smashing, he fell asleep.

Later, Larissa woke him up. The evening had turned blue and

shadowed. "Hey, *papito.*" She smoothed his hair off his forehead. "How was your day?"

"It was good," he said, stretching. "Here, you gotta read this." The note was still pinned to his shirt, even more crumpled than before. He'd fallen asleep with it tucked under his chest.

"What's this?" She unpinned it.

"Miss Jackson said I need to bring it back tomorrow with *signature.*" He said the word carefully, hoping he got it right.

She unfolded and scanned the page, frowning. "You know what this is?" She looked up at him and then back down at the paper.

Curtis resented that she could decode the patterns of the words and understand their meanings so quickly. He could spell his name, and simple stuff like *duck* and *run*. But that wasn't real reading yet. "It means that I get to play a musical instrument." *Instrument* was another big word, but that one he knew. "I get to pick it out. And then I get to play it."

"How come your mama didn't sign it?"

Curtis shrugged. "She said it was for Daddy."

"She did, huh? Why am I not surprised," she said, more to herself than to Curtis as she reread the note. "You want to do this?"

He nodded. "Opportunity to play a music instrument," he told her.

She read aloud, "The Delaney Foundation is offering your kindergartner the opportunity to play a musical instrument." A pause. "Did you memorize that?"

Curtis nodded again. A smile crept onto his face.

"And you wanna do it?"

Another nod.

"There's a meeting on Friday," she said.

"At seven o'clock," Curtis said. "Can you go?"

"We'll have to get your daddy to go. I ain't your mama, baby."

"Mama said she won't go," Curtis said. "She said daddy has to. Will he?"

"I don't know. I hope so. But we won't ask him tonight, that's for sure. He had a bad day."

Curtis nodded. He'd heard all the banging and yelling. "What happened?"

"Oh," Larissa said, looking away, "he came up short when he was trying to sell some things."

Curtis hated when they talked down to him and didn't explain precisely what they meant. "Sell what short things?"

"Oh, just some things," Larissa repeated. "Nothing you need to worry about."

Which made no sense, since Curtis wasn't, and hadn't been, worrying about short things. He shook his head. It wasn't important, not when *signature* needed to happen. "Can he signature now?"

"We're gonna wait on that," Larissa said. "We're gonna wait till he in a better mood."

"When he sells more short things?"

"Yeah," Larissa said. "When he sells more short things, he'll be in a much better mood. Now let's get some food into you and get you into bed."

Half an hour later, comfortably full of the hot dog and macaroni that Larissa had boiled for him, plus three vanilla wafers and a glass of red Kool-Aid, and now again curled up in bed, he asked her, "Where's that paper for *signature*?"

"I got it right here," she said, showing it to him.

"What you gonna do with it?"

"We'll keep it right here till tomorrow morning." She put it on the cardboard box next to the door, where she stacked his underwear and shirts.

"He gotta signature," Curtis told her.

"Okay. Got it." She looked over at him, and the dimple on her cheek flashed. "You want this real bad, don't you?"

He nodded.

"What kind of instrument you wanna play? You even know what an instrument is?"

Afterward, for the rest of his life, he never knew where the words came from. Perhaps he'd heard of saxophones and drums, but probably not the names of most of the other instruments.

And yet when he opened his mouth to tell her this, the word

came, whole and complete, from some part of himself that he didn't recognize.

"The *cello*," he told her, even pronouncing it correctly— although neither he, nor his father, Zippy, nor his father's girlfriend, Larissa, had ever seen the word, let alone said it out loud. "The cello," he repeated, liking the way the word sounded in his mouth, round and full and utterly delicious. "That's what I wanna play."

They started with cardboard instruments: heavy paper forms that Curtis assembled with blunt-nosed scissors, glue, and tape. His quarter-sized cardboard cello was already almost as tall as he was, so Miss Daniela let him keep it in a storage closet instead of taking it back and forth from home. In the evenings, since he couldn't practice his "cello," he worked on his bowing—holding a yellow no. 2 pencil parallel to the floor, four fingers pointing down and the thumb pressed against the back the way Miss Daniela had showed him.

"What you doing?" Larissa asked him one morning when he was using a spoon to practice his bowing. She leaned around him, pouring his Cheerios into a bowl.

"I'm playing," he explained. "This is my cello bow grip."

As she poured the milk, she kissed him on the top of his head.

In the weeks that followed he learned to count basic rhythms, then the names of the notes: C, D, E, F, G, A, B, and another C. Miss Daniela just had to show him once, and he could do the right fingers. He never made a mistake in naming notes or counting rhythms.

A few weeks later, the real instruments came in a U-Haul van. Miss Daniela stood in the cargo bed and read the kids' names aloud from the open back door. When she pulled out one of the biggest black instrument cases and said "Curtis Wilson," his heart almost burst with excitement. He was too short to take it from her, his little hands reaching up, so Miss Daniela climbed down from the truck and lifted off the case herself. She opened it for him on the asphalt parking lot as he danced around her.

Years later, at Juilliard, Curtis would play on fine instruments: Bergonzi, Amati, Testore, and many others. The wood grain shimmered as if lit from within; the fingerboards and details were sometimes inlaid with special woods, ivory, or mother-of-pearl. Seeing them, let alone touching them, would be a body blow, a punch directly to the solar plexus. But nothing, ever, punched him harder than the sight of that first quarter-sized cello, nicked and beaten up, its back scarred and its fingerboard discolored with faded black paint.

"Pick it up," Miss Daniela was saying. Around her, the kids stirred impatiently as they waited for their instruments, but Miss Daniela was watching Curtis. He could feel it. She seemed far away and unimportant. Everything—*everything*—in Curtis's universe lay cradled in that scratched and battered case, rested on the scuffed blue velvet.

He picked it up and—in the deepest sense—never let it go.

That night he refused to leave it at the school. Larissa had to haul the cello on the bus with them, and then bring it back to school the next day. Curtis practiced his bowings and his fingerings until way past his bedtime.

"You need to go to sleep, *papi*," Larissa told him.

He wanted to have the cello sleep in the bed with him, but Larissa put her foot down. Curtis compromised by letting her leave it on the ground. He fell asleep with one arm hanging down, his fingers caressing the cello's face and f-holes.

Miss Daniela told him that he had to practice every day, so soon Mama or Larissa—whoever picked him up that day—got used to hauling the cello on the bus back and forth to school. "You better start growing if you're gonna keep playing this," she told him. "I think it weighs more than you do." When he played, he had to sit on a dictionary to reach the bridge. But he practiced every single night, without fail, and on Saturdays and Sundays too. When Daddy or Larissa told him that he had to go somewhere or do something, he couldn't go or do until *after* practice, because that was what Miss Daniela had said.

But he couldn't play all the time. Larissa made him go out and play with the kids, especially the Bookers downstairs, or took him on errands with her. Never to Larissa's work—"that's not for kids," she'd told him.

Right before Thanksgiving, his mama didn't pick him up on Tuesday like she was supposed to. Miss Daniela had to call Larissa, who was working and had-to-drop-everything-but-it-was-okay-honey, she told Curtis. That night his daddy tried calling mama to find out why she didn't pick up Curtis, but he had to leave her a message.

The day after Thanksgiving, Daddy was waiting for Curtis at the breakfast table. It was first thing in the morning, before cereal, and he had the whole day ahead of him to practice his cello. Daddy was normally busy with his papers or his phone, but today he didn't have anything in front of him. Curtis sensed that Daddy had been waiting for him. "Hey, buddy," Daddy said, and raised his right thumb to touch his forehead. Curtis did the same. They touched thumbs. "Hey, remember how I told you how it's always going to be you and me?"

"And Larissa," Curtis finished for him.

"And Larissa," Daddy amended. "You remember that?"

Curtis nodded.

"Well, now it's just us three. Even more than it was. Your mama won't be coming around very much."

"Why not?"

"Well . . ." Daddy trailed off, looked over Curtis's head to where Larissa stood in the doorway, mouthing something that Curtis couldn't make out.

"Mama decided that she needed to live someplace else," Daddy said. "But that's not gonna change anything with us, okay? It's always gonna be us."

"Where's she gonna live?" Curtis asked. "When's she coming back?" Mama lived with two other ladies in an apartment building that smelled like fish and pee. He hated to visit. Hopefully Mama would move somewhere nicer.

"She's gonna tell me when she gets settled," Daddy said. "But everything is cool. This means we get to spend more time together. I'm gonna take even better care of you, and Larissa's going to be here to help. But it's always gonna be you and me, tough guy. Okay?"

Curtis thought about this. "Is Larissa going to leave too?"

"No!" Daddy said, and Larissa chimed in from the doorway. She was next to him now, hugging him from behind, her breath warm and sweet on his cheek.

"You're my number one, and you always will be," Daddy said. He touched his thumb to his forehead again, and Curtis mimicked him.

"I got your back," Daddy told him as they touched thumbs. "Always."

Curtis hugged him tight.

The next day Larissa came to pick Curtis up. They stopped by the grocery store, and as they headed home Larissa paused in the middle of the sidewalk. "Yo, baby, I got a surprise for you today."

"What?" Curtis asked skeptically. He wasn't a big fan of surprises. He liked everything to be organized and in its place.

Instead of answering, she pushed open a nondescript door between a liquor store and a convenience store. Curtis followed her down a corridor with a grimy linoleum floor, leading to a fluorescent-lit shop. It sold comic books. Curtis had seen kids with comic books and had looked at the pictures of X-Men once with Keyshawn Booker, but he'd never been in a comic book store before. Bright covers with heavily muscled men on them stretched seemingly to the ceiling; and around the walls in display cases stood action figures withs arms in the air or posing threateningly. Posters sported teams of heroes. By now Curtis knew the alphabet and many words, and he deciphered names like *X-Men* and *Avengers*.

He breathed in the smell of paper and cool air and glue, and a word came into his head: *power.* He didn't understand why he thought it, but he took a breath so deep he thought perhaps his ribs would crack.

"I thought we'd get you a comic book," Larissa said. "You can choose any one you want."

"For real?" he asked. "Just one?"

"How many you want?"

He shrugged, eyes wide, peering into the shelves. "A hundred?"

"How about three for starters," she said.

Almost at random he chose a big muscled Black dude on the cover of *Power Man and Iron Fist*; an *Avengers* with a huge black bird-man battling an enormous guy wearing yellow and green; and an *X-Men* comic book with Wolverine flashing his claws. He recognized Wolverine from Keyshawn's comics.

That night at home, he made Larissa read the comic books several times to him, and he forgot to practice Beethoven's Second Cello Sonata like he was supposed to.

2

LARISSA

LARISSA WAS LATE to the appointment with Miss Daniela, and it wasn't her fault. At all. It was Crisette. Again. As hard as Larissa tried to help her, she knew, just *knew*, that Crisette had started using. Again. That was the only explanation for why Crisette wasn't at the drop point off Sixteenth by two p.m. at the latest. Larissa got word at almost a quarter to three that Crisette hadn't shown up. Larissa figured that she could still handle the drop-off before the five thirty meeting with Miss Daniela.

In dealing with Crisette, time was of the essence, so she swung by Crisette's pad first to confront her directly. Always be direct and firm, that was Larissa's motto.

She let herself into Crisette's place—she had a key. Had a key to most of her crew's pads. Larissa, after all, had made the arrangements with landlords. Sometimes her boss T Block—through a series of intermediaries—rented out derelict townhouses, too. So the apartments were more Larissa's than anybody else's, she figured. Of course she'd gotten keys.

Crisette's bedroom was on the main level, off what once had been the parlor, a spacious room with high ceilings, heavily carved crown moldings, and a once-majestic fireplace dominating one wall. But now charred floorboards near the fireplace were too fragile to bear weight; mold left a sinister tapestry of decay on the ceiling and crept down the walls; and a solitary mattress lay propped in a corner, stinking of pee and worse.

Larissa knocked on a door that maybe once had led to a library. "Hey, you in there?" No response, but Larissa could sense move-

ment. "Crisette? You in there?" The doorknob didn't latch prop-
erly. Larissa tried to shoulder it open, but it wouldn't unlock.
"Hey, it's me, open this door, you okay?"

Shuffling, and a minute later the latch slid back. Crisette—older
than Larissa, probably in her midthirties—was already retreating,
shambling back toward her own mattress on the far side of the
little room. She wouldn't look at Larissa. Her chestnut-brown
hair, which only last week looked radiant, now hung in unkempt
strands, wisps escaping the loose ponytail. She wore a mismatched
array of faded colors and worn fabrics, and her hands trembled.

"Yo, girl," Larissa said, trying to convey both warmth and
authority, "I know things are getting tight. What did we talk about
last week?"

The only light crept in from tattered shades pulled down
against the world. Crisette staggered back to her mattress. The
air was thick. On the other side of the room, tucked in a corner, a
child-size mattress had been fully made up. A pink plastic unicorn
lay on the pillow.

Larissa followed Crisette to the adult-size mattress, grabbed a
plaid blanket that had been pushed off, snapped it straight, and
draped it over the sheets. She settled in next to Crisette. Choosing
her words carefully, she said, "I know this journey ain't easy. It's
walking on a tightrope, and there's a lot of temptation. But you've
got the strength in you—I've seen it."

Crisette sighed, rubbed her eyes with the palms of her hands.
"Yeah, but sometimes that rope feels like it's gonna to break. I'm
barely hangin' on."

Larissa leaned over, draped an arm around her, pulled her
close. "I get it. I get it. It's okay to feel like you're on the edge.
But remember, you ain't alone. I'm here, ain't I? And we got each
other's backs. You're stronger than you think. You know you are."

Crisette, gaze dropping to her trembling hands, mumbled,
"I'm trying. I swear I am."

"I know," Larissa said. "But you got to think it's not just you,
you know?"

"I got Jamila," Crisette agreed.

"You do. Where is she now?"

"She at preschool. I dropped her off at preschool just like we talked about and then I was gonna go to the drop like we talked about but then I—" Crisette gulped—"then I almost slipped. I couldn't fight the craving, you know? I don't even know why I'm fighting."

"You know why," Larissa told her. "You totally know why. Tell me."

Crisette shrugged.

"You're fighting for you. For Jamila. That's something worth holding on to, ain't it? You don't want to lose sight of that."

"That little girl needs her mama," Crisette said, and began to cry.

Larissa hugged her tighter. "You remember. You ain't the slips you make. You are the strong woman who gets back up. And you got that strength."

Crisette wept harder, mumbling into Larissa's neck, thank-yous and apologies. "We only got each other," Larissa said, rocking her. "I told you, I'll always be on your side."

They sat there for ten minutes or more. Larissa wasn't focused on the clock. She imagined herself a sun, pouring healing radiant rays onto the older woman. After a while, Crisette snuffled and wiped her nose with the back of her hand, sat up.

"You better?" Larissa asked.

She nodded.

"Girl, if you get makeup on my blouse, we gonna have a problem. Now go make some tea and say that affirmation. I know you think it's lame, but you know it works, right?"

Again Crisette nodded.

"And you trust me, right?"

Crisette wiped at her face, tried for a smile. "Always."

"Next time you call me instead of going down to the corner and looking for stuff. Don't you make me have to hear from anyone else that you're struggling, you hear me? If you need me, call me. We're in this together. Remember that."

They sat together for a while longer, until Crisette was strong enough to stand, make her tea, compose herself. Larissa gave her new instructions for a new drop. "You gonna be there on time, right?"

Crisette nodded.

"Okay then. I'm right here if you need me," Larissa said.

Ten minutes later she was on her way. And only then thought to look at her watch—it was after five, and she was supposed to meet Miss Daniela at five thirty. She had to navigate D.C. in rush hour. Now she'd be late.

Mentally she kicked herself. She hated having to choose between crew and Curtis, and tried to never put herself in that position. Well, she was in it now. She wished she had Miss Daniela's phone number, but Miss Daniela was only a volunteer and it was after school—would there be anybody there still? It was too complicated to figure out, so Larissa just drove as fast as she could to the elementary school.

She knew everything that Miss Daniela was doing for Curtis— which was why she was dreading the conversation. Miss Daniela was a nice lady, but more important, Curtis utterly revered her. It was always "Miss Daniela says this, Miss Daniela says that" all night long, as soon as Larissa picked him up.

She was fifteen minutes late. But when she burst through the door, full of nerves and apologies, Miss Daniela didn't seem at all flustered or angry. She and Curtis were sitting on the far side of the room, Curtis with the cello propped against his shoulder, and Miss Daniela was explaining something.

When Larissa came in, Miss Daniela rose, smiling. She was a pleasant-faced woman in her midforties. Then Miss Daniela asked Curtis, in a heavy Guatemalan accent, to wait for them in the hall.

He trundled out obediently, and moments later a cello melody seeped faintly through the closed door. Miss Daniela and Larissa grinned at each other.

Larissa switched into Spanish. Might as well get the bad news over with as soon as possible. Direct and firm, as always. "I'm sorry," she said, "but Curtis's daddy won't let him play on the TV."

Miss Daniela shook her head, not understanding. "Not let him play? What father doesn't want to see his son on TV? Do you realize how exceptional he is?" She leaned in. "I sometimes feel like I could be teaching the next Mozart."

Larissa wasn't sure what a "mote-sart" was, but she gathered it was a good thing. "His daddy says no," she said, shaking her head, trying to figure out how to not anger Miss Daniela. She was with an organization that offered free after-school music and instruments to inner-city kids. With all the budget cuts, Taylor Elementary School in Ward 8 didn't have a music program or music teacher anymore. If Larissa made Miss Daniela angry and she threw Curtis out of the program, Larissa couldn't even imagine how Curtis would react. She cleared her throat. "I'm not even sure how they found out about him."

"People talk," Miss Daniela said. "Especially when it's something like this. You can't blame them."

If Larissa didn't want to imagine Curtis upset, she wanted to imagine even less how Curtis's father, Zippy, would react. "Zippy ain't gonna do it," she said.

"Zippy?" Daniela repeated.

"His daddy. Zacchariah. We call him 'Zippy.' He's super private. He don't want nobody up in our business."

Daniela glanced from Larissa to the classroom door, as if she was expecting to see Curtis, or perhaps Zippy, standing there. "I'm sure that he wants what's best for his son—"

"Oh, it ain't about that," Larissa reassured her. "He loves that little boy. It's just that—well, it ain't gonna be easy. Zippy has a lot going on, and there's people in and out all the time. He won't want Curtis on TV, and won't want no TV people sniffing around the house. I can guarantee that."

She wanted to tell her that Zippy was only twenty-three, a low-level drug dealer hanging out on street corners and trying to make it big time. Larissa herself had her own crew, like Crisette, about a dozen women who provided escort and other services—sometimes sexual, often not, like bagging or being lookouts. Neither Larissa nor Zippy could afford to have a television crew showing up and filming them like they were something out of a *Cops* TV show.

"This is the kind of opportunity that could change his life," Daniela said.

"I hear that, but—" She shrugged. "He ain't my boy. Don't know if you know that. You met his mama, right? And she's out of the picture now. But he ain't mine, and I don't got a lot of say in this."

"He must want Curtis to succeed, though?"

"Oh, he does," Larissa assured her. "It's just—well, this isn't something that he's ready to deal with. You know where we live. Zippy ain't somebody who'll take many risks. Especially when they can end up backfiring."

"But this isn't a risk at all. It's—"

"He'd see it as a risk," Larissa said firmly. "I know he would."

"I'm sure you know that this school isn't the greatest," Daniela said. "If this was in a different neighborhood, Curtis would have a music program, teachers, opportunities that he won't get here. I've been doing this for nineteen years, and believe me when I tell you, I've never seen a kid like him."

"You don't have to tell me," Larissa said. "I see it every day."

"He's got an amazing talent. This would be national TV. This could mean scholarships to the best music programs, the best conservatories, in the country. He's only five and he's playing like this—who knows where he'll be when he's ten?" Miss Daniela laughed, and then said earnestly, "You can't cheat him out of something like this."

Larissa didn't say anything for a moment, and in the silence the wistful strains from the cello seemed louder—as if it, too, were pleading with her.

"Okay, I'll try," Larissa said. "I can't promise anything, though. I'll let you know on Monday."

3

ZIPPY

ZIPPY CAME THROUGH the door thinking about how many more kilos of blow he could sell. Now 18ST extended all the way to Eighteenth Street SE. Fourteen more blocks. A million square feet more than a month ago. So if three new middlemen bought two kilos per week, that could mean an extra twelve for Zippy.

He just needed to convince The Man. T Block.

Next to the door, he tossed the duffle bag with tonight's stash. Forty-eight bags. Four kilos. Zippy could always tell the exact weight of the product. It was like a party trick. The duffle was worth about $75,000. Zippy's cut would be close to $4,000.

Easier said than done, since T Block always kept his distance. Zippy got his orders from his direct higher-ups—JFunk, Scotty, and Tremel.

Now Tremel said that T Block wanted Zippy over at Thirty-Eight doing pickups. Zippy didn't have long for dinner.

As soon as he got in that evening, the smell of fried chicken—his favorite—buffeted him, and he breathed in deep. He was tossing his coat on the back of a chair when Larissa appeared in the kitchen doorway. "About time you got here," she said. "I got you some fried chicken."

"I can smell it," Zippy said. "And damn that does smell good." She came up to him, and he put one arm around her, drew her close, and kissed her. "And damn, so do you," he told her.

She grinned at him—they were exactly the same height—and leaned back into his arms. What a fine woman, he thought again.

Beautiful, yeah, but smart and funny and full of sass. He often felt grateful that he'd found her.

"I got some news for you," she said. "And it's gonna be great for Curtis."

"Curtis?" Zippy repeated. "What's going on?"

"You ain't gonna believe this, but that son of yours is almost as talented as his daddy. Some people came to the school today to ask him to be on the TV."

"TV?" Zippy repeated. "What're you talking about?" Zippy was still thinking about those kilos of blow. T Block needed to increase production in order to widen distribution. Cut it up more. That was the ticket.

She handed him a sheet of paper. Zippy glanced at it but didn't read it. "What it say?" He could read well enough. He was just busy. Had to get over to Thirty-Eight.

Meanwhile, the powerful scent of fried chicken was curling out of the kitchen. His mouth watered. He started toward it.

She followed him. "There's a TV show that wants to film him. They wanna come next week to school. And then come here when we're home."

He was in the kitchen now, a brown paper bag rolled up tight on the counter. Grease splotches darkened one side. "You telling me that somebody actually wants to come here?"

"Stop talkin' so loud," Larissa hissed. She'd followed him into the kitchen. He'd opened the bag, inhaled a thick puff of fragrant steam. "Don't talk like that where he can hear you."

"That kid can't hear anything but that thing," Zippy said. He could barely hear the melody coming from Curtis's room, but he kept his voice down anyway. He pulled out a wax-paper bag of fried chicken. Dug around for a fat piece of breast meat.

The kid came home and practiced the same way every single day. "It ain't like he's makin' real music. He could get out here and listen to some real shit." Curtis wasn't bumping Drake and Lil Uzi. Or Post Malone. When Zippy was Curtis's age, he was already rhyming to his own beats. But Curtis? The only time he came out of his room was to go to the bathroom. And for dinner.

Larissa had to force Curtis to go outside and play basketball with the other kids.

"Shut up. He is playin' real music. You think it ain't music if it ain't Jay-Z."

He shrugged. Zippy didn't think being a dad was going to be like this. When he'd learned Quenella was pregnant and wanted to keep the baby, he'd been a junior in high school. Sixteen years old. He'd been thinking about taking accounting classes when he graduated. But even when she'd told him the news, he still imagined a cozy life. Being a dad, with a wife and a kid. Sitting around the dinner table saying grace before talking about the account he just landed. Zippy was well on track to being valedictorian. He'd scored a 1490 on his PSAT. His math score was nearly perfect. He could rattle off calculations. He had a chance to make it out of the hood.

But, as soon as Quenella told him that she was having his kid, he was determined to be around for the baby. For his *son*. He imagined basketball games, baseball tryouts. His parents hadn't been around much. His dad had taken off when he was little; and his mom, Patrice, cleaned offices at night. So she wasn't around much either. Zippy'd imagined a much different life for his kids when he was a dad.

What he hadn't ever imagined was this intense, quiet little boy hauling around a violin bigger than he was. Okay, it was a cello, he knew that now, but still.

He and Quenella were going to live with Zippy's mom until they finished high school. Then Zippy was going to go to community college. Get his associate degree in accounting. He could do it if Quenella worked too, and his mom took care of the baby some.

But Quenella never wanted the baby to live with her, and she never wanted to live with Zippy and his mom. He wasn't sure how it happened, but at seventeen he was the father of a newborn baby, dealing with diapers and trying to figure out what kind of formula was the closest to breast milk. Quenella didn't want to breastfeed.

Alone, and with Patrice, he'd been there for Curtis. Larissa, who he'd started seeing when Curtis was less than a year old, had been as in love with Curtis as she was with Zippy, and now Zippy had hopes, again, of having a real family. Especially after Quenella called Zippy last fall to say she was getting married and "starting a new life," and would be in touch in the future. He hadn't heard from her since.

"This is a big-deal TV show," Larissa was saying behind him. He'd bitten into the chicken. It was delicious. Salty and crispy and the inside juicy. He wiped one hand on his jeans and headed back into the living room, chewing.

Larissa had followed him again. "It's the one on Sunday morning where they go all over doing interviews. She says that people will see it and will offer Curtis scholarships and who knows what."

"No," Zippy said. He looked back at the living room, imagining a TV crew assembled in front of the couch. Kicking the kilos of cocaine out of the way. Moving the baggies of uppers so they were more photogenic. He imagined what T Block would say about that.

Larissa straightened. "Do you even know what this is about? This is about his future. I know you want what's best for him. I do too. Daniela really thinks if he gets this exposure, it could—"

"Are you high right now or somethin'? Can you imagine what Tremel would say if I'm on TV?" Zippy thought a minute. "He wouldn't say anything. He'd just smoke me. He'd just put a bullet in me so fast that I'd be dead before the end of the show. And you, too. And Curtis." He shook his head. "Sorry, baby, but I can't have Curtis all over the TV. Not here."

"That's exactly why he needs this, *papi*. This could be his way out. A real chance for him. Miss Daniela says he could get a scholarship."

"He's five," Zippy said. "He don't need chances yet. He needs a daddy who loves him. And a mama—isn't that you? He needs a roof over his head. He needs the security of knowing he is loved. That's way more important than some fancy school or some private teacher."

Over the past months Larissa had mentioned, almost casually, that a kid with a talent like Curtis's needed to have that talent nurtured. He needed the opportunities, the exposure to other musicians. He needed private teachers, conservatories, boarding schools, music camps. "Ain't no way we can afford that," Zippy had said dismissively. There was no chance his son was going to a music camp or a boarding school. Nobody was gonna take his son away from him. Nobody. Not happening.

"I don't know if you've looked around here lately, but there ain't too many opportunities at the front door." Her voice was rising. He realized she was actually serious. "This might be his big break. Hell, it might be a break for all of us."

"I'm gonna get my big break," Zippy tried to say. He was not hungry anymore. He stared down at the half-eaten piece of chicken as if daring it to speak too.

But Larissa talked over him. "Your son might really be something, you know that? Daniela keeps saying it every time I pick him up, and she doesn't say that about nobody else. You want him to just hang around at home and take over the family business? Be a loser and run smack on the corner?"

"What did you just say to me? Cuz it sounded like you just called me a loser."

"Oh, *papi*," she said, coming up and rubbing his shoulder, "you know what I mean."

He shrugged away, rage beginning to surge in him. He was always sensitive to people thinking he was less than he was. "Was I a loser when I took you in? Does a loser provide? How do you think you ate this morning? Where do you think you got the money for this chicken?" Now fury frothed up in him. He was smaller than the other men, only five-seven, with a slight frame, and he only came up to the chests of some of the guys he ran with. He'd had to fight to be respected. Had to fight to get where he was. And now this woman was calling him a loser?

"What are you talking about?" She looked at him incredulously, her face flushed. "And for your information I pay for myself, you know that? I work just as hard as you do, plus I take care of your kid—"

He put the chicken down on the armrest of the couch. "I pay

the bills to keep this place over our heads and the lights on, but I guess that makes me a loser, huh?"

"I didn't mean—"

"Well, this loser ain't gonna destroy everything he built just so his kid will be on some lame-ass TV show." And no way that some lame-ass boarding school was going to take Curtis away from him. Not happening.

She tried again, coming up to him. "No, baby, that is not what I meant. I know you take care of us the best you can."

He backed away, eyeing her and the duffle bag half-pushed under the couch. "It *is* what you meant. You think I'm just gonna be some low-level street rat all my life—"

She reached out to embrace him. But just as her arm stretched around him, his arms flew up and out, hit her square in the chest, knocking the breath out of her and pushing her back against the couch. He'd shoved her harder than he intended, and the chicken fell to the floor.

And so did Larissa: she flipped over the side of the couch.

It was an accident, and at another time it could even have been funny. At another time they would have laughed about it afterward. But it wasn't funny now. Not at all.

Her head and shoulder hit the floor with a sickening thwack.

She cried out, splayed half on the couch and half on the rug.

Zippy knew he had messed up. He'd never hit a woman before, let alone the woman he loved. The woman who loved his son like her own. He leaped toward her. "Oh, shit, baby, I'm so sorry, are you—"

"Get the hell away from me," she said, cradling her skull in her hands. The corner of the couch had cut her cheek.

"Baby, I—"

"I said don't touch me." She scooted away with a groan. "Don't you come near me."

"I didn't mean—"

"Now I get it." She tried to stagger to her feet, clutching her shoulder. "You got priorities. You showed me I'm not one of them. Neither is Curtis. You ain't gonna be tossing me around like some bag of trash."

"Baby, hold on, I didn't—"

"I don't know who you think I am. But you're gonna have to learn the hard way, little boy. Go ahead and keep the lights on. Don't worry about food neither. You won't need to feed me anymore. I'm out."

"Little boy" stung, but he tried not to show it. "You can't be serious. It was an accident." He couldn't figure out how everything had spiraled out of control so quickly.

"I told you if you ever laid a hand on me I was out of here. You think I'm joking? You think I'm a loser like you?"

"It was an accid—"

"It's always an accident with you. You're always yelling, and now you're hitting me. That is one thing I ain't ever gonna stand for. Never."

"Baby, I—"

"There ain't no way I'm doing this," she told him. The blood on her cheek was dripping down her jaw, and she wiped at it, not even looking. The smear took over half her face. "I'm out," she repeated. She stumbled to the door, and then paused. Reconsidered. "I think it would be better for all of us if I took Curtis with me. You can't take care of him by yourself. You don't even know where his school is."

"You ain't leaving," Zippy said. "And there is no fuckin' way you are taking my son anywhere. You ain't his mama."

"I should have been," she said. "Piece of shit garbage you fucked ain't never been a mama to him. And you ain't no kinda daddy either."

"Bullshit," Zippy said, now stung. "I'm a good father to that boy. I make sure he has everything he needs. I always have."

"Well, now you gonna get to show everybody how great you are."

"You know what? You wanna go, go. Ain't nobody stoppin' you."

And a moment later the door slammed.

The apartment was shockingly silent. Curtis wasn't playing his cello.

Zippy stared accusingly at the half-eaten piece of fried chicken, now wedged against the couch leg, as if he expected it to climb up, rearrange the furniture, put his life back in order. Instead it just lay there. The silence was deafening. Finally he went over, picked it up, and threw it in the garbage.

An instant later, the cello melody started up again.

4

CURTIS

"RISE AND SHINE, tough guy." Daddy turned on the overhead light, and Curtis rolled over, blinking.

"Where's Larissa?"

"She's not here today," Daddy said. His voice seemed very loud and hurt Curtis's ears. He pulled the covers over his head.

"It's you and me, buddy," Daddy said. "Time for breakfast. I made you a surprise."

Curtis clutched the blankets more tightly. He *hated* surprises. "I just want Cheerios," he told the mattress. "Larissa makes me Cheerios." With his special Spider-Man spoon.

"Well, you haven't tried my surprise," Daddy said. "You're gonna love it. Let's go." He yanked the blankets off, and Curtis was clutching at air. Daddy scooped him up and dangled him by the ankles, head down, fingers sweeping the floor, to the bathroom.

Despite himself, Curtis laughed and scrabbled at the cold tile floor, trying to walk on his hands.

Daddy deposited him in the bathroom, right side up. "Now you do your thing and you get yourself dressed and meet me in the kitchen."

"You have to watch me brush my teeth," Curtis explained. "To make sure I'm doing it right."

"I'm sure you're doing it right," Daddy said. "You're five. You've been brushing your teeth for years. You've got this."

"Larissa always watches," Curtis said.

So Daddy leaned on the door frame as Curtis peed and washed his hands and brushed his teeth.

Then he had to get dressed—Larissa hadn't laid his clothes out, and Daddy chose the wrong Batman underwear—and then the *surprise* for breakfast, which wasn't Cheerios with chocolate milk, as Curtis had hoped. Instead, it was French toast. With honey. Curtis poked at it with his fork. "I don't want it," he said to the plate. "Larissa wouldn't make me this." On the crust, a white strip of fried egg hugged the edge like a slug's trail on a sidewalk.

"Yeah, well," Daddy said. "It's you and me now, buddy." He scooped up the plate and took a bite. "Yum," he told Curtis with a full mouth. "This shit is good. You don't know what you're missing."

Curtis stared back at him.

Daddy shook his head, chewing, and put the plate on the counter. Then he poured Cheerios into a bowl. Got out the Spider-Man spoon. Curtis sighed with relief.

As Daddy set the bowl down, he did the thumbtouch. "Got your back," Daddy said.

Curtis nodded.

"You know *when* I have your back?" Daddy asked.

Curtis stared at him, not sure of the answer.

"I got it all the time," Daddy said. "I got your back *all the time.*"

Curtis nodded, thinking.

"Because it's you and me now, partner. And I'm not going anywhere."

Daddy put his thumb to his forehead, and Curtis mimicked him.

"Got your back," Daddy said.

"All the time," Curtis told him.

Curtis didn't know where Larissa had gone. Now it was just Daddy, and Daddy didn't do anything right. Curtis was late to school because Daddy didn't know where to go. Curtis kept asking where Larissa was, and Daddy kept saying it was just them two now.

That afternoon there was a new lady to pick up Curtis: Tanya, who pulled out her hair in clumps, and had big buck teeth. And after that it was a different lady, Yolanda. He never knew who would be picking him up. Sometimes it was Tasia, but other times it was Moni and sometimes Yolanda and sometimes Grandma and sometimes Daddy.

But at least Curtis had Miss Daniela. She taught after-school music, and she convinced Daddy to let Curtis take extra lessons with her. On those days she brought him home herself.

Curtis liked school okay, but he loved Miss Daniela's lessons. And even more than the lessons, he loved his cello. He loved the cool, smooth wood and the intricate spiral of the scroll. His fingers barely wrapped around the neck and his fingertips sometimes still blistered from the strings, but Curtis didn't care because sometimes—and later it would happen more and more—when he played, he could feel the sound resound so deep in his chest that it wasn't even in his chest anymore. When he was holding the cello and the music came out, he felt huge and powerful, like Ironman or the Sentry.

Every night, when he'd have to stop playing, he'd put the cello to bed in its blue-velvet-lined case, and he'd be proud that he was keeping it safe, even if he felt a little sad when he couldn't look at it and touch it when the lid was closed.

He also had started a list of his favorite superheroes, which he kept in the blue notebook that Larissa had once used to schedule the ladies who worked for her. There were lots of blank pages. One week, number one was Batman and number two would be the Flash; and the next week number one would be Spider-Man and number two would be Iceman. Sometimes there was a tie, because that week Wonder Man and Captain America both looked incredibly cool, and Curtis couldn't decide who was best.

March soon came around. He'd lost count of the ladies who were helping take care of him. At least once a week he went to Grandma's—which was nice because Grandma always had good food waiting for him, better than the stuff that Daddy or his ladies made. But the problem with Grandma was that she smoked, and all her old friends smoked, too. And Grandma would tell him to go to her room and watch TV when her friends came over to play cards. So he'd go in and read his comic books—she called them "funny books"—until he had them memorized. Grandma told him she'd take him to get a new comic book, but she never did. And she never let him practice the cello, either.

Sometimes at Grandma's when he'd finished the comic books he'd pretend that he was a superhero—Spider-Man, usually—and he'd jump off Grandma's bed and try to stick to the walls. He always slid down, and Grandma would yell from the front room where she was playing cards, "Curtis, what you doin' in there? You better not be breakin' anything."

He sure wished there was a superhero who played the cello.

One Saturday, he was home in the apartment with Deandra, who he liked well enough. She had long braids that she'd whip around when she was being funny, and they'd smack Curtis like tiny ropes. He'd been in his room practicing, but the Popper etude wasn't going well. He was having trouble shifting into fourth position, even though he'd done it fine the day before. But no matter how many times he tried, the melody came out sounding flat and jagged. Ms. Daniela was expecting to hear it on Monday. If he played well, she'd give him a new solo piece, Dvorak's "Humoresque."

He went to the bathroom. Larissa had showed him how to take his own bath. He hadn't seen Larissa since after New Year's, and he missed her something fierce. It was the same kind of ache in his chest that he felt when he played the cello, but this ache hurt in a different way.

When he came out of the bathroom, he looked for Deandra. She was usually on the couch, bopping her head to some music on her headphones. Now he found her face down in front of the refrigerator. She'd thrown up all over the countertop, and it was dripping onto the floor. She was groaning. He ran down to the Bookers and they called Daddy, but Daddy wasn't around so they called Grandma, and he played with Keyshawn until Grandma came, even if he couldn't really pay attention to what Keyshawn was saying because he kept thinking about Deandra.

Finally Grandma came over, a cigarette hanging from her lips, and marched upstairs to see what was going on. Curtis followed.

She took one look at Deandra and used a whole bunch of words that Larissa told Curtis never to say, no matter what. "We gotta find your daddy," she told Curtis. "Where is he?"

Curtis shrugged.

Grandma pulled out her ancient cell phone and, lips pursed, laboriously typed a message on it. "Lord, I swear. I can't believe I'm missing my card night to come look at some stank girl half naked on the floor. Did you eat yet?" she said to Curtis.

He shook his head.

"Well we sure can't be cookin' in here." Grandma stared daggers at Deandra, who was still groaning. A whitish drop of vomit splattered next to Deandra's open hand. Curtis was sure he was going to be sick too.

"You want some chicken? Is that carryout place on the corner still open? Go get your funny books."

While Curtis was in his room getting his comics—he chose *Iron Man* and *Fantastic Four*—he heard Daddy coming in. "Whoa," Daddy said. "What you doin' here?"

"I sent you a message," Grandma said. "Did you even look at it?"

"I was driving."

"Well, you come in here and see what kind of mess you got," she said.

Curtis, comic books in hand, followed Grandma and Daddy back into the kitchen.

"Boy, you need to get this girl up and into the shower, then clean up this mess before somebody else gets sick."

"Dammit," Daddy said. "Girl can't hold her liquor."

"Mmm-hmm," Grandma said. "That's more than liquor. A lot more. This is pathetic."

"Curtis, go get me a towel," Daddy told him.

"No you don't," Grandma said to Curtis. "You go back there—" she gestured to the living room—"and read your funny book." And then to Daddy: "This is your mess, hear me? How you gonna let that boy stay with this junkie? Ain't no tellin what she's on. You leave your little boy here with this? And that's the kind of father you are? Keep goin' the way you're goin' and them Social Services gonna come take Curtis away from you. Disgraceful is what it is. I know I raised you better than this."

"Mama, stop trippin'. He's fine. She only—"

"They only after what little money you got. I can't believe you still messing with them. Where is Larissa?"

Curtis sat on the couch and thumbed through *Fantastic Four* as Daddy hauled Deandra into the bathroom and then came back to towel up the mess.

Grandma did take Curtis out for Tony's fried chicken and seafood. They each ordered the two-piece dark meat with fries and a Coke. Grandma usually didn't let him drink Coke, and her cooking was better, but she knew how he liked Tony's.

Curtis didn't talk much. He chewed and swung his legs, banging against the table.

"Whoa, easy there," Grandma told him. "You gonna knock everythin' clean over if you keep kickin' like that."

"Would they really?" Curtis said. He'd been thinking hard about what Grandma had said to Daddy.

"Would they really what? Get knocked over? You gonna knock everythin' on the floor, and I ain't buyin' you more dinner. You stop kickin' now, hear?"

"Would they really take me away?" Curtis said. The chicken had turned cold and lumpy in his mouth. With difficulty he swallowed.

Grandma stared. "Would they what? Who?" She paused, mouth open, teeth yellowed from smoking. "Who take you away?"

"The social people," he said. "You said to Daddy."

Grandma leaned across the table and laid a hand on his shoulder, pulled him toward her. "Oh sweetheart," she said, "ain't nobody gonna take you away. Don't you worry about that. Not an instant. Your daddy just needs to understand the consequences of what he doing, is all. He needs to understand. But you're not going anywhere."

"Promise?"

"Promise," Grandma said. "If things don't get better maybe you'll come stay with me for a little. What you think 'bout that?"

He thought. Grandma only had one bedroom. She hated when he practiced the cello. It would take a lot of figuring out. But it was better than the unknown social people taking him away and

maybe not letting him have a cello at all. "Okay," he said, nodding, meeting her eyes. "That'd be okay. If I can bring my cello."

"That'd be okay, huh?" Grandma repeated, taking a big bite of
her chicken. "If you can bring your cello, huh? You just gonna be
my little maestro, ain't you?"

He nodded. Yes, he'd be her little maestro.

When they got back home, Deandra was gone. Curtis asked
where she was, and Zippy just shook his head. Grandma sniffed,
unconvinced and unappeased. "You better get your act together
because I'm gonna take Curtis out of here if you can't control
your ho's," she told Daddy, lighting up another cigarette.

Curtis didn't sleep much that night. After Daddy put him to
bed he pulled the cello out of its case, and even though he wasn't
allowed he dragged it under the sheets with him. He finally fell
asleep with his head tucked against its neck.

One Saturday afternoon in April, he went to the refrigerator for
a hot dog, but there were just two beers, a tomato, some lettuce,
and a jug of water. No hot dogs, no macaroni and cheese. Not
even milk. He'd finished the Cheerios that morning. In the cabinet under the sink he found an open sleeve of saltines. He sat on
the couch to eat them. Katrina had bought him the latest edition of *The New Warriors*, but he'd already read it, so now he just
thumbed through, checking out the panels he liked best. Like the
Night Thrasher on his skateboard, and Namorita pulling back her
arms as a towering wave threatened to engulf her.

A few minutes later, Daddy came out of his bedroom, went into
the kitchen, and then returned and sat next to him with a cup of
coffee.

Curtis thumbtouched, and Daddy did too.

"Who's got your back?"

"All the time."

Daddy was out super late last night, like he usually was on
weekends. Now he'd just woken up. He smelled faintly sour, of
smoke and morning breath, even though it was after lunchtime.
The coffee smelled good, though.

"What you doing out here?" Daddy asked him. "You finished playing already?"

"Yeah," Curtis said. "I was hungry so I came out."

"You're really into those comic books," Daddy observed, leaning over and looking at the page with Curtis.

"Yeah, they're cool. This is Firestar. She controls microwaves."

"She does, huh?"

"Yeah, and this one is Speedball—he bounces around like crazy. But his jokes are so lame."

"They are, huh?"

"Yeah," Curtis said. Then neither said anything for a while. Curtis studied the page, brushing cracker crumbs onto the couch and the floor. Daddy stared off into space.

"Daddy, when's Larissa coming back?" Curtis asked.

"Ah, buddy, you know this already. She ain't coming back," Daddy said. "She's got some other stuff to do. You saw Katrina, right? She's going to take care of you."

Katrina had been around for maybe two weeks. "Is Larissa gone forever?"

"It doesn't matter. 'Cause it's you and me, right? I got your back. And you know what? You know what I think?" Daddy asked. "I think you need to start playing some different music. Like stuff that I do. Mix it up a little, you know? Rap. Hip-hop. Beat boxing." Daddy demonstrated, rapping his knuckles against the coffee table.

Sometimes Daddy would have his friends come over, and they'd open their beers and light up their blunts and they'd mess around with their phones. Everybody had their own mixtapes and they all thought that they should be producers. "Listen to this," they'd say. "I came up with this beat yesterday." And they'd play a little. The rhythms felt elementary and amateurish compared to Bach or Beethoven, but Curtis wouldn't say anything. The other guys, though, would say, "That's fire," or "That beat is dope," even when Curtis knew that Haydn had used the same rhythm three hundred years ago, and it was nothing special.

Now Daddy took out his phone. "Like check this out. I did this yesterday when I was driving home. Rap is like poetry. It's about finding the rhythm in your soul and letting it flow through your fingers."

Daddy turned on a rap track. The beats filled the room. He tapped his knuckles on the arm of the couch, his foot keeping time. Daddy's eyes were unfocused. "You feel that?" Daddy asked him.

Curtis tapped alongside him. The rhythm was in 6/8 time, like a ship swaying on the sea. He'd learned it a few months ago when he'd played *St. Paul's Suite*. He wanted to grab his cello.

"Yeah," Daddy said. "Yeah man. Now, listen to the words, the way they fit into the rhythm. It's like a puzzle. You find the right pieces and put them together."

Daddy's phone blared with a rap verse, the lyrics cascading in a rapid-fire flow. He started to rap along, his words weaving into the music. "Why don't you try spittin' somethin'?"

Curtis took a deep breath and thought for a moment. "Um . . . I'm Curtis with a C, I play the cello with a C, up and down the fingerboard it's where I be."

Daddy's laughter rumbled through the room. "That's more than a start, little man. That's your truth right there. Keep going."

Katrina came out of the bathroom in one of Daddy's T-shirts, her legs bare. She'd been in there a long time. Curtis hadn't even realized she was home. Now she sat next to Daddy, tucking a foot underneath her. A few hours ago she'd had long thick blondish-black hair, but now her hair was shorter than Curtis's. She didn't say a word, just kept sniffing and sniffing like she had a cold. She probably had to sneeze.

Curtis and Daddy ignored her. "What you rappin' next?" Daddy asked Curtis.

He thought a minute. The rhythm filled the air. "Larissa, where'd you go? I miss you more'n you know. With my cello, I want to play, bring you back, in my own way."

Daddy didn't say anything.

"You always goin' on about that ho," Katrina said. She reached under the coffee table and pulled out a bag of white powder.

"Don't you call her that," Daddy said, but Curtis was looking at the white powder. Daddy and Larissa had told him, *Always stay away from the white stuff. It ain't sugar.*

"She has that white stuff out here," Curtis said, pointing. "It's not good for you, right?"

"Girl, what's wrong with you?" Daddy asked her. "You know better." He jerked his thumb toward the bathroom.

Katrina got up. Took the white bag with her.

But she'd broken the mood. Daddy sighed and turned off the phone. He didn't seem to want to be around Curtis anymore. He disappeared into the bedroom.

Curtis returned to *The New Warriors*. The apartment seemed more silent and empty than ever. He unpacked his cello as a cockroach darted out and immediately swerved back toward the baseboard. He whacked at it with his bow. "Take that! Now you citizens are safe. The Bowman—no, the Maestro—will protect you!"

He swished his bow around like a sword, and then remembered Miss Daniela told his class to never swing their bows like toys. So he picked up his cello by the neck and used it as a shield to protect himself from the villainous foe. "The Little Maestro will protect you from the alien invaders!" He laid down the Shield of Music and the Wand of Dissonance, pulled the pillowcase off his pillow, and tied it around his neck like a cape.

In front of his mirror, he flexed into his best superhero poses. The roach found new life and scuttled toward his closet.

The Maestro, cape flowing, leaped to the dresser and grabbed the *Little Lulu* comic that Grandma bought him. Nobody read *Little Lulu*, but Curtis said thank-you when she gave it to him. He'd thought she was kidding until he realized she wasn't.

Now he rolled it up super tight and slammed it down on the cockroach. The first blow stunned it again, but several more devastated it.

Triumphant, he stood over his adversary, his hands on his hips. "The Maestro has utterly defeated you, foul creature!"

———

Kindergarten ended, and Curtis was devastated. Miss Daniela would be going to Guatemala until the end of August. There had been talk of summer camp or another music teacher, but without Larissa around, none of that happened.

Daddy said that Curtis could hang with the other kids and maybe go to the pool sometimes. He didn't have to play that *damn violin* all the time. That's what Daddy called the cello when he was mad at it.

More and more white powder was around the apartment. Daddy's ladies really liked going into the bathroom with it.

Grandma started fighting with Daddy and refused to pick Curtis up from school. "I ain't bein' a part of this mess," she told Daddy, and Curtis could hear. "It is disgusting around here. Pathetic. Them ho's ain't nothin' but trouble. Curtis is gonna stay with me is what gonna happen."

Before she left, Miss Daniela gave Curtis a whole pile of music—sonatas, excerpt books, and position technique books. She drew up a daily practice schedule for him: in the first week of July he would focus on technique, in the second, he'd do tone and position work, and so on. He had only nine weeks to get through before Miss Daniela came back.

Daddy's lady at the beginning of the summer was Anjelique, and Curtis liked her okay. She'd take him out to play with the other kids, take him to the pool, even over to the Golden Corral a few times. She was short and round and loved mint chocolate-chip ice cream. She made sure he said his prayers. And even when she forgot, he said them from bed: "Bless Daddy, bless Miss Daniela, bless Anjelique, and bless Larissa. God, please make Larissa come back home. Amen."

He learned Bach and Marcello, and loved the Mozart Minuetto, which he played as often as he could. Finally, nine long weeks later, Miss Daniela returned and school started up, and Anjelique took him to first-grade orientation, where he met his new teacher, Miss Johnson, who was pretty and tall and soft-spoken. "I heard all about you," she told him when Anjelique introduced him. "You're the little Mozart, right?"

"I want to be Luigi Boccherini," Curtis said. Mozart played

violin. Boccherini played the cello, and did guitar, which Curtis thought was really cool.

But then a couple weeks later Daddy and Anjelique had a big fight that involved a shattered chair, a mint-green smear on the kitchen wall, and a "get your fat ass out of my house." Pretty soon it was a string of ladies again. After ShaTara forgot twice to pick him up, Daddy finally let him take the city bus. Keyshawn Booker, from downstairs, took the bus, and Daddy said he could go with him. It was a little scary but Keyshawn had been doing it since he was in kindergarten. And this way they could look at comic books together. Keyshawn was a huge Spider-Man fan, even more than Curtis.

More and more, as the school year went on—Halloween, then Thanksgiving—he spent time in his room practicing, or reading comics, or pretending to be the Maestro. Rescuing an imaginary Keyshawn Booker from the clutches of the nefarious Crescendo by furiously playing the magical Sonata, the sonic vibrations creating ripples of harmony that extracted Keyshawn from the Crescendo's darkness. His room became a battleground of musical prowess, where each stroke of the bow became a strategic move in the fight against the forces of evil.

Music was safe. Miss Daniela's hand on his bow hand was safe. And the noises outside the door—the banging, the screaming, the gunshots, the sirens, the raucous laughter—weren't safe. He didn't trust any of Daddy's women, no matter how many times they told him that he was the cutest thing and they could just eat him up.

In those weeks and months, his imaginary Maestro character evolved and blossomed. At the beginning he had been vague, blurred, a shadow of harmony. But the more time Curtis spent alone, the more the Maestro solidified. He wore a long brown duster coat like the X-Man Gambit, and a cowboy hat like the cowboy hero Jonah Hex. His skintight, fingerless black Gloves of Power allowed him to absorb the music when he played. Unlike mere mortals, he could store up musical energy.

Curtis wasn't sure quite when the Maestro's name changed into the Dark Maestro. Just like Speedy became the hero Arsenal. How Robin grew into Nightwing. The evolution had begun.

Inside his room there was harmony and order. Outside was chaos and loud music. Daddy had always played his own rap and hip-hop, and when his friends came over, they'd all drum beats on the table and come up with rhymes.

Yo, here we go, like I'm running from a hitman.
In and out and up and down while you're mucking in the
quicksand
Gimmie gimmie gimmie everybody think they want some
Tell all of them suckas they can't handle where it's comin' from

They'd rap for a while, and drink and dap each other up. Curtis would listen. Often he could imagine putting notes to those rhymes—low D, E, G, A, B♭, using different rhythms—and other times he just let Daddy's rhymes soak in.

A few days before Christmas break, after the last bell, he made his way with the other students to the music room. Next to Miss Daniela stood another figure, so familiar and so sought after that he froze in the doorway. Lamel Smith bumped into him. "Hey, watch out," Lamel was saying, but Curtis barely heard.

"Larissa!" he shouted as he ran to her, giving her knees the biggest hug he could muster.

"Hey, baby! You got so big," she said as she leaned over and hugged him back. She smelled of wool coat and makeup and fruity gum. She smelled like warm honey. She smelled like herself. He wanted to breathe her in forever.

He grabbed her hand and started to tell her everything that he was doing—the music he was playing, that he was reading big-boy books and already had a comic book collection, even if he only had twenty-eight, and that he was taking the bus all by himself. "Are you coming home? Because I can show you how I take the bus."

"No, *papito*," she said, and her face went all funny, but not in a happy kind of way. "I have another home now."

"Whatever I did, I'm sorry," Curtis said. "I brush my teeth all by myself too. Every day. Promise."

"Aw, you didn't do nothin' wrong. Me and your daddy just had a disagreement."

He thought about this for a moment. "You want to hear me play? Miss Daniela says—"

"I can't stay, baby. I need to go. I wanted to see you and let you know how proud I am of you. Miss Daniela told me you got a concert coming up. Imma try to come see you play, okay?"

"Okay," Curtis said, trying to hold back tears. He wasn't going to cry in front of all these kids, who were running around getting their instruments ready but were listening to them too. "I love you," he whispered to her.

"I love you too," she whispered back, hugging him harder.

He didn't want to let Larissa go. But from the front of the room Miss Daniela said, "Okay, time to get started. Where's my little Boccherini superstar cellist?"

He hurried to the storage closet, pulled out the cello case, keeping an eye all the time on Larissa, who smiled wetly at him. He tuned and rosined his bow, got into position. Miss Daniela led them through their warm-up drills, and then into an easy Bach chorale. Larissa watched him the whole time.

He kept an eye on her as he played. But somewhere in the chorale, where he had the melody—a tricky bit that required shifting into fourth position—he looked down at the music. When he looked back up, Larissa was gone.

5

LARISSA

AFTER LARISSA moved out of Zippy's place, she still saw Zippy occasionally—after all, they were both still in 18ST. She'd sometimes hear about Curtis from her crew, some of whom became Zippy's girlfriend-du-jour. For a few hours, or days, Larissa would be jealous and angry, but she got over it. Whenever Zippy's name came up, she kept her expression blank and neutral. After all, her crew was just looking to survive, and Zippy was a success story— had his own apartment, took care of his kid—and good-looking, even if he was on the small side. Larissa understood the attraction. The girls respected her enough to not share any details about what they did with him.

Guys in the hood fell into a few categories. They were low-level thugs who prided themselves on the number of times they'd been shot; or they were bagmen who blindly followed orders— even to kill. None of them had a future.

Zippy was different. He was a follower too, but he was meticulous, focused in a way that most of the other men weren't. When he was tasked with something, it was done to a T. She admired that in him.

But more than anything—perhaps even more than Zippy—she missed Curtis. Missed his obsession with his cello and how he refused to eat his cereal if he didn't have his Spider-Man spoon. Missed the weekly trips to the comic book store, how excited he'd get on the ride home, paging through each one, eyes wide and serious, lips moving with the words. Missed how he'd look up at her, barely nodding when he understood or agreed with her. She felt like the bond with him, his connection with her, remained as tangible and durable as concrete. He'd been six months old when she'd come into his life. She, not his mama, Quenella, had handed him his first spoon—long before the Spider-Man spoon; and Larissa had held his fat little fist for his first steps. She established his routines and always told him how important it was to follow through. "What do we say about rules, *mijo*?" Larissa would say when it was time for Curtis to brush his teeth. "Rules keep us together!" Curtis would shout with that beautiful smile of his.

She missed him unbearably.

But running her crew was all-consuming, and once she was out of Zippy's apartment it just got worse. In 18ST, she had the unique position of trying to make sure the women in the gang knew how to survive in the hood without going to jail. So many lived only for the next minute—the next hit, the next beating, the next meal, the next joyride. Larissa tried to give them something more than just survival. So as they ran drugs or worked as look-outs or sometimes prostitutes, she tried to also instill in them the same kinds of values that she wanted Curtis to have.

Crisette, for instance, who years before had gotten caught stealing TVs and microwaves to buy meth, and did four years for grand larceny before her daughter was born, now had managed to stay clean. Larissa had hooked her up with a night class, and she'd gotten her GED. Now she was trying to finish an associate degree. Larissa worked out a schedule where Crisette could study at night, with her daughter. They moved out of the crack house and into a tiny studio apartment.

The dozen or so young women that Larissa "took in" were usually about to hit strike three. She knew they desperately needed to get their lives together, and she wanted to give them a chance. She didn't know why this was so important to her—why she didn't just go about her life and let other people go about theirs. But it was an involuntary reaction. If she saw a toddler wandering toward an unprotected balcony, she'd lunge for their hand the same way she lunged for these women, dragging then back from the precipice of drugs, abuse, and hopelessness.

Often—daily, sometimes hourly—she felt mentally wiped out

from dealing with them all. Acting as their counselor, mentor, doctor, therapist, referee, chef, babysitter, personal trainer, and supervisor all rolled up into one. She never turned anyone away and always made herself available to anyone who needed her. Some of the girls tried to nickname her "Energizer," but Larissa put a stop to that quickly.

Life was easier now, without trying to juggle Zippy and Curtis on top of everything else. She was living over on Thirty-Sixth Avenue SE, in a ramshackle apartment with Quanae and Jemilla, next to a crack house and above a takeout Chinese food joint. Curtis's school was almost half an hour away, and she had no reason to get over that way much. She kept telling herself that she shouldn't see him again. It would be better that way for him. And for her.

But she wasn't a quitter. It wasn't in her nature to give up on anything, least of all being in contact with the child she loved like her own.

So, despite all the competing demands for her time, she kept finding excuses to drive over, especially when he was getting out of school.

She never saw him, though, until she showed up in his classroom.

She figured he'd be shy, turn his curly little head away. She thought maybe he'd be angry at her, pretend to ignore her.

She should have known better: his heart was always open. When he ran and hugged her, it was as if the past year had disappeared. He was taller but he was still *Curtis*, and he still adored her. She left that afternoon with a warm knot in her chest that she hoped would never go away.

Curtis usually took the city bus to get home, but Larissa started to casually rearrange her schedule to pick him up. She'd double-check to make sure he had enough money for lunch, or had a snack in his backpack for the next day.

As the year went on, she'd come to pickup early. If she could find parking, she'd go inside and watch the last few minutes of his music lessons. Daniela was constantly saying how good a player Curtis was, but it took Larissa a while to figure out what that meant. The first time Daniela called Curtis a "prodigy," Larissa had to look up the word on her phone.

"I'm happy you think Curtis is doing good," she told Daniela. "But you know what? I hear this kinda stuff every day from people comin in', blowin' these kids' heads up, makin' them think they're the next Kobe Bryant. And when that don't work, they end up on the street with everybody else."

"I know you must think that," Daniela said. "But the last kid that I saw who had this kind of talent now teaches at the Oberlin Conservatory, and she had a lot more advantages than Curtis has. She had a stable home, and her parents could afford to pay for a Buffet R13 clarinet. And I think Curtis is better than she was. Way better. Even now."

Larissa didn't know if she believed Daniela or not. After all, Curtis lived in the projects in Southeast D.C. Drugs and guns could kill, but the thing that killed more than anything was hopelessness. Kids and adults hung out on street corners smoking weed, throwing down flamin' hot Cheeto wrappers, fighting.

So many people she knew fell off and did nothing with their lives. They were stuck. Some had jobs, others didn't, but none had education, and none had much of a future. Going to the other side of D.C. was a big deal. Going as far as Alexandria, Virginia, was like going out of the country. That's why she was trying so hard with her own crew—to give them a chance.

"I don't want him hurt," Larissa said. "I don't want him chasing dreams he'll never see come true. I want him to have practical skills that he can actually use. That can make a difference in his life."

"I don't either. But I really think he has a shot. He's really something special." Daniela hesitated. "And even if he's not the next Yo-Yo Ma, we're still giving him the tools to succeed."

"Like what?" Larissa asked.

"The opportunities are out there. We're showing how to take advantage of them."

"Those, you mean," Larissa gesturing toward the musical instruments that the kids were packing away.

"No, not those," Daniela said. "Those instruments are just a way to get started. We're teaching them how to practice. We're teaching them responsibility."

"Life skills," Larissa said, nodding. It was the same thing she was doing, with the crew. She knew something about instilling life skills.

"Yeah," Daniela said, "but it's more than that. I think that music"—she gestured vaguely into the air—"can give people a purpose." She shook her head. "So many of these kids don't have anything to really look *forward* to."

Larissa thought about Curtis. Always hungry to play the next sonata, to practice some technique she didn't understand.

"At this age," Daniela was saying, "the world is wide open. No shade to the parents, but so many of them feel lost. Like they have nothing. Some of the stuff I've heard come out of their mouths would make you cry. One little girl told me her grandma's birthday was coming up, and I asked how old Grandma was. I was thinking maybe sixty or sixty-five. She told me her grandma was turning thirty-six. Girl, I almost passed out."

Larissa had taken in so many women, so many families, like that. Moni, the former crack addict from Baltimore; Cheryl, a battered wife with six kids by six different men; LaShay, a heroin addict; Quanae, who got caught jacking cars. And the others—Jemilla, Delisha, Briana, Kelly, Elena. Larissa stopped her mind from reeling out still more names, more histories.

She felt like she and Daniela were fighting the same fight in different ways.

If Daniela could give these kids a little bit of a purpose, a little bit of hope . . . maybe it could go somewhere. Even if the kids weren't musicians, they'd learn self-discipline and responsibility, and how to succeed—even if "success" meant only playing "Row, Row, Row Your Boat." Maybe that would be enough to have them try a little harder at school, or at finding a job. Maybe it would lead to something other than back to a street corner in the hood.

A little hope would be enough for Larissa, if that's all music was for Curtis.

But she knew already, like Daniela, that for Curtis it was so much more. Music wasn't just a casual thing with him. It was everything.

She didn't know how he learned discipline, this single-minded ability to practice, but somehow he had it. She wondered if he even liked sitting in his room for hours, playing the same music over and over again. How boring it must be to play one phrase fifty or sixty times until you got it right, and then move on to the next phrase before you were finally satisfied with it. And none of it making any difference because you'd have to do the exact same thing tomorrow, playing that same music again.

And yet: *he would.* Larissa had the sense that if the Delaney Foundation hadn't stuffed an instrument into his open fist, he would have glued one together with a Cheerios box and rubber bands.

How could Larissa *not* want to do everything she could to help that kind of single-minded passion?

Okay, so it was true that Larissa had broken up with Zippy. She lived miles away. Curtis wasn't even her biological child. But all of those objections were just details. She felt chosen. She understood that this odd little boy was something more, something special, and to not do what she could to help him would be as much a betrayal of herself as of Curtis.

Everything changed one afternoon when Daniela texted Larissa, asking her to pick Curtis up from school that day. Larissa rearranged her schedule and, at five thirty, poked her head into the music room. This was one of many unused classrooms in the school, given the plummeting enrollment. The ceiling tiles, many mottled with uneven brown stains, were held together with duct tape. The pencil sharpener on Miss Daniela's desk seemed like the only new piece of equipment. A few tattered posters hung on the walls: *Here are the instruments in your orchestra!* And *Look how you can read music!* Three of the overhead fluorescent bulbs were out, and another flickered and hummed.

When Daniela saw Larissa, she ushered the other parents and kids out of the room. Then she said to Curtis, "Why don't you go pack up and sit outside in the hall for a minute? I just want to talk to Larissa some more."

"Can I read *Iron Man*?" he asked Larissa.

"You can," Larissa said. "We'll be right out, okay?"

When they were alone, Daniela said, "I have some exciting news."

"Every time you got some exciting news, my blood pressure goes up."

"Well, you might want to call 911 because this is a game-changer. Curtis has been selected to perform with the American Youth Symphony."

"That's good? Who are they?"

Daniela handed her a thick packet of cream-colored heavy paper with an embossed logo on the cover. "It's a group made up of students from across the country and Puerto Rico. Normally each state will have two student musicians representing them, as long as the students reach a certain level. The last time D.C. sent a kid to the youth symphony was back in 1998. I checked."

"And Curtis made it?"

"He did. Do you know how big this is?"

"Where is this at? When? How much is it gonna cost?" Larissa asked, bracing herself.

"Normally, it would cost around five thousand dollars, but—"

"Five thousand dollars? Girl, bye. You didn't tell Curtis about this, did you?"

"No, I wanted to tell you first. I sent his audition video on a whim, hoping he'd get in but not wanting to get his hopes up."

"Zippy's gonna hit the roof when he hears you did that," Larissa said.

"His father signed off on it when he signed that permission slip."

"He probably didn't even know what he was signing." Larissa briefly closed her eyes.

Daniela shrugged. "Don't matter now. In any case you don't have to pay a dime. The Delaney Foundation is paying for everything. He'll travel to Chicago to rehearse and perform. This could be the thing that guarantees his future. Ninety percent of the kids get full rides to conservatories. Schools will be lining up to recruit him."

"Lord. This is too much. Who's going to be in Chicago with him? He can't go by himself."

Daniela smiled. "Remember when I said Delaney pays for everything? I mean *everything*. The hotel, the taxis, the flights, the meals. I can go as an official chaperone. Or you. Or his dad can. This is not only good for Curtis, but it's good for Southeast D.C. It'll be in the news for something other than carjackings. It might motivate some people in a good way."

"I just don't know. Curtis ain't never been away from home before. He's still a little boy." She thought a moment. "When is it?"

"In spring, right before school gets out."

"That's just two months away!"

"You think you can convince his dad?"

Larissa exhaled. She kept playing the words over and over: *This is for Curtis.*

Which was why, the following Tuesday evening, Larissa found herself outside her old apartment, knocking on the door after she'd picked up Curtis from school. She'd texted Zippy earlier in the day, telling him she would be bringing him home.

OK, was all he texted back. They still saw each other occasionally on the street, and were always cordial. She closed her eyes briefly, opened them. Her pulse felt thin and thready in her veins.

"Why don't you just go in?" Curtis asked at her elbow. He pushed the door open. "Hey, anybody home? Daddy? Larissa's here." He bounded into the living room, little red backpack bouncing on his back.

Zippy was splayed out in the living room, chewing something. He looked up when they came in, kept chewing but tapped his thumb to his forehead and held it out. Curtis echoed him.

"Who's got your back?" Zippy asked.

"All the time," Curtis told him.

Larissa looked from one to the other. "Y'all are crazy."

Zippy reached out to give Curtis a one-armed hug. "That's my dude," Zippy said to him. "How was school? Did you learn a new song today?"

"I did the whole second movement of Beethoven number one. In third position," Curtis informed him.

"You did, did you?" Zippy said.

"Yep. And then I got the runs right."

"That's good," Zippy said. "Great, actually."

He was different than he used to be, Larissa noticed. He seemed actually interested in what Curtis told him. Maybe her leaving him hadn't been such a bad idea after all, if it brought Zippy and Curtis closer.

But now Zippy was eyeing Larissa, stone-faced, and said to her, "Whattup. Watcha want?"

"Can I talk to you for a minute? It's important."

The apartment looked different, but exactly the same. The couch had more food stains, and the gross gray-and-yellow rug under the coffee table was blue and orange but equally disgusting. The laminate floor curled up even more in the corners.

"I already picked up today's drop," Zippy said.

"Hey, Curtis," Larissa said, squatting down to his level, "you wanna take a bath before dinner? Maybe I'll tuck you in tonight."

Curtis nodded.

When he'd disappeared into the bathroom, Larissa said, "We need to talk. He just got a big award." She felt like they were repeating the same conversation that they'd had a year ago, but she tried to explain as carefully as she could. The youth orchestra. Representing Washington, D.C. "This is huge."

She thrust the cream-colored packet at Zippy, who took it but didn't try to read. "Is he gonna be on the TV? I still don't want him on the TV." He looked up at her, sorrowful. "I'm sorry. I never should have put my hands on you. It was an accident. But that boy can't be on TV. It could mess me up for real. And you too."

"Would you listen to yourself? This ain't about you. This ain't even about me. This is about Curtis. All this drug runnin' ain't gonna do nothin' but get him killed."

"What are you talking about? I make sure that—"

"I'm talking about Curtis making it out of the hood. You know why he practices all the time? He practices because he loves it. His teacher thinks he can make it out."

"You sure know a lot about what's going on with him. And he's always talking about Larissa this and Larissa that—"

Larissa sighed again. "Because I make sure he gets everything he needs. Do you?"

Zippy stood up now, staring at her. The couch separated them. "I take care of that boy. I make sure he has everything he needs."

"Seriously—listen to yourself: I, I, I. Nothing about Curtis. It's all about you. You're trying to prove to T Block how much of a man you are. You need to be focusing on Curtis. I know you love him. I do too. Selling blow ain't gonna get him out of the hood."

As she'd driven over, rehearsing what she'd say to Zippy, she'd felt that the conversation would be a waste of time. Surprisingly, though, it felt as if she was actually getting through. So she went on, "This youth orchestra is a big deal. His teachers are saying that he really has something."

"Yeah," Zippy said, "I know. The kid's nuts about that cello."

The fact that he actually called it a cello made Larissa reach out and touch Zippy's hand. "We can't punish Curtis for our decisions. But we can give him the chance we didn't have."

Zippy looked at her, looked over her shoulder, at the wall, thinking. After a minute he said, "Okay, but they can't come here. No cameras. I can't go on TV."

"I know. It's all about Curtis. I'll make sure that nobody says your name or talks about anything except Curtis."

"You're something else. You know that?" Zippy said. He reached out then and grabbed her other hand.

She shrugged away. "Curtis. All for Curtis."

"I got one more thing to say before you dip out." Zippy said. "You hungry? I know it's late but why don't we go out to eat. All of us."

Larissa gave Zippy a side-eye and said, "Golden Corral? You know that's my jam."

6

ZIPPY

"yo, come out here for a minute." Zippy stood outside his son's door. Closed, as usual. No response from inside. "Ayo, Curtis!"

He two-knuckle tapped. Strained to hear the faint sound of the cello. Barely audible, drowned out by next door's Chuck Brown go-go music. What's up with a little kid having his door closed? It wasn't a bad thing, come to think of it, since the kid repeated the same music over and over and over all the time.

He respected closed doors. From the days when his mama would have men over. Some of them taught Zippy to respect a closed door.

Finally, silence from inside. The door opened a crack. Curtis peered out. Little eyes wide and blank. The kid was a billion miles away.

"We got shit happening," Zippy said. "Come out here. You're gonna meet a friend of mine."

"Who?"

"My boss."

Now Curtis was paying attention. "T Boom?"

"Yeah. T *Block*," Zippy said, realizing how rarely he spoke the name. He'd only met the Big Boss a couple of times. "Now go get changed. And I need your help before we go."

"Now?"

"Yeah," Zippy said, "now."

Curtis glanced back, and Zippy could have sworn the kid looked like he was gonna apologize to the cello. "Can I come out in a few? I just wanna try this—"

Zippy stood his ground. "Now," he said. He put a little bass into his voice. Zippy might be on the smaller side, but he was a lot bigger than Curtis. He jerked his head toward the living room. "I told you, we got to meet T Block, and I want to show you a few things first. You're getting an important lesson today."

He had no idea why T Block had called five minutes ago, but he could guess. The phone call had been brief, as the few other previous calls with him had been. "Hey, it's T Block," the voice had said. "Can you swing by today?" No "sup man," no "howyadoin." Since T Block used burner phones, Zippy hadn't recognized the number.

"Yeah man, of course," Zippy had said. "When is good?" He kept his voice low and even. Wasn't going to give away his excitement. He'd never met one-on-one with T Block. He didn't know anybody who had. JFunk or Tremel met up with him usually. T Block liked to rule from a distance.

But Zippy had sent so many messages over the years, through JFunk and the others, and all that persistence had finally paid off. T Block was finally going to take Zippy's plans for expansion seriously. Zippy was sure of it.

"How's that kid of yours doing?" T Block had asked, unexpectedly.

Zippy didn't realize that T Block even knew he had a kid. He wanted to ask why it mattered but didn't want to question the Big Boss. "He's good," Zippy said.

"Why don't you bring him along?"

Zippy's pulse suddenly sounded loud in his ears. The Big Boss not only wanted to talk to Zippy, he wanted to meet his family. Zippy had finally made it. "Uh, sure," he told T Block, "I can do that."

"Cool," T Block said. "Be here before six. I got stuff to talk to you about." He gave Zippy the address, off Pennsylvania Avenue, on Capitol Hill. Zippy scrawled the address down on his hand. He didn't have any paper handy and was lucky he found a pen. "Don't park out front, you hear me? Park a couple blocks away. And come in the back door. There's an alley." T Block described it. Zippy tried writing it down on his arm, but the pen ran out of ink on his skin.

T Block hung up without saying goodbye. Zippy was left playing out multiple scenarios in his head. They could expand the
blow biz farther north. They could go after the white students at
Catholic and GW, hell, maybe all the way to Georgetown. Zippy
tried to remember all the ideas he'd floated up the chain over
the past few years. Must've been two dozen or more. Enough
for T Block to finally take notice.

But wanting to meet Curtis took things to an even higher level.
T Block wasn't just interested in Zippy—he was interested in
Zippy's family. Larissa was already a trusted gang member; now
T Block wanted to meet the son. Which meant, Zippy guessed,
that T Block would ask Curtis, "Your dad's showing you the
ropes?" T Block liked to get the kids involved early. Act as look-
outs or bag product.

And what would Curtis say? "No, sorry, I gotta practice my
music."

Zippy couldn't imagine how that would go over with T Block.

Curtis was only eight, but it was time he got started. Some kids
in second grade were already going on runs. A couple were look-
outs. And Curtis was in third already.

Larissa was against it. She wanted him practicing the cello.
Luckily she was out now. Doing something with her crew. Still, he
couldn't wait to tell her about how T Block summoned him.
They'd celebrate tonight.

On the coffee table, Zippy had already stacked the baggies,
scales, masking tape, and Sharpies. There were two kilos of product to put into ninety-six baggies, label, and tape securely closed.
On the street it was worth about forty thousand. Zippy's take
would be fifteen hundred. It was time Curtis started understanding the economics of life. How selling blow would pay for electricity, food, water, clothes. Curtis needed to learn how to budget.
How far the value of a hard-earned dollar actually went.

"Daddy, what do you want me to do? I gotta practice—"

"You can practice later. Right now you need to pay attention."

Curtis looked around. "Where's Larissa? She knows what—"

"She's out," Zippy said. "And you're *my* son, I know what's best for you. You're gonna just watch today. I'm gonna show you how this is done. You watch."

"Daddy, I—"

"Now," Zippy said, gesturing. He felt like T Block was already looking over his shoulder, approving. He wanted to believe Larissa, wanted to believe that Curtis could become a musician and make a living out of it, but Zippy knew the reality of the streets. Kids like Curtis—like Zippy had been—don't just leave Southeast and become accountants. They become thugs and gangbangers if they're lucky enough to not get shot on the corner. In Southeast, there were only three ways to succeed: you were a seven-foot-tall basketball player; you had the connections and the means to make a dope rapper; or you pushed product.

Curtis would never break six feet, and would only hang around the edges of a pickup game when Zippy forced him outside to play with the other kids. He'd tried to make the kid love rap, but that hadn't happened, and Zippy didn't have the connections anyway. So the one thing that Zippy knew, the one thing that Zippy could give his son, was street smarts. Was working knowledge of how to thrive in the projects. Teaching Curtis now—and it was long overdue—was Curtis's best shot. Even if Larissa disagreed.

So now Zippy gestured firmly to the couch; and after a long hesitation, Curtis sat.

Zippy showed him how he loaded up a bag. Weighed it. Taped it closed. Labeled the finished product.

"I don't think Larissa would want me doing this."

"Larissa works for T Block too. Now watch. We makin' moves and money." Now Zippy was psyched to show Curtis the ropes. The ins and outs of how to survive in the hood. Once Curtis got a taste of how the world really worked, he'd pay less attention to the cello. Zippy was convinced it was just a phase. A long-ass phase and Curtis would get tired of it eventually.

Zippy showed him how to pour into the baggie until it was two ounces. A teaspoon could adjust if there was too much or too little.

Zippy started playing Jamie Foxx's version of "Gold Digger," and the music helped get him into a rhythm: opening the bag, pouring the product, sealing it. He was in the groove. Zippy tapped a counter-rhythm to the beat. Curtis joined in, grinning.

This was father-son bonding. This was better than what Zippy had imagined.

But before the last bag had been sealed and labeled, Curtis was on his feet. "I'm just gonna go back real quick and run through—"

"Hold up," Zippy said. "You practiced enough. Go change your shirt. I told you, we're gonna meet my boss. And we gotta drop this shit off on the way." He was arranging the product in his duffle bag. Flat bricks in five rows.

In a few minutes Curtis was back, wearing a clean hoodie. Zippy looked him up and down. He looked all right. "Let's go." Zippy could see them doing this more and more. Teaching Curtis the family business. Rising in the ranks. Becoming T Block's lieutenant, and Curtis eventually becoming Zippy's lieutenant. That's how Greg was doing it with Mica, and now they *owned* Third Street.

The elevator was broken again. The stairs smelled like pee. In the stairwell, they stepped over an empty fire extinguisher. Plastic bags leaking pickle juice. A half-eaten bologna sandwich. A few broken vials. From high up on the walls, out of reach, roaches warily waved their antennae.

His family wasn't going to be living in these projects much longer. If Zippy played his cards right, soon he wouldn't be just a two-bit hustler selling drugs. Soon he'd be one of the bosses. Maybe he'd get one of those townhouses that Larissa had her eye on.

He tossed the product in the trunk, climbed into his ride. A beat-up gray Honda Civic with a beige side panel from where he'd gotten into an accident a couple years back. Though it wasn't his fault. Zippy was a careful driver.

They swung by Ninth and F. The corner that JFunk ran. He was hanging with his homies, Vernell and Big Mike. Smoking weed and talking smack. JFunk was one step higher on the rung. A skinny black dude who spent his money on shoes and jewelry. Today he was rocking green and white Nike Airs that probably cost $300.

Zippy pulled up next to him. "Hey man." They dapped. "Brought you somethin'." He thumbed toward the trunk.

"I thought you was bringing it tomorrow?" JFunk leaned in the driver's window. The mildewy smell of weed blew in with the stench of car exhaust. "Whattup man? All good?" His eyes were on Curtis, sitting in the passenger seat. "How ya doin'."

Curtis reached across, dapped him up. "Wassup."

"We chillin'," Zippy said. "I figured I'd drop it by on the way to T Block's." Zippy'd been waiting to say that. JFunk needed to know Zippy was a player. That Zippy was coming for his job.

JFunk squinted, studying Zippy more carefully. "For real?" He nodded to Vernell to retrieve the duffle bag from the trunk. Vernell sauntered over, pants hanging below his ass, and peered into the back seat, where Curtis sat. "What up, what up," he mumbled, popping the trunk.

Zippy eyed him. "Yeah," he said to JFunk, "keeping it in the family. He asked me to swing by."

JFunk didn't say anything for a minute. Then, reluctant: "Cool."

Zippy knew that JFunk didn't think it was cool at all. Leapfrogging over him and Tremel. Going directly to the Boss himself. But there was nothing JFunk could do.

A minute later they were heading up to Capitol Hill.

Eight years ago, when Zippy was a lost seventeen-year-old father with no prospects, no way of finishing school, and no way of earning money, T Block had reached out. Not directly—through Tremel. But Tremel let him know it was T Block. And Zippy had never forgotten. Now Zippy felt a dedication bordering on worship for a man that he'd only met three times. Yet T Block had given Zippy so much. T Block commanded respect. Zippy hungered for people to look at him the same way. He was always conscious about how short he was. Skinny. Not a big dude that people would look twice at.

Now he wanted to be worthy of T Block's trust. He didn't piss away his money on jewelry or ho's or the latest kicks. He'd gotten his priorities straight. He was going somewhere. He was thinking like a boss. Like T Block himself.

They left the trash-strewn streets of Southeast. Zippy kept

checking his arm for the directions to T Block's house. A straight shot up Pennsylvania Avenue. Past busted-ass row houses. Boarded-up or barred windows. As they ascended toward the homes of senators and congressmen, the potholes disappeared. Blowing trash and ripped-up McDonald's bags transformed into ladies in Lululemon sportswear prancing along with dogs on leashes. The houses grew pristine. Manicured lawns and flower gardens. It was a magic trick.

Curtis hadn't spoken the whole car ride over, which was okay. Zippy was bumpin' Drake so Curtis could be exposed to something other than Beethoven and other dead white dudes.

They wound their way through the neighborhood. The people they passed, white and Black, looked clean. No homeless people anywhere. No packs of brothers hanging on corners. Trees, bare now, stretched branches to the sky.

"We gonna be livin' up here one day," Zippy told Curtis.

"Like the Avengers mansion," Curtis said in awe. One enormous palace—big as a hotel or a castle—shouldered the next.

They passed a cream-colored brick townhouse. Its front porch had freshly painted maroon carvings and blue railings. "That's where we're going," Zippy said, double-checking the address on his arm as he gestured to the building with his chin. He drove farther down the block. Parked a few streets over, as T Block had instructed. Zippy didn't blame him. Zippy wouldn't want any jacked-up cars out front of his townhouse, either.

T Block went to rooftop bars with famous athletes. Sat in the owner's box for Nationals games. Hung signed pictures of congressmen on his walls. And now T Block wanted to hang with Zippy.

On foot, they approached the townhouse. Zippy tried to decipher what he'd written on his arm. Weren't they supposed to go down an alley? He thought so but now couldn't remember. Couldn't see an alley. Panic rose in his throat.

He led them past the front walkway. Curtis had stopped. "Wha—why aren't—"

"We don't go in that way." Zippy hoped he was right. "We go a different way."

They turned down the next street. Halfway up the block, casually stretching between two more beautifully painted townhouses, lay an unmarked alley that Zippy first mistook for a driveway. He gasped with relief. Headed in. Past garbage bins and garages. Wood-slat fences screened off backyards. He tried to decipher the scratches the pen had made on his skin. Was that an "8" or a "3"?

Halfway down the block, they paused in front of a wooden door indistinguishable from the others, with a wrought-iron "23" discreetly to one side. Above, the bulbous eye of a security camera gleamed down. The address matched the address on Zippy's arm. This had to be right.

He pressed the button. Leaned against the wall. Very casual. Very at-home. He was showing Curtis what kind of life was possible.

The latch clicked.

They were in.

Down another flagstone walkway, through a well-groomed lawn, past a stainless-steel barbecue, up on the back porch. Zippy looked for a doorbell, but before he could find one the door opened. An enormously muscled man looked at Curtis. Nodded at Zippy.

"You the kid?" the guy asked Curtis, ignoring Zippy.

Curtis looked up solemnly at him. "I'm Curtis," he said.

The man nodded, dapped him. "My man." He didn't introduce himself but gestured for them to come in.

T Block had even told his bodyguards that he and Curtis were coming, Zippy thought. It gave him a sense of pride that T Block was talking about him. *My new right-hand man is comin' over with his kid. Let 'em in.*

They slid into a gleaming kitchen with immaculate marble countertops and brushed steel cabinet knobs. Zippy tried to swagger in as if he belonged.

"T Block's ready for both of you," the big man said, pointing with his chin toward a doorway, and took the lead. They followed him into a hallway where impressive-looking paintings lined the walls. There were pedestals with smooth stone statues.

The big man knocked on a half-open door and pushed it open

with his foot. Inside, facing them, gleamed an enormous desk. The chair behind it sat empty. On top of the desk, beside piles of papers and an oversized computer monitor, a French bulldog snored on a cushion.

Zippy paused, flummoxed. Where was T Block?

"Yo, T," the big man was saying. He leaned around them into the room, looking at someone out of Zippy's line of sight. "They're here. The kid and his dad." He drew back and gestured for Zippy.

Zippy put his hands on Curtis's shoulders, and they shuffled in. "Yo, T," Zippy said, maneuvering Curtis inside. "Howyadoin'." On the other side of the room, a wraparound leather couch took up all three walls. A coffee table piled with electronics was barely visible in the center.

On one side of the couch slouched a handsome older guy in a tracksuit, a potbelly pushing at the fabric. His feet, in blue socks, were up on the coffee table, next to three or four cell phones. Another cell phone was on his chest.

A younger bearded man sat across from him. He had an iPad out, showing the screen to an elegant woman in her midthirties, her hair elaborately braided.

They all turned to look at Zippy and Curtis.

"Zippy," the older man said, not standing. A real power move, Zippy thought. He'd have to do it too, when he became the Boss.

"So this is your famous son." T Block was examining Curtis.

"Famous?" Zippy said. Not following.

"Aw, come on," T Block said. "American Youth Orchestra. And he played for the British Embassy, right?" T Block was saying to Curtis. "That was you, wasn't it? The cello? I saw it on TV."

Curtis nodded.

Zippy prodded him slightly. "What do you say?"

"Yes, sir," Curtis said obediently. "That was me."

"Hot damn," T Block said, delighted. "When they said, 'Curtis Wilson, who lives in Southeast D.C.,' I thought, 'How many Curtis Wilsons could there be?'"

None of this was making sense to Zippy. Weren't they here to talk about Zippy's ideas? Ways of expanding the business? Not

Curtis on TV. He hadn't even known that Curtis was on the TV again. Curtis had been on several times by now—and Zippy had learned to be okay with it. As long as nobody interviewed him or Larissa, and stuck to Curtis in school, it had been okay. Now Zippy tried to wrap his head around the ramifications of T Block knowing his kid was on TV. A sick feeling poked its fingers into his stomach. *Curtis Wilson of Southeast Washington, D.C.* Was that enough for people, for the police, to trace him back to Zippy? Was Curtis—and, really, Zippy—putting all of T Block's network in jeopardy?

Then again, T Block didn't seem angry or upset. He was beaming like a proud father. Was that just an act? And now he'd have that big dude take Zippy out into the manicured backyard and shoot him, right next to the stainless-steel barbecue?

"They say you're a musical genius," T Block was saying. "You playing with the National Symphony?" Zippy knew he was playing with a symphony, but somehow the way that T Block said it made it seem way more important.

"Just the youth symphony right now," Curtis amended.

T Block guffawed. "Just the youth symphony. You're how old?"

"Eight."

"Eight, huh? Well damn." Finally he looked at Zippy. Who tried to meet his gaze no matter how the terror and anxiety were constricting his throat. He needed to use the bathroom. "You're a sneaky one, Zip, keeping this from us. Larissa too. Damn!"

"We don't let them do interviews with us," Zippy said hastily. "They only film him when he's playing, and right after."

T Block nodded, vague, not listening, turning back to Curtis. "Is it true what they said about you? The ones who interviewed you?"

Curtis shrugged. "I dunno. I didn't hear. We didn't see the show either."

"What was it like to play for a king?" T Block asked.

"It was okay," Curtis said. "He had a big nose. There was so much security, and we had to get there hours ahead of time."

"Big nose, huh?"

Curtis nodded.

"Well, young man, they said you have a brilliant future ahead of you. That's what they said. 'Brilliant.' Did you know that?"

Curtis shook his head, smiled.

Zippy didn't know that, either. The sick feeling was going away. Who'd have thought that the cello could be the reason that T Block was beaming at them?

Maybe here was another way that Zippy could get himself out of the hood. Up the ranks. He rubbed Curtis's shoulders briskly. "This boy practices all the time. I mean *all* the time. He loves it."

"I should've had you bring your cello. Why didn't I think of that?" T Block asked the room.

The bearded guy nodded. "That'd be great, T."

"We could've had a private concert," T Block was saying. "Would you give us a private concert?"

"Yes, sir," Curtis said.

"We're gonna do that, okay?" T Block only had eyes for Curtis. "What grade you in? Fourth?"

"Third."

"My daughter Trishelle's in fifth. She goes to Sidwell. I got two other little girls younger than you. Two older kids, too—they're grown. Five girls, total." T Block paused like he was expecting someone to chime in, but when no one said anything he went on, "I'm gonna have you come over one night for a barbecue. Would you play for my girls? I think it'd be good for them to see." He chuckled. "Zip, we're gonna have you all over for a barbecue. But you gotta bring the cello, aight?"

"Aight," Zippy said.

"How you feel about that, young man?"

"I'm good with that," Curtis said. "I like to play. I'm working on a Beethoven sonata right now."

"Oh yeah? Which one?" T Block asked. Zippy had the impression that T Block wouldn't know a Beethoven sonata from Taylor Swift.

"Number three."

"That's great. Can't wait to hear it. Do you know—what's that one—the bird one—*Swan Lake*? No—"

"*Swan Lake* is Tchaikovsky," Curtis said. "I just played the 'Chanson Triste.'"

"Isn't there another sonata about a bird? With *Swan* in the title?" T Block asked. His eyes seemed fixed on Curtis's face. Focused. He hadn't even glanced at Zippy.

"'The Swan,'" Curtis told him. "That's Saint-Saëns, though."

"Okay," T Block said, head bobbing enthusiastically. "You can play 'em both, all right? I'm really looking forward to it. We'll make sure it happens soon. And now you're playing for royalty. At eight years old."

It didn't seem to be a question. Curtis just looked at him. Zippy wasn't sure if he should prompt him for an answer, so didn't.

"How do you have time for all that?" T Block asked Curtis. "You get special lessons? Music lessons?"

Curtis nodded. "Larissa takes me."

"Takes you to practice?"

Curtis nodded again. "I have to go to Virginia."

A couple times a week and on weekends, Curtis would practice with the Alexandria, Virginia, youth orchestra. But since Zippy wasn't home much in the afternoons or weekends, Larissa had handled all of that.

"Larissa takes you," T Block repeated. "What time do you get home?"

Curtis looked up at Zippy. Zippy didn't know what time they got home. He shrugged.

"My girls," T Block said, "they're in bed by eight. Lights out."

Curtis nodded again.

Zippy had no idea why they were talking about T Block's daughters' bedtime. "Listen T—" he started.

"Where do you live again?" At last, finally, T Block looked at Zippy.

Zippy told him the address, in Southeast.

T Block refocused on Curtis as he calculated. "You come all the way from there to Virginia?"

"Yes, sir," Curtis said.

"You have private teachers? How do you learn all this stuff?"

Curtis shook his head. "Miss Daniela tries to help me when all the other kids are practicing. And then there's youth orchestra."

"You don't have a private teacher," T Block repeated.

Curtis shook his head again.

"Would you want a private teacher?"

"Yeah," Curtis said, and Zippy could hear the excitement in his voice. Who was going to pay for a private lesson, Zippy thought.

T Block must have had the same idea, because he glanced at Zippy again. "I bet that would really help him," T Block said to Zippy. "Exceptional teachers. Private lessons. The best that money can buy."

"Miss Daniela says that that's what the rich kids have," Curtis volunteered. "That's why they get better faster."

"Do you want to get better faster?"

Curtis nodded so vigorously that Zippy could feel the air moving on his arms. "Yeah," he said. "She told me last year that she taught me everything she could. So I try to learn from youth orchestra. Like last week? Miss Daniela showed me how to do thumb position, but in youth symphony I had to do a whole section in thumb position and it was really hard. See? I got a blister." He showed T Block his thumb.

"Huh," T Block said, studying the thumb as if he'd expected it to sprout wings. "So private lessons would really make a difference. What else would really help you?"

"A new cello," Curtis said. "The Delaney Foundation got me an okay one, but Miss Daniela said—"

"These things are expensive," Zippy interrupted. "She talked to us about it. Like ten Gs. Maybe more. And it's not even a full-sized cello."

"Ten Gs for a cello?" T Block repeated.

"It's an investment," Curtis said. "That's what Miss Daniela says. An investment in my future."

"Well, we certainly want to make sure you have a good future in front of you, young man," T Block said. "Right, Zip?"

Now Zippy found his own head nodding, wondering where he'd come up with $10,000. "You bet, T Block."

T Block thought a moment. Stood. Leaned over the coffee table to shake Curtis's hand. "My man, it's been an honor to meet you. We're gonna set up that private concert, though. And I want to hear—what is it again? The duck? The flamingo?" A little smile creased the corners of T Block's eyes.

"'The Swan,'" Curtis said. "Yes, sir. I'll practice it when I get home."

The interview—audience, interrogation, whatever it was—was over. They were being dismissed.

T Block hadn't wanted to talk to Zippy at all. Zippy wondered if any of those ideas had ever made it up the chain.

"Hey man, can I have a word?" he said hastily, before they were pushed back out into the shadows.

T Block paused, glanced at him.

"Got some business I need to talk over with you," he went on.

"Business?"

Zippy nodded. He tried to play it cool but had the sense that his head was bobbing a little too frantically. He tried to slow it down to just a chin lift.

T Block shrugged, looked back at Curtis. "Hey, bro, me and your dad got some business to talk about. So would you be okay going with Dre for something to drink? You look like a bourbon man."

Curtis half smiled, sought out approval from Zippy, who nodded.

"We're gonna get together soon, okay?" T Block repeated.

"Okay," Curtis said. There was a pause, and then he asked, "Can I pet your dog?"

T Block bellowed laughter. "Can he pet the dog? Sure you can pet the dog. His name's Buddy."

Curtis turned to pet the snoring French bulldog, who woke, snuffled his hand. Licked it.

"I knew Buddy would like you," T Block said. "He don't like many people. If he didn't like you, though, I'd have to get a new dog," he said, laughing to himself.

After a moment, the younger woman and the guy led Curtis out. They were alone. Zippy had never been alone with T Block before.

"Quite a kid you got there," T Block said. "He's gonna make something of himself."

Zippy nodded modestly.

"You and Larissa are doing a good job. Nurturing him. Giving him some real culture. The lessons, the symphony, the teachers, all that shit. Not everybody would do that. It's impressive, you know? You're a man after my own heart. I know what it's like to have kids. You want what's best for them."

Zippy smiled down at nothing, waiting for his chance.

"I'm serious about that concert. And the barbecue," T Block went on. "You like ribs? Mambo sauce? Ever have Junior's? I'll talk to my wife and we'll set something up. Maybe next weekend. When's his next concert? Maybe I'll take the kids and go see it."

Zippy shrugged. "Larissa keeps track of all that. I'll let you know."

"Oh, okay," T Block said. He leaned back on the sofa. Stretched out both arms across the back, waiting.

This was Zippy's chance. "Look, T," he started. "I got some ideas. Ways of growin' the business. Expanding."

T Block didn't move. Didn't seem to want to hear more, but didn't stop him. That was enough for Zippy to keep going. Briefly he explained a few of his ideas—how to increase production by bringing in Matty and Deshaunda; cut in the fetty more efficiently and sell it to the college kids in Northwest; and a couple of other ideas that he'd told JFunk and Tremel about months ago, but that they'd apparently never relayed to the Boss.

The whole time, he never let his eyes stray from T Block's face. At the beginning it didn't seem like the Man was listening, but soon it was clear he was, and he nodded along as Zippy went on, asking questions.

"I'm glad we've had the chance to talk, Zip," T Block said at last. "I feel like God had a hand in all this, bringing you to me. Seeing Curtis on the TV was His hand in it."

T Block leaned toward Zippy, tapping one finger on the paper on the coffee table. "Don't think I haven't noticed. Your territory's running like a well-oiled machine. You've been bringing in everything you said you would. Down to the penny, my man. To the penny."

He reached out and dapped Zippy again.

"Yeah, I'm doing it. Told you I would."

"But these ideas here? These are good. Not sure about the one with the Ravens, that feels a little risky. But the others? I'm liking them."

"Good," Zippy said. "Great. Let me do 'em, T."

There was a moment where T Block stared expressionless into Zippy's face, and Zippy stared back, feeling his stomach flip again. *The question is, can I trust you?* the older man seemed to be saying, and Zippy wanted to be worthy of that trust. He didn't move. Didn't do anything to display weakness or uncertainty.

After a moment T Block seemed satisfied. "Rob?" he said, his voice not loud, but it carried. A moment later Rob poked his head around the closed door. "Get me that stuff we were talking about."

Rob disappeared and came back a few seconds later with a manila folder, like something out of a banker's office, or a lawyer's.

"Rob was going over the weekly numbers and seems to think there might be some skimming off the top. Not you. But I'm thinking maybe you can give me some insights." T Block opened the folder. Slid a spreadsheet across to Zippy. Rob took a seat next to him. Pulled out his iPad and brought the spreadsheets up electronically. "Do me a favor and let me know if you have an opinion on this, okay? Rob's thinking that this is a simple mistake. You know how JFunk's turf is poppin' off."

Zippy studied the spreadsheets. Grabbed Rob's iPad for a couple of them. He mouthed some calculations. Wrote down a few figures. "These are JFunk's numbers from two weeks ago, right?" He double-checked his math. "Yeah, he's off by"— a beat—"nine thousand six hundred and fifty dollars. Can I look at the one from a month ago? Cause if that's happening twice a month, you're losing close to twenty Gs."

T Block looked at Rob, then back at Zippy. "You did that awful quick," T Block said to Zippy, and then to Rob, "Is that what you came up with?"

Rob looked at his iPad, nodded. "Yeah. I have nine thousand six hundred fifty too."

"And you did that all in your head?"

"Yeah, I know numbers." Zippy shrugged.

"Damn. I'm gonna be hitting you up again." He chuckled. "This is some family. The Black Beethoven and the human calculator. I see you, Zip. You're doing good work. One word of advice: don't get too ambitious too quick. You'll get yours soon enough."

Zippy dapped him. "I got you, T. Whatever you need."

"My man. I'll be in touch soon to figure out that barbecue."

A few minutes later, back in the alley, past the dumpsters, Zippy slung an arm over Curtis's shoulder. "Now that's how you do it."

"Do what?"

"Make moves, son. Make moves. We're going out tonight." He texted Larissa from the road: Meet us at Golden Corral. We're celebrating.

7

CURTIS

IT ALL CAME TO A HEAD when Curtis was ten, in the fall of fifth grade, barely a month after school had started.

All last year he sensed what was coming but had managed to slip beneath the radar, slide beneath the surface of the water so the maelstrom passed him by. He'd kept thinking, magically, that everything that had happened up till then—and especially all of the events that summer—would somehow insulate him from what was waiting for him that fall.

Because over the summer, the summer before fifth grade, he'd felt like a prince.

T Block's brother Rodney owned an enormous mansion out in the country, almost three hours from the projects where Curtis and his family still lived. It seemed like a fairy tale, too good to be true, that every couple of weeks Curtis would receive an invite—a summons, really—to spend the weekend in the country with T Block's daughters and their cousin Ralph.

And then, a couple hours later, Curtis would be sitting in the back seat of T Block's Lincoln with the other kids, being driven like royalty to a mansion set in the foothills of the Blue Ridge Mountains. There, on the side of a spring-fed pond that stretched out on one side of the house, reflecting water lilies and sky on its surface, there would be picnics. There would be outings for ice cream. There would be horseback riding and swimming and long rambling walks through the honeycomb of bridle trails that stretched in all directions, linking the estates.

But above all else, there would be music. Curtis's cello received as much, if not more, of an invite as Curtis himself.

There were performances on the terrace at dusk, and there was practicing in the afternoon. Two of Block's three daughters—Trishelle and Lyndsay—now played the violin and the oboe, and all three would practice together with the local teacher that Ralph's father had hired. Crista, the youngest, only six, wanted to be a ballerina and refused to play an instrument. While the other kids practiced she'd twirl in a pink tutu that her parents had bought at Ross.

Curtis could not believe that a life like this could exist, so far away from the grimy streets and hopelessness of Southeast D.C.

By then he'd seen other parts of the city. He practiced several times out in Annandale, Virginia, on the campus of Northern Virginia Community College—he was there so often, staying late, that the custodian actually gave him the security passcode to the building.

He performed concerts with the youth symphony and warm-up shows before he played in New York, Chicago, and Boston.

But always, always, he'd come home to the projects, where the sweet rot of weed competed with the stench of neglect and something beyond despair. He'd climb the stairs past discarded needles and worn-out crack pipes, the echoes of fighting and laughter reverberating in the stairwell.

When he was nine, in fourth grade, he won the inaugural $20,000 Lyric Virtuosity Prize, a much-touted fellowship partially subsidized by T Block's brother. The prize was awarded via nomination and audition only, for kids ages nine to eighteen who demonstrated "striking musical prowess" and "exceptional citizenship." Curtis didn't know what "exceptional citizenship" meant. But in any case 90 percent of the prize money had to be used to further the winner's music education.

The awards ceremony took place on T Block's brother's estate. The mansion was large enough to have a thousand or more people on its grounds. The LVP Awards Committee would commandeer dozens of limousines to drive the winners and runners-up out to the country for an evening under the stars, with an elegant dinner and a performance from the winners, along with special guests who flew in on private jets—guests like Joshua Bell, Mitsuko Uchida, Yo-Yo Ma.

As an award winner, Curtis was invited to attend every year, and adored the ceremony: the winners played a musical program, and often invited him to participate as well. All the handshaking and holding of wineglasses ("You got this," T Block told him that first year, handing him a glass of white grape juice in a champagne flute) intimidated him at first, but it seemed like an overture come to life. All the like-minded people were in the same place. All loving what they did. All the tuning of instruments and shuffling of pages that, with the conductor's raised arms, transformed into the opening strains of the symphony, that first glimpse into the musical world they would soon venture deep inside. So if drinking from crystal goblets would allow Curtis to enter that world, he would hold the glass high.

Only later, much later, when he'd had more than enough time to brood, did he wonder about T Block's real motivations. At the time, T Block had seemed like a fairy godfather waving his drug-funded wand to make many of Curtis's dreams come true. At the time, it didn't seem odd that T Block would drag a kid, no matter how talented, out from the projects for golden summer afternoons in one of the wealthiest and most beautiful places in the country. At the time, Curtis didn't question that T Block would lift him up out of the city streets but demand that Zippy continue to live there, to be close to the heartbeat of his burgeoning drug-running business.

Later, he wondered. He wondered about the satisfaction T Block must have felt, showering the poor kid with what was possible but remained out of his reach. Curtis may have had talent, but the money and power belonged to Trishelle, Crista, Lyndsay, and Ralph.

At the time, though, at the beginning of fifth grade, ten-year-old Curtis was too young to realize any of this. So when school started up, he still felt insulated. Coddled. Privileged. As if knowing how to sit on a horse or swing a badminton racket could protect him from the fists and neck slaps of Southeast D.C.'s Kramer Elementary School, one of the most dangerous elementary schools in the country.

He knew something was up as soon as he came through the doors in late August. He could barely believe he was back. The fiberboard ceiling tiles seemed even lower, the linoleum floor even grubbier. Nothing had been repaired over the summer break. Most of the fluorescent lights on the second floor were still out.

Most familiar was the smell, a funk of body odor and weed that set Curtis's stomach roiling the second he breathed it in. He tried to pull back his memories of the summer fields at night, dotted with fireflies and stars; of playing an impromptu sonata on the terrace overlooking the pond. The smell of honeysuckle and hope. But try as he might, it might as well have happened to some other kid on some other planet.

Then came a voice: "Move, bitch."

And although the hallway was wide, and although there was no one near him, before he had a chance to get out of the way, a shoulder rammed and flung him almost to the wall.

"I told you get out of the way, bitch ass," Antoinne Marley said, baseball cap turned around menacingly, his tattoo of Chinese characters disappearing under his T-shirt.

Of course, on Curtis's very first day, it had to be Antoinne Marley. He too was in fifth grade, held back for the third or fourth time, Curtis wasn't sure which. All he knew was that Antoinne was bigger than the other kids, and shaving, with the Hammer Edge gang tattoo on the back of his elbow.

Last year, Antoinne and his crew had left Curtis alone. Curtis's dad was Zippy Wilson, who was way up in the 18ST ranks. So Curtis should have been untouchable. They spoke to him with respect, calling him "man," asking his opinion and inviting him out, figuring—Curtis guessed—that being a friend of Zippy's son could only do them good.

But Curtis hadn't come with them to hang at the carryout on Eighteenth and Minnesota Avenue. Curtis wasn't smoking weed with them in the stairway. Curtis wasn't joyriding with them at night, or boosting cars with them on weekends.

Curtis had cello practice.

He didn't talk about the cello at school, but that didn't matter. Everyone knew. Every once in a while someone saw him on TV and dapped him the next morning at school.

The cello, and Curtis's fame outside Kramer Elementary School, must have enraged Antoinne. "Why you play that thing? You tryin' to be white? You think you're the shit because you been on TV, don't you? Stuck-up bitch."

They teased him tentatively at first—expecting him to throw the first punch, Curtis guessed.

Curtis wasn't a fighter. Even though he cheered when Batman faced off against the Joker in hand-to-hand combat and he applauded when Wonder Woman clashed with Cheetah, he knew very well that he was just reading a comic book.

The possibility of five bigger guys piling onto him in real life was too much. No matter what Antoinne or his crew said, retaliation wasn't worth the risk. Curtis hadn't fought back.

So they teased him, and from teasing grew contempt that the great Zippy Wilson's son was such a pathetic bitch, flouncing around on stages with some kind of big violin.

They'd yanked chairs out from under him. They'd slapped the back of his head, knocking off his cap. They'd thrown food at him in the cafeteria. And always, always, the insults they lobbed at him everywhere, with everyone hearing them: *White boy. Punk ass. Fag. Bitch ass.*

But until this year they hadn't gotten violent.

Last spring, Curtis had figured that he'd be done with Antoinne, that Antoinne would graduate to middle school, but somehow, impossibly, Antoinne was still there. Grinning at him contemptuously. "How's your little white-boy music going, huh? Kiss any bitch clarinets over the summer?" At his shoulder, D'Andre, Quintin, and Tayquan laughed evilly.

Clenching his fists and not answering, Curtis angled across the hallway like he was heading for the classroom. When they swaggered on, he took the south stairway up, across to the other side of the building, and back down to avoid them. Not a teacher or security guard in sight.

He managed to avoid them for weeks and thought perhaps he

could keep avoiding them for the whole school year. Whenever he saw Antoinne Marley's baseball cap, he'd slide into the bathroom or disappear into a classroom. Once Antoinne came toward him, and Curtis opened a door and jumped into a fourth-grade science class. The kids were all seated, with Ms. Anderson at the whiteboard. They'd all turned to stare. He dropped his books. The fourth graders burst into laughter as Antoinne Marley stalked by, and it took Curtis a few moments—until he was out of sight—before he managed to gather them up again.

But there was no avoiding him that Monday morning in PE, when Curtis opened the locker-room door and heard the voice that he couldn't honestly believe belonged to Antoinne Marley. He wasn't in this class! He shouldn't be here!

But here he was. Bare-chested, snapping a T-shirt at Raizell. Antoinne's body was muscled like an adult's, with a tattoo of a spider crawling up one shoulder and Chinese letters creeping down his neck to meet it.

Curtis tried to duck out of sight, but he stood there stupefied an instant too long, and Antoinne caught sight of him. "Ho, ho," he crowed. "Look who's here. Robofag! Guess we got gym together." He sauntered over while Curtis tried to vanish between the lockers. "We gonna have fun, ain't we?"

"Quit playin' with me, man," Curtis muttered. "Leave me the fuck alone."

"Leave me the fuck alone," Antoinne repeated in a high singsong voice. "Or what? You gonna tell your daddy, is that what you gonna do? He gonna come take care of you? Scrawny little bitch-ass punk."

Curtis didn't know if Antoinne was talking about Zippy or about Curtis, but it didn't matter. He ignored him. Stuffed his backpack into the locker just as Coach Mickens strode in, blowing his whistle. Antoinne retreated.

But that was just the beginning.

That morning, as they ran the perimeter of the gym, Antoinne bodychecked him every chance he got. Either Coach Mickens was looking the other way or he'd gone blind. Then again, Antoinne was bigger than Coach Mickens.

The next week, they were playing basketball. Curtis hadn't ever played basketball in gym. He ran laps instead.

At the end of class, he got a head start to the locker room. He wasn't that sweaty and would forgo the shower, grab his clothes, and get out hopefully before Antoinne had even shrugged off his T-shirt.

But the moment Antoinne hit the locker room, he was yelling, "Yo, Robofag, where you at?"

And Curtis, stupidly, froze, one leg half in his jeans, his tighty-whities gleaming.

"You too good to play basketball?" Antoinne was saying. "You better than us? You ain't nothing like your daddy."

Curtis was dressing faster now, sliding his jeans on, and Antoinne was looming over him. "That it? You too good now?"

"Leave him alone," someone else suggested.

Curtis knew he was on his own. His only friend in the class, Georgio, was even more afraid of Antoinne than Curtis was.

"I'll leave him alone," Antoinne said, tattoos shining with sweat. He slapped Curtis, almost lightly, on the shoulder, and Curtis crashed back into the lockers. The bang turned all heads. Coach Mickens was nowhere in sight.

"You like that, huh?" Antoinne said. "You like that, bitch?" He followed it up with a punch to the gut.

Curtis doubled over, coughing.

Antoinne stepped back, waiting for what surely would be Curtis's pathetic flailing punches. Antoinne was ready, daring him to retaliate, hands loose at his sides, grinning that toothy grin.

Instead Curtis tried to gather up his clothes. One of his shoes had fallen, and he groped under the bench for it. As he turned, Antoinne punched him again, in the kidneys.

Curtis went flying under the bench.

"Come on, faggot," Antoinne was saying. "Get up. You ain't nothin' but a bitch. I'm gonna kick your ass. Does your daddy know how much of a bitch you is?"

Curtis dragged himself to his feet.

The next punch he saw coming.

Time slowed.

For a moment he almost put up his hands to block.

He could see the fist, see his own hands in the air, desperate to catch it.

With almost superhuman will, he pulled his hands down, lifting his head and turning his chin as the blow took him square in the collarbone.

Half an hour later, Curtis was in the nurse's office. Zippy and Larissa had been called in, along with the principal and Coach Mickens. An ambulance was on its way. The nurse thought his shoulder might be broken or dislocated. A scary-looking bruise pulsed near his spine. The blood from a cut on his skull had bled all over his shirt.

They had all—all but Curtis—been yelling for a while now. Antoinne Marley would almost certainly be suspended but likely be right back in school in eleven days. Curtis tried to take some comfort in knowing that he wouldn't have to see Antoinne for at least two weeks.

Larissa was kneeling in front of him, tears in her eyes. "What is it, *papi*? What is it with you?"

"We gotta make you into a fighter," Zippy said. "I can't believe it. What kinda school is this? Where are the teachers who are supposed to be stopping this shit? Where's the kid that did this? Where are his parents?"

His dad's voice grated over him, sending up a tingling feeling on the back of his neck. The pain throbbed everywhere, but mostly in Curtis's guts. He was so *embarrassed*. How could he not fight back? His dad didn't understand, and Curtis felt like a failure, like he'd never possibly succeed in any way that was meaningful. His dad just wanted a kid who wouldn't get picked on like a little girl. Instead he got Curtis. He wished he could open the gray Red Cross locker next to him and disappear inside it forever.

"What is it?" Larissa repeated, holding Curtis's gaze. "They say you didn't fight back."

Curtis was old enough by now—he was ten—to identify the issue. In *The Amazing Spider-Man*, Flash Thompson bullied Peter

Parker daily, but Peter never fought back. Curtis *knew* he needed to fight, but it was as if he was five again, or younger. Mute with despair and embarrassment, he wanted to tell her. Larissa more than anyone. He thought she would have already understood.

So he did the only thing he could think of. He opened his hands and looked down at them.

She followed his gaze, then looked back up to his face. "What, *papi*?" And then her eyes widened as she looked down again. "You didn't want to hurt your hands," she said, so quietly, almost to herself.

Curtis nodded.

"Oh, *papi*."

He couldn't tell her—couldn't tell any of them—what seemed so obvious. That his whole body could be battered and destroyed, but even a broken finger might mean that he would not be able to play.

And if he could not play, his life would not be worth living. Far better to have Antoinne Marley beat the rest of him to a bloody pulp.

But he would not go down again without a fight. He vowed that, too. He thought about the street superheroes Luke Cage and Daredevil, and Nightwing, who did acrobatics. He was going to start seriously weight lifting. He was going to make himself invincible, like the Man of Steel. A cello-wielding superhero, that's what Curtis would be. Until now Dark Maestro had just been a figment of his comic book imagination—he'd whisper Dark Maestro phrases like "Pizzicato for power!!" and "Dark Maestro, Vivace!" He'd hold his bow and pose, threatening the malevolent lamp in his bedroom or a kitchen chair, but he didn't really *believe*.

Dark Maestro needed to be more than just a whisper at night. He needed to be real.

Larissa was still hugging him as the paramedics arrived to take him to MedStar Washington Hospital. He hugged her back, his head already full of plans.

8

LARISSA

THE REPORTER from the *Washington Post* first called Larissa when she was just shy of three months pregnant. She and Zippy had been trying for a baby for the last several years, and now it was finally happening.

Larissa didn't recognize the number, but she was always answering numbers she didn't recognize. She never knew how the women—99 percent of them were women—found her personal cell phone, since the nonprofit had a dedicated line, but more likely than not they'd call on her number.

So she didn't say "Hello" like she otherwise would have. "Bright Horizons," she said. She was now the executive director—which sounded far more impressive than the reality: her, two counselors, an assistant, and several part-timers in a narrow four-story with offices on the ground floor and dormitories and classrooms in the floors above. The organization, which provided a safe haven for domestic abuse survivors, offered music therapy sessions to survivors and organized events to raise awareness about domestic abuse, the proceeds of which went toward helping the women at the shelter.

It was a lot of work, but Larissa loved it. And she owed it all to T Block: at one of his barbecues, he introduced her to the Manning family, whose foundation was looking to expand their reach into domestic abuse. One thing led to another, and now, eighteen months later, Bright Horizons sheltered fourteen women and eight children and had put on two programs in D.C.

But now the voice on the line wasn't a woman choking back sobs or whispering in terror. This voice was clear, crisp, commanding. "Hi, I'm Diane Jamison from the *Washington Post*. I'm looking for Larissa Stokes, who's listed as a guardian of Curtis Wilson," the voice was saying. "Are you Ms. Stokes?"

"What's wrong? Is he okay? What happened?" Larissa asked. She thought she could feel the baby turn, an elbow or a knee bumping against her insides.

"I believe he's fine," Diane said. "I'm calling to get your response to a story I'm working on about him."

Now relief and unease surged through her in equal measures. *A story?* This was a *reporter*, not someone from the subscription department. In the five years since the first time Curtis was on TV, very few reporters had ever reached out to her directly. Zippy had made it very clear to Curtis and to the schools that Curtis was to be interviewed about school and music, but that his home life and parents were off limits. Somebody at Ellington had not gotten the message. Larissa was going to give that school a piece of her mind.

"We don't talk to reporters," Larissa told her. "I'd appreciate it if you didn't call here again. We are very proud of Curtis and you are welcome to talk to him about his cello and his music, but his dad and me, we ask that you respect our privacy."

"I understand," the woman said. "But my story will also be covering you and Mr. Wilson—I believe he goes by 'Zippy'?— and I'd like to give you the opportunity to go on the record so readers can hear your side of things."

"No thank you," Larissa said, and hung up.

She told Zippy about it that night.

"What did you say to her?" Zippy asked. Larissa told him. He cornered Curtis later, when he got home from orchestra practice. Curtis said he hadn't talked to any reporter in weeks.

"You only talk to reporters about school and about your music," Zippy told him.

Curtis nodded, a little sullenly, Larissa thought. He was only eleven, but sometimes he was already acting like a teenager.

"You think we should tell T Block?" Larissa asked Zippy later, when they were in bed.

"No," Zippy said immediately.

"Why not? I bet he knows somebody there—"

"Too bad," Zippy said. "If I told him he'd think I can't handle my own house. I'd look weak. I ain't sayin' nothing."

"But nobody's ever called the house before," Larissa said uneasily. "The lady said she'd be writing about both of us."

"You shut her down, right?"

"Yeah, I told her we weren't interested."

"All right," Zippy said. "We did our part."

But neither of them slept much that night, or for several nights after. A week passed, and then another. The tension began to uncoil.

And then the woman texted her.

> Hi Ms. Stokes this is Diane Jamison from the Post. I just wanted to let you know that the article about Curtis will be running on Sunday. It's the lead story in the Style section. If you or Mr. Wilson would like to get in touch with me beforehand to provide your side of the story, our deadline is Friday at noon. Thanks!

Larissa didn't reply, and forwarded the message to Zippy, and called him. "You gotta call T Block. Now. You aren't gonna look weak. You're gonna look proactive. Call him now."

Zippy didn't come home. He texted her at one point—"At T"—but that was it. She finished early with the crew and came home and waited. Curtis was in Alexandria, and although he'd had a ride home she drove the hour out of town to pick him up.

Eleven o'clock and Zippy still wasn't home.

Just after midnight the story ran in the online version of the *Post*, with the headline: FROM GANG TURF TO SYMPHONY HALLS: TALENTED 11-YEAR-OLD CELLIST SHATTERS EXPECTATIONS. The print version would be on the streets in the morning.

Her insides clenched, and she wondered if it was the baby kicking again. She couldn't believe the words she was reading.

The article started off innocuously enough. Leading with photos of big-eyed Curtis, both with his cello and in the halls of the Duke Ellington School of the Arts, it all sounded like stuff Larissa had seen before—about how he was the youngest person playing in this symphony or with that quartet; how he'd won the Rockville Competition for Young Artists three years in a row, got a first and second at the Handel Society, and won a bunch of other awards that Larissa honestly had forgotten about. Then it discussed his remarkable tone and his characteristic vibrato; how Ellington made a special provision to take Curtis two years early, when he was in sixth grade; how music schools like Juilliard, Berklee, Eastman, and Oberlin were already scouting him out.

And then came the section that would change her life.

But that's only part of Curtis's story. Because every night, after leaving Ellington, Curtis returns home to Potomac Farms, a public housing project at Minnesota and 46th Street Southeast, infamous in the District. The neighborhood has a fearsome reputation, with some of the most violent crimes in the city, 411 cases, and the highest number of robberies, 253, last year alone. "You more likely to get shot than you is to find a grocery store," Camilla Jones, a resident, noted.

Curtis's father is rumored to have affiliations with one of the city's most concerning and rapidly expanding gangs, 18ST. Accusations range from illegal firearms possession to orchestrating an extensive network of drug dealing and other criminal activities. In the ongoing street conflict against rivals such as 5 Bloods and Street Demonz, 18ST has been gaining ground, claiming victory one street at a time. D.C.'s surge in cocaine and heroin over the past three years is partially attributed to 18ST. As of press time, these claims remain unsubstantiated.

The story continued for another four paragraphs. Larissa couldn't even read them all, she was feeling so nauseated.

"This is bad," Larissa mouthed as her insides knotted up again. Zippy wasn't even home. She texted: Where u? 911

A moment later Zippy responded: You ok? Baby???

Larissa: Baby's fine. Just read WashPo article

Zippy: Yeah

Larissa: Are u w T Block?

Zippy: Yeah. Be home soon

Larissa: What's he saying?

Zippy didn't respond.

She tried to plan, to get ahead of what she feared might be next. This was everything he'd worried about: a spotlight shining directly on him and on Larissa.

Most terrifying: T Block himself. She wondered how he'd react, even if he wasn't mentioned by name. Since the article was about Curtis, would T Block somehow try taking it out on him? That seemed unlikely. He really liked Curtis. He had him over for dinner. Invited him to Trishelle's and Lyndsay's birthday parties. Curtis played at events in T Block's house. Surely he would understand that it wasn't Curtis's fault.

Curtis was asleep in bed, his cello lying next to him on the floor, one hand drifting down and touching the case. She watched him for an instant, wondering what would happen next. Whatever it was wouldn't be good.

"Hey," she said louder than she needed to, "I need you to wake up. You gotta help me with something."

He woke, slowly and surly—he really was turning into a teenager—but once she explained the situation, he stopped looking sullen.

"We gotta ditch anything that can pin us," Larissa told him. "That means phones, computers, anything that could get us into trouble. Plus anything that connects us to T Block. Wipe them and dump them. I'm calling Cheryl and Marie to come help get rid of all this. The police aren't on to us yet, but we ain't gonna make any stupid moves."

"Where's Dad?" Curtis wanted to know.

"He's with T Block. He'll be home soon."

She felt physically worse and worse as they worked to pack everything up. She had a headache, and her limbs felt achy. But she ignored it.

Zippy stumbled in. T Block had sent him home. Most terrifyingly, T Block was calm and friendly, and that scared Zippy far more than rage.

"Think about it," Zippy told her, even though that was all she was doing. "They got details. Someone was talking. T probably thinks it's us."

"We didn't snitch," Larissa said. "He should know that."

"Well, somebody did. T Block's got to suspect us. At least."

"There could have been dozens of people who could've ratted him out," Larissa said.

"And we're two of them," Zippy said somberly.

She wished she'd made Zippy tell T Block about the reporter. T Block could have threatened the reporter to back off—done something.

Mostly, journalists and law enforcement steered clear of Southeast. Despite tough talk about "eradicating crime" and "cleaning up the streets," the cops and politicians left them pretty much alone. After all, if the police cracked down on this neighborhood, the drugs and crime and gangs would only migrate somewhere else, somewhere closer to the wealthy and powerful. Far better to keep the crime where it was.

For the next two hours, they removed anything that the police could use as evidence: the old coat in the hall closet, the stash kept in a hole in the bedroom floor covered by a cheap Ikea rug, the framed pictures hiding holes which housed stacks of cash, the floor-model TV that had been hollowed out and served as storage space, and on which the new flatscreen TV leaned.

It was almost four in the morning when Larissa at last fell asleep, shivering.

Zippy and Curtis were both gone when she awoke. She'd told Curtis he could stay home from school, but his orchestra class was starting on a Mendelssohn symphony, and he wasn't going to miss it. The apartment was dark, all the shades drawn.

She had forty-two unread texts, including:

LaShay: We know you, we know Zippy. They don't know squat.

Quanae: Just saw that news. We got your back. Dont let those fancy papers get to you.

And more kept pinging her.

But beyond the texts, there seemed to be no immediate ramifications. No police showed up on their doorsteps. No other media outlets tracked them down to ask for comments on the story. Curtis went to school and orchestra and music lessons as usual. Larissa felt like an idiot, making everyone stay up all night, even if doing so now allowed her to feel some small measure of control. Larissa and Zippy hung out at home or met their crew in out-of-the-way places. They imagined faceless governmental ears listening in on their phones, eyes peering at their texts. They checked for people following, but the grimy streets seemed always the same, the usual mix of homies and homeless all circling in their usual orbits. T Block hadn't been in touch with Zippy directly since the article ran, which Larissa convinced Zippy was a good sign. "If he wanted to do something, he would've done it by now. He knows you got his back," Larissa kept repeating, trying to make herself believe it too.

They were all starting to relax, all beginning to think everything had blown over and Larissa was being overdramatic, when, just after eleven p.m. on an overcast April night ten days after the article ran, a knock thundered at the door.

Larissa jerked up in bed, clutching the sheets and knowing what was coming.

The knock came again, and a muffled voice: "Zacchariah Wilson, open up!"

Zippy looked at her, holding her hand, before getting out of bed.

Half an hour later, after the cops finished tearing apart the apartment (they found nothing but confiscated the new cell phones and Curtis's new laptop) and led Zippy away, Larissa was on the neighbor's phone. She called Cheryl and Marie, telling them to reach out to T Block.

By three in the morning the apartment lay quiet again. Curtis was in his room, but she didn't know if he was sleeping. The apartment felt suffocating, the shadows dancing with uncertainty.

A sudden, stabbing pain seized her abdomen, stealing the air from her lungs. Beyond Zippy, beyond everything else that had happened that night, something was terribly wrong.

Gasping, Larissa sat up, her hands instinctively moving to her stomach. The room blurred as physical pain intertwined with her misery and terror, and everything intensified.

The knocks on the door and the image of Zippy being led away in handcuffs now seemed distant, as if it happened long ago to an entirely different person. Each wave of pain carried away a fragment of hope.

Alone in that dark hour long after midnight and long before dawn, she navigated the heart-wrenching reality of a miscarriage. Her world was loss: loss of the baby, loss of Zippy, loss of certainty. The night crumbled around her and she faced it alone.

Later that morning, after she'd sent Curtis to school and after she'd gone alone to her doctor to confirm what she already knew, she met T Block in an anonymous office in an anonymous office building on P Street Southwest. She struggled to walk, with cramps still periodically buckling her legs.

It was the first time she'd seen T Block in months. Over the past few years, Zippy and T Block had grown close. T Block no longer worked through intermediaries like Tremel or JFunk—he reached out to Zippy directly. Larissa wasn't sure of the extent of the relationship, but whenever she saw them together—T Block invited them over for barbecues, and every once in a while out to his brother's house at the base of the Blue Ridge Mountains—T Block and Zippy possessed an easy, comfortable familiarity together. Larissa herself had gone out for ice cream and drinks with T Block's wife and kids. No, the two families weren't friends, but she felt that they trusted one another. She needed to use that trust now.

"T, I know it looks shady. You gotta trust me. This ain't Zippy. You know him. You know he doesn't want anybody to even look at him. He'd never talk to a reporter." She eased herself gingerly into one of the guest chairs. Her belly and pelvis felt raw and bloated, but she didn't let on.

She studied the room. Couldn't tell if this bland office was T Block's or not—there was nothing personal in it. It might even be an office share.

Now T Block sat across from her, his face expressionless. She'd thought about bringing Curtis with her but didn't want to put him through any more stress. It was bad enough that everyone in D.C. now knew more about his home life than they should have. She didn't want to use him as leverage. What would that say about her?

"Zippy been holdin' it down for you for years," she went on. "He'd never betray you. And you know what? He's takin' the whole rap. He's saying he's behind the drug sales, the guns, whatever. You won't even come up. That's loyalty. Trust."

T Block leaned forward, looked her up and down. After a moment, he said, "I know that. Zip's my boy. I know he wouldn't screw me." He sat back, thinking. "But I didn't think he'd take the fall for this."

"I told you, T. He's loyal. We both are."

"How long we been working together? You and Zip and me?"

"Curtis is eleven," she said. "So Zip's been rollin' with you for almost eleven years. Me, a couple less. Why?"

"Zippy has never let me down." A beat as he mulled something over. "Imma get him a lawyer. A good one. Not one of them sorry-ass public defenders. He's looking at a minimum of ten years."

"Yeah," Larissa said. "I know. I was checkin' out lawyers this morning." A confusion of emotions roiled in her—gratitude for T Block's offer and fury that it was T Block's fault they were there in the first place. That Curtis would have to endure the shame and humiliation of a drug-dealing, gang-banging father just as his musical career was taking off.

"My guy's solid. He won't do ten. Nowhere near," T Block went on.

"You think?"

"Trust. I'm droppin' stacks on his lawyer. She's gonna get him off easy, just a slap on the wrist. Prob'ly a few years and probation."

Zippy being locked away meant that Larissa was suddenly juggling a lot more than just her crew: she was also Curtis's sole parent. Legally and technically, since she and Zippy weren't married, Curtis should be living with Patrice, but from the beginning it was clear to them all that Curtis would stay with Larissa; Larissa would shuttle him to his cello practices, and Patrice would step in if absolutely necessary, or when the state-appointed social worker stopped by for a wellness check. Curtis could always come over, as long as his presence didn't interfere with bridge night. Or spades, or hearts, or tonk.

Once Zippy's sentence had been handed down—"twelve years with a minimum of eighteen months to be served prior to eligibility for parole"—Curtis withdrew into himself even more. He was monosyllabic at breakfast, stirring Cheerios around in his bowl and staring down at a volume of sheet music, turning page after page, never looking up. He was silent, staring out the window, when Larissa drove him to Annandale for his orchestra practice.

And yet, when she was early to pick him up and caught sight of him onstage, he shone. He vibrated with concentration, with passion, his bow taut against the strings, swaying slightly to the music, eagerly watching every movement the conductor made. Fixated. He'd always been focused before, and by now Larissa was used to musicians' absorption as they played, but this seemed like a whole different level.

His grades dropped. He'd always been a B+ or A student, but

now he was getting Cs, and even a D in history. "He's just not engaging," Mrs. Meadows, the history teacher, told Larissa. "He just stares out the window. I was hoping the D would wake him up, but I don't think he cares."

"It's hard on him right now," Larissa said. "With his dad away." Everyone knew where Zippy was.

Mrs. Meadows nodded. "I'm doing my best to accommodate him, but he needs to keep up." She sent him to weekly sessions with the guidance counselor, but nothing changed.

The B in Math—which last year had been Curtis's best subject, with an A+—now turned into a C, and then a C-.

Six months after Zippy's sentencing, she drove Curtis back from practice. He was, as usual, turned away from her, staring out at the evening and the rain and the cars flashing past. "Hey, I thought the percussion was really on today," Larissa said to him.

He didn't respond.

"Did you like the gong? It made me jump," she went on.

No response.

It was late, and it was a school night, and she needed to take him home and check in with her girls. But as she passed a late-night miniature golf park, on a whim she turned in. "Hey," she said. "You never done this, I bet. Wanna play a round?"

He looked up, into the rearview mirror. "We gotta get home," he said.

"Yeah, we'll get there. We're not in hurry. I bet we have time for one game. You should try this, you know?"

"I don't know how to play," he said.

"About time you learned," she told him.

Underneath the festive, multicolored lights, they lined up their shots at the start of a neon, jungle-themed course. They were the only ones playing—the park was closing in half an hour—and silent except for a soft electronic hum and the swish of cars out on Route 1. Towering fake palm trees bobbed gently in the night.

Larissa gave the ball a sharp whack. It bounced off a monkey's extended foot, looped around a volcano, and dropped neatly into the hole. Hole in one. "Sorry, *mijo*, the golf spirits seem to like me more," she said.

Curtis stared down at the ball, more serious than it warranted.

"Take your shot," she told him. He hit the ball, and it bounced off the monkey's foot and returned almost to where they'd started. He tried again, and after four shots managed to reach the volcano. Seven shots before the ball dropped into the hole.

They moved on to the next hole—beach themed, with sand traps and a lighthouse. This time it took Larissa six tries, and Curtis four. He seemed more like himself now, focused on lining up his putter and the ball.

On the third hole, spaceship themed, Larissa thought she might as well give talking to him another try. Occupied with the game, Curtis might be distracted and let his guard down. "A little birdie told me you're feeling blue, *mi vida*," she said softly, nudging him with her shoulder. "You want to talk about it?"

He swung. His neon-yellow ball zoomed toward the rocket ship, and then skittered across the course and caromed off the curb.

She waited a beat before trying again. "I care about you, you know? And I know it's hard for you right now. Not having your dad around."

Curtis looked up, then stared off at the ball, his silence cutting through the steady murmur of the park.

"It's not forever. Just another eighteen months. You know that, right?"

He nodded. Hit the ball again, which this time dipped around Saturn's rings, in the right direction this time. He trudged after it.

"And he loves you very much. He wants to see you." And then, almost as an afterthought, she added, "He hasn't left you."

His chin was tucked against his chest as he lined up for the next shot, and he spoke so softly that she almost missed it. "But he did."

She came up next to him. "No, he didn't. He's still here. He still loves you. He wants to see you very very much."

He hit the ball again, an angled shot that went off in the wrong direction. She followed him over to Jupiter and Mars, and a sign saying SHOOT THE MOON!!!! After what felt like an eternity to Larissa, he responded, almost too softly to be heard, "Why does everyone leave?"

The words hit her hard, and she thought back to that year when she'd moved out. She wanted to hug him, but he seemed so isolated there, framed by the glow of the fluorescent lights, so she kept her distance. "Not always," she said. "And not for good."

"My mom," he said. "Now dad. And even you left me." His voice hitched a little.

Now she leaned over and wrapped one arm around his shoulders. Her smile faltered. "Well, *mijo*, if it makes you feel better, I only left because I wanted to join the circus."

"What?" he looked up at her, puzzled.

"I thought I could become a trapeze artist. But I'm scared of heights . . . and clowns. And elephants," she said with a shudder. She wagged a finger at Curtis, "And plus, they wouldn't let me bring my makeup kit. So I figured . . . nah, I'll just rough it with you and your dad."

Despite everything, Curtis let out a smile.

"But I won't lie," Larissa said seriously. "People come and go, and that's a hard lesson. It's just life. But remember something else. They're not leaving *because* of you. We all have our demons. Our flaws. Our behavior is because of what we do. Not what you did."

Curtis said nothing, looking down and tapping the golf ball lightly with his club. "Why did he leave? And . . . Why did you leave when you did? For years I thought it was me."

Larissa leaned in and hugged him even tighter. "Nothing you could ever do would make me leave. I'm sorry. We should have talked to you sooner. Your dad and I—we had an argument, and I left. But I never wanted to leave you. And I've never stopped loving you. Just like your dad will never stop loving you. Even if he's not here to tell you. He still does."

He stared at her, not fully convinced, but listening. "But Dad said he'd always have my back. Always. And he's gone. And he doesn't."

"Yes he does," she said. Now she knelt in front of him, so she was looking up into his face. His eyes were enormous. He was going to be a handsome man someday, she realized. "Just because you can't see him most of the time doesn't mean he's gone. He's waiting for you. He's still here."

She waited a beat. "Let's go see him, and he'll tell you that himself. Okay?"

After a moment he nodded, just slightly.

"Sometimes people can't be there when you want them to be. But that doesn't mean they don't love you. It just means you have to be strong for yourself, too. And you are, you know that?"

"I'm what?"

"You're strong. So very strong. And I don't just mean physically. I see it every time you pick up that cello of yours. That music . . . it's a part of you that nobody can ever take away, understand?"

"Yeah, I'll always have the cello," he said to her, or to himself.

"You do. You'll always have your music. Always."

Another long pause, but this one felt softer, more contemplative.

"Let's finish up this game. I'm thinking we should get you some private golf lessons because you're terrible."

"This is my first time, and I almost beat you. Maybe you need the lessons. I know a guy."

Then he lifted the putter and took his shot.

9

ZIPPY

CURTIS REFUSED to come see him.

Refused.

On the first visiting day, Larissa—and his mom, Patrice—made the drive, and made excuses. *Curtis has a concert.*

It happened again two weeks later. *Curtis has to practice. He sends his love.*

Zippy thought his son's absence might actually, physically, destroy him.

Curtis was eleven now, but for years—Zippy didn't even remember how it started—they'd do that secret handshake thing. Thumb to forehead. Zippy saying, "Who's got your back?" and Curtis answering, "All the time."

But now Zippy didn't have Curtis's back. Would perhaps never have Curtis's back again.

"He's young," Larissa said. "He'll get over this."

But Zippy didn't know if Curtis would. Zippy didn't know if *he* would. He'd betrayed the person he loved best in the world, and he couldn't escape himself. Not in the confines of his cell or in the exercise yard or in the shower or in the cafeteria. Zippy was always, always himself, and a failure.

He barely tried to navigate the prison. He was afraid of the unknown, of the merciless hierarchy that governed the prison walls. The fear of violence, betrayal, and the constant watchful eyes of the other inmates kept him awake for the first three nights, but he almost welcomed them—they were distractions from the relentless sting of failure in his lungs.

He spent most of each day waiting: to be let in, to be let out, to eat, to be done eating. The days stretched endlessly, with no purpose or direction. As much as he could, he spent time in the library, learning about music, trying to understand everything about it. He read about Baroque cellos and listened to Boccherini. He played Boccherini's Fourth Concerto over and over again because it was Curtis's favorite—and perhaps if Zippy could love it the way that Curtis did, he'd be able to connect again with his son.

It didn't help. Curtis didn't appear.

In his free hours, whenever he wasn't in the library, he hung out with the same group of eight or so guys in the yard. They told stories of their lives on the street, of sexual conquests or their wishful thinking about sexual conquests, and they passed rhymes back and forth. Many of the guys had dreams of becoming rappers.

Zippy recognized some of the lyrics from J.O. Blanco or early DMX, but never said anything. They'd constantly try to top each other. "Please don't come in here with that weak sauce. That might fly on the street corner but it ain't hittin' in here," Zippy would tell them, rhyming.

Comin out the projects looking like a reject
Always getting upset when I hit the outlet
You're ready for a reset. Way too late for regret
You're childish like a playset, losing Russian Roulette
Go back and learn the alphabet before you shoot a weak threat.

They'd laugh and fist bump and keep rhyming.

One day, while browsing the prison library, Zippy discovered a dog-eared accounting textbook. He'd always been good with numbers, but life on the streets running drugs was an easier option than trying to go to school as a seventeen-year-old father. Now, as he flipped through the pages, he found himself intrigued. He checked the book out and spent hours in his cell devouring every word, every formula, finding solace in the structured world of numbers. The discipline of bookkeeping provided him with a sense of control.

Days turned into weeks, and weeks into months. He enrolled in an accounting correspondence course. When he needed a break from the monotony, he'd ask the guys for a word to freestyle from. They'd try to stump him with words like *soapdish*, *fried liver*, or *candlebox*, and Zippy would come back at them with:

> *You turn into a paradox talking everyday*
> *Your rhymes are weak like monkeypox keep that shit at bay.*
> *Hate to hit you with the madness, just brings up the sadness*
> *You gotta take it easy cause your mouth is full of badness*

But most important, while he was listening to the music, he kept up his studies. Not that there were many alternatives. But with each passed test and completed assignment, he gained confidence. The courses taught him about financial management, budgeting, and recordkeeping far beyond what he'd figured out on his own. He learned how to handle financial transactions, create balance sheets, and prepare financial statements.

The trick to prison was to stay unnoticed and unnoticeable, and that's what Zippy tried to do. It wasn't as hard as he thought—he was a smaller guy, and didn't have a big personality, so except for the rapping, often people just overlooked him. In the meantime, he prepared tax returns for several of the inmates, and for most of the guards. Pretty soon the other prisoners started calling him "Buckz."

Once he finished the first course, he spent several hours a day at the commissary under the constant supervision of "OG." He helped manage finances, assisted with invoice processing, reconciled cash, and recorded sales.

Mack "OG" Siler had been in prison for the past thirty-six years and by now had gained special privileges, including unfettered access to the library and no cellmate. Posters of places Zippy didn't know—but which OG told him were of Rome, Cologne, Cremona, and Berlin—had been taped to the walls. He even had his own bedsheets. "OG" stood for "Original Gangster," since he was the oldest person in the cellblock. In his early sixties, he seemed much older, with bright white hair. His well-manicured beard seemed to glow in the shadows. OG had taken a shine to Zippy, especially when Zippy continued to apply himself to all of the financials that OG put in front of him.

Zippy spent hours with him. They joked that OG was old enough to be Zippy's father, and Zippy sometimes called him "Dad," but a part of him that he wouldn't quite admit actually did think of OG as a father figure. Zippy had never known his own father. His mother had never been married, and had had a revolving series of boyfriends after Zippy was born. So this steady relationship with an older man was both new and special for him.

One day, after a visit from Larissa, who towed along another excuse for Curtis's absence, Zippy slammed into the tiny office off the kitchen supply room. He was in a foul temper. The upstairs neighbors, high on crack, who loved taking baths, had flooded the apartment again when they passed out in the tub with the water running. Larissa said that she'd spent hours trying to clean up the mess.

And: Curtis still hadn't come to see him.

Zippy felt powerless and guilty. Curtis's absence and Larissa's complaints he took to be *his* fault. If only he weren't in prison. If only he'd done something worthwhile in his life. If only. But he hadn't, and all of his loved ones' problems were because Zippy was a Class-A Fuck-Up.

Now he flung himself in the desk chair across from OG, so frustrated and pissed off with life that he wanted to just rip up the ledger book—Who used ledger books these days? Shouldn't the prison be computerized?—and overturn the desk.

"Whattup, youngblood," OG said mildly.

Zippy didn't answer right away. He stared down at the ledger, closed and tried to force himself to open the pages, grab a pencil.

"How was the visit?" OG said, once it was clear that Zippy wasn't going to respond.

"Aright," Zippy said at last.

"Just aright?"

"Yeah."

A pause. Zippy clenched his fingers, willed them to pick up the pencil. To open the faded black-and-white book with its even columns of numbers, so sane and clear and accountable.

"Seems like it wasn't aright," OG said at last.

"It was cool," Zippy said. "It was aright." He managed to force the ledger book open and dragged over a pile of receipts and work orders: 300 cans of crushed tomato, 175 cans of tuna in water, 14 boxes of romaine lettuce. After a few moments he said quietly, "My son hates me."

"*Hate* is a strong word."

"I haven't seen him since I've been in here."

"That Larissa needs to make him come. He's eleven."

"I think she's tried. She won't talk about it."

"Well, why does he hate you?"

Briefly Zippy explained how he'd vowed to always be there for Curtis. To always have Curtis's back. Zippy demonstrated the thumb-to-the-forehead.

"He's the cello player, right?"

Zippy nodded. He'd told the OG—he'd told everybody—about Curtis, and although they nodded like they understood, Zippy knew a concert cellist wasn't even in their universe.

"It's natural that you'd think he hates you. You're in here instead of out there with him. You're too smart to be wasting time here. Time you ain't never gonna get back."

"I sure ain't," Zippy said. Frustration, familiar as his own stench, washed over him. He finished processing the receipt and turned to the next one. Olive and canola oil. "What am I supposed to do?"

"You're gonna reach out to him, is what you're gonna do."

"I've tried. I tried calling, I wrote him letters, I told Larissa—"

"And nothing worked?"

Zippy shook his head, numb, staring down at the neat columns of numbers that didn't even seem to be his own handwriting anymore.

"When you called. Wrote. You wrote to him as a prisoner. You need to do that as a father."

The OG's words washed over him. He didn't understand, and yet he did.

"He loves that cello music, right? Is there some song he loves best? Some composer?"

"Boccherini," Zippy said immediately, a reflex.

"Who?"

"He was this cellist. Lived in the 1700s. Curtis knows everything about him. Wanted to be him. And get this—turned out that the guy traveled around and composed music with his dad. How cool is that?"

The OG looked at him. "So why are you telling me? Tell him."

Two weeks later, at the next visitor's day, Zippy pressed a thick paper wedge into Larissa's palm. It was a sheet torn out of his ledger, folded and refolded and wrapped in Scotch tape. On one side, in Zippy's neat, careful script: TO THE NEXT BOCCHERINI.

My Little Boccherini,

I thought of you today when I heard your Second Concerto, the one you used to practice all the time. I don't know how you manage to catch it all, the buzz, the step, the spirit of the street. It's pure magic, my son, and you make it happen.

Curtis, you know this already, but I've come to learn that what comes out of your cello is not only music, but life itself. You're painting sounds of joy, hope, sometimes sadness and regret. Your cello is magic and your ticket to freedom.

I know you do not wish to see me these days, but I want to tell you this:

Keep going. Keep finding new melodies, new stories. The rhythm of life might change, might shift, but it all fits together.

You will remember a promise I made. I made it every day, many times. I promised to always—always—have your back.

That promise has not changed.

It has not diminished.

It has not vanished.

It is here with every beat of my heart and every note in your cello.

I love you and I always will.

And I will always be here for you.

Be proud, Curtis, just as I'm proud of you. I know Boccherini would have been too. Don't forget, no matter where I am, that my heart's always with you and your music.

In admiration and love,

Your Father Z

10

CURTIS

THE FEDERAL CORRECTIONAL INSTITUTION PETERSBURG was a two-hour drive from D.C., far from civilization, in a barren sunny corner of nowhere. Curtis and Larissa made the drive in silence. Larissa parked in an enormous, mostly empty parking lot. Curtis followed Larissa into a bland reception area that could have led to a doctor's or insurance office.

He'd been here only once before, although his dad had been in jail for six months already. His dad the jailbird. The convict. The felon. The kids at school all knew about the case. It was on TV, all over social media. "Convict Dad, Maestro Son: A Tale of Two Pathways." "Dad Serves Time, Son Serves Tunes."

For a while he stumbled daily, sometimes hourly, over someone referring to his dad. Kids whispered in the hall, eyeing him with amusement. Several times he had to rip off paper taped to his locker, decorated with prison bars and a hanged man, a crude knife in his back, tongue sticking out. And dozens of other reminders every day: on the way home, at orchestra, at school. Each time, a white-hot blade of shame and fury stabbed into Curtis's rib cage. It wasn't enough that his dad ran in a gang, but he had to fail so spectacularly. He couldn't imagine any of the schools and conservatories wanting him now.

He hated his dad.

During the trial, Mrs. Dotsner, the Ellington guidance counselor, made him come in twice a week to "just sit and talk." She was a nice lady and he liked going there, and she'd ask him about his dad and how he felt and he tried to tell her. But the tight tumult of emotions—fury, betrayal, embarrassment—never faded. When he played a piece that touched these emotions—the *Kol Nidre*, or the Elgar concerto—he bowed so angrily that he snapped his cello strings, sometimes several times a week.

"You just channel that," Mrs. Boswell, the chamber music coach, told him once. He'd been playing an ugly-ass Brahms sonata but thinking about his dad, about *Who's got your back*, and somehow during the allegro section tears dripped down his nose and actually splashed onto the cello's face. "That was the first time I really felt your emotional connection to the piece," Mrs. Boswell said afterward.

Now the guard confiscated their phones. Larissa had told Curtis to bring reading material, so he lugged in a stack of his latest comic books, the covers already battered and shiny: *Runaways, Generation X,* and *Crisis.* Wedged in the center of the stack, unfolded, taped edges still ragged, was that letter Zippy had written. *To the Next Boccherini.* Curtis didn't need to read it again. He'd carried it around with him for the past two weeks.

Who's got your back.

All the time.

They waited, the only people in the vast cavern of the reception area. Beyond sparklingly clear windows, the main prison facility loomed, spirals of barbed wire delicately probing the sky. It smelled like Pine-Sol and musty old upholstery.

Only yesterday he'd worn a coat and tie as he played in a string quartet at an event for prospective Ellington students from all over the country. The dean of admissions had stood in front of him and said that Ellington combined "a full college-preparatory curriculum with intensive pre-professional arts training." The words had stuck with him, so far removed from the world he lived in, where a woman once OD'ed in the kitchen, or where piss-smelling junkies lay in the halls, terrifying him as he stepped around or over them. Where gunshots, not fireworks, blasted the night.

And now he was here. The Duke Ellington model student visiting his dad in the joint.

Curtis didn't know who he was anymore.

After half an hour, a guard came for them, led them through a warren of passageways to a grimy cubicle with two orange vinyl chairs and Plexiglas partitioning the room. It smelled like stale smoke. They waited another twenty minutes. Eventually Zippy appeared in orange coveralls, chin up, swaggering, looking hard-core, eyes searching. As soon as he saw them, his face lit up.

His hand scrabbled with the phone, eyes never leaving Curtis.

Larissa elbowed Curtis. "Pick up the phone. Go ahead."

The phone was heavy and cold and stank of bad breath. He put it to his ear.

"Hey." Zippy's voice came through, tinny and electronic. "Looking good. Where'd you find those shoulders?"

"I picked them up at a two-for-one sale," Curtis said, not missing a beat.

"You have a coupon for some biceps, too?" Zippy said.

"They threw those in for free," Curtis said. Ever since Antoinne Marley had broken his collarbone, Curtis had spent an hour or so a day working out. The Ellington gym was state-of-the-art for the actors and dancers, and the phys ed teacher had given Curtis a training regimen. He hadn't noticed the difference for months, but now new muscle padded his shoulders and thighs, and veins stood out on his arms.

"I hear you've been helping Larissa a lot."

Behind Curtis, Larissa—who must have been able to overhear Zippy on the phone—chimed in, "He helps out all the time. Even when he knows he should be practicing."

"I'm proud of you," Zippy said. "And I thought the solo you did in the Borodin quartet was really spectacular. I really liked your interpretation. You really milked the melody. Seemed like you made everybody else play up to your level."

"What are you talking about?"

"Yesterday. At the open house. For the new students."

"How would you—"

Zippy shrugged. "I heard it."

"You couldn't have heard it. They didn't tape it—it was just an in-school thing."

"Well," Zippy said, "how would I know that your quartet played at the open house, right after Mrs. Gradinger's dancers? I really think you should keep playing Borodin. You have a knack for it."

"I don't understand," Curtis stuttered. "How did you—were you there?"

Zippy's eyes twinkled at him. "I got my ways. It's not important how. What's important is that I told you I'd always have your back."

His eyes never left Curtis's, and Curtis clutched the phone more tightly.

He was afraid he was going to cry, could feel the tears in his eyes, and then he was crying. "I don't know what to say—"

"You don't have to say anything," Zippy said. "Just know I love you, okay? And that I meant it when I said I'd always have your back."

Curtis found his thumb reaching for his forehead, and Zippy echoed him. They touched thumbs, the Plexiglas cold and unforgiving between them.

"I got your back," Zippy told him.

"All the time," Curtis said.

He'd walked in here wondering who he was—up-and-coming musician or the son of a felon. He realized that he was, and always would be, both of these. But even more importantly, he was Zippy's son. His heart was full.

His father showed him that he belonged, and the sensation was like the sweetest melody he'd ever heard.

11

LARISSA

THREE DAYS after Curtis's visit to the penitentiary, Larissa was upstairs at Bright Horizons, dealing with the latest black eye and busted lip, when her phone pinged. A text from Cheryl.

Larissa wasn't a nurse but had spent so much time these past years patching up women that she knew basic first aid. This latest wasn't that bad. Maria—a Nicaraguan refugee—had a mouth on her, and she probably was sleeping around, but that didn't justify her boyfriend beating her up. He'd probably been high, or jittery from the latest gun or drug drop, but that was no excuse, either. Larissa always wished she could figure out how to give these women more self-respect. "If they lay a hand on you, you get out of there," she would always tell them, thinking of the one time that Zippy had laid his hands on her. But unlike Larissa, it often would take a catastrophic event to propel them to leave.

So when the text from Cheryl came in, Maria was pissed off and swearing, and Larissa was distracted. It wasn't for another half an hour that she'd realized what she had read. By then Maria was in bed with a bag of frozen corn on her face, and Larissa remembered.

Cheryl: Urgent. Can you talk????

Larissa: wassup

Cheryl must have been staring at her phone, because her response was instantaneous.

Cheryl: Can you talk?? Important

Larissa: I'll call you in 2 mins

She went downstairs to her office to have some privacy. Then she dialed. "Hey girl. Wassup?"

"You alone?" Cheryl said. "Anybody around?"

"I'm in my office. What's going on? You good?"

"I'm straight. I got that info you wanted. About Zippy. Can you talk?"

Larissa understood her immediately. "Yeah I can talk." When the terrible *Washington Post* article had come out, Larissa knew that someone had snitched on them. Since then, she'd put out the word, quietly, to her crew to keep their eyes and ears open.

The thing about this culture of gangs and crime was that people didn't stay silent, Larissa knew. They had to brag, had to top each other, had to prove they were more of a man, swinging a bigger dick. She'd hoped it would be just a matter of time until someone got drunk enough, high enough, or stupid enough to say something about who fingered Zippy.

She was right.

"JFunk ratted you out. He was the one running his mouth to that newspaper."

"What? How you—"

"My cousin Chavonne was over at his spot on Thirty-Eighth. Him and his crew was snorting and shooting up everything. She said he pulled out his piece, talking about taking over T Block. Bragging about how he put Zippy in jail and he was gonna get his shot at T Block."

"How'd you find that out? JFunk might be a fool, but he ain't dumb enough to say that mess in front of Chavonne." Larissa stared blankly at the poster on the opposite wall: "You Are Strong, You Are Worthy, You Are Safe Here."

"I'm telling you. She's sharp. Acted like she was knocked out." A pause. "She's scared. Said he was losing it."

"Where she at now?" Larissa asked.

"She bounced. Headed home."

"All right," Larissa said, pondering. "All right. I'm gonna talk to her. Keep it on the low, you hear?"

"Yeah, for sure."

"Drop her a text, let her know I'm swinging by." She cut the call, practically sprinted upstairs to check on Maria. "Hey, you good for a bit? I need to do somethin'. If you need anything, hit me up, aight?" She texted Maria the number of one of her lesser-used burner phones and headed out.

She grilled Chavonne for a good half hour, asking for as much detail as she could get, before she used another burner phone to contact T Block. When she got his anonymous voicemail, she hung up and texted. I have info you need to hear ASAP.

He called her twenty minutes later, and minutes after that she was driving Zippy's beat-up Civic over to Anacostia, near the waterfront. She didn't ask T Block what he was doing over there.

She found him in an enormous run-down warehouse, alone, although she had the sense that his men were nearby. She hadn't seen him in person since that day in the anonymous office building, and knew that although he professed to believe her and Zippy, he was keeping his distance. Curtis hadn't been invited to any more impromptu concerts or barbecues, either.

"Good to see you, darlin'," he said when he saw her. "How's Curtis? We need to have you all over one of these days."

Larissa didn't believe him, and didn't dance around. "One of my girls caught wind of something."

T Block stood there, listening like a monolith. He was dressed casually in jeans and a black windbreaker, so dark it somehow seemed to suck the light from the room.

"Wasn't sure at first, but after talkin' with her, I'm convinced. She's solid."

"Who's this girl?"

"That don't matter," she said. "She's one of mine, and I vouch for her."

T Block waited.

She took a breath. "So, she spilled that JFunk fed info to that reporter. JFunk's gunnin' for you. They wanted Zippy out, seein' how tight you roll with him. How loyal he is to you. JFunk's mad about you handin' over Twenty-Seventh to Thirty-Third. They think you're gettin' soft in your old age."

"Bullshit."

She shrugged. "That's the word on the street. I'm just tellin' you what I got."

"How do I know I can trust this?"

"Don't take my word then," she said. "Zippy's already doin' time for you."

"Maybe he's gettin' out soon. The lawyer's talkin' about—"

"Lawyers talk, but it ain't real until it happens," she cut in. A beat passed as they sized each other up. "Look," she said finally. "JFunk's on the move. He had to clear Zippy to climb. It adds up. Squeeze him, he might spill."

T Block thought for a long moment. "Go home. Get some rest. Appreciate you being straight with me." He turned toward the open warehouse door, and she followed. "Tell Curtis I'm looking forward to the concert. Got it marked on my calendar. Bringing Treshelle."

Larissa was speechless. That was it? This was loyalty?

Shaking her head, she headed back to Southeast. Back to Bright Horizons.

But a week later it was all over the news. Larissa heard about it moments before, from Cheryl.

Cheryl: JFunk got smoked

                                                                    Larissa: ??

Cheryl: Girl, He's dead. Look @ Citizen.

Larissa opened the Citizen app on her phone.

Incident Alert: Multiple Fatalities in Southeast DC
Location: 18th and F streets, Southeast DC
Citizen Alert: Multiple Fatalities Reported
Multiple gunshots were reported in Southeast DC at the
intersection of 18th and F streets. Six Black males have
been confirmed dead. Authorities currently responding, and
incident is under investigation.
Residents are urged to exercise extreme caution and avoid
the vicinity. Anyone with information should contact DC
CrimeStoppers.

Larissa put her phone on speaker. "Dang. You sure it was JFunk? Who else? The 5 Bloods in on this?"

"I can't say for sure," Cheryl told her. "But you know where my thoughts lean." Larissa could almost feel Cheryl glancing over her shoulder.

Suspicion hung heavy between them, the idea that T Block might have ordered the hit.

"If you hear anything else, let me know," Larissa said.

"Got it, girl. I'm with you," Cheryl assured. "No worries. I got you."

12

ZIPPY

IT COULD HAVE BEEN a dentist's office. Or a furniture wholesaler. Right off the highway, one of several dozen low-slung single-story brick buildings. Angled parking out front. A landscape designer had limply tried to transform utilitarianism into small-town charm, with cream-colored signs that had a "ye olde village" theme. The looping cursive was difficult to decipher, so Zippy had to drive even slower. The car behind him honked. He gave the driver the finger. Just past JEFFREY HARRINGTON DDS, Zippy pulled up in front of 84-183.

The door was unlocked, and as Zippy entered, a bell jingled. Just like at a doctor's office. There was a small carpeted reception area, with six chairs pushed back against the walls. All were empty. He could hear voices. "Yo, T, you there?"

The voices fell silent.

Zippy had texted T Block on the ride back to D.C., as soon as he'd gotten out of the pen. He was on parole, had served only eighteen months instead of the twelve years he'd been handed.

Yo T, made it out. Tx for the lawyers

Before they hit the D.C. line, T Block's number chimed in Zippy's phone. Glad you're out. You're a good man. I got a business proposition for you.

A second later, another text: an address in the Virginia suburbs, near Dulles Airport, and a time: 2 PM.

So here Zippy was, dressed in a clean hoodie and brand-new

joggers. T Block appeared in the doorway. Alone. He hesitated an instant and then came forward. Hand outstretched. "Zippy." T Block's voice rumbled with a mixture of authority and delight that seemed real. "Good to have you back." A one-armed man-hug.

Zippy had never felt so short. His head barely reached T Block's neck, which seemed wrapped in another layer of muscle and fat since he'd last seen him. "Good to be back. I owe you one."

"You owe me several, Zip." T Block bellowed a laugh.

Zippy swallowed a lump in his throat. He'd rehearsed on the way over. But now words failed him. Gratitude surged. He owed T Block everything.

"I dunno how to thank you," Zippy finally managed to say. "You came through. Handled that lawyer. Thought I was done."

"I take care of my peeps," T Block said. "You're one of mine."

"I am," Zippy agreed, fervent. "I'm ready to get back to work." He wanted so much more than to work for T Block. He'd taken the rap for him. So T Block, in all fairness, should be grateful to Zippy. It didn't make sense that Zippy had such a sense of obligation. It felt stuck in his chest, enormous and round.

"I've been thinking about this for a long time," Zippy said. "I appreciate everything you've done for me. You know that. I paid my dues. You know that too. But—" He hesitated.

T Block said nothing, just looked at him.

Zippy looked at the floor. "But I want more. Want something bigger. I really want to roll with you."

T Block leaned back, studying him. The silence stretched, testing Zippy's resolve.

"You're hungry for more, huh?" T Block's voice hinted at a smirk, eyes narrowing. "What's 'more' lookin' like to you?"

Zippy's voice grew firmer as he met T Block's eyes. "I've shown my loyalty. Did time for you. You know you can trust me. I didn't break in jail. I never snitched on you. I understand what loyalty means. I'm ready to ride or die."

He drew a breath, went on. "I took classes in the joint. Numbers, bookkeeping, accounting. All that shit. I officially got skills now. Now I can really have your back, man. I have some ideas on how to reinvest, how to take what you're doing and really blow it out."

A moment of contemplation passed between them, the weight of the room bearing down.

"You're an ambitious man," T Block said, studying him, two little lines between the thick bushes of his gray eyebrows. "Ain't you?"

Zippy nodded.

"You're a solid soldier. You grasp loyalty. Punks like JFunk never got that. That's why he and his crew are no longer in the picture." T Block's lips curled into a smile, and he nodded. "Seems you grew up. You've earned your shot. There's more beyond these streets. A world that demands trust and discretion." He paused, choosing his words. "And the ability to navigate complex alliances." It sounded like he was quoting from someone else.

Zippy's heart was pounding. This was the moment where his gratitude would evolve into a tangled web of loyalty, power, and danger.

"I been talking to some folks," T Block said. "They're looking for a recommendation. They want someone they can trust. I mean really trust. And in exchange for that trust, they're offering serious rewards."

"What kind of rewards," Zippy asked warily. "And what kind of risks?"

"It's a day job," T Block said. "Regular hours. Nine to five. Paid vacation time. Health insurance."

"401(k)?" In prison Zippy learned how important retirement funds were.

"401(k)," T Block affirmed. "There are a couple of retirement programs."

"So what's the catch?" Zippy asked. He'd also learned, long ago, that if it seemed too good to be true, it always was.

"The catch is that it's very private. It's not something you can talk about. Not even to Larissa."

"You recruiting me to the CIA?"

T Block guffawed, a bellow that went on a little too long.

"Just one thing, though. I want to work for you, but I ain't going back to prison," Zippy said. "I ain't doing anything else to put my boy at risk."

"I know these people—they're not asking you to. They need someone who is good with numbers and who can keep their mouth shut. As soon as they told me about what they needed, I thought about you. You've earned my trust."

"Why don't you want me to work with you, then?"

T Block hesitated. "These people—they're good friends of mine. Very good friends. I owe them. If I can make this work with you, I'd be doing a mitzvah for everybody."

Zippy wasn't sure what that meant, but T Block seemed sincere enough. Zippy studied him closely.

"And the money is good, Zip," T Block was saying. "Regular steady income. Enough to give Curtis the kind of cello he deserves. Enough to buy Larissa the house she always wanted. I don't know the exact salary, but it's generous. They can tell you about it if you want to meet them."

Zippy had already made up his mind. "I'm your man," Zippy said. "I won't let you down."

"I know you won't," T Block said. "But here's the deal. Once you're in, you're in. They can't have any squeamish, weak-ass pussies working for them. These people, these friends of mine, do not fuck around. There ain't no such thing as a trial run."

Zippy nodded. His anxiety grew.

"I ain't talking guns or blow. You're about to start makin' real money." T Block moved closer. Zippy could smell his breath. Sausage, or meat of some kind. "I'm taking a chance on you, Zip. I know you want to do this for Curtis. You stay focused, you get everything you need."

T Block paused. Zippy waited.

"But you mess with these guys at all, what happened to JFunk will look like amateur hour compared to what will happen to you and Larissa. And Curtis. And you know what? That'd be a damn shame." T Block waited a beat, as if to let Zippy contemplate his future. "You in?"

Zippy nodded, forcing his eyes never to look away. He knew how to work hard and impress his superiors. He wasn't going to cross these people and endanger Curtis. In fact, this could give Curtis the opportunity he deserved. He forced himself to inhale T Block's meaty breath. "I'm in."

"Good." T Block stuck out a fleshy hand. Zippy grabbed it. They shook. Hard.

"Let me see when these folks are free." T Block pulled out a phone, texted. "How was the concert?" he asked. "Curtis play the Saint-Saëns concerto?"

Zippy nodded. "The kid was killing it. They called him out for another solo. 'The Swan.'"

"For real?"

"Yeah, he's got that special something."

"I tried to get Crista into music, you know? Got her a violin, a pricey teacher, the whole deal. But she wasn't feeling it. Just wanted to paint her face and hit the shops." He chuckled. "But that girl's got a voice. Thinking of starting her on some vocal lessons soon."

His phone pinged. He read the message, nodded. "Good. They can talk." He led Zippy into the rear of the building, past rooms that seemed empty and bland, and out the rear door, into another empty parking lot that seemed a mirror image of the front.

Across the parking lot, the building they approached also seemed identical to the one Zippy had just left. The door opened as they came up the pathway, shouldered past a broad bald Black man in a suit. T Block didn't nod or acknowledge him, stalked right past, through another corridor and series of rooms that seemed similar to the building they'd just left.

A group of people sat huddled around a conference table. They all turned.

"Here he is," T Block said. He pushed Zippy forward into the room, and people were standing up and leaning over the table to shake his hand.

Part 2

GATHERING CLOUDS

13

CURTIS

"I THINK you're in my chair," Curtis said to the young man in the white shirt and tie. The kid—an upperclassman, Curtis was sure—was warming up with one of the Bach suites, head down, and, Curtis thought, being a little overdramatic about it all. Every time the guy hit the C string he whipped his head around, blond bangs flying.

"Excuse me, dude, you're in my chair," Curtis tried again. The guy didn't seem to hear him, even though Curtis was almost sure the other cellist had caught sight of him through those half-closed lids. He tapped the kid's left shoulder.

The Bach screeched to a halt. "What is it?" the kid said, looking up, bow at the tip of the D string. "Can I help you?"

"You're in my seat," Curtis repeated. "Dr. Docker showed me the audition results." He shrugged. It was out of Curtis's control.

The blond kid shook his head. "I doubt it. You must be thinking about prep orchestra. They're upstairs." He flicked his blond locks dismissively toward the ceiling and, duty done, returned to the previous measure of the Bach.

"Trust me, buddy," Curtis said, louder. "You're sitting in my seat."

Now he'd pissed the guy off. The bow hand stopped again, holding the bow as if he personally held Curtis responsible for his inability to warm up his instrument. "You're that freshman from D.C., right?"

"Hi, yeah. I'm Curtis." He extended a fist for a fist bump, but the guy didn't meet the hand with his own, so Curtis's paw hung limply in the air for a second before he pulled it back.

"The Beacon Scholarship, right?"

Curtis nodded. He'd won the most prestigious scholarship to Juilliard: full tuition plus a generous stipend to cover all living and travel costs.

"Well," the guy said, "congrats on getting in, but here's lesson number one. Around here, we don't just do what we want. There's a hierarchy. A procedure. You got to follow the rules, *buddy*." He echoed Curtis now, but Curtis could hear the scorn.

"Yeah, I know," Curtis said. "It's called an audition. And this is the seat I earned."

"Okay, look," the guy said. "You might be a Beacon, but there's no way that you got first chair. I find it hard to believe that a freshman beat me."

The room, which moments before had been alive with the warm-up strains of a hundred instruments, had fallen silent. Everyone was watching them. Curtis realized that he should be intimidated: here he was, a freshman, in an upper-level symphony class. But, he realized at the same moment, he was far from daunted. Years of walking over junkies and living in the projects, plus his own well-muscled physique, grounded him and made him sure of who he was. No Antoinne Marley would ever beat him up again.

He shrugged. "Look," he said, "you can either move now on your own, or you can wait for Maestro to tell you to move. Since we're following *procedures*."

He waited. The moment was almost surreal, and yet felt utterly grounded. Wealth, privilege, and seniority no longer scared him. He knew he belonged.

So, at that moment, when Maestro Fleary, the symphony conductor, strode in and casually glanced at the blond kid, saying, "Del Buono, you've been dethroned, you're second chair now," Curtis didn't feel any triumph.

Del Buono's scowl, his gathering up the cello and moving one seat over, didn't fill him with glee.

Instead, it felt right. It simply confirmed what he already knew. Curtis had made it.

He was in.

14

LARISSA

MARTA GONZALEZ was supposed to be one of Larissa's success stories. She had two kids, a seventh-grade education, and a husband—now ex-husband—who liked to extinguish his cigarettes on her shoulder when he got drunk. She'd spent three months in Bright Horizons, and Larissa had found her Section 8 housing in the nice part of Southwest, had hooked her up with pooled childcare that Bright Horizons offered, and had worked with Marta to help her get her GED and associate degree.

She'd practically guaranteed Marta a job if Marta did all these things, but the kind of job that Larissa had promised—a receptionist, an executive assistant, something in a nice office with lunch breaks and free coffee in the break room and paid health insurance and paid vacation time—hadn't materialized. Instead, Marta could work the french fry machine at a fast-food restaurant or join the night janitorial crew to clean office buildings, all for minimum wage.

Marta had worked too hard, had come too far to clean toilets. Larissa, illogically, blamed herself, even though she couldn't figure out what else she could do to help. "Give it another month," she told Marta, and agreed to have Bright Horizons pay another month's rent, even though that was against policy.

Leaving Southeast had changed her perspective. One thing she noticed about her new neighbors was that most had some sort of education. Maybe not a college degree or a PhD, but most had their GEDs or high school diplomas. Many had certificates or diplomas from vocational schools or community colleges. It made all the difference. It opened doors to jobs, to steady paychecks, to security.

So Larissa encouraged the women to study. She worked out daycare programs—sometimes just a new runaway acting as a babysitter—so the women could take night classes. Some couldn't hack it—Jemilla tried taking evening classes but never studied and got caught smoking crack; Marti tried to seduce one of the teachers and they kicked her out—but most of them, given Larissa's encouragement, had been thriving.

But they still weren't landing jobs.

It was after eight when she unlocked the apartment door and slipped off her shoes. She could feel her shoulders slumping in defeat.

"I'm back here," Zippy called from the kitchen. She hung her coat in the closet and went to find him. The rich smells of roasting meat wafted out to greet her.

They'd moved out of the projects four years ago, when Curtis was a sophomore in high school. Although Larissa had wanted an entire townhouse, that proved to be too expensive, so they bought the top two levels of a brick 1890s Victorian on Sixteenth Street Northwest. In a *nice* part of town. She only wished that Curtis could have had more than two years of it before he headed off to college.

Still, though, the lamps and antique furniture that she'd culled from secondhand shops filled her with delight: the apartment was warm and cozy. Without a roach in sight.

Zippy was in the kitchen, something savory bubbling on the stove while faint crackles and pops came from the oven. She didn't know when he'd become such a good cook but was thrilled he did. She hugged him from behind, kissed his ear as he stirred a pot of some kind of rich-smelling soup, then sat down at the kitchen table.

"How was work?" he asked her.

She put her head down on the table. "Don't ask."

"I'm asking," he said.

"I feel like a failure," she said.

"Girl, you ain't hardly a failure."

"It doesn't matter how hard they work. I can't seem to get them placed in a decent job that doesn't involve cleaning grease traps or mopping floors."

"Babe, what do you expect? Most of them girls wouldn't know a mop from a tablet. You're doing right by all of them."

"I used to think so, but these girls are really smart and ambitious. They want to do better. To have more. Every office job they apply for finds a reason not to hire them."

She sipped a glass of white wine that Zippy brought to her as he set the table for dinner. "I told you, you're making this too complicated. Instead of going for the fancy office jobs, have them apply for hospital jobs. There is tons of admin work there. Or even medical jobs. There's always high turnover because people keep getting promoted or transferred."

"And I told you, I've tried. I think I placed maybe one woman in the past six months."

"Maybe you're doing it wrong," Zippy said.

"Well, what's the right way to do it?"

"I don't know," Zippy said. "But I talk to medical people all day. And they always need more warm bodies."

"So *you* ask them," Larissa told him. "I'll get you a pile of résumés. You can pass them on."

"I can't do that," Zippy said.

She closed her eyes. "I know. That's the point. None of these women can get a toe in the door."

He put a bowl of the soup, steaming and fragrant, in front of her. She inhaled.

"But I can ask around," he said. "I can find out if they're hiring. The problem is that so many places I work with aren't in D.C. They're in Philly or Baltimore or across the country."

"Yeah, well, it's a place to start," Larissa said.

"And if you could train them to do medical procedures, that would be huge. They always need trained staff. Like phlebotomists. Billing techs. MAs. If you don't faint at the sight of blood and you have a pulse, you're in."

"Would you really ask around?" Larissa asked him. "See if they're actually hiring and not just talking about it? And if they'd hire some of my girls?"

"Sure," Zippy said. "Consider it done."

15

ZIPPY

UNTIL THE FBI SHOWED UP, that Tuesday seemed like an average workday for Zippy. He'd arrived at three minutes to nine with two cups of coffee—his own, with cream and sugar; and his assistant Colleen's, black—and let himself into the office on H Street. It was a tiny place, a former car rental spot, sandwiched between a check-cashing store and a liquor store. He flicked on the lights, powered up the computer, and started going through the emails that had arrived from the night before.

There were sixteen: three from medical facilities in Romania. two from Israel, and eleven from India. Each dealt with procedure status.

The first, from a Romanian doctor, Octavian Radulescu, included encrypted photographs. So the procedure was done—and a success. Zippy scanned them quickly, double-checked the photo of a liver held in gloved hands, labeled with date, patient name, and relevant information. Then checked the others—of the suture site and of the patient awake, time stamp indicating twelve hours after the initial photograph.

Radulescu's accompanying email was brief. By now Zippy didn't even need the translation app to read "Procedure completed" and "patient stable."

Zippy typed back a quick acknowledgment: "Mulțumesc. Fonduri transferate." Thanks. Funds transferred. He flicked over to one of the dozens of banking programs. Years before, he'd created a labyrinth of shell companies and nonprofit organizations through which he'd donate lavishly to the targeted hospitals, clinics, and medical personnel. It built goodwill, earned him plaques on honorary boards, and more importantly, access to certain administrative privileges.

Now he selected the proper company, "Borealis Unlimited," and used the account to wire the monies to Radulescu's Cayman Islands account—another bribe that greased the wheels and kept the machinery moving.

Six years ago, when he'd gotten out of prison, T Block had introduced him to a man and a woman, Ricky Lyman and Jordan Parlavamian, who were working out of an anonymous strip mall on the outskirts of the Virginia suburbs.

Jordan was a tall willowy blonde with wide-set gray eyes, a vaguely Eastern European accent, and thin lips that never smiled. In her forties, she was perhaps ten or fifteen years older than Zippy. She moved with a sharp brittleness that reminded him of one of those electric puppies yapping in mall gift shops—there was nothing cute or cuddly about her. She was austere, would hold his gaze for long moments without speaking, and there was no warmth on her face. Only calculation and sharp cunning.

Ricky Lyman was Zippy's usual point of contact. Where Jordan would stare coolly without saying a word, Ricky would jump in with a laugh; where Jordan would hold back and concentrate, Ricky would launch in apparently without thought or consequence. They made an effective team, one playing off the other.

Together, they explained to Zippy their business.

They were selling hope.

Daily, hourly, people were dying because they couldn't get the treatments they needed. Perhaps it was a cancer victim who needed bone marrow; or a twenty-five-year-old gymnast whose kidneys, inexplicably, failed. Or a doting grandmother who, without a new heart, wouldn't see her granddaughter sing in the high school musical. Or the teenager whose love for extreme sports resulted in a devastating accident and urgent need for a lung transplant.

Normally, too often, these people joined the ranks of all the thousands of others on the Organ Procurement and Transplantation Network. The OPTN was a massive nationwide web that managed organ donations and the list of patients waiting for transplants. Like the DMV, it was a government-designed system filled with frustration. People waited years for a donor. The OPTN justified the wait using factors like medical urgency, tissue matching, and location, but the reality was that people waited forever, feeling lost in bureaucratic paperwork and forms and contradictory demands and requests. The complex and drawn-out game seemed to never end: offering hope, in theory, but in reality often offering relentless anxiety and despair.

Jordan and Ricky had figured out how to bypass the bureaucracy. To make that bone marrow, that liver, that kidney, possible for those who needed it most.

The donor part was easy—they could always find someone who'd be willing to donate a kidney for $25,000, or a small piece of their liver for $50,000. The tricky part—and what they needed Zippy for—was to handle the medical, financial, and logistical aspects: the complicated process of finding and paying the right medical personnel, outfitting the right treatment facilities.

"This shit is complicated," Ricky said. "Lots of moving parts, and we need somebody who can handle it all." Which included compensating doctors and reimbursing facilities and coordinating recipients and creating shell companies to reinvest the proceeds.

The work was, technically, illegal, they told him. Five years in prison or $50,000 fine—per offense.

But, in reality, not a lot of law enforcement resources focused on organ transplants. The chances of being caught seemed very low. And they were already working with many law enforcement personnel, helping officers' relatives find their own kidneys or hearts when they needed them.

Zippy found himself accepting their offer. And, bottom line, Zippy honestly, truly believed that he was doing good in the world. He was helping people who needed to be helped. It didn't make sense to him, in this capitalistic society, that the wealthy and the desperate couldn't pay to be healed—had to wait at the bottom of a list, to rot and die as the bureaucratic wheels of the OPTN ground ever more slowly onward—when Zippy had the power and the ability to heal them, almost miraculously.

So for the past six years, from nine to five, this was what Zippy did. From Philadelphia to Tucson to Bangladesh and Bethlehem, he worked with medical personnel to make the transplants happen, interfaced with world-class hackers who tapped into and manipulated medical databases, and so much more. He pulled strings, pushed buttons, and paid off whoever he needed to keep the operation safe and successful. All the while telling himself it was for a good cause.

And the money was great. They sold the two-level apartment on top of a townhouse and bought their own townhouse. He took Larissa on vacation to Seville, Paris, Buenos Aires. He saved for retirement. He bought rental properties in Northwest.

And he bought Curtis a $75,000 Melanson cello.

He told them that some prison buddies had started an investment firm and wanted him to help out—and the "investment firm" kept getting more and more successful. He even gave them a tour of the office and introduced them to Colleen.

There was much that Ricky and Jordan didn't tell him, and that he never asked. For instance, how the recipients found out about the organization. Or where the donors came from. Or who recruited the doctors, and how. And what happened to the hundreds of thousands of dollars that Zippy would regularly make disappear into dozens of offshore accounts.

But he had his hands full just keeping track of his own little piece of the puzzle. Sometimes he paid off the medical facilities directly, and other times he arranged for the supply shipments to the facilities; sometimes he coordinated travel for the recipients, and other times reimbursed the recipient or the recipient's travel company. In any given moment, two or three procedures were actively in process; and it took all that he had to keep track of all that he did.

Everything disintegrated one late-April Tuesday after work. Zippy, as he often did when the weather was nice, sat at an outdoor table at a café on H Street, a few blocks from the office, his gaze plastered to the financial section of the *Washington Post*. Dressed in his usual crisp white shirt and perfectly knotted tie, he fit the part of the quintessential D.C. businessman.

He'd finished a plate of calamari and was sipping his beer, preparing to head off home to Larissa, when a woman slid into the chair across from him. He glanced up, startled. The woman must have made a mistake. She was tall, long smooth hair pulled back, her features vaguely Asian—elegant eyes and a small nose.

"I hope you don't mind if I sit here, Mr. Wilson," she said, and he almost replied, "No, be my guest, I'll be leaving in a minute" before he registered that she'd called him by name.

"Who—" he started.

"Let me introduce myself," she said, rising slightly from her chair and leaning forward to shake his hand. As he reached out automatically to take it, he caught sight of what she held open in her other hand: a case, like a wallet, with a clear screen on one side. Beneath the plastic was a silver oval that he recognized in a moment as a badge, and a moment after that deciphered the words "Federal Bureau of Investigation." "I'm Teddi Slager," she said. "Special Agent Slager. FBI."

He stood up.

"I wouldn't go anywhere if I were you," she said. "You have a choice—if you attempt to walk out of here I'm going to arrest you right now. Alternatively, you have a chance to make up for what you've been doing with minimal risk to yourself."

He shook his head, hands raised, backing away. "I'm not going to—"

"I thought as much," she said. "So I'm going to have to place you under arrest."

To one side he caught sight of two men, one in a tan suit and one in a gray suit, standing a few feet away. There was nowhere to run.

"It doesn't have to be like this," she said easily. Too easily. "It doesn't have to destroy your life—and Larissa's, and Curtis's. But you'll have to cooperate."

"Curtis?" his voice came out, cracked.

Got your back.

All the time.

He sat back down. "What do you want from me?" he said.

She leaned forward, murmuring, her voice barely audible over the sound of the street and the pounding in Zippy's temples. "Here's the situation," she said. "We already know a lot about the people you work with. We know about the organ transfers, and payoffs and how things move around. We have enough to put you, Jordana Parlavamian, Richard Lyman, Elspeth Johnson, Terrence Delvecchio, and a dozen other people—do you want me to list all their names now?—away for many years. But we need you to fill in a lot of the gaps."

"You want me to snitch," Zippy said. "I ain't no snitch."

"That's what I told my colleagues," she said, nodding. "I said you wouldn't cooperate, but here's the thing. The alternative is that you're going to be arrested, right now. And tonight we're going to raid your offices and confiscate all the computers. We're also going to simultaneously arrest everyone else who's been in and out of the office the past six weeks.

"And here's something else. It may look like you cooperated with us, and you'll get the blame anyway." She let that sink in for a moment.

"On the other hand," she said more brightly, leaning in even closer, "we're going to do our best to take out everyone in the organization all at once. Have them all arrested immediately. We can make it look like you're one of them, but we'll let you off with a slap on the wrist. We're your last best hope. Honestly, we're your only hope if you ever want to go to Carnegie Hall and listen to that boy of yours playing the $75,000 cello you bought him. Which we'll be confiscating. Along with that fancy townhouse of yours. Illegal gains."

She sat back, her face smooth but friendly, looking at him. "What's it gonna be?"

Got your back.

All the time.

Part 3

THE STORM BREAKS

16

CURTIS

MOMENTS BEFORE, the halls outside of Curtis's dressing room in Lincoln Center had been filled with people—stagehands, orchestra members, the press, the public, who knew who else. But now, Federal Bureau of Investigation Agent Mitchell pushed open the door onto an empty corridor gleaming under anonymous fluorescent lights. None of it seemed real.

Mitchell led the way—Curtis hauling the Melanson—with the gray-suited woman hovering close at his heels. He tottered out, bewilderment and panic growing with each step. "Hey, is my dad okay? Is Larissa? What's going on?"

Agent Mitchell said something that Curtis didn't catch, and he realized that the older man was speaking into an earpiece. So he tried to talk to the woman behind them. She seemed sympathetic, smiling encouragingly as they'd ushered him out. "Is my dad okay?" he started again.

"Sir, we'll answer all your questions in just a minute, but right now we've got to get you to safety," she told him.

They passed a maintenance worker, who looked at them curiously. Curtis nodded, said nothing. He tried to remember the name of the cute stage manager. The comic book fan. He couldn't remember.

They descended levels deeper. A man in a blue suit loomed before them, nodding at Mitchell as he pushed open an emergency door.

Now Curtis recognized where they were: in a small glassed-in vestibule abutting the parking garage. No one manned the security desk. Curtis had the sick feeling that everyone in the world had disappeared. The fluorescent strip lights sputtered and hummed.

Directly outside, a car with dark-tinted windows waited, engine idling, so close to the door that Curtis couldn't catch a glimpse of the license plate.

Mitchell gestured for him to get in. "You can put your cello in the trunk."

"Um, no," Curtis told him. "The cello stays right here with me."

Mitchell measured the cello with his eyes. "It'll be a tight squeeze."

Curtis stuffed the Melanson in and wedged himself next to it. Mitchell and the woman were having a conversation he couldn't catch. Then the woman slid in the back, behind the driver's seat. He could barely see her around the cello but caught a glimpse of that smile, and again the gleam of pearls. Incongruously, he felt like he could trust her. The driver was a round-faced Hispanic man also with an earpiece. Mitchell clambered into the front. The car took off—the interior felt strangely dark—and another car fell in behind them. They pulled out into the warren of streets that Curtis knew so well, having just spent four years at Juilliard nearby.

There was the cinema where he saw *Avengers: Endgame,* and there was the Chinese place where he and his friends would get late-night takeout. Down that side street was the French restaurant where he'd gone on a first date with that dancer whose name he couldn't remember, but he could still remember how rude the waiter had been. It had taken forever to get mussels and french fries. How crazy that he could remember what he'd ordered but couldn't remember the girl's name or her face.

Now everything was blurring by with a terrifying finality.

He tried again. "Will you please tell me what the fuck is going on?" He wished he could remember the woman agent's name, too. Everything felt jumbled. One minute, he'd given an incredible performance, one that Daniil Shafran himself would have been proud of; now, all he had was his cello, Captain America socks, and terror.

"We're taking you to your family now," the woman said to him.

"And where's that?" he asked her.

Mitchell, who'd been mumbling into his headset, turned around from the front. "Delaware."

"Delaware," Curtis repeated, as if it were Mozambique or Thailand, some place far away and exotic.

Mitchell nodded. "The lead agents are with your father," he said. "We've been assigned to bring you in and keep you safe. So they'll explain everything. Your dad is involved in providing evidence about an organization we've been keeping tabs on."

Of course Zippy was involved. "What was he mixed up in?" he asked. "What's this organization? I thought he worked for an investment company."

"Bad group of guys," Agent Mitchell said, still turned around. And then, looking at the woman, amended this to "A bad group of people."

The car headed up the West Side Highway. Agent Mitchell spoke into his headset again.

"Look," Curtis said, "I've got to call people. Tell them where I am. There's a big reception I'm supposed to be at. And a dinner afterward. People are going to go nuts if I don't show up."

"Is there a single person you can call? Assure them you're all right?"

"I guess my manager," Curtis said, thinking. Having a manager was still so new that he wasn't quite sure how to navigate. "I guess he can tell them I got sick or something."

"Do it," Mitchell said. "Better yet, text him."

Curtis pulled out his phone. There were six missed calls and eighteen unread texts.

"Here's what I want you to write," Mitchell said. "That you're okay. And you'll be in touch in the future. But you can't make whatever events you're supposed to be at tonight. That's it."

Curtis typed, I'm okay but I can't make the reception tonight. Back to you soon.

"Let me see," Mitchell said.

Curtis handed over the phone.

Mitchell pressed Send and looked at Curtis. "Is there anyone else? Anybody urgent?"

He thought about his on-again-off-again girlfriend Katie. She'd be home. She was a flutist trying to break into the film score world out in Hollywood.

"There's my girlfriend," he said.

"Is she waiting for you?"

"Not right now. She's in L.A."

"Good," Mitchell said. "You can text her later." He slipped Curtis's phone into his breast pocket.

"Yo, can I get my phone back?" Curtis now felt vulnerable on an entirely different level. He hadn't thought once about his phone until now, but its absence panicked him. His last lifeline with the outside world.

"Mr. Wilson," the woman said, "we're trying to keep you safe. We understand this is scary and very disorienting. Until we can assess the risk, it's better you're not on the phone."

"But people will wonder. They'll be worried."

"Right now our priority is your safety."

"Is my dad gonna be where we're going?"

"Yes, he'll be joining you."

"What about Larissa?"

"She's already there. And your grandmother."

"My grandmother?" Curtis repeated. A whole new realm of panic opened up as I-95 spooled out in front of them. "Why is she there?" The car turned off onto a two-lane road, heading south, and city lights fell away.

"We're trying to keep you all safe," Mitchell said.

For the next two hours, Curtis tried to learn more, but the agents either couldn't or wouldn't tell him anything further. He had no phone, and no other way of reaching the outside world. The silence inside the car stretched on, broken only occasionally by one of the agents muttering into their headset or, a couple of times, on the phone. Their heads were turned away, so he could only catch a few words: "Martin" and "we're going." He thought about asking them to play some music, but for once in his life he didn't want to hear anything.

So, because there was absolutely nothing else to do, he stared out the window. He had never felt so powerless. And so frightened. He thought about the comic book, half read, on the hotel nightstand. "Can I get my stuff?" he asked. "My clothes? They're at the hotel."

"We've made arrangements to have them picked up," the woman told him.

After another half hour, his initial panic faded, replaced by emptiness, and then exhaustion. He'd been up early—he never could sleep in hotels, and he'd wanted to practice before the concert—and had gone to bed late the night before, hanging out with Thomas and Neil over in the East Village. Finally, he fell into a light doze, awakening only when the car slowed and took an exit.

He blinked awake. Looked for highway signs. The road was ending in a T intersection. North Adams Street to the left, South Adams Street to the right.

"Where are we?" he said. "Are we almost there?" He felt like he was eight years old again.

"Yes," the woman told him; simultaneously, Mitchell leaned back and said, "We're almost there."

Signs for Selbyville, Delaware. The car slipped down one street and then another. They were in suburbs now, row upon row of small houses and developments blurring beneath irregular street-lights. Then the car turned in between two brick columns bearing an innocuous sign that read WELCOME TO EDGEWATER: A PLANNED COMMUNITY. Beyond lay a gatehouse. The car took the right lane and barely slowed as the orange-and-white-striped traffic gate lifted up.

"This sure doesn't feel that safe," Curtis said. "Is that it? Just that little gate? Shouldn't there be better security?"

"There's a lot more than you think," the woman told him.

The car circled past rows of adjacent townhomes, many with front porch lights on. *We'll leave the light on for you*, Curtis thought, trying to remember the name of the hotel that the commercial advertised.

The agents in the car were rustling. He could sense relief and renewed focus.

The car slid into a parking spot in front of a townhouse that looked like all the others, except here no porch light glowed. They came to a stop. The car doors clicked open. Curtis bundled the cello out of the car, into the cool night air.

"This way, sir, please," Mitchell said.

Curtis wasn't wearing a watch, but caught sight of Agent Mitchell's. It was almost two in the morning.

In a moment they were inside, and the door slammed behind them.

Immediately, a woman blocked his path: tall, gaunt, wearing a black suit and running shoes that had seen better days. She had a smooth face and heavy-lidded, elongated eyes. The features were both strong and delicate. "Curtis Wilson? I'm Special Agent Slager. In charge of your briefing." Her voice was low-pitched but filled the room. "Come on in. You can leave that here." She gestured to the cello, indicating that Curtis could prop it against the wall.

"Thanks, I'm good," Curtis said, not relinquishing the Melanson. "Are you someone who can actually tell me what's going on?"

Beyond Agent Slager, the living room looked like it had been designed by a retired couple back in the nineties—brown corduroy overstuffed sofa, dark-blue La-Z-Boy chair, cream-colored carpet. It seemed crowded with people, all turning to look at him. "Is my dad here? Larissa? Grandma?"

Agent Slager said something that Curtis didn't hear, because from the living room another voice cried out, "Oh, baby, I'm so glad to see you!" Then Larissa was bounding toward him and wrapping him fiercely in a hug. The top of her head came up to his chin, and he breathed in the clean cucumber smell of her hair. For the first time in the past several hours, he found he could take a breath.

"*Mijo*," she said to his chest, "I'm so glad you're okay!"

"Hey, I'm okay. What's going on? Where's Dad?" He'd shifted positions as she hugged him, and now counted three other people, two women and one man, all in business clothes, ties loose around their necks, all typing on laptops or on their phones. Could they be working at two in the morning? He wondered if they were just playing solitaire but got the impression that they'd all been waiting for him. When they saw him watching, they turned back as if to give Larissa and him the illusion of privacy.

"Your grandma's upstairs," Larissa said. "She went up maybe an hour ago."

"Where's Dad? What is going on?"

She broke free of his arms, led him to the brown corduroy couch. "Sit down."

Agent Slager had been watching them, and now said to the room, "I'll introduce you to the team, but right now we'll give you a moment." She gestured, and the others stood up, gathering their laptops, and disappeared deeper into the interior. Slager, though, didn't move. She stood, arms crossed, in the doorway from the foyer.

"What's going on?" he asked Larissa, conscious of Slager's presence. "Why are we in the middle of nowhere with a bunch of FBI dudes—um, agents—barking orders?"

"I'm not even sure I understand," Larissa said. When she got stressed or exhausted, she often would lean into the person nearest her; and now she put her head on his shoulder, her thigh against his own. The warmth of human contact felt good. "Your dad hasn't been himself lately. I been noticing things, you know? He ain't been talking too much, and he's been away more. Even when he's here, he's not really here, you know? But I thought everything was straight." She took a breath.

"So what happened?" he prompted.

"He texted me after work, said he was going to stay late and he didn't know what time he'd be getting home. Then he texted me at like eleven and said he was going to have to pull an all-nighter. So I go to work the next day, and the next thing I know folks are showing up at Bright Horizons, talking 'bout pack your stuff, leave now. I'm like, 'What the hell?' They got Patrice and told me they were coming for you." Curtis kept an arm around her. She felt delicate, brittle, a late-autumn leaf.

He said to Slager, "What did he say? What did he do?"

"Your father has gotten himself mixed up in a black-market ring." Her face gave nothing away, but her eyes at least looked sympathetic. "He's providing evidence to the government to take them down. But until we're able to get the ringleaders, we thought it would be better to hold you here."

"Why me, though? I'm just a musician. And he works for an investment company. He doesn't know anything about a black market." Apart from the drugs his dad had sold when Curtis was a kid, Curtis didn't even really know what people sold on the black market. The latest cell phones or souped-up laptops?

"It's a well-funded group, and if they hear that your father is cooperating with us we're concerned that they might retaliate. You're the most visible person to go after. Have you ever heard of Dr. Benjamin Pembroke?"

"She's joking," Curtis told Larissa. "Tell me she's joking. The only doctor Dad knows is Dr. Pepper. I mean I know he's not a model citizen but—"

Slager interrupted, "He's a prominent nephrologist at the Quaker Ridge Medical Institute, outside Philadelphia. He's one of the top in the nation. Your father has provided evidence that implicates him. We think he may have ties to organized crime. There are a lot of other people involved. A lot of moving parts. We thought that it would be better to have you in protective custody."

"Wait," Curtis said, bewildered. "Why would a doctor be involved? Can't he just buy a laptop? What's my dad selling? Medical equipment?" Now he was envisioning an enormous warehouse in D.C. with boxes bearing indecipherable labels.

"Organs," Agent Slager said. "Black-market organs."

Curtis first thought of was musical instruments—pipe organs or church organs. How could there be a booming cutthroat business in those? "You mean human organs, right?" he said slowly. "Like lungs? Hearts? That kind of thing?"

Agent Slager nodded. "Yes. Exactly. They specialize in kidneys and hearts."

"Did you know about this?" Curtis asked Larissa. From where he sat, one arm around her, he could only see the part in her hair. He had no idea what black-market organ harvesting even meant.

"I didn't know it was about that," she said. "Not until I got here. I thought it was about managing investments. And some of the clients were doctors."

"This is crazy. I need to go. I have a press conference tomorrow morning, and I'm supposed to be heading to Chicago tomorrow afternoon."

"Well, that's going to have to wait," Slager said. "We need to assess the risk before you can return to your regular life. We hope it'll just be a couple of days."

"A couple of days?" he repeated incredulously. "I don't think you get this. I have concerts booked already. People paid for tickets. You need to let me out of here."

She shrugged. "We'll have a better sense of timing tomorrow. Your father and the DA should be here. In the meantime I'd suggest trying to get some rest. It's going to be a long couple of days."

"Let me make you something to eat," Larissa said, standing.

He tried to argue but could get no further information out of them. Larissa dragged him back to the kitchen, where two of the other agents were hanging out. They introduced themselves as Agents Lombardi and Kowalczyk, two men in their midthirties. Lombardi was short, with curly dark hair and a strong jawline, and Kowalczyk had receding hair and a paunch. Larissa made turkey sandwiches for everyone. They all talked, with Curtis trying to wrap his head around what was happening. He told them about the performance that night, his first time playing solo in Lincoln Center. How transporting the orchestra had been. He wanted to tell them that the maestro said he hadn't heard the Kabalevsky played like that since the fifties but figured he'd just tell Larissa later.

He swallowed the last of the turkey sandwich. Larissa took the plate and stowed it in the dishwasher while Curtis grabbed his cello. They both headed upstairs, with Slager close behind them.

His bedroom felt impersonal, a cross between a guest room and a hotel. No pictures hung on the walls; a bed and a single nightstand sat on beige shag carpet. His suitcase, from his hotel, leaned next to the door. Everything seemed to be inside, including his *Nightwing* comic book, with the notepad from last night's hotel still marking his place. He showered, put on a T-shirt and boxer shorts, and curled up in the alien bed. Despite how wired he was, despite the utter disorientation, the adrenaline from the performance and all that had happened afterward had exhausted him. He was almost amazed that he fell asleep.

The next morning, the banging of pots and the muffled sound of raised voices woke him. He lay a moment disoriented, trying to get his bearings. And then, almost before he'd realized it, he was up, shrugging into a pair of jeans and a sweatshirt and bounding barefoot down the stairs.

His father must be back and would clear all of this up. Curtis figured he could be on a flight to Chicago by midmorning. What was the closest airport?

But in the kitchen, he saw that his father was not there. Halfway down the stairs he realized that the voices were those of his grandmother and others that he didn't recognize. Patrice, wearing threadbare sweatpants and a blue Nationals sweatshirt, was at the stove, stirring something in a saucepan. One agent he recognized from yesterday leaned back in a chair by the window and another was on a laptop.

"Hey, Grandma." He gave her a hug, which she submitted to, patting his back gingerly. She didn't like hugs. "Is my dad here yet?" he asked the two people in the chairs. The one from last night, pudgy, with a long Eastern-European-sounding name, had greeted him warmly; the new one, a Black man, was stockier, with a beard. He introduced himself as Agent Pierce.

"We heard later this morning, at the earliest," Agent Pierce said.

"God knows what your daddy been up to," Patrice said, waving a spatula. "And I got my Spades game tonight and it's my turn to cook. So I gots to do these"—she gestured at the eggs—"and I gots to cook tonight, too, for the girls. Did I tell you it's my Spades night tonight?"

She stirred the saucepan once more, then tilted it over an open plate. "I told these people I wanted scrambled eggs," Patrice said. "How hard is it to make a scrambled egg? Making some for you and Larissa, too."

"Is she up?"

"No, she ain't up," Patrice said.

"Then they'll be cold by the time she gets up," Curtis said.

"Then she should have been up," Patrice said, now scowling at the two agents.

"Ma'am," the blond agent said, "we offered to get you takeout."

"Takeout," she sniffed. "As if I'd want to eat cold takeout. I didn't know I was gone be cooking for all the FBI. Don't think I'm doin' this every day neither." She'd filled up several plates, tossed them in front of the agents, who didn't seem to want them. She handed another plate to Curtis. "Here, you eat."

He wasn't hungry but knew better than to refuse her. She sat down across from him. "Took me out of my house, made me come here even though I said I wasn't coming."

"It's just for the day," Curtis reassured her, chewing. She did make good scrambled eggs, delicate and light. "Just until Dad gets here."

"I swear when that boy gets here Imma put my foot square up his ass," she told Curtis.

"I think we all want to talk to him."

"Got me in this mess! Came in and busted up my tonk game. Me and DuPree was winning for once."

"I thought you said you were playing Spades," he said.

"Tonk was last night. They busted up that game. Tonight is Spades night. They better not bust that one up too. I'm cookin' tonight and all the girls is comin' over."

"That's messed up," he told her. And then, to the agents, "How long does this usually take? Shouldn't he be done by now?"

"It takes as long as it takes," the blond one said.

"Sometimes a few hours and sometimes a few days," Agent Pierce added.

"Hmmmf," Patrice scoffed, glaring at them, especially Agent Pierce, as if she blamed him personally for everything that had happened. She fumbled in her pockets for her cigarettes and lighter.

The blond agent noticed. "Ma'am, I told you that you can't smoke in here. And you can't go outside and do it."

"I know," she said, scowling. "I'm standing right over there"— she gestured to the far end of the living room—"just like I told you I would. It's not like you ain't all up my ass everywhere I go anyhow. Y'all need to chill. Damn! Can't even have a cigarette in peace round here." She stomped across the living room, carrying her cigarettes and a mug of coffee. The blinds were half down, but someone had cracked the top of a window for her. She sat in a chair and smoked, breathing out into the cool morning air, glowering at everybody.

Finally Larissa came down, ate the now-cold eggs, and they all talked a while. There was no news, so finally he returned to his room, pulled out his cello and warmed up. He played through some of the Kabalevsky, closing his eyes and trying to recall the glow of last night's performance, and then worked on the Dvorak concerto he was slated to play in Chicago in two days.

His flight from JFK was this afternoon at two thirty. He didn't let himself think about that, immersing himself instead in the piece that had been described as the perfect concerto for cello. At least here, in the confines of this cream-colored room, he found some measure of peace in something that he could control—something familiar and welcome and accepting.

After an hour he took a break, knocked out a hundred push-ups and two hundred sit-ups. He tried to work out regularly. Professor Belovarov told his class, "Strength in the body and melody in the mind equals harmony of the soul."

At almost noon, a door thumped and voices rattled up from below. Curtis stuffed the cello back in its case and took the stairs two at a time down to the main level.

They were all in the living room. Zippy with his coat still on, Larissa hovering near him, and what seemed like dozens of other people there as well—which soon sorted into three agents and Patrice.

Although Zippy wasn't yet forty, he looked older. Curtis took two strides over and hugged him. He breathed in Zippy's familiar odor, closed his eyes for a moment. "What the F is going on?" Curtis said. "I'm supposed to be heading to the airport to get to Chicago. What are you doing?"

Zippy tapped his thumb to his forehead and with everyone looking on, told Curtis, "Got your back."

Curtis was only slightly embarrassed. He'd been doing this since he was a little boy, no matter where. Instinctively he tapped thumb to forehead, met Zippy's thumb with his own. "All the time," he told him. "But what the F are you doing?"

"Trying to do good," Zippy said. "Trying to do the right thing. They said your concert was great. Congrats. I'm really pissed that I had to miss it."

Finally Zippy sat down on one side of the couch with Larissa next to him. Patrice commandeered the La-Z-Boy. The two FBI agents from earlier leaned against the wall, and Agent Slager again stood tall and watchful at the doorway to the foyer. Curtis brought in a kitchen chair.

Over the next couple of hours, as the plane from JFK that Curtis should have been on departed on schedule, without him, Zippy's story emerged. The job he'd gotten out of prison, which Curtis had always thought was working investments, turned out to be the front of a black-market organ-harvesting organization. The true source of the serious money Zippy started bringing in.

Agent Slager then interrupted. "We've been monitoring this group for a while. So two days ago we approached your dad and offered him a deal."

"Wasn't much of an offer," Zippy mumbled.

"It wasn't," Slager allowed. "We offered to keep him out of prison in exchange for information."

His dad the felon. Curtis felt the old resentment boiling in his guts. His father, again, playing fast and loose not only with his life and future, but with Curtis's. And Larissa's. "And what happened?" Curtis said, trying to keep his voice neutral.

"Yesterday we went in with a warrant, confiscated the computers, took Colleen Perkins into custody, and went to apprehend some of your father's other associates." She hesitated, impassive, and he had a sense that she was alert to all of them, sensitive to every shift in position. When Patrice coughed, Slager's eyes went immediately to her, assessing, but otherwise unmoving.

"Okay, and?" Curtis said.

"And we couldn't find them. Jordana Parlavamian, Richard

Lyman. We'd had them under surveillance, but somehow they slipped through.

"Slipped through," Curtis repeated. "How?"

Slager shook her head. "It just happened."

"So—"

"So until we can locate them, we don't think it's safe for you to be on the street. It's fair to know that they might suspect your dad at this point too."

"Oh, Lord," Patrice said, and lit up another cigarette.

17

LARISSA

FOR THE NEXT TWO WEEKS, Larissa, Curtis, and Patrice could not set foot outside the townhouse in Delaware. Only Zippy was allowed to leave—he'd go off in a safe car and return two or three days later, exhausted. Larissa would ask him what was going on, and at first he just stared past her, unspeaking. Finally he said, "It's all dead ends."

"What do you mean?"

"All the accounts. The bank accounts. All the info on the computer. It was all on the cloud, and it's all either gone or the accounts are closed. I've been going around and around everything with those FBI guys. Forensic accountants, they're called. They're all trying to figure out what happened."

"I don't understand," Larissa said.

"I don't either," Zippy said, his voice a whisper. "It happened instantaneously. Everything closed down. As soon as they raided the office. Boom. The FBI guys haven't seen anything like it."

"So what does this mean?"

He looked at her, sorrowful. "It means that nobody knows what the hell is going on."

"So you don't have any leads on where Jordan and Ricky are, huh?"

"That's just one of a billion things they don't know." They were in the bedroom, and now Zippy went out, thumped down the stairs, and spent the night with Agent Kowalczyk watching TV.

During the day, Patrice took over the only outdoor space: a grubby, weedy patch of ground enclosed by a tall wooden-slat privacy fence. A chipped plastic table, gray with mildew, crouched between two sagging vinyl chairs. Patrice took the less mildewy one and would sit there for hours, shivering, smoking sometimes three packs a day, playing endless solitaire games.

Larissa was at a total loss. She didn't know what to do with the time. She was normally busy every day at Bright Horizons from morning till night; besides the administrative work, one of the women always needed something—tending to a busted lip or dropping off a child or getting a driver's license renewed. Now she didn't know how the organization was functioning, how they were coping, since she had no access to the Internet.

For something to do, she threw herself into cooking. Although she'd left Puerto Rico as a child, her mother made wonderful dishes that Larissa had never forgotten. So now she would whip up a batch of mambo sauces, or savory half-smoke chili, or mini cupcakes infused with the essence of sweet potato pie. She became obsessed with creating half-smoke empanadas, which were more difficult and complex than she'd first imagined. Crafting the dough to the ideal consistency was an art in itself. Larissa couldn't get the balance of flakiness and tenderness right. Then she tried to infuse the empanada filling with the smoky essence of half-smoke, and that never seemed to work out as well as she'd imagined. She tinkered with spices, experimenting with various meat blends, and kept a running grocery list. The agents had to pick up different achiote seeds, or different types of chorizo.

While she cooked, she befriended the FBI agents on duty— Agents Mitchell and Gustavson, who were from Maryland; Agent Pierce, from Pennsylvania; and surprisingly more frequently, Special Agent Teddi Slager. Agent Slager wasn't around as much as the others but often accompanied Zippy, and would linger a few minutes, chatting, once she'd dropped him off.

In the few weeks since Larissa had met her, a distinct impression of Slager had crystallized. To Larissa, she was a relentless force, a midforties dynamo. She didn't speak a lot about her home life and family, only that she was divorced and had no children. Larissa detected a nuanced blend of empathy and steely determination—a potent cocktail that made her not just an investigator but a crusader against crime.

As Larissa would work on her latest culinary experiment—"Cooking Disaster no. 49," she'd call it with a laugh—Slager would sit at the kitchen table, keeping her company. Teddi always had a laptop that she wouldn't show Larissa, but that she pored over with her characteristic intensity. Larissa saw her more and more as their advocate, a beacon that would cut through the murky depths of criminality and rescue them.

They needed to be rescued. Desperately. Because if Larissa and Patrice struggled with what amounted to in-home imprisonment, it was nothing compared to Curtis.

He'd appropriated the townhouse's top floor—tucked under the eaves, perhaps designed as a home office, the space became his impromptu concert hall and practice room. He rarely left it, moving his belongings from the guest room. The building thrummed with Dvorak, Fauré, and Beethoven, which became so much a part of their day that when he stopped playing, even the FBI agents would pause and look around as if something was wrong.

Larissa would bring him up bowls of her *pollo guisado* ("Disaster no. 83, eat up!"), a chicken stew he loved, along with strawberry lemonade. But often the food would still be there, untouched, when she'd return for the plates a few hours later. He'd still be hunched over the cello, sawing away, his back to the stairwell, facing where the beige dormer wall slanted down to meet the beige carpet.

But as soon as he heard Zippy come in, he'd bound down the stairs to ask what the latest was.

Larissa and Patrice would crowd around too as Zippy fell into a chair, or sat down for dinner. He'd soon provided the FBI everything he remembered, but still they drilled into him for more.

He and Slager provided updates. The FBI and other government organizations were arresting, or bringing in for questioning, dozens of people that Zippy had paid off in the past—medical personnel, doctors, hospital administrators, travel agencies. They were interviewing organ recipients. The transplant facilities in Romania, Israel, and other countries were under investigation.

Still, the Wilson family stewed in limbo, waiting, trying to imagine what would come next.

Two weeks in, Larissa went up to Curtis's lair, sat on the top step, and listened to him play. She'd heard the piece before—dark and somber, repeating and branching off and turning back into itself again. Then it became more lively, more optimistic, before twisting into something intense and dramatic. Finally it slid into quiet resignation. She didn't think she'd ever heard music as profoundly sad. It was gorgeous, and it broke her heart.

When the last note had died away, he sat slumped and unmoving.

"That was beautiful, *mijo*," she told him.

He jumped a little at her voice—he must not have realized she was there—but all he said was "Thanks."

"You play it a lot."

"Yeah," Curtis said.

"What is it?"

"It's the *Élégie*. By a guy named Gabriel Fauré. It's better with a piano."

"I think it's beautiful," she said lamely, not knowing what more to say. She wished she understood classical music better.

"He wrote it after a girl he was engaged to dumped him," Curtis said. "She broke his heart."

The pain in his voice made Larissa choose her words carefully. "I know this isn't the best situation. I'm so sorry this is happening to all of us. Is there anything I can do?"

Curtis had been staring at the corner of the room, but now turned around and looked up at her. "Give me my life back," he said. He spoke with such an eerie calm that Larissa shivered. She had never seen him so blank, so detached. "Catch these guys and let me go back to playing. They've postponed all my concerts indefinitely now."

She knew this already but nodded as if it was new. Slager had allowed Curtis one brief call with his agent, that was it.

She stood, trying to figure out if there was anything she could do. She felt powerless and frightened.

"I'm gonna practice some more," he told her, turning back to the cello.

Before she was even halfway down the stairs, the *Élégie* started up again.

Agent Pierce was in the living room on his laptop. He'd told her to call him "Matt" when no one else was around. "Hey," Larissa said, dropping into the recliner across from him. "I'm really worried about Curtis."

"I know." Matt was in his early fifties, and also a parent. He had two kids in college, and his wife was a manager at Whole Foods. He sometimes brought Larissa special packets of ingredients. "There's nothing you can do."

"How much longer can this last?" Larissa said, echoing Curtis. Echoing all of them, every day, day after day.

He shrugged, as he and the other agents always did. "Your husband's pretty much gone over everything he knows. Now it's just us doing our job."

"And how's that going?"

She knew he wouldn't answer, and he didn't. "It's a process," he said. Another shrug. She wanted to stand up, yell, flip over the coffee table. Instead she said, "Can you get me almond extract? I'm gonna make those *mantecaditos* again. Get ready for Inedible Experiment no. 806." When Curtis was a child, he'd loved the little shortbread cookies.

"You made them yesterday," Matt said.

"Yeah, and you and the others"—she meant the other FBI agents—"sure enjoyed them. I'm gonna make a batch just for Curtis. And pick me up strawberry jelly, too."

It all came to a head the next day. Teddi Slager arrived late morning. They were all around, including Zippy.

Slager called them all into the living room.

The other two agents, Pierce and Kowalczyk, stood next to her. "There have been developments," she said. Today she didn't lean against the wall or slouch in an armchair. Larissa realized that she was more dressed up than usual, in a charcoal-gray, impeccably tailored pantsuit. Today, Teddi was a professional. The casual woman who lounged at her kitchen table, munching Mistake no. 16 or commiserating with her over Curtis's depression had disappeared. Now the slim, notched lapel jacket, paired with pressed trousers, conveyed a commitment to precision. Subtle silver FBI insignia, a white button-up shirt, and polished black heels completed the look.

"I have some great news and some not-so-great news," Slager was saying. "Thanks to Zippy's courageous actions, our investigation has led to the identification and apprehension of fourteen people in nine hospitals throughout the Northeast, as well as in Ohio and Kentucky. We've also opened investigations in India, Israel, Romania, and Brazil. Several people are in prison, and others are taking plea deals." She pulled out a piece of paper and read names and hospitals, including Dr. Benjamin Pembroke.

The revelation hung in the air, momentarily lightening the atmosphere. "You've single-handedly disrupted the organ trade," Slager went on, looking at Zippy. "There's a lot to feel proud of."

Larissa reached over and took Zippy's hand, squeezed. He squeezed back. She wondered for the millionth time if he was far more afraid than he let on.

"More troubling, though, is that, despite our concerted efforts, we've been hitting a lot of roadblocks. All of the accounts, both payable and receivable, that Zippy had access to were shut down within seconds of us entering the office that day. We have forensic teams working on going through past records, but I'll be honest with you—there's very little to go on. Accounts that were either paid or received funds have disappeared. Going through past records, and looking at those transfers only leads to other accounts which have now gone dead. We're hitting dead end after dead end."

"So what are you saying?" Curtis interrupted. "That you don't know where the money is, and that you can't catch the people who did this?" He was leaning forward, hands on his knees. Incongruously Larissa found herself focusing on his hands—they seemed larger than they usually did, covering all of his knees in a way that seemed somehow ominous.

Slager met his eyes. "Yes and no. We actually have found the people who—as you said—'did this.' Jordana Parlavamian and Richard Lyman."

All of them sat up straighter, and Zippy twisted around in his chair. "Where are they? What did they say? Did you tell them about me?"

"They're dead."

The air went out of the room.

"Suicide," Zippy said. "They must have realized you were going to get them. Ricky once told me that he wouldn't ever go to prison."

Slager continued as if Zippy hadn't spoken. "Three days ago, their bodies were found in a house about three miles outside Meadville, Pennsylvania. They'd been there for some time. We received confirmation of their identities earlier this morning."

"So we're done!" Curtis said, standing. Larissa had the impression he would momentarily be bounding upstairs to grab his cello as he called for a taxi to take him to the nearest airport.

"Not so fast," Slager said. "The house they were found in was owned by Augustus Development, LLC. One of the corporations that Zippy created. We've been systematically tracking down every lead we can find for any of these entities."

"Okay, and?" Curtis prompted.

"And they've been dead for weeks. We won't be able to pin it down with total accuracy, but we believe that they died right around the time when we took you all into custody. The suicide was staged. They were murdered. Single bullet each. To the head."

Larissa groaned, horrified.

"So obviously there's someone else involved," Agent Pierce chimed in. "Possibly several others. But we don't know who."

"It's got to be T Block," Zippy said.

"We don't have anything to tie him to this. Only the introduction he made, and that's not illegal." Slager adjusted the lapel of her suit.

"Did you look at his bank accounts? Follow the money," Zippy said.

"We've been following. He remains involved in the drugs and

guns in Northeast, but we're not seeing a tie to the organ trafficking or to these murders. We believe now that Parlavamian and Lyman were intermediaries. Not the brains of the outfit. We've monitored their bank accounts, and it's clear that most of the money is going somewhere else."

"Meaning?"

"Meaning we're only seeing one part of the picture," Slager said. "Whoever masterminded this group is not only well funded, but is also incredibly careful. Every piece has been siloed from the others. Zippy told us about the medical side of things, the recipient side of things, but we don't have any idea what happened to the money when it left the accounts he worked with. And we don't know how they procured the organs in the first place."

"But I told you—" Zippy started.

Teddi Slager was nodding. "Yes, you gave us as much as you could. Patterns, details when you remembered them. But we don't have anybody coming forward claiming to have received payments for organs. We don't know how the organs were found. We have the actual organs in the living recipients, and we're trying to track down DNA through those, but that's going to take a while."

"So who knows the rest of the picture?" Larissa asked.

"That's what we don't know. That's what we're trying to figure out. Who set this all up. Who's ultimately been profiting. We don't know who the masterminds are."

Larissa's mind raced, grappling with the implications.

"It's got to be T Block," Zippy said.

"Based on what?" Slager asked him. "Did you ever see him associated with the group? Is there any reference at all you can remember?"

He shrugged. "It's just got to be."

Larissa asked, "Did you try talking to him? He's got to know something."

"Of course we brought him in for questioning," Slager said. Larissa could hear the frustration in her voice, which didn't seem directed at them. "That was one of the first things we did. He came with a lawyer and denied everything. He's lawyered up very heavily, and we're pushing as hard as we can to get through and search everything of his. But in the meantime we've got to figure out how to get you all back a life."

Curtis guffawed. "So you don't have shit, is what you're saying," he said.

"In light of these challenges," Agent Slager continued, ignoring him, "and prioritizing the safety of you and your family, the Federal Bureau of Investigation deems it imperative to recommend your entry into the Witness Security Program, or WITSEC. This program, commonly known as 'witness protection,' is designed to safeguard individuals who are willing to provide testimony against criminal organizations. It will keep you safe."

"What you talking about? I ain't going nowhere." Patrice said. "I ain't leaving my house and my friends forever. That's crazy talk."

Curtis was already standing. "Y'all are straight trippin'," he said. "I got shit to do. I got concerts, flights. The record is releasing. People are waiting for me. I'm not going into any bullshit witness protection program."

"Entering into the program is entirely optional," Slager said evenly.

"So I'm not in prison? You're not holding me here?"

Larissa's heart hammered in her chest, as if she'd been running. They'd been living this life of forced isolation, but she'd always known—thought—that after a few weeks she could step back into her real life again, text Cheryl and Crisette and the others, go back to Bright Horizons. Not disappear forever. Not never see her friends again. This was unimaginable.

"No, of course not," Slager was still talking to Curtis, but also talking to all of them. "You're free to leave at any time. But if you do decide to go, we won't be able to protect you."

"You guaranteed our safety," Zippy told her.

"I thought I could," Slager said.

"So if we do what they tell us, we can go on with our lives," Zippy said to Curtis, Patrice, and Larissa.

"You know something," Curtis told him, "I really don't want to hear anything else from you." He strode past Slager to the front door, as if he were going to walk out right then, but hesitated.

Probably to go upstairs for his cello, Larissa thought. "If you can't hold me here," he said to the room at large, "can you give me my phone back so I can call an Uber?"

"My people will drop you at a train station so you can get back to New York," Slager said. "We can give you your phone then."

"Thank you. *Now* you're talking."

"I'll need to set some ground rules, though," she went on as if Curtis hadn't said anything. "First, you'll need to know that when you say goodbye to your family here, it's permanent. You'll never see them again."

"At least until you catch the people. Take them to trial," Curtis finished for her.

"Yes. When that happens. If it happens. We certainly will do our best to make it happen, but you need to prepare for the alternative. We don't know how long this will take. Going into witness protection isn't a temporary measure. We're going to have to relocate your family, find them other names and professions. There will be zero contact between you, ever, moving forward."

"Yeah, I'm through with this mess," Patrice said, also standing. "Where's my cigarettes?"

"Here's the problem," Slager sighed, and now it seemed personal to her. "The problem is that in our rush to keep you all safe, we've also shone a spotlight on all of you. Unintentionally, but there it is."

Larissa shook her head. "I'm not following."

"I am," Zippy said. "It's because you guys"—he was talking to the agents—"didn't figure out who the leaders of the group are, right? You promised to keep me safe when you first talked to me. But instead I've disappeared. I'm supposed to be in prison, more like. Like Colleen. And none of you should have disappeared. You should be going about your regular lives. Visiting me in jail. But you're gone too. Which could mean only one thing—that I was involved."

"So they know it's you," Larissa said.

"Yes," Teddi said. She turned back to Curtis. "So, Curtis, be careful. As careful as you can possibly be. People could be waiting for you at the airport. Until we can figure out who killed Jordan and Ricky, your life is in serious danger."

Terror made Larissa's fingers go numb. "Curtis, you can't—"

Agent Slager spoke over her. "It's my belief that they won't kill you, though—"

"Well, at least there's that," Curtis said, taking a few steps further into the room. He was going to get his cello, Larissa was sure of it.

Now Agent Slager spoke over Curtis, "—because you're more valuable to them if you're alive. My guess is that they'll kidnap you. Maybe cut off your fingers, one by one, see if they can get a message to your father that they'll just keep cutting pieces off you until he either shuts up or kills himself. Or maybe figure out a way of using you as bait so they can kill him themselves. Yeah, they're gonna definitely want to find you."

It was as if someone had slammed Larissa face first into the coffee table. She couldn't catch her breath. Something about Teddi Slager's flat, matter-of-fact delivery made it impossible to even think. She clutched Zippy's arm.

"Pieces of me? What kind of *Pulp Fiction* shit is this?" Curtis said.

"Nah-ah," Patrice said. "Ain't nobody cutting up my grandson."

"They do organ transplants," Slager said. "Keep in mind that this is a group that is particularly good with blades and other sharp objects."

"Holy shit," Curtis leaned against the doorframe. Looked blankly at Larissa and Zippy, looked away. "How long is it going to be like this?"

"We don't know," Agent Pierce said. "But realistically you should plan on forever. Your entire family needs to vanish. Permanently. You need to go with them."

"When do we gotta do this?" Patrice asked. "When we gotta make a decision?"

"Participation in the program is one hundred percent voluntary, and you can always leave. But if you do want to enter the program, you'll need to let us know in the next twenty-four hours." She unfolded several documents that she pulled from her lapel, hand-ing a copy to each of them. Including Curtis. "This one outlines the terms and conditions of your entry into the Witness Security Program."

Larissa scanned the document but couldn't concentrate on the wording.

"In entering this program, each of you will undergo a metic-ulous relocation process," Agent Kowalczyk explained. "New identities will be assigned, and you will be relocated to a secure and undisclosed location. Once you enter the program, you'll be assigned a U.S. marshal to assume responsibility for your secu-rity and well-being throughout the duration of your participation."

As the other agent was speaking, Teddi met and held Larissa's gaze. "I understand how hard this will be. But it's the best way of keeping you alive."

"How will it actually work?" Zippy asked.

"We have to put in an application for the Federal Witness Security Program, plus all the backup paperwork. It's a long pro-cess. If the program accepts you, the U.S. Marshals Service will take over your protection and relocate you to a different part of the country."

"How long will all this take?" Curtis asked.

"At least three weeks. Probably closer to six."

"Six weeks! Are you kidding me? We're going to be here for six weeks?!"

"It's complicated. Inventing a new life," Slager said apologeti-cally.

"Fuck. That. Shit," Curtis said. "I am not the one. No. Nope. Sorry, Dad. You fucked up. I'm not doing this. I got concerts. I play for a living. I don't disappear and go to work at Wendy's in Bumfuck, Illinois, for the rest of my life."

"It doesn't need to be a Wendy's," Larissa said, flailing for some-thing positive. "There are other things you can do. You can—"

"I'm a musician. I play. I play in front of audiences. I play with orchestras. I don't fucking work at Walmart or some lame-ass job like that."

"You do if you want to stay alive," Agent Slager said.

"Look, we don't know what's going to happen—" Zippy started.

"Yeah we do," Curtis said. "She just said this is for the rest of our lives. This means I can't play anymore."

"Of course you can play. Just not publicly," Agent Slager said. "Not under your own name."

"What do you mean, 'not publicly'? You want me to play under your name instead?"

"You won't be playing under any name in any public venue," Slager said. "As a young Black man with a characteristic musical style, you'd be too easily identified."

"Thanks for the compliment. So what am I supposed to do?" Curtis had stalked over to her, now stood inches from her face. She looked up at him, unintimidated, seemingly unimpressed. "Play with a bag over my face? That's what you're saying, isn't it? Because how many concert-level Black cellists are there? You want me to tell you? Sixteen. Sixteen in the whole goddamned country. I have a fucking bull's-eye on my back."

"So you will need to figure out something else to do," Slager told him. "There's more to life than music."

Curtis just stared at her, dumbfounded. Larissa couldn't even imagine what was going through his head. For him, there wasn't anything else in life except music. The comic books were fun, entertainment. But they weren't critical to his existence the way that music was.

The room had broken into chaos. Everyone was speaking at once—Zippy, Patrice, Curtis, and the agents, who were trying to answer their questions. Larissa sat silent, mind spinning. She tried to imagine what was to come. She didn't think about Bright Horizons right then—she thought about her own family. She had a sister, Loretta, up in New Jersey. They weren't close, but she'd see her a couple times a year. Would she never see her again? Her niece and nephew were both in high school, and her niece wanted to be a beautician. Her nephew didn't know what he wanted to do—would Larissa never know what he'd decided?

And that didn't even begin to deal with all of the women she'd nurtured and helped through the years. These were her friends, her colleagues, her family.

Curtis was in the middle of an argument with Slager, standing inches from her face, yelling down at her, when suddenly he just stopped. Stopped speaking, stopped moving, his face locked into a broken grimace.

Then, still saying nothing, he turned and left the room, fled to his lair upstairs.

Moments later the Fauré started up again.

Larissa fell into Zippy's arms and wept.

18

ZIPPY

ALMOST TWO WEEKS LATER, the tests began—a series of cognitive evaluations from the witness protection people to assess how Zippy and the family were coping. They all met with a psychologist who asked questions about their mental state. *How often do you experience fear, anger, sadness, or guilt? How do you cope with these emotions? Do you have any symptoms of depression, anxiety, or posttraumatic stress disorder? Do you have any history of substance abuse, self-harm, or suicidal thoughts?* Tests to measure stress level, to gauge coping skills, to identify personality traits and mental disorders.

Zippy had always tried to play a part—the alpha male, able to handle whatever the world threw at him. Black? Check. From the hood? Check. A criminal? Yep, got that. And even when he got out of prison, people would still see him as a criminal. Impossible to save. And not worth the effort.

And despite this—because of this—he'd grown balls big enough to handle it all. Maybe if you're born poor and Black in the projects, people can only see you one way: and you can only see yourself that way, too.

But, simultaneously, he also saw himself as the man he could—should—be. Financially successful. A loving father and supportive partner. An identity far beyond what he was *supposed* to be since he was "just" a Black dude from Southeast D.C.

The U.S. marshals' cognitive evaluations made him think about all of this as never before. So much of who he was had always been determined by where he'd come from, by the color of his skin, by the opportunities—or the lack of opportunities—that presented themselves to him.

He'd started over so many times already. Bright student who became a single father. Gangbanger who became a criminal. Businessman who became a fugitive. This was his chance, again, to start afresh, and he was determined this time, at last, to do it right.

So when he was battered with questions about what was in store, he answered eagerly, impatient to get started on this next phase. *What are your expectations and goals for your new life? How prepared are you to leave behind your old identity and start over? How willing are you to follow the rules and guidelines of the program? How confident are you in your ability to adapt to a new environment and community? How attached are you to your current name and identity? How willing are you to cut off contact with friends and relatives? How adaptable are you to new situations and environments? How much do you trust the U.S. Marshals Service and the program?*

As he answered the questions, a part of him was excited about what would come next—but another, bigger, part of him felt overwhelmed by guilt, frozen by grief. He'd destroyed his son's life—the one life he'd vowed, above all others, to treasure and support. The one person in the world—even more than Larissa—he wanted to do right by.

You make a choice, and you make another, and you think you're doing right, and you think you're helping. And it turns out all you're doing is fucking up. Royally. All you're doing is destroying the lives of the people you treasure most.

So how would *they* answer these questions? It was *his fault* they were in this mess. It was his fault that their identities were being scrubbed away. They didn't see this as a fresh start, as a chance to start again.

Curtis saw this, quite literally, as a death sentence. He wouldn't even look at Zippy anymore, and never spoke to him if he could help it.

And what could Zippy say? "I'm sorry"? What good would an apology do? How would acknowledging past mistakes put an audience in front of Curtis, give him a record deal and a career and allow him to do the one thing he loved—which was to perform for real, live listeners?

Zippy spent hours listing his family, education, work history, hobbies, interests, skills, and languages. He indicated his preferred geographic region, climate, urban or rural setting, and type of community. *Did he have any chronic or serious illnesses or injuries? Did he have any special dietary or nutritional requirements? Did he have any physical or mental limitations or impairments?*

Then there were the job-related questionnaires. *How do you communicate with different types of audiences, such as customers, colleagues, managers, or stakeholders? What role do you usually play in a team? What are your leadership style and values? How do you use creativity and innovation to find alternative solutions?*

And then all the financial information. They'd lose all of their belongings—except Curtis's cello—and would receive a six-month living stipend. The USMS would find them a house and create new driver's licenses and birth dates and backgrounds. It was like something out of a movie, but it was real. The Zacchariah Wilson he knew was already ceasing to exist.

He would no longer be Buckz, a former felon. He wasn't even forty years old yet—a lot of people started over at his age.

A few weeks later, an unfamiliar voice summoned them downstairs. Larissa had been lying down, napping, and Zippy had to wake her up. She was sleeping ten or more hours a night, and told him that she was still exhausted when she woke.

They followed the voice down to the kitchen, where a scrawny thirtysomething guy with bad skin introduced himself as Marshal Dubek. At first it was just Zippy, Larissa, and Patrice—Curtis as usual refused to come downstairs. The sound of the cello seeped faintly through the walls. Larissa trudged halfway up the stairs, yelled for him on the landing to come down. After a moment his footsteps creaked in the stairwell.

"Well, I have some good news for you," Marshal Dubek told them when they were all assembled. "Looks like you've been officially accepted into the witness protection program."

Curtis had been standing in the doorway, broad shoulders almost filling the space. He stalked around the table to the fridge, opened it, closed it again. He looked larger than he had—Zippy knew he was taking breaks between playing to work out. Push-ups, sit-ups, other body-weight and isometric exercises. He'd even gotten the agents to procure him a pull-up bar, which he hung in a doorway. Zippy sometimes came upstairs to find him hanging from the pole, lifting himself over and over, as if trying to see beyond the horizon, and finding only the tiled wall of the bathroom.

Now he sat down heavily in one of the chairs. Everyone else tried to ignore him.

"What this means is that you're leaving tonight, after dark," the marshal said.

"Where are we going?" Patrice asked. "I hope it ain't some-place hot."

Dubek told her, "It's out in the country. Great view, great air. You'll love it there. You can go fishing. There are miles of hiking trails."

"I ain't hiking nowhere, and the only fish I'm catching are from Long John Silver's," Patrice said.

"There's a porch," Marshal Dubek offered.

"I bet it ain't even screened in," she said. "There's probably mosquitoes everywhere. I hate mosquitoes. I can already tell I ain't gonna like this place. Why can't we just go home?"

"Mom," Zippy said, "you know we—"

"It's up in the mountains," the young man cut in, speaking quickly so they couldn't interrupt him. "Lots of fresh air. And it's just for a few weeks, as you get oriented in your new lives. So get yourselves packed and be ready to hit the road around midnight."

All this time Curtis hadn't moved. Stared down at the tabletop impassive. Zippy's heart would have broken even more, but there was nothing left to break.

That evening they assembled in the living room, waiting on the corduroy couch and La-Z-Boy chair. Patrice sat next to the window, smoking and glaring at everyone. Her wig was slightly askew, but Zippy didn't want to mention it. Curtis stomped down-stairs, suitcase in one hand and cello in the other—the boxes of music, and the box of comic books, would meet them there.

"We're ready to move," Marshal Dubek said, his voice barely audible. "The cars are waiting outside."

Zippy nodded, swallowing the lump in his throat. He looked around the living room, said goodbye to this temporary sanctuary, oddly grateful for the safety it had provided them.

Marshal Dubek motioned them to follow, and the group made their way to the waiting vehicles outside. The darkness enveloped them, and Zippy felt like a shadow lost in shadows.

After a while, he dozed off, awakening after they turned down a highway and followed a series of switchbacks around hills. BLUE RIDGE PARKWAY, 15 MILES. He couldn't remember where the Blue Ridge Parkway was. North Carolina? Virginia? The journey felt long and yet swift, as if time itself was slipping through their fingers.

The car took one unnamed road after another, climbing up and around. Finally they turned onto an unmarked gravel driveway with no mailbox at the end. Dubek got out, unlocked a chain with a "No Trespassing" sign dangling from it. Dawn was lightening behind the hills.

The car parked in front of a small cluster of houses, all a weathered maroon. The view was spectacular. They were somewhere in the Appalachians, where gray-blue smudged mountains piled on top of one another, losing themselves in the clouds. A few birds spun into the air.

Up a small front porch with creaky steps and, inside, into a simple, tidy living room. A faded rug covered wooden floorboards. The furniture was old, mismatched, and stood stoically against the walls, each piece seemingly holding memories of its own.

"Here we are," Marshal Dubek said.

They'd arrived in late August, with several weeks of intense heat still in store, and would be there for several months. Perhaps they'd be out by Christmas, but perhaps not. It took time to create new identities, to work with various departments to create all the relevant records.

Curtis's new name would be "Connor." Larissa became "Lorna," Zippy was "Zeke," Patrice was "Pamela."

Zippy discovered that he was married, too.

"It's less complicated that way," Marshal Dubek told them. "Unless you both really don't want to be married to each other?"

Zippy looked at Larissa, whose dimple flashed in her cheek. "I guess I'll have him, since nobody else will," Larissa said.

"Use your new names constantly," Marshal Dubek told them. "The more you use them, the more they'll imprint in your subconscious."

"Connor, can you pass me that fork?" "Sure, Lorna." They'd laugh, uncomfortable, the first times they did it, but Zippy and Larissa soon got the hang of it. Zippy'd had enough different identities for this to be easier on him than it could have been; and Larissa was always eager to adapt. Patrice either couldn't or wouldn't get the names right; more than half the time she either forgot or she obstinately used their old names.

As for Curtis, he never called anyone by any name. It was as if, for him, they'd all lost the trappings of what made them themselves; and now they—all of them, including Curtis—were nameless: "Hey, you," or, more often, "Pass me the fork."

Once, after the first week, Zippy tried to do the thumbtouch routine. He'd put his thumb to his forehead, and Curtis had just stared at him, walked away. Zippy had held that thumb in place for another few moments, wishing yet again that the world were a different place as Curtis stalked over to his cabin.

There were three cabins: the family cabin, a cabin for the U.S. marshals, and a third, which an agent told them was used for overflow if a larger family unit was going into witness protection. Curtis commandeered this one for himself, and moved out of the main cabin, so he could play his cello and sulk in peace.

If he wanted to survive, his career as a concert cellist was over. He spent long hours closeted with Larissa, going through possible job options, each one worse than the last, Larissa told Zippy later.

Finally, he decided to become a sound engineer. He told Larissa that, as a classically trained cellist, he already had a solid foundation in music and sound-related knowledge but had to gain technical expertise in recording, mixing, and producing for various media platforms. So he begrudgingly enrolled in online courses and workshops. As he immersed himself in digital audio workstations and virtual lessons, Curtis found a faint glimmer of hope—perhaps he could find meaning and fulfillment in this other aspect of music. He sure hoped so.

At least, here in this cabin in the middle of nowhere, they had Internet again. It was monitored, though.

He watched as Larissa followed Bright Horizons' social media feed, which was limited, since many of the women were hiding from their abusive partners. But she was able to determine that her former assistant, Shana, got promoted to temporary, and then permanent executive director; and that the machinery that Larissa had created—for education, therapy, support—continued to thrive. She found several women from Bright Horizons back on social media, no longer in the projects or at Bright Horizons housing, holding jobs as nursing assistants or a manager of a hobby shop, or working inventory in an auto parts store.

The U.S. Marshals Service gave the family their invented back-story. Zippy, now "Zeke," had moved on from a troubled past as a former drug dealer and became a bookkeeper for local busi-nesses. "Lorna" had previously managed a community center that supported at-risk youth. They'd decided to leave Baltimore in search of better opportunities, and "Connor" had come with them. "Pamela" had come as well, because she'd always wanted to move somewhere less humid. "Finally I can go someplace where I don't have to do my hair every ten minutes."

"But where are we going?" Larissa asked.

"Yeah, about time you tell us," Zippy said.

They'd all—well, everyone except Curtis—speculated on where the USMS would move them. As part of one of the questionnaires, they'd listed where their close family and friends lived; and where the greatest danger would be of someone recognizing them.

"Phoenix," Marshal Dubek said.

"Phoenix?" Zippy said. "I don't want to go to Phoenix." He tried to remember what the classical music scene was there—he'd spent hours reviewing different cities, hoping they could go someplace where Curtis could at least be near a major symphony. From what he remembered, the Phoenix Symphony was pretty good. Not top tier, but all right. Maybe that would be enough for Curtis after all. He breathed easier.

"We're putting everything together for you in Phoenix, but before we can take you there, we have one final intensive orientation, to make sure you're all ready for your new lives. So get ready, you're moving tomorrow to the final stop before your new home."

The car windows were heavily tinted, so Zippy never knew the location of the last halfway house—a kind of peculiar hotel, one step down from a Holiday Inn, with faded brown carpet and smooth vinyl-paneled walls. Cameras bulging every few feet from the ceiling seemed to watch them stagger down the hall—Zippy felt eyes on him, and it felt like prison again, and his skin crawled.

Every movement he made, from eating to going to the bathroom, was being monitored. The doors bolted electronically and could only be opened if you tapped the keypad and someone in some control room somewhere opened the door. Corridors deadended into other barred doors that Zippy never went through.

For the next two weeks, they got "oriented." They faced yet another battery of physical exams to make sure they were healthy. They received their new paperwork and spent hours with the analysts going over it all in detail. They each met with another psychologist for further assessments.

Zippy found himself talking to "Dr. Bowen"—Zippy was convinced that wasn't her name—for a couple hours a day. He tried to articulate his grief, terror, guilt.

Guilt was such an odd emotion, digging weirdly into even the most mundane parts of his day. Because what had happened to all of them was very clearly Zippy's fault. With the best of intentions he had stumbled down the path. He felt like he was doing good, working with the organ transplants. Yeah, it was illegal, but he was *helping* people. Now it seemed so obvious that—of course—the FBI would descend.

But even so, Zippy had tried to do the right thing. He'd given up the incriminating information so they could bust Jordan,

Ricky, and whoever else was involved. Zippy was still convinced it was T Block, even if he didn't have any proof. But in any case, he'd imagined that this was how it would go down: the police would round up everyone, there'd be the show of a trial, and the bad guys would be off to prison for a few years or a lifetime. That's how it had happened with Zippy.

Instead the bad guys were free, probably partying it up on some Caribbean island, drinking mai tais and casually telling the guys who worked for them to keep watching out for Zippy and his family.

With the best of intentions, Zippy had destroyed everything. His son's career—his son's *life*—had all but disintegrated. Now, despite the therapists and the heavy doses of antidepressants, Zippy's guilt ate at everything.

But there was no going back.

To make things even worse, he also realized that he had it the easiest of all of them. Everyone else had lost so much: Larissa had lost her sister and the rest of her family; Patrice had lost her friends and the familiar world she loved; and Curtis had lost, well, everything except the cello that he sometimes dragged with him to meals as if it were a giant wooden teddy bear.

For fun, they watched videos of Phoenix, Arizona: the bustling downtown with its towering skyscrapers and modern architecture; the Arizona State University campus; artsy Roosevelt Row; the historic district of Heritage Square; the street festivals like Chinese New Year in the Asian District and the Día de los Muertos festivities in the Hispanic neighborhoods; and on it went. Zippy couldn't keep most of it straight but figured he'd learn it all soon enough, anyway.

Finally, sixteen days after they'd arrived, with Thanksgiving bearing down upon them, it was over.

"Congratulations," Marshal Dubek said. "You're going home."

To Phoenix.

19

CURTIS

"I'M GONNA SELL MY CELLO," Curtis announced to Larissa one afternoon in late October. She'd come over with a Tupperware of still-warm lasagna. He'd popped the top and was eating it right from the container.

He almost never came over to Larissa and Zippy's place these days—he still didn't want to have much to do with Zippy. *Got your back, my ass*, he'd think when he'd allow himself to go there. The fury and frustration he'd first felt toward Zippy had subsided into a dull aching numbness, a constant effort to forget about Zippy's existence. It was easier to do than it should have been, he sometimes thought. He just focused hard on something else, on his music or trying to learn this new job, and anytime the thought of his father would slip across his mind, he'd drown it out with Bach's Cello Suite no. 1 in G Major or Tchaikovsky's *Rococo Variations*—both were robust, intricate, and required complete focus. No thought to spare for the father who betrayed him.

As part of the deal with WITSEC, he'd been allowed to keep the cello. Most of their other personal possessions had been sold off, and they'd gotten a check for them. "This is our whole life," Zippy said when he opened the envelope and stared down at the amount. "This is how much we're all worth, you know that?"

Now, when Curtis announced his decision to sell the Melanson, Larissa jerked her head back as if he'd hit her on the chin. "Are you sure? You don't have to—"

"I do," he said. "I'm going to sell it and get a cheaper one. It doesn't make any sense for me to have a cello that expensive anymore. Plus there's the insurance." He'd been struggling for weeks to figure out the logistics of paying for it, which cost him $1,963 a month. Until now it had been insured under the name "Curtis Wilson," but the renewal was coming up. He'd have to renew it under his new name, with a proper bill of sale. If someone got access to the insurance company's records, the new name would be an easy way to identify him.

"I'm sorry," she said.

He could feel her sympathy and shrugged it away. "It'd be good to have the money, right? I can get a new one, maybe one I could put a pickup on. And maybe a couple of pedals to play around with the sound." He still practiced daily—Dvorak, Haydn, Boccherini, Lalo, Vivaldi, Schubert, Schumann, and dozens of others—but struggled to find a reason to continue.

For Curtis, it wasn't just the actual physical playing of the instrument that he found so compelling: music had become a way of connecting with the world. When you play the Kabalevsky with the New York Phil, you're not playing a cello in a vacuum. You're playing with the orchestra, you're playing with the maestro, he's leaning into a phrase and you're answering him, and the orchestra is echoing and challenging you and pushing you harder. And you're playing on a stage: you're playing in a vast chamber where people are listening, and shuffling their feet, and coughing; and you're hoping that your playing will make them forget the uncomfortable theater seats, forget the tickle at the back of their throat. Your music—the music that comes from your hands and your heart and your soul—will transport them, will suck them up into the vortex of your sound, and they'll come away changed. Perhaps more joyful, perhaps more thoughtful. You've taken them, emotionally, places they've never been. Places only you can take them, because those places are woven into the fabric of who you are.

He'd once diagrammed a performance as a square—with performer, orchestra, maestro, and audience in each of the cor-ners. But that wasn't right; that didn't do a performance justice. Because every individual orchestra member was a vertex, a corner. Each audience member, too. It wasn't a square as much as a multifaceted, multicornered diamond glittering in space. And he had been the glue, the focus, the spirit that sent everything spinning.

After everything in his life had disintegrated, he'd first struggled with fury and despair, and then he'd settled into a sort of bafflement. Music had been his way of *connecting*. He wasn't good with people; he wasn't warm and engaging like Larissa, and couldn't shoot the shit like Zippy. He was introverted, shy, a guy who used his cello to communicate how he felt. How could he talk to people, how could he explain how he felt and make them like him, without music? It just didn't seem possible. For the past year, here in Phoenix, he'd been trying to learn a whole new language, and he felt like he still didn't know even the most basic words.

Because—especially at the beginning—he was so afraid. Terrified that, pulling out a bag of frozen peas at the supermarket or ordering french fries at a restaurant or handing his keys to a parking lot attendant, someone would stare at him and point and scream. He never was sure what they'd scream—perhaps his old name, Curtis; perhaps "liar"; perhaps "imposter" or "Caught you!" But whatever they would shout, he spent months bracing for it.

Every interaction, however mundane, required a delicate wariness, an assessment of how to blend in. The Marshals Service had taught them to maintain a certain distance; to avoid, especially in the first crucial years, forming deep connections that could unravel their carefully constructed facades. Their new identities came with preestablished histories and social connections, and Curtis was constantly afraid he'd forget everything that had been drilled into him.

Luckily, the marshals were there for support. For the first months the family had to check in with Marshal Thomas Michael daily; and then, after a few months, weekly. But they knew that Michael was monitoring them. At times, the isolation and secrecy were welcome; at other times, suffocating.

For so many reasons, he retreated more and more into the music: as a way of escaping the marshals' scrutiny; as a way of escaping this bizarre world he now found himself in, his loss of who he was, how he'd always thought of himself. No longer *musician, cellist, going-to-be-a-soloist.* Now audio engineer. Loner. Weight lifter.

He tried to tell himself that it was for the best. That's what people said, in times of loss and grief: *It's God's plan. It'll make you stronger.* He tried to believe this now. He'd heard stories of animals caged all their lives suddenly confronted with freedom. The dolphin from SeaWorld, released into the open sea, leaping above the water; the group of former circus elephants who trumpeted and rolled in the grass, touching their trunks repeatedly to the earth; the laboratory chimp who saw the sky for the first time and could not look away.

That's what he tried to hope would happen if the cello was out of his life. No more practicing the same phrase over and over! No more hauling the huge thing around with him! He was free! Free! Because sometimes that's how he felt. Resentful of it, sick of practicing, bored. Not always, but often enough that he hoped—maybe even expected—that once the cello was gone, he'd see the sky.

Instead, he became aware as he never had before of these new cage bars, of cheap foam ceiling tiles now hovering inches above his head.

Only now did he realize that when he'd been a cellist, he'd seen the sky.

He tried to distract himself with comic books. He lurked at a couple of local bookstores, buying rare editions and vintage issues. He discovered the first appearance of Spider-Man in *Amazing Fantasy,* no. 15; the iconic *Detective Comics,* no. 27, featuring Batman's debut; and the emotionally charged *X-Men,* no. 94. As he purchased each magazine, he reveled in their tangible magic, even if they couldn't quite create for him the magic that music could.

So he'd sell the cello. Try something different.

"Might be good to have a new cello," Larissa agreed. "Start fresh, right? Can you take it to that music place out on the highway, see if they can sell it for you?"

"That's the thing," Curtis said. "I can't just take it to a music store out here. I wouldn't get the best price. Plus I don't trust the marshals with it."

"They're *marshals*," Larissa told him, amused. "They're probably the most trustworthy people in the universe. You don't *trust* them?"

"There is no way I'm sending my seventy-five-thousand-dollar cello with some dudes who don't know the difference between a Melanson and a ukulele. I should sell it myself."

"So sell it yourself. How hard can it be?"

He shrugged. If he did have to sell the cello, he wanted to get as much for it as he could. Many music dealers sold instruments in this price range or above, but he'd become fixated—probably irrationally—on one stringed instrument dealer in New York. At Juilliard, the students and teachers had spoken with reverence about Rowland's Fine Instruments over by Carnegie Hall. The proprietor carried some of the most valuable stringed instruments in the world and had some of the best clientele, including Joshua Bell, Ray McMillan, and Pablo Ferrández. If anyone could command top dollar for the Melanson, it would be Rowland's. "There's a music shop in New York that—"

"You know you can't go to New York," she told him.

"I thought about it. I can go incognito and—"

"You know you can't. They told us over and over about—"

"Yeah, I know. But just think of how far that money would go." He said it as if he were trying to convince himself.

"Have you talked to Marshal Michael?"

"A little."

"What did he say?"

Curtis barked a laugh. "Same thing you said. Word for word."

"I think you should try to sell it locally," Larissa told him. She unpeeled the foil off the garlic bread she'd baked, and the steam poured out, fragrant, into the room. "I agree that the cello is probably holding you back. You need to move on. You're putting us all at risk with it."

He knew she was right.

He'd gotten in trouble a couple times with the marshals' office. He didn't mean to, but it just kept happening. He didn't think about performing—he just did it.

He'd gotten a job at Desert Studios—a local sound and video

production company—as a low-level sound engineer, mixing and recording local commercials and wedding videos, mostly. He wasn't loving it, but at least he was able to listen to music, and it kept him busy.

But he was already getting into trouble with the marshals. Just last week, he'd been helping a couple of clients promote a local recital at one of the big churches south of town. They'd all gone to the park, and he'd pulled out the cello and played for half an hour behind a big sign: CONCERT SUNDAY. Someone in the gathering crowd had given him a business card, asked if he played for social events. He shook his head, kept his head down, made sure nobody was filming him. This was good for the church, good for the audio studio, and a good way of meeting other musicians. What harm could a little innocent playing do?

Apparently it could do a lot.

That night Marshal Michael showed up at his doorstep, irate. "Look," the man said, "this is your third warning. That's it, you hear me? If you ever pull this kind of crap again, it's over. Period. We can't keep you safe if you don't try to keep yourself safe."

Curtis backed away. "Calm down, man," he said. "I was helping out some clients. I'm keeping a low profile. Don't worry, I know."

"You don't know enough," the older man said, inches from his face. Curtis could smell the coffee on his breath.

"Okay, okay, I'm sorry," Curtis said, trying to show him how contrite he felt. How had the marshals' office even known?

But it took more than a month to melt the iciness when they met every week—and another three months after that before he broached the subject of selling the Melanson.

When he finally did, Marshal Michael was surprisingly receptive but had to go through the proper channels. Which meant another month of planning, and arguments, and calls to USMS bosses.

But eventually, in mid-November, Curtis found himself in the back seat of a black SUV with the Melanson beside him, the car idling in the bus lane on Fifty-Seventh Street. Around him Manhattan glittered and honked in the evening light.

He was not permitted to go into Rowland's—there was too

strong a chance that he'd be recognized as the now-vanished Black cello prodigy Curtis Wilson. Instead, the U.S. marshals would handle the sale, and Curtis would listen in.

Marshal Ben Hailey turned around in the driver's seat. "You'll hear every word," he repeated again to Curtis, and Curtis could feel the irritation in his voice. After all the tutorials that Curtis had gotten on the earpiece he was wearing, he felt he could teach a course on espionage. "Don't talk, just listen. If we have any questions for you, either Marshal Navarro or I will come out to you. Don't even think about coming in."

Agent Luis Navarro raised his eyebrows and nodded sympathetically. He and Curtis had become if not friends, then something closer than acquaintances. He was younger and could relate more easily to Curtis's situation. Curtis found out he played viola through college. They talked music every now and then and were supposed to play a duet sometime.

Rowland's had regular hours, but also could be open at other times, for "discriminating clientele." So Navarro had booked an appointment at eight thirty p.m., half an hour after the curtains went up in theaters and concert halls all over Manhattan. Better if no one else would be stopping by.

The town car pulled up to the curb. Curtis could only imagine the incredible instruments that waited patiently inside. Stradivari, Guarneri, Del Jesu, Montagnana—names of instruments he'd only read about or seen. Now not only could he not see them close up, but he had to say goodbye to his prized cello that his father worked to get him. Consigning the Melanson for sale was like a death, like abandoning a puppy to a humane shelter. He stroked the Tonareli case as if to reassure the cello inside, locked it as if it would be stolen over the course of the twenty feet between the car and the front door of Rowland's. With some difficulty he maneuvered the instrument into Agent Navarro's grasp.

And then before Curtis was quite ready, the cello was gone, floating down the sidewalk. He wouldn't think about it. He stared straight ahead, at the back of the headrests, focusing on the ear microphones.

He closed his eyes to concentrate, and it was as if he was standing right there, listening to their footsteps, to the knock on the door, to the buzzer letting them inside.

Greetings and introductions. The proprietor, Mischa Rowland, had a deep, booming voice with a foreign, perhaps Eastern European, accent. He thanked the gentlemen for coming. A rattle and click as the key unlocked the case, as the clasps opened. A rustle as the cello was removed. Silence. Curtis assumed it was being examined.

"Nice instrument," Mischa Rowland said after a few minutes. "Melanson, of course. In good condition. Set up very well. The photos you sent did not lie."

Another pause.

"Ferraz here, she may play it?"

"Of course," Marshal Hailey said.

More rustling. She played the open strings, then broke into a C major scale, tested the harmonics.

"The tone is open and resonant," Curtis heard her say. "Definitely a soloist's instrument."

More rustling. Curtis wondered what they were doing.

"Thank you," Rowland said, with a note of finality. Ferraz was being dismissed. "Thank you for staying."

She said goodbye, and a moment later the front door opened and a small dark-haired woman hurried away into the night.

Meanwhile, Mischa Rowland was saying, "You mentioned seventy-five thousand dollars. That seems like a reasonable price. I will list it for eighty-five, and of course my commission is ten percent. That is agreeable to you?"

It was agreeable to the marshals.

"Now it is just a question of the paperwork, yes?" Rowland said.

Another rustle. The marshals must have handed over the envelope with all of the documentation that had accompanied the Melanson—the certificate of authenticity, the appraisal from when Zippy had purchased the instrument eight years before, a list of the previous owners, and so on.

A pause.

"Interesting," Rowland said. "You didn't mention this is Curtis Wilson's. I have heard he simply disappeared. Why are you selling his cello?"

Agent Navarro cleared his throat. "Mr. Rowland, I am not at liberty to discuss anything other than that Mr. Wilson is safe and that he authorized the sale of his cello. It's all right here." Another pause. Curtis imagined him brandishing the document that Curtis had had to sign.

"What if this cello is stolen? How can I be sure you are not thieves? That you have not harmed him?"

"Mr. Rowland, please, can we continue with the business at hand? I assure you Mr. Wilson has authorized this sale," Marshal Navarro said. "See? It's notarized. This is a perfectly legal transaction."

"No," Rowland said after a pause. "This is, how do you say? Sketchy as fuck."

"Mr. Rowland—" Marshal Hailey said. "Wait. Put down the phone, sir."

"I am going to have to ask you to leave. This is trouble. Or I call the police and we can sort it out with them."

"Put down the phone, sir," Marshal Hailey repeated. "We *are* the police. We're with the U.S. Marshals Service."

Another pause, and Rowland said, "Can I see some identification, please?" And then, "Is the young man in trouble? Is this why you are selling his cello? What happened to him?"

"Sir, with all due respect, we are asking you to facilitate the sale of this instrument, at Mr. Wilson's specific request."

Curtis pulled his hoodie up over his head, opened the car door, and in moments was banging on the door to the shop. After a second, a tall man with blue eyes and slicked-back salt-and-pepper hair opened it. "We are closed," Mr. Rowland said. His voice echoed weirdly—both in Curtis's earpiece and in his ear. He yanked the ear microphone off.

"I'm with them. It's my cello," Curtis said. He pulled back the hood to reveal his face a little more clearly.

Agent Navarro moved past Mischa and dragged Curtis into the shop. "Have you lost your mind?" he said. "Do you know what would happen if someone sees you?"

"Yeah, I know. You guys are screwing this up. I figured I could move things along so we can get the hell out of here."

"You are Curtis Wilson," Mischa Rowland said.

Curtis looked at Marshal Navarro for approval, and then said, "Yeah. I am. Look, let's get this done." He met Mischa Rowland's eyes.

After a moment, the taller man nodded. "Okay. Let us do this."

The day after he arrived back in Phoenix, Curtis drove out to the music store in downtown Scottsdale. For the past weeks he'd canvassed all the cellos within a five-hour drive and had settled for a $3,000 Knilling. It didn't have the Melanson's rich, velvety tone and he'd never win a competition with it, but then again, he'd never be in a competition, for all he knew. It was a solid instrument. He'd downgraded from a Mercedes to a Volkswagen, but this Volkswagen could still drive him around.

A few weeks passed, with him playing at the recording studio every morning and every evening, and whenever he had a break during the day. The new Knilling helped—as did the recording equipment he'd picked up secondhand, along with a pickup and three pedals. During breaks at work, he'd tweak what he'd recorded, duplicate it, dub each part, turning his single cello into a symphony. Although he ached for the immediacy of a performance, this was kind of fun.

He bought another pedal, which played in fifths. Then another, which played in octaves. He'd perform each part, recording them, blending them together to create his own quartet.

After a time he found he could breathe easier, wasn't as surly. When Mark and Dave from the studio invited him out for a beer, this time he accepted. He went home from the bar that night with a woman named Kathy, and woke up with the sound of her breath in his ear instead of the memory of the Haydn Cello Concerto no. 1 in C Major.

Four weeks after his trip to New York, $72,128.24 appeared in Curtis's bank account. The Melanson had been sold.

Ten days later, his social media feeds trended with the disappearance of a prominent New York City music dealer. Curtis's heart hit his throat. He clicked on the link.

Mischa Rowland had vanished two days before. He'd stayed

late at the shop, as he often did, but never made it home that night. His wife, a tiny blond woman, pleaded for him to come home. Police had no suspects.

Curtis called Marshal Navarro. "What the FUCK. Did you know about this?"

"Hey, man, calm down—"

"Go fuck yourself. Did you *know* he'd disappeared? Rowland? Did you—"

"Yeah, we heard yesterday."

"Why the fuck didn't you tell me? What are you guys doing about it?"

"It's a local police matter."

"What about the FBI?"

The bureaucracy of the witness protection program was mind-boggling. The family had no further direct contacts with the FBI; if any of the FBI—mostly Agent Slager—wanted to talk to them, they had to go through proper channels, interface with the marshals' office. The marshals would create a secure link to a video-conference line, and the FBI, marshals, and the family—usually Zippy—would jump on a brief call.

Periodically, over the past months, Curtis would bug Zippy for information. It was the only time he reached out to his father these days. Zippy said that the FBI had no further leads. That the prosecution against the medical personnel he'd worked with was moving forward, but that the FBI was no closer to finding who killed Jordan Parlavamian and Ricky Lyman—which meant that they were no closer to finding the people after Zippy.

The people who, now, seemed to have abducted Mischa Rowland.

"Is it my fault? Did they kill him because of the cello?"

"Look. We don't know anything yet. Rowland seems to have vanished on Thursday. We're interfacing with local law enforcement."

"You need to tell me if you hear anything, okay? Anything."

He hung up, sick with fear and weak with guilt. Why had he consigned the Melanson? Why had he shown up in New York? Did his appearance in the shop end up costing a man his life?

Marshal Navarro was off the next day. So Curtis learned through social media that Mischa Rowland's body had been found halfway to New Jersey.

He didn't sleep that night. He wondered if he'd ever sleep again.

Guilt and terror gnawed at him. He paced around the house. Stuffed the Knilling in a back closet as if it were a dead body. The idea of playing an instrument, of listening to music, filled him with horror. He stood next to the window and watched cars slowly cruise past, almost called the police when one car's brake lights flashed and slowed right before his driveway.

Had his pig-headedness killed the large, gentle man with the urbane accent? It didn't seem possible.

Suddenly, in a way it never had before, the threat of the people hunting them seemed impossibly real.

At six in the morning, his phone chimed. He jumped, grabbed it. Marshal Navarro. *I'm coming over.*

Twenty minutes later he showed up, and Curtis let him in. "What's going on? You asshat, you promised you'd tell me as soon as you knew something."

"Dude, chill. That's why I'm here now," Navarro said. His handsome, dark face was somber. "To tell you what you're not going to hear on social media."

Curtis waited.

"He was tortured. Surgically. I'm going to spare you the details, but it was pretty bad. They're not releasing that to the media."

"Surgically?" Curtis repeated the word as if he wasn't sure what it meant. None of this felt real. All of it felt real. He wanted to cry and wanted to smash something. Instead he imagined— as he often did—playing a few scales on a cello in his mind, tasting the movements in his imagination even if he never wiggled his hands. Then he thought about how Mischa Rowland's person had played the Melanson, and he stopped. Tried to take a breath instead.

"Yeah," Navarro said.

"You think it was them?"

"Yeah," Navarro said. "It was definitely them."

20

LARISSA

ONE SATURDAY AFTERNOON about three months after Mischa Rowland's murder, Larissa stopped by Curtis's apartment with a plate of her chicken taquitos, another of Curtis's favorites. He was watching TV while casually curling a pair of enormous dumbbells. His thighs, thick and well-defined, pressed against the fabric of his shorts. A tattered muscle shirt hung from his chiseled torso, loosely revealing an eight pack and sculpted chest.

"Hey, come on in," he greeted her, continuing the reps. On the TV screen—he'd bought a large-screen, the first he'd ever owned, with some of the money from the sale of his expensive cello—buildings exploded. Caped, costumed people threw cars at each other. Another one of the Marvel movies.

Larissa had always been grateful that she'd bought Curtis that first comic book so long ago. As a child, he'd always been such an intense, private little person, so focused on his music, and always a little awkward around other kids. The world of comic books gave him another community. Another group with shared interests. He'd told her that he had joined a local comic book club and was planning on going to a comic book expo in a few months. So he was adjusting. He was moving forward.

Or he had been, before the news broke about Rowland.

After that, he'd sold his new cello, too. Larissa had argued with him. "Just keep it, *papi*. You don't have to sell it."

"I don't want to get near that thing," he told her.

"Then just put it in the back bedroom," she said. "Put it in the closet. But maybe you'll want it someday."

"Would you want to stuff a dead body in the closet?" he asked her. "Because that's what you're saying. That thing is a death sentence. It caused somebody's *murder.*"

"It didn't—"

"He had three grandkids, did you know that? Three. Two live in London and one's in Hungary. The London one is a girl three months younger than me."

"Your cello didn't have anything to do with it."

"Close enough. I paid for it with blood money. The guy is *dead.* And it's my fault."

"*Papi,* you—"

"No," Curtis told her, tone final. "I don't want that thing anywhere near me."

To Larissa's knowledge, he hadn't played since. Instead, he mimicked being a regular guy. To an outsider, it might look as if Curtis were adjusting, moving on. Possibly even Curtis would describe himself that way. She wondered if the therapist that the U.S. Marshals Service had found for him also believed that he was improving.

Larissa herself was terrified for him.

She didn't know how to articulate the fear—she didn't think he'd do anything drastic like hurt himself—but still she brooded. Brought him food every day or so. He wasn't himself any longer. She didn't know how else to describe it, but that's how she felt. That's what she told Zippy so many times.

Most people trudged through their lives and they were fine. She was probably like this herself. It's how people *were.*

But some people seemed to breathe different air, look out the same window or at the same page and arrive at an entirely unforeseen conclusion.

Curtis had suddenly, somehow become like everyone else, and that terrified her. Ever since he'd been small, he'd seemed to glow with a different kind of intensity than she'd ever seen before in anyone else. Part of it was his single-mindedness, his love of music, but she wasn't sure what came first—that intensity or the love. Was he so intense because he loved music, or was music just the way that his intensity manifested?

But now, after Rowland's death, that intensity was gone.

And she had to get it back. She had to bring him back. It's what she did—it was her job. It was what she knew how to do.

Since the move to Arizona, Larissa had found work at Safe-Harbor Phoenix, a shelter and recovery center for battered women. These were the kinds of people she already knew how to help. Native American women, fleeing the reservations, whose husbands hit the sauce and then came home and hit them. Or migrant women hauling a couple of children, fleeing a boyfriend or a gang or a father who would pin her down with one hand while the other hand unbuttoned his pants.

Larissa had worked with women like these all her life, and she knew how to engage them. How a small act of kindness—complimenting a blouse or admiring the shape of a hand or handing them an already-peeled orange—could be the first step to circle out of whatever grim place they'd retreated into.

One of her crew, Moni, had been a runaway. The marks from her stepfather's hand were still black around her throat when Larissa had first met her outside a bar where she was giving blow jobs for ten bucks. It had taken months before Moni would confide in her, but eventually she had—it was slow but inevitable. That was the human spirit, Larissa believed. Coiled and gray and all but dead, but give it warmth and human contact, and it would unfurl.

Until then, though, those desperate women had retreated somewhere behind their eyes, their souls curled up like fetuses, numb and desperate to forget.

You'd think, just looking, that Curtis wasn't like them at all. He had a good job. He was a weight lifter, and a hunk. He was joining comic book groups. He'd even begun dating. He was *fine*. Larissa kept telling herself this: He was more than fine.

But that light, that glow, had gone.

With her crew, and at Bright Horizons, Larissa had used common sense, easy affection, and therapy to break down their barriers. But at SafeHarbor, the therapists had additional tools and techniques, including art therapy, which Larissa became involved in. By painting or drawing, or using some of the computer pro-grams that the shelter had installed on iPads and laptops, the women and children were able to express their emotions, fears, and experiences without having to talk about them. It helped them to learn about themselves, but also empowered them by giving them a sense of control over their stories.

Since starting with SafeHarbor, Larissa had watched and helped and learned. Today she was going to try her own version of art therapy.

"Here, have a taquito," Larissa told Curtis, setting down the casserole dish and her laptop on the cluttered coffee table, where the latest editions of *WildC.A.T.S.*, *Titans*, *Photon*, and *Uncanny X-Men* were spread out, taking up most of the available horizontal surface. These, she knew, were the ones he hadn't read yet. The ones he'd finished were stacked on one corner of the table, ready to be filed.

"I don't want a taquito."

"I made it extra spicy."

"I said I don't want a taquito."

"Okay fine, no taquito," she said, sitting down in the armchair across from him and opening the SafeHarbor laptop she'd borrowed. "I have this crazy idea that I was hoping you could help me with."

"Oh no. What now?" Curtis was still watching the television, where now an enormous blue monster stepped over buildings while minuscule helicopters buzzed around it like gnats.

"I want you to help me make a comic book," she said.

Whatever he had been expecting, that clearly wasn't it. She had his full attention now. His mouth was slightly open. "What are you talking about? You don't even read them."

"Well, I'd like to," she said. "I've been thinking it would be a good thing for me to make one. Do a whole series of them."

"Why?" He sounded incredulous and dismissive. "How?"

"Because I think it would help the women I'm working with. At the SafeHarbor. And they've got this program. It creates really good graphics even if you're not an artist. You can choose from thousands of images and then modify them however you want. That's what we teach the women to do, if they don't want to draw and like using computers."

He just stared at her.

"So I was thinking," Larissa said, "I could make a comic book to give to some of the women, or their kids. It'd help with their English, too."

He was at least listening. She went on: "If I knew how to do it, I could teach them to make their own books. Visual books. Maybe of something they loved, or maybe as a way of expressing their own trauma. First, I have to figure out how to do it, and I want to have samples that I can show them."

"So you want to make a comic book," he repeated, still skeptical.

"Why not?" she said. "And it's something you know something about. So I figured you could help. But yeah, I want to do a couple of them."

"Okay," he said, doubtful.

But that was enough for her to get started. She logged into her account, pulled up the graphic software that she'd found incredibly complicated. She'd already spent over a week just trying to figure it out. Now she roughly had the hang of it: how to choose images and modify them, choose illustration styles. Then she could animate them, add text, animate the text, resize it . . . The process went on and on.

It had taken Larissa a couple of hours just to decipher the drop-down menus, but Curtis seemed to effortlessly understand what to do. Within an hour, they had a couple of rough mock-up comic book panels with random images and words, just as practice.

And he'd devoured all the taquitos.

Now he was hunched over the laptop, meaty hands poised over the keyboard. He'd turned off the movie sometime ago. "Okay, this really isn't that bad," he said. "Now you just have to decide what kind of comic book you want. What do you have in mind?"

"I don't know," she said. "You tell me."

"You've got your classic superhero stuff, like Batman and Superman, where capes and powers rule the day. Then there's the darker side, like noir comics. Antiheroes. Mysteries. If you want mind-bending, there's sci-fi. That's alternate realities, future tech, crazy imaginative stuff."

"*Mijo*," she said, "I don't know. No idea what would be the best way to start."

"Well," Curtis said, "I know that sometimes they're more inspiring. With a positive message. You should check out *Ms. Marvel* or *Jessica Jones*. Or *Bitch Planet*. They're all about healing from traumatic pasts."

"Maybe I'm crazy," Larissa said slowly, "but I keep thinking something superhero would work with the kids, especially. Let them make up their own superheroes. Invent whatever magic powers they like."

"Okay, superhero it is," Curtis said. "What's the superhero? And what's her superpower?"

"I have no idea. This is why I came to talk to you to begin with. You know all this stuff."

He thought for a minute. "How about something like Mind-shifter? She's telepathic and helps people find inner strength in times of great need. Or the Elemental, someone who can manipulate the elements—you know, fire, water, air, earth—to restore harmony?"

"You're really good at this, you know that?"

He laughed. "I've just been reading the stuff since I was six. All your fault."

"The thing is," she said, "that for these women to really buy into this, it has to really mean something. Has to mean something to us. So when they read it, they know. They'll be able to connect with it."

"Like what?" he said,

"I have no idea," she said. "We have to figure out a superhero that really connects with me. Or you."

Over the next hours they created the backstory and a few panels of *Ink Enchantress:* Valeria Diaz, who crafts fantastical worlds offering a temporary escape for those seeking refuge from real-world dangers.

Curtis was having so much fun thinking about the plot and the characters, that she didn't want to cut it short. She stayed for dinner. Zippy could make his own. When, at almost ten, she finally left to go home, Curtis was clearly disappointed that she had to take her laptop with her.

"Why don't you buy the software yourself?" she asked him.

It was expensive. "What's the point?" he asked her. "You can do it yourself now."

"Nah," she said. "You do it better. You know all about this stuff."

Over the next week, she labored when she could on the comic book, but without Curtis it wasn't as much fun, and she wasn't creative. Valeria Diaz would get herself into impossible situations, and she'd call Curtis to help her get Valeria out of them. He took her call more readily than ever, though, eager to help, to plot. His musician brain loved the intricacy and the stories' multiple levels.

They only had one issue—it took a lot longer to create these than she'd imagined!—but she'd shared it with the women at the shelter, and surprisingly they all enjoyed reading it. She assembled an English and a Spanish version, and one day found one of the women—Monica, a scrawny blonde from Pasadena with three kids by three different men—reading to all of them.

"In this realm of dreams and ink, I control the narrative," Monica read in the voice of the Ink Enchantress. "Your darkness can't bind me."

And then, as Shadow Stalker, the enemy: "You think your illusions can protect you? I am the essence of nightmares, and even your art can't save you from the shadows."

She showed them the page: an otherworldly landscape, air filled with swirling colors, with dancing surreal creatures of ink and dreams spinning around Valeria. In her superhero costume, she stands confidently as she faces an imposing, shadowy figure emerging from the abstract background.

Larissa had closed the door quietly on the reading family, feeling a tightness in her chest that was wonderful.

"So I have this idea," Larissa told Curtis now. "This one's pretty crazy though."

"Yeah?"

"What about making it a YouTube channel? *Ink Enchantress*, I mean."

"You're tripping," he said.

"No, I'm not. I think it's a good script. I think it's fun. I think other people would be interested in reading it. We could get a wider readership." She told him about a few other YouTube comics.

"So here's my thought," she went on. "Could you put together a music soundtrack?"

"What? I'm not playing—"

"No, don't worry, I didn't mean play. I was thinking you could create something. In the studio. Some kind of cool upbeat music, themes, to play underneath the audio. I'll read it aloud, and we could have hip-hop or something, some good beat, going."

"That doesn't sound very difficult. But the marshals will have a fit if you start posting online."

"I thought of that," she said. "I'll post it under the SafeHarbor's name. My name—our names—won't be anywhere on it."

Curtis started work on the soundtrack that afternoon. A week later they posted their first comic on their new InkEnchantress YouTube channel.

21

ZIPPY

TEDDI SLAGER always set up a phone call via the USMS at night, after hours, when they were home and wouldn't be overheard. The investigation had been going on forever, it seemed, and Zippy could detect the frustration in her voice even as she tried to remain impartial, casual, friendly.

"Hey," she said that night. "You have a sec?"

Zippy hated when she took this casual tone. Setting up the call wasn't as simple as just her dialing him up—the USMS had to figure out the time, had to sort out the right videoconference protocol. Nothing was casual or easy. But he tried to play it cool, like she did. "Of course," he told her. "Any news?"

Larissa was on the laptop she'd been bringing home every night, working on some kind of comic book for her job, but she was listening in as usual.

"Any updates?" he asked the agent. "Breakthroughs? Anything?"

"I know you're frustrated," she said. "But just take a minute and realize all you've accomplished."

"Besides destroying my life? And my son's life? And—"

"You've decimated a well-funded, well-run organization. You've cut them off at their knees. All their hospitals and doctors are under investigation. They're not doing the organ transplants anymore."

"You still don't know who is behind it all," he pointed out.

"We're working on that. Just be patient. How's Curtis holding up?"

Curtis had not been holding up well. He was already on thin ice with the Marshals Service for compromising their safety. Before the New York dealer's death, he'd had multiple run-ins for being videoed, or playing in public. Once one of the marshals, doing a spot check, just happened to be driving by and hustled him inside. For a week they were more or less on lockdown, waiting for a video to surface online, where facial recognition software could identify Curtis. Luckily no video existed. Yet.

The only good thing to come out of Rowland's death, Zippy'd decided, was that Curtis no longer wanted to play the cello, either publicly or privately. Zippy wasn't sure how his son now spent his time—Curtis hadn't really spoken to him much ever since WITSEC started, and their exchanges were always cool and formal. They hadn't thumbtouched in ages.

"He's doing okay," Zippy said to Agent Slager, wondering if it was true. "What's going on with the investigation? You getting anywhere?"

"Do you remember anything involving Delta Services Limited or Zenith Enterprises Company?"

He thought for a moment. "Not really. They sort of sound familiar, but they sound like everything else, too." He forced a laugh.

"No problem. How about Eclipse Dynamics or Stellar Medical Solutions? Any transactions or dealings with them?"

"Sorry. Not really ringing a bell. What are you looking for?"

"Just seeing if anything sparks."

Larissa had gotten up, was hovering in front of him, mouthing questions that he couldn't decipher. He shrugged at her.

"Okay, just thought I'd ask. Another question. The medical personnel you paid off. You've said that they never told you how they were recruited. Did your bosses ever discuss how they chose people to target? Why them and not someone else?"

The FBI always asked questions that he didn't know the answers to. That he felt that maybe he should have asked at the time, but he'd been focused on other issues. He was the guy who did the day-to-day job, and didn't know the big picture—the whys and what-ifs. Didn't want to know. "No," he told her. "I just handled the financials, not the recruitment. I just paid people off."

"Fair enough," she said easily. "Any chance you recall handling payments to something like NorthStar Medical Group?"

"Definitely NorthStar," he said, relieved. "I'm pretty sure I told you about them. I transferred funds at least once every couple of weeks."

"You remember how much?"

"It was usually about twenty thousand dollars. Sometimes up to a hundred thousand, though."

"Did you ever receive funds from them?"

"From them?"

"Yeah."

"Not that I remember," he said. "It was always one way, I think."

"Did you deal at all with blood banks?"

"Blood banks?" he repeated.

"Yeah. We've been looking into them."

"No, that wasn't a major focus. Organs were the main game."

"Right. Just figured I'd ask. Ever hear anything about blood banks, even in passing?"

He shook his head.

"Well?" she prompted.

"No," he said. "No blood banks."

"No worries. Shifting gears here. When it comes to finding donors, did they ever mention methods beyond the medical staff? Anything that caught your attention?"

"I've answered that a million times," he said. "They never went into details about the donor process. That was beyond my scope."

"We're just trying to piece things together. Every little bit helps, you know? And of course if anything comes to mind, give me a shout."

"Will do," he said, eyeing Larissa. She was holding out her hand for the phone, since the call was clearly wrapping up. "My wife wants to talk to you."

"Oh, okay, great," Slager said. "Thanks for taking the call."

"Let us know if you hear anything, okay?"

"Of course."

"Anything at all."

"You bet," she said.

He handed the phone over to Larissa, who tucked it under her chin and turned away, "Hey," she said. "I'm glad you called. I was just thinking about you. What ever happened on that date a couple weeks ago? You never said."

Muffled words from Slager, and Larissa laughed. "Yeah, typical," she said. "Where did you go?"

Zippy shook his head. How Larissa befriended people was beyond him, but of course now Larissa was involved with Special Agent Slager's love life.

He turned the TV back on but couldn't focus. His frustration was like a brick in his guts. Why couldn't they move the case forward? Why couldn't something *good* happen for a change? It was about time for Zippy to catch a break—he sure hadn't had many of them.

Part 4

THE RISE OF THE DARK MAESTRO

22

CURTIS

THE MOMENT that Larissa said, "Let's make a comic book," the idea erupted in his head—as transformative as when ordinary high school student Peter Parker had got bitten by a radioactive spider.

He'd actually assumed, before she explained herself, that *his* world-transforming idea was what she'd been talking about; but instead she'd gone in an entirely different direction—a comic book about broken, lost women trying to reclaim themselves.

That night he went to sleep brooding; and woke up in that dark empty hour around three with scenes and scraps of dialogue floating almost tangibly in front of him, glowing bright against the gray wall opposite.

All the next day at work, as he mixed the audio tracks for a local hotel commercial, he couldn't focus. At lunch, when Marq and Elizabeth invited him to the taco truck down the street, he shrugged and said he had stuff to do.

"You going back to the gym?" Marq said knowingly. In the early days, he'd gone to the gym every day at lunch. WITSEC had impressed upon him the need to keep his distance from work colleagues until he'd grown comfortable in his new identity; plus he wanted the burn of his muscles to silence the nauseated churning of his brain.

"Nah," he said. "I gotta do some research. I'll just pick something up. But thanks."

The idea of creating an online comic book wouldn't leave him. *It wouldn't hurt to just look,* he told himself. *Look, but don't touch.* He imagined what the marshals would do if they caught him—

posting online material like comic books, which could clearly be attributed to him, was out of bounds. During his orientation— the multiple orientations—WITSEC had been utterly clear with them: the witness protection program was optional. You could leave it anytime. But as long as you were in the program, you stayed within the clear boundaries they set for you. As soon as you started to color outside those lines, you were gone, and on your own, and anything that happened afterward was your problem.

His fingers still ached for the Melanson, its smooth honey-colored back, the distinctive flame pattern of the maple grain perfectly symmetrical. Those flames had rippled with the slightest movement. He could even now feel the ghost of its weight pressed against his chest.

He thought, too, of what it had meant to sit in a concert hall and play the cello, and feel so vastly more than himself. He was part of the orchestra and part of the audience and part of the air. He was all of these things, and yet more. Something ineffable happened when bow touched strings. What a marvel it was, the cello. Four tender lines hovering in space—lines which, with the right pressure and force, could create music to rival the gods'. Those four strings, those miracles of physics, had been the closest he'd ever found to immortality. Touch them and their response would leap back at you. They could connect this world to the next. Connect this world and the world you had lost. Their heartbreaking resonance could echo down the long passage of years.

But perhaps—just perhaps—there were other ways for him to connect with the universe.

Now he tapped his search into the search bar. An instant later, possibilities exploded on the screen.

Within minutes, he knew he could do it. Within an hour, he'd figured out basic protocols.

Within three days, he'd purchased the basic electronics and supplies, assembled them.

Within a week, he'd created a rough first draft of *Dark Maestro*, "Sound-Shattering Issue no. 1, featuring the Allegro Appassionato by Saint-Saëns."

23

LARISSA

LARISSA WOULD HAVE said that she stumbled upon *Dark Maestro* by accident, but really there was no accident about it. The next time she saw Curtis—she and Zippy had dragged him out for Chinese food—she sensed immediately that something was different.

His glow was back.

He didn't say anything out of the ordinary, act in a way that she could immediately put her finger on; but she could tell even then that some of the tension had left his enormous shoulders; and how, when he ran his finger around the lip of his water glass, the gesture now possessed a new, relaxed thoughtfulness.

She wanted to ask him what was going on—maybe he found a girlfriend—but she knew that when you're working with battered people, you give them some space.

That lasted almost a week.

One night after work, she again showed up unannounced at his apartment, knocking on the door and opening it immediately, her SafeHarbor laptop under her arm. She'd been struggling to figure out how to animate a slide for her Ink Enchantress and knew that Curtis could probably do it in an instant.

And maybe, just maybe, she wanted to check up on him and see how he was doing.

She froze in the doorway. The screen door banged against her back, but she didn't notice.

When he'd first moved in and was constantly practicing on his Melanson, the living room had been sparsely furnished, with a couch and a coffee table, where he usually sat and ate, flipping through his comic books. A large-screen TV had hung on the opposite wall, but he barely turned it on. When he wasn't playing, cello music piped in through speakers that surrounded the room; and the cello, in its case, leaned elegantly in a corner next to a chair and a music stand. The cello had always been the focus of the room, the heart of it, from where all the energy emanated.

Later, after Mischa Rowland's death, Curtis dragged the chair next to the coffee table, and the music stand vanished. The corner was just the corner of the room again, glaringly empty. Comic books, not music, stacked in precarious piles on the coffee table; on the floor kettlebells and fat dumbbells waited like enormous Easter eggs for her to stub a toe or trip over.

Now the room had transformed again.

From the second bedroom, he'd pulled out the bookshelf with his comic book collection, all neatly boxed and organized. She'd barely seen those containers open, but now gaps had emerged in the shelves; and a few boxes lay scattered on the floor between the kettlebells and weights. Two yawned open on the couch next to him.

On the coffee table, a shiny new tablet computer perched on a stand; and an enormous close-up image of a comic book figure filled the screen.

Curtis didn't even notice when she opened the door, he was so focused on the tablet in front of him. He snapped it shut when she said, "Hey, what's going on here?"

An instant later the image vanished from the TV screen. He said, as if trying for nonchalance, "What are you doing here?" and then, "I've been just working on some stuff."

"I can tell." She tried to be casual, tried not to look at a cello— when did he get a cello?!—again propped in the corner with the chair and the music stand, as if they'd never been moved. She wanted to hug him. Tell him how happy she was that he was playing again.

"You can't keep coming over here without letting me know," Curtis said. "Just walking in. What if I have company? People need their privacy."

"You're right," Larissa told him. "You're absolutely right and I'm sorry. I'll definitely text ahead next time. Do you have a sec? Because if this is really a bad time I can come back or we could probably just do it on a call. I was just coming back from work and couldn't figure this out and thought I'd take a chance and come over." She knew she was talking too much.

"What's going on?"

She closed the door behind her, explained the situation with the software, careful not to look at the cello vibrating in the corner. She put the laptop in front of him.

As he studied her computer screen, she asked, pointing with her chin at the comic books, "What's all this for? You doing research for Ink Enchantress? You are such a sweetheart."

He guffawed. "I think Ink Enchantress is all you. I'm just here for help and support."

"So what's all this then? All these shiny new toys?" She read his expression, which had closed up. "Or is it better I don't ask?"

"It's better I don't tell you," he said, grinning, but she could tell he was serious.

She studied the legal pad next to him, could decipher "DM Slaymaster? Scissors? Schrz Tarant? Branden#3." But she didn't push him. He'd talk when he was ready.

A few minutes later he fixed her software issue—she hadn't set the permissions correctly on an image—and she closed her laptop, left him to whatever he was working on.

A week later, she was just starting her shift at SafeHarbor when he texted.

Curtis: Hey you free tonight?

Larissa: At work wassup

Curtis: Have something to show you

Larissa: ?

Curtis: Come over when youre done. Dont mention to dad?

Larissa: C U 530

At 5:28 she pulled into his driveway, marched up the sidewalk. This time knocked.

"It's open!" Curtis yelled from inside.

The living room had been straightened up. All the comic books were back in the storage boxes, neatly lining the bookshelf. Kettlebells and dumbbells, organized by graduated weight, flanked the baseboard.

All this she noticed afterward: after Curtis, grinning (How long had it been since he'd smiled like that? The whole room lit up), gestured for her to check out the large-screen TV.

She thought it was turned off, but then realized that the screen wasn't completely dark. As a solo cello melody began—she recognized Curtis's characteristic vibrato—specks of light appeared, swirling and evolving into musical notes. They spun, faster, melding into the silhouette of a caped figure with a broad-brimmed hat. The silhouette split, drained into color, and now the figure held a cello in one hand; in the other, a bow like a wand waved and flashed.

"*Dark Maestro*," she read. "Issue no. 1."

The opening melody transitioned into music she recognized: Saint-Saëns's *Allegro Appassionato*.

Then, panel by panel, she watched his video comic book develop.

PANEL 1: Scene: A dark alleyway. A group of thugs are surrounding a helpless victim.

THUG 1: "Give us your money, or else!"

VICTIM: "Please, leave me alone!"

PANEL 2: Scene: The Dark Maestro appears at the entrance of the alleyway, holding his cello.

DARK MAESTRO: "I don't think so, gentlemen. It's time to face the music."

PANEL 3: Scene: The Dark Maestro sits and begins to play the cello. The thugs are affected by the sound waves and start to feel remorse for their actions.

THUG 2: "What are we doing? This isn't right."

THUG 1: "I'm so sorry. We should go."

PANEL 4: Scene: The Dark Maestro continues to play as the thugs leave the alleyway.

DARK MAESTRO: "Remember, there's always a better way."

VICTIM: "Thank you, Dark Maestro. You truly are a hero."

PANEL 5: Scene: Conventional living room. Mild-mannered man sitting on a chair takes out his cello and begins to practice the cello part to the Schubert Ninth Symphony. He is glowing as the music seemingly surrounds him.

WHO IS THIS MYSTERIOUS HERO?

"This is gorgeous," she told him as the last notes died away. "You make my Ink Enchantress look pretty pathetic."

"Nah," he said. "It's just a different thing. And I kept this first one super simple." Typical musician, he had to explain the music first—he used Saint-Saëns's *Allegro Appassionato*, with a pedal to play it in octaves, to sound like two cellos. But he wanted to keep the visuals simple on this first one. "I took it one step at a time. To see if I can do it."

"Well, you can definitely do it," she said.

He told her that he wanted to create channels in all the social media feeds. He'd need to be totally anonymous—so the U.S. Marshals Service wouldn't get wind of what he was doing. Curtis was already on thin ice with them. But if the USMS didn't know about it, and if Curtis could keep the anonymity, then Zippy's former bosses wouldn't know either.

"Have they done a house check and seen all this, though?" Larissa asked. The Marshals Service regularly showed up at their house, alert for new electronics that could potentially be violating the agreement.

"Yep," Curtis said. "I ran it all by them."

She searched his face, wondering if he was lying.

He explained how he'd spent hours researching the best, most foolproof, ways of posting online—and then double-checking what he'd found. He'd created a series of anonymous Google accounts, none going back to his real identity, and then used a series of VPNs to encrypt everything.

Once he'd assured himself that he couldn't be discovered, he brought *Dark Maestro* to life. He loved the idea of his childhood alter ego, a cello-playing superhero. It made him laugh out loud when he thought about it.

The story would center around the best cellist in the world. He's playing Schubert's Ninth Symphony when the nefarious Mr. Scissors uses a chloroform-soaked cloth to drug him. He awakens in Mr. Scissors's secret lair. He's not alone: Mr. Scissors has kidnapped three other musicians—the two best violinists and the best violist—to create the ultimate string quartet. But when they play together, their combined talents erupt into a previously undiscovered energy force, a type of living sound wave that the cellist will later call "Vidawaves." Exposure to the Vidawaves kills three of the musicians. The cellist barely survives.

In the explosion and confusion, the cellist escapes Mr. Scissors's clutches. He disappears, goes into hiding.

Soon he realizes that the Vidawaves have now transformed him.

He has become the Dark Maestro, able to harness sound waves and frequencies through a psionically created cello.

He now can produce disorienting or distracting melodies to confuse his enemies; or empowering music to enhance his allies' powers; he can use precise tones to neutralize threats, and other notes to heal and restore the wounded. Sometimes he can even see eight seconds into the future, anticipating the patterns of what is to come.

He now has a mission: to bring truth, justice, and peace to anyone who the seedy, corrupted underworld has wronged. He will use his gifts for the good of everyone who is willing to listen.

"So now what?" Larissa asked.

"I wanted to get your take on it. And then I'm gonna upload it."

They stared at each other. It felt like a big step.

"Well," she said, "I think the graphics could use a little more work."

He shook his head. "You do, do you?"

"Yeah," she said. "I did notice a few things. Can I see it again?"

He hit Play, and this time she took notes. She thought that the alleyway could benefit from more dynamic lighting to enhance the atmosphere and create a stronger visual impact, for instance. And the thugs seemed pretty stereotypical—could they be more interesting? She'd been looking at a few other comic books that week, and saw one that had great background detail—maybe *Dark Maestro* could add more elements to make the scene visually richer?

And on it went.

"Stop," he said. "Holy crap. I thought I did a good job on this."

"You did do a good job," she said. "But you're a musician. You spent a lot more time focusing on the music than you did putting the visuals together. Even though the animation is pretty awesome," she admitted.

"How about this," he said. "Let's do this together. I'll do the music and the words, and you do the graphics. I'll help animate them, but you have a way better sense of this than I do. Waddya think?"

She agreed without hesitation. They spent the next week expanding the initial comic panels to seven, bulking up the animation.

Finally they decided they were ready. Curtis pressed Upload.

Then they sat back, waiting for the U.S. Marshals Service to descend on them, for Zippy's former bosses to fire missiles through his sliding glass door.

Instead, nothing happened. No one seemed to notice.

Larissa checked the next day. Thirty-five views, one like. Hers.

And three comments: "This is lame," "interesting soundtrack but the story sucks," and "The tree that made that cello wants its wood back."

No further views for several days. Then, finally, a positive comment: *"I have spent all my life listening to classical music and*

*I've NEVER heard Saent-Sans performed so beautifully!!!!!! Dark
Maestro you are my hero!!!!! BRAVO!!!"*

Curtis called Larissa at work. "We got a good comment for a
change," he told her.

"You did? That's great!"

"It's from K448AB," he said.

"That's good." She tucked the phone under her chin, nodded to
the woman she'd been talking to.

"K448AB has never had any other posts," he said.

"So?"

"So I think I'm probably talking to K448AB," he said.

"What do you mean?"

"I mean you posted it."

She shook her head, even though he couldn't see it. "Um,
guilty."

"How many Gmail accounts do you have?"

"As many as I need."

"Okay," he said. "We're doing a Beethoven sonata next. I'm
gonna use a pedal that makes it sound like an electric guitar. *Dark
Maestro*, Issue no. 2 is happening!"

Larissa turned off her phone, smiling. Finally, he'd found
something that he could love again. Even if nobody was paying
attention.

Maybe especially because nobody was paying attention.

24

ZIPPY

WHEN ZIPPY GOT HOME from work that night, Larissa had her noise-canceling earbuds in and was focused on the computer screen. He liked to think of himself as enlightened, but it was her night to cook. Ever since they'd moved to Phoenix, they alternated making dinner. She was much better in the kitchen, so he'd been looking forward to whatever she came up with.

Except tonight the computer screen absorbed her. He stood behind her, expecting her to sense him and turn around, but that wasn't happening. She flicked from one screen to another. On one tab he saw a half-finished black-and-white line drawing that looked like the beginning of a comic book panel. He leaned in to read the text over her shoulder, and she noticed him.

"Hang on, just give me a second," she told him.

"What are you doing?"

"I'm being creative. What are you doing," she said, clearly sarcastic, and clearly not interested in his answer.

"That looks dope," he said. As usual, she was always doing this art therapy stuff after hours for the women at SafeHarbor. He didn't pay it much attention. But he also had his own plans for the evening. He was compiling a comprehensive list of medical clinics, treatment centers, blood banks—he'd spent the past few weeks, every night, making lists and gathering details from the Internet. "When's dinner?"

"Give me a minute," she said. "Or go start making something yourself. I want to get this done."

"You do you," he said, retreating to the kitchen. "I'm just gonna be over here not knowing how to cook this chicken." He turned on the oven, found some potatoes in the fridge, and set to cleaning them.

She told him she needed a "minute," but hours passed. The chicken had cooked, and the potatoes boiled and cooled. He'd repeated to her that dinner was ready, but she just needed "another second."

He marched over to her with a plate, set it next to the keyboard. "So today's special is cold chicken and mushy potatoes. A brother is hungry. What are you doing?"

Now she looked up at him. "Check this out." She pulled out her earbuds, and music instantly erupted from the computer's speakers. The rich sound of a cello. Zippy instantly recognized the vibrato. "What the fuck," he said. He leaned in, studied the computer screen, a black-and-white cartoon illustration of a young man sitting on top of a car, cello in hand. A glow encircled him.

He read the screen. *Who is this mysterious figure calling himself Dark Maestro?*

PANEL 1: Scene: Clinging to the shadows, a tall figure watches citizens from a rooftop when he hears a scream.

PANEL 2: Scene: A man is being assaulted by a group of dog-like creatures. His girlfriend has been thrown to the ground.

GIRL: "Someone please help us!"

PANEL 3: Scene: The man swings a stick at the three dog creatures. One of the creatures bites down and snaps the stick in half. Dark Maestro swoops in with his bow drawn.

PANEL 4: Scene: Dark Maestro jumps in front of the pack of dog creatures and points his bow. The bow releases a high-pitched tone that causes the creatures to howl in pain and eventually pass out.

PANEL 5: Scene: The police, along with Animal Control, show up and collect the creatures while Dark Maestro reassures the man and woman that he will be vigilant against these strange monsters.

MAN: "Who are you?"

WOMAN: "How can we thank you?"

DARK MAESTRO: "I'm the harmonic hero, Dark Maestro!"

"What is this? Is that Curtis? Are you writing some kind of crazy comic book about him?"

"It's not Curtis," she told him. "It's the Dark Maestro. Waddya think?"

"Dark Maestro? What? Who? That's Curtis! What are you doing? This ain't going online, is it?"

"Chill," Larissa told him. "It's all cool."

"You know you can't post anything, right? The marshals would have our asses in a sling. Curtis can't mess up again or we'll get kicked out of the program." Anxiety bubbled in his guts.

"Not if nobody knows who he is," she said.

"What?"

"It's anonymous. We've done all this research and it's safe. Nobody knows who he is. And even if they did, they wouldn't know *where* he is."

"Well, I fuckin' know who he is," Zippy told her. "He's unmistakable. You can't post this." His panic rose. "They'll *find* us, don't you get it? And if the marshals get wind of this—"

"First, stop cussing at me," she said. "Next, will you calm down? I told you, it's anonymous. It's through a series of FTP servers. It's safe."

Zippy had no idea what she was talking about. "What the hell you know about FTP servers?"

"More than you," she said.

"Well, I don't care if it's an FTP or an STD or PCP. It's not safe," he said. "It can't be."

"Look," she said. "He needs this. And you know what? I do too. You gotta give him something. If we don't, we'll lose him. He's depressed, and I think he's thinking about leaving the program. We've got to give him something to believe in. He's got to play. And you know how he loves his comics."

Something about her tone made him not want to argue. All he wanted to do was to heal his son. Zippy was the reason his son was in this situation; how could he not let Curtis have a little bit of joy now, especially when they'd seemed to anticipate the risks?

"And I'm doing these comic panels for the visuals," she said. "He came up with a crazy idea. The Dark Maestro. You remember he used to call himself that when he was little? A cellist with superhuman powers who fights the bad guys. Sound familiar?"

"Look," he said, trying again. "I know he's been through a lot. We all have. But this is too much. Y'all are putting us all at risk."

"Sometimes you've gotta take a little risk," she said. "You should know that better than anybody."

Ouch. "How's this? You can make as many comics as you want. Just don't post them online."

"This is already in motion. You've gotta trust him. Trust us. He wants to perform. He wants to play for people. He wants to make music. This is a way he can do it."

"This could get us killed. What don't you understand? What does *he* not understand?"

"Do you trust me?" she asked.

"Trust? What does trust have to do with anything? It's not you I'm concerned about. It's *them.*"

"If you trust me, you'll let us do this," she said. "If he doesn't do this, he's gonna do something else. Maybe something more reckless. Right now he's in his element, and I'm doing it with him. And we've put so many protections on it that I really do think it's safe. Just give him a chance, is all." She put his hand in both of hers and looked up at him.

"Do the marshals know?"

"He's run the laptop and equipment by them. They don't know the full extent of it, but they know most of it. And he's tight with Navarro, so I bet he cuts him some slack."

"And they're okay with it?"

"According to Curtis they are."

"Okay," Zippy said. "All right. But the moment anyone starts asking any questions, it's done. No arguments. Don't fight me on this."

She kissed the palm of his hand, and he took that to mean that she agreed with him.

"Now you want some of this cold-ass chicken?" he asked.

Later, Larissa showed Zippy the two online *Dark Maestro* issues on YouTube and several other social media channels. It had taken them a month to create both of them. Issue no. 2 was the Dark Maestro's origin story—Mr. Scissors's kidnapping the cellist, the explosion of Vidawaves, and his rebirth as Dark Maestro while playing Schubert's Symphony no. 9.

In Issue no. 3, the Dark Maestro, now working in his day job as a sandwich maker at the Bigger Tuna Sandwich Shoppe, is in a back room when gun-toting thugs appear in the restaurant. As the customers shriek in fear, the Dark Maestro appears, manifesting his psionic cello. "You've reached your finale," he says, as Bartók's *Allegro Barbaro* swells. In moments the thugs have returned all the stolen goods, and ordered a twelve-inch hoagie, toasted, with cheese.

Over the next few weeks, Zippy surreptitiously kept his eye on social media and came to see that *Dark Maestro* was getting only a handful of views, and not much interest. The marshals didn't pick up on it either.

Lame AF, Zippy thought to himself. Seriously lame AF.

But it was harmless. The view counts for each of the pieces moved slightly up to twenty-eight and then forty-three, but never much more. Zippy never told Curtis that he knew.

One Saturday afternoon when Larissa was out, Zippy clicked onto the YouTube channel, where the Dark Maestro had just posted *Dark Maestro*, "Sound-Shattering Issue no. 4, featuring Dvořák's Ninth Symphony, Allegro con fuoco."

The beginning sounded like the theme from *Jaws* as the Dark Maestro's archnemesis, Mr. Scissors, reappears. His blade-like hands can cut through concrete and trees; and when he's in a foul temper (as he usually is), he slices through puppies and cuts straight through the hair weaves of unsuspecting women.

Zippy shook his head. It couldn't get any cornier. But the melody was big and bold and undeniable, and Zippy tapped it out on the table. He listened to the first chunk, and then started rapping.

Hit it high hit it tight step to me and get yo lights
Knocked out, here we talking bout The Dark Maestro
Gettin' in the right space, takin' up the right case
Drop it in the wishing well, jack 'em up up and go to hell

Dark Maestro on the move, cello in his grip,
Hears a sound, something's not right on this trip,
Turns the corner, sees a sight so dire,
Mr. Scissors slicing through a bridge like fire.

With blade-like hands, he cuts with skill,
Through steel and concrete, causing people to shrill,
In a foul temper, he's often heard,
Chopping through the bridge without a word.

Dark Maestro confronts him, with music and fight,
Ready to battle for what is right.

"You freestyle that?" Larissa leaned in the doorway, grinning.

"Girl, you know me," Zippy told her. "Yeah. I still got some skills. Even working at that lame-ass bank, your man gots skills."

"You seriously do," she said. "That was good."

It *was* good, Zippy realized. "And you know something? That Mr. Scissors, I tell you, that's definitely something."

"Oh you like that? I came up with that myself."

"Yeah," Zippy said. "I could totally tell."

He wanted to be part of it. And when he'd added the rap, he could imagine it on a whole new level.

That evening, Zippy drove to his son's with a foil-wrapped plate of *pollo guisado* steaming next to him in the passenger's seat.

Curtis's Fiat was parked in its usual spot. Zippy pulled up alongside. He wondered if this was just a bad idea. He could leave the plate on the porch, just so he and Curtis didn't do their usual dance—the sullen *Hi dad, yeah, all's fine, howabout you?*—one more time. A needle stabbing, sharp and sure, into his gut. He trudged up the walkway, the plate still uncomfortably hot on his hands, so he held it by the edges.

Curtis was playing, of course. Fauré's *Pavane*. The melody floated through the open window, so arresting and so pure that Zippy halted, plate burning his fingertips.

He knocked. The music cut off. Eventually Curtis came to the door. "What are you doing here?"

The relationship between Zippy and Curtis had been cool since the whole witness protection nightmare began. Zippy understood how much Curtis resented him. "Yo, Dark Maestro," Zippy said. "You interested in a collab? Your playing is hella dope. I really enjoyed that Dvorak."

Curtis froze. "What are you talking about?"

"I know all about *Dark Maestro*. And it's hella dope. Completely corny, but hella dope."

"Are you going to take that away from me too?"

"No. Nothing like that," Zippy said. "With everything you've been through, this is the closest thing to therapy that might actually work."

"So you're not mad? I figured you'd go tell your pals at the Marshals Service. We all know you got loose lips."

Zippy led it slide. "Fair enough. You got me on that one. But I'm being for-real here. I'm serious. I want to do a collab."

"What do you mean? You learn to play the cello while I wasn't looking?"

"I have an idea," Zippy said. He set the plate down on the ground, thumbed open his phone. He pulled up the *Dark Maestro* page on YouTube, started rapping over the music:

See you from the very start, this is comin from the heart
Maestro is a work of art, I think you gon like this part

"Where did that come from?" Curtis asked, clearly taken aback. "That wasn't that bad."

"You like that, huh? I was thinking. Maybe we could do some songs together. You play and I spit some bars. And Larissa's corny-ass artwork will tell the story. And we post *that*. What do you say, Maestro?"

Curtis looked Zippy up and down. "That's Dark Maestro to you, son."

"Thank you, Dark Maestro." Zippy said. "You're my hero."

Zippy thought, took the risk.

Touched thumb to forehead. "Got your back."

And this time—after over a year—Curtis touched his own thumb to his own forehead, and then tapped Zippy's waiting thumb. "All the time," he said.

25

CURTIS

CURTIS CONTINUED to dive into the *Dark Maestro* comic, although even with Zippy's rap lyrics they barely broke fifty eyeballs per issue, if that. Some didn't hit twenty.

"That don't make any sense," Zippy argued. "Don't people watch the first one, and then the second? So it don't make any sense that number eight would have more eyeballs than number four!"

Curtis shrugged. "Who knows."

Meanwhile Curtis modified his music to make it less classical and more hip-hop, with a more apparent bass line and less intricate fingerings. Then his dad rhymed on top of what he was playing. Larissa's comic book panels, though computer generated, were stylish and edgy. It was really a family affair. "We just need to get Grandma in on it," Curtis said.

She rolled her eyes. "That's gonna be a hard no."

Patrice had settled in surprisingly well to Phoenix. She still complained about her girls being gone, but she'd met some ladies at church and started a couple of regular card games. She'd also become a Tuesday Night Bingo player, and had won almost two hundred dollars over the past few months.

Everyone was adjusting. But although the sound engineering wasn't bad, and although the comic book was a good outlet, Curtis still hungered for the live connection between an orchestra, him, and an audience. The online comic book, the number of views and comments, didn't seem real to him, no matter what the number. He found himself replaying, over and over, that last Kabalevsky, drawing out each note and trying to relive each phrase. In the second movement, had the oboes done a trill or eighth notes? Had the violins done the phrase pizzicato or arco?

He read online that Elisabeth von Hohenberg had passed away. She was the tiny first oboist he'd played with that night who'd congratulated him and said that they would have to get dinner, and Curtis had imagined a luxurious white-table-clothed restaurant in midtown Manhattan and agonizing over the wine choice.

And here he was in Phoenix, a million worlds from Manhattan, and his cello was gone and his career vanished and Elisabeth von Hohenberg was dead.

The Saturday after her death, he drove two hours to Tempe, pulled a baseball cap low over his forehead, and busked on the sidewalk, playing Fauré's *Élégie* in the hot desert wind as an homage to her. What harm could it do? He was just a Black dude with a cello. He kept telling himself this, as if he could make himself believe it. But he knew the risks. He just couldn't resist. He needed to play, to be heard in the world, to engage with an audience. It felt as necessary as blinking: a reflex, something he didn't think about, just did.

But then a couple of tourists held up their phones to record him, and he stopped, packed up for fear that they'd post the video on social media. Because identification was always, always, possible, especially with the new advances in facial recognition software. So he drove two hours back and went on a date with a barista named Megan.

He knew that playing in an orchestra would be a nonstarter. No doubt his dad's ex-pals would be looking for any Black cellist in any orchestra anywhere—it's not like there were hundreds of Black cellists. But he couldn't shake the thought of playing in an orchestra, or maybe a quartet. Maybe if he grew a beard he'd look different enough. He felt like the last years had aged him a dozen years, and that it showed in his face. It might work. It was worth the risk—if for nothing else, to get this craving out of his system.

The big thing would be to stay far away from the guy known as Curtis Wilson. Mischa Rowland had known his name, had held his cello; Curtis couldn't have anything like that happen again. He'd have to stay anonymous, do nothing to lead anyone to believe he was once an up-and-coming cello prodigy.

So the following Thursday night, when the Phoenix Symphony was doing a benefit concert for the kids of St. Jude, he lingered and introduced himself to William Thomas, the concertmaster, as Connor Jones, who'd gone to a tiny college in North Carolina and majored in music. Connor was a sound engineer, but in case they ever needed a substitute cellist, maybe they could keep him in mind?

"I know all the major literature. I used to take lessons," he said. Mr. Thomas nodded.

"I could send you an audio file if you want?" he went on. He knew he sounded desperate—and now he *was* desperate. Just being in the concert hall had awakened the hunger in him: to play for an audience, to play with a trained group of musicians. To be part of something bigger than himself. To fit in.

Mr. Thomas looked at him for a moment, as if considering, then gave him his email address.

That night Curtis sent a file that he recorded when he'd gotten home—just a few selections of some of the pieces he played all the time—and figured that was the end of it, that Mr. Thomas had forgotten him. But not two weeks later, William Thomas called to ask if he was available to try out as a sub. He immediately accepted.

He didn't tell his dad and Larissa. The last thing he wanted to hear was that he couldn't, shouldn't, play in the orchestra. He wanted to keep this going as long as he could. With any luck, the FBI would finally collar the ringleaders of the gang and Curtis could go back to a normal life. They all told him that this was forever, that this *was* his normal life, but he was sure that something would change.

Dark Maestro was fun, sitting in his living room playing multiple variations of a piece, and it made him appreciate the genius of Mozart or Vivaldi even more, but *Dark Maestro*'s end result—a tiny thumbs-up, for instance, at the bottom of the screen—wasn't in the same planet as the rush he got from playing with an orchestra. From sitting in the middle of other trained musicians, all of them focused and intent on creating a moment so clean, so pure, so fleeting, and yet so concrete and resonant.

Issue no. 9: "In the Clutches of Villanova!" (Borodin's Polovtsian Dances):

PANEL 1: A cellist is playing in an orchestra when he senses, with his precognitive abilities, that a supervillain is after Dark Maestro. Quickly he leaves the stage, transforms into Dark Maestro. Now he stands poised with his cello, facing the supervillain in a dimly lit alley beyond the stage door. The supervillain is none other than Villanova—he who can see through disguises and illusions, can burrow beneath the superficial to sense someone's true nature and turn it against them. Villanova smirks, his eyes glowing with malicious intent. "I've got you, Dark Maestro! Or should I say—"

PANEL 2: Before Villanova can speak the cellist's name, Dark Maestro begins to play his cello, tapping into his precognitive abilities to anticipate Villanova's moves. He sees glimpses of the future, calculating his actions with precision.

PANEL 3: Villanova lunges forward, but Dark Maestro effortlessly sidesteps his attack, his movements fluid and graceful.

PANEL 4: With a swift motion, Dark Maestro strikes Villanova with a blast of sonic energy, sending him staggering backward, his eyes wide with shock.

PANEL 5: As Villanova lies incapacitated on the ground, Dark Maestro stands victorious, his cape billowing behind him in the night breeze.

PANEL 6: Dark Maestro approaches the fallen Villanova cautiously, ready to deliver the final blow. However, Villanova suddenly springs to his feet, his eyes burning with fury. "You think you can hide from me? You and your pathetic mortal disguises? No one can hide from me! No one!"

PANEL 7: Villanova unleashes a devastating counterattack, somehow able to anticipate Dark Maestro's every move. "You'll never take me," Dark Maestro says. "Your mission shall fail!"

PANEL 8: Dark Maestro struggles to defend himself against Villanova's relentless assault, his precognitive abilities pushed to their limits. Villanova laughs. "The dark powers who have asked me to find you shall reward me well when I bring you to them!"

PANEL 9: As Villanova gains the upper hand, Dark Maestro begins to doubt his own powers, realizing that Villanova's ability to see the truth, and manipulate it, may be his undoing. And more frightening: who are these dark powers that hired Villanova in the first place?

PANEL 10: With a triumphant smirk, Villanova delivers a crushing blow to Dark Maestro, sending him crashing to the ground. As darkness closes in around him, Dark Maestro wonders if this is truly the end of his heroic journey, and––most terrifyingly––who the shadowy forces are behind Villanova.

Curtis thought Issue no. 9 was a huge success—he used Borodin's whirling Polovtsian Dances to accompany the battle.

Even Larissa noticed. "You're getting good at this," she said as she ran a mock-up.

"Well, I did have a pretty good teacher." Curtis told her. She rolled her eyes.

Two weeks later, he was onstage with the Phoenix Symphony and was beyond nervous. At the dress rehearsal earlier that afternoon, as with the prior three rehearsals, he kept a low profile. The woman he sat next to made that very easy to do. She didn't acknowledge him. Her playing was proficient but lifeless, with zero expression or finesse. Curtis didn't complain. His biggest challenge was hiding his excitement. During the Bacchanale, it almost seemed as if he would snap his bridge in half as he played the driving rhythms to set up the rousing final allegro.

"You need to take it easy. This ain't a solo," his stand partner sniffed. She hadn't introduced herself, but he saw in the program that her name was Michelle.

He wished he could have said, "Why don't you try getting into it more? This music is awesome," but he just ignored her.

The performance went well, and as he packed up the cello, he could feel something loosen in his chest, almost as if he could take a deep breath for the first time in years. He turned in his folder and headed toward the exit.

En route, the conductor, Ian Hargis, stopped him. "You did a great job tonight. I'll see you at the reception?"

"Can't make it," he said. "I have to be at work early tomorrow." He shook Hargis's hand.

"Oh, okay. Maybe after the next one then. I have an email all ready to go out to you, but since I have you, I'd like to tell you in person that the orchestra board would like you to join the orchestra permanently. The next concert is Vivaldi-themed. I've programmed the two-cello concerto in G minor. I was going to ask if you and Brandon Lauer would do the solos." Lauer was the principal cellist.

"I—uh—" he stuttered, unsure what to say and so incredibly tempted. But if he sat in the back, it was much easier to be inconspicuous. If he was out front playing, it was much easier to be videoed and caught. "Thanks for the offer. Let me think about it?"

"It's all in the email I'll be sending you," Hargis said. "But I hope you'll seriously consider it. You're a remarkable talent. Great job tonight!"

That night he brooded. Should he take the offer and do what he'd wanted to do since he was five, or just make it a one-and-done? Should he talk to his dad? To Larissa?

He spoke to no one. He knew what he needed to do.

Dear Mr. Hargis and the Orchestra Board,

I very much appreciate your offer and your faith in me, but my time commitments are such that I can't commit to a full-time position with your orchestra. I do hope you'll keep me in mind to fill in for substitute gigs as necessary, though.

Yours sincerely,

Connor Jones

For the next months, he filled in at several performances, always sitting in the back, always head down. A few times Hargis approached him to do a solo performance, but each time he demurred.

In the meantime, he continued to work on *Dark Maestro*. Sometimes the views were as high as seventy-five. He wondered why they continued to slog on with it, since obviously nobody was interested. Or it was just a dumb idea.

And then one morning on the way to work, after what he'd thought was a fairly mundane performance the night before— an uninspired *Rosamunde Overture*, followed by a pretty rote Beethoven Symphony no. 1—his phone buzzed the distinctive ringtone of the U.S. Marshals Service.

He picked up. "Hello?"

Navarro didn't waste any time. "How the fuck could you do this? Seriously, man. I thought we were friends. I trusted you, for crissake. But now you've done it. You've really screwed it up."

Cold horror splashed him. "Wha—what's going—" Had they discovered *Dark Maestro*? Discovered the orchestra?

"We're moving you."

"Where?" Curtis looked around frantically, as if the marshals were descending to haul him away.

"Don't know yet. And I probably won't know anyway. You should be grateful to me, man, you hear me? They wanted to just toss you out of the program, but I talked them into giving you one more chance. Don't bother going in to work. I'm heading your way and will be there in ten."

"What happened? What—"

"Your little concert got blasted on YouTube."

"Which concert?" he asked, not sure if the marshal meant the Phoenix Symphony or *Dark Maestro*. Or both.

"*WHICH CONCERT?*" Marshal Navarro was screaming at him now. "How many of those have you done?"

"I—"

"Don't tell me," Navarro said, cutting him off. "I don't want to know. The bottom line is that Ray Charles could see it was you, beard and all. I don't know what it's going to take to get you to understand what's at stake. You know that Rowland got killed for less. Start packing." He hung up.

Curtis turned around, heading away from work, away from what had become his regular life, and drove to his dad's little house. Marshals Navarro and Michael were already there.

Larissa gave him a kiss on the cheek. "We've got to get going. They gave us two hours."

"I'm sorry. I didn't mean—"

Zippy was suddenly there, in front of him. "Dude, shit happens," Zippy said. "It sucks to move, but it's okay. I screwed up last time, and you screwed up this time. It's gonna be fine. We'll get through this." He gave him a hug.

"We will," Larissa said. "We'll get through it together."

"Go get the stuff you need," Zippy said meaningfully, and Curtis realized that he meant all the electronics with *Dark Maestro* on them.

He nodded, headed out, Marshal Navarro following behind. Back home, he pulled down the suitcase he'd brought eighteen months before, when he arrived in Phoenix. He started packing essentials. Navarro followed him in, watched every move. His usually sunny disposition had soured. He was no longer a friend, just a lawman. Silent, unhelpful.

"Hey," Curtis tried, "I'm sorry man. I shouldn't have done it. I screwed up."

"Yeah you did," Navarro said. "Guess we won't be playing together anytime soon."

"You're a good guy. It's my fault."

"You're a maniac," Navarro said thawing slightly. "You just can't stop playing, can you? You have to keep testing the boundaries."

Curtis didn't answer. He focused on coiling up some of the cables and stowing them in a suitcase.

"You could've played with me anytime," Navarro went on. "But somehow you got yourself in the symphony? How do you manage to do that?!"

"It's like an addiction," Curtis said. He'd been thinking a lot about this—not just in the past hour, but in the past months. "It's like some part of me needs the rush of performing to just live. Like the cells in my body won't work right unless they get their fix. I don't know. I need it. Need to play. Need to engage with an audience. With other performers."

"You're not the best candidate for WITSEC, you know that?" Navarro asked.

Curtis's grip tightened a moment on the cables. If only this world were different. If only he could just get up in the morning, practice for a couple of hours, go have lunch with some musician colleagues, play with the orchestra that afternoon in preparation for an evening performance—that should have been his life, bathed and breathing in music. That's what he loved, what he knew, what he wanted. "I know," he said. "I'm trying, though."

"I know you are," Navarro said. "I just hope you try harder in your next location."

Despite the turmoil whirling through Curtis, he hung on to one thought: *They hadn't discovered* Dark Maestro.

At least not yet.

26

LARISSA

"GIRL, I ain't goin' nowhere. It's bad enough I had to give up my apartment and come to this hot-ass state and have everybody call me 'Pamela.' Now you want me to move again? You must be drunk. I told that FBI and I'm telling you. The answer is no." Patrice took a sip of her ice tea and swallowed loudly, as if that was that.

"But we gotta leave," Larissa repeated yet again. "We told you how dangerous it is. They killed that guy in New York, remember? They'll be coming after us. They might even be in Arizona already."

"I ain't gotta do nothin' but stay Black and die," Patrice said. "I told him and Imma tell you. Ain't no way I'm movin' again."

Patrice stood up and went to the fridge, opened the freezer, and pulled out a blue plastic ice-cube tray. "All this ain't nothin' but a bunch of silly mess anyhow. It don't even involve me. The FBI or whoever they is will catch anybody before they get to us. And yes, I know, I know—" she overrode when Larissa tried to break in—"I know Imma get kicked out of the program and that's fine by me."

She twisted the tray to break the ice seal, fished out three cubes, and dropped them into her glass. She didn't offer any to Larissa, even though Larissa's tea glass had sweated through the ice cubes just as quickly as hers. Larissa thought of asking for more and decided not to bother.

"I'm tired of moving all around the country anyhow. Them crooks ain't gonna touch me." Patrice added more sugar to the tea.

Larissa put in, "These people might know where we are, and Zeke says—"

"And don't tell me my son is Zeke. He was born Zacchariah and as far as I'm concerned, he gone be Zacchariah till the day he die."

"Patrice." Larissa tried one more time, using the woman's real name in hopes of somehow reaching her, "These people are killers. They don't care how old you are. You have to leave with us." She could feel the hysteria and tension rising in her own voice.

Patrice must have sensed it, too. She reached out and patted Larissa's hand with fingers cool and wet from the ice cubes. "Come here, sugar," Patrice said, softening her tone. "Look, I ain't nobody. I ain't done nothin' wrong. I ain't worried. I was talking to my friend Lisette yesterday, and she didn't know why I left in the first place. Bottom line is—"

"You called Lisette? In D.C.?" Larissa asked, horrified.

"Yeah. Girl, ain't nobody thinking 'bout me or Lisette. We's old ladies that can't do nothin' to nobody."

Larissa didn't know where to start. It felt like the floor had shifted. Not only was Patrice unwilling to leave, but she'd been talking to her friends back in D.C.—which would get her kicked out of the program in no time. Not to mention get all of them killed.

"But we'll never see you again," she tried. "You understand that, right? We'll have new names and new identities. This will be it."

"I like it here," Patrice said obstinately. "It ain't home and it won't never be home, but I'm makin' friends and this is a good place to be an old lady. And you know what, they'll prolly send us to Mississippi next. They don't know how to treat Black folks down there. And it's humid. I can take the heat, but that humidity is on another level."

"Why do you think we're going to Mississippi? Nobody said anything about Mississippi."

"That's where they'll send us. You mark my words. Them FBI don't know how to treat Black folks."

"It's the U.S. Marshals Service," Larissa tried.

"Whoever. I'm stayin' right here."

"You won't have us around, though. You'll be on your own."

"Girl, you think I ain't been on my own before? Zacchariah's daddy wasn't never nothin' to speak of. Been alone my whole life, and I like it here. I ain't movin'." She sucked in her lips in a way that spoke of finality.

Larissa reached for her phone, texted. "I'll at least have your grandson come to say goodbye. And your son." She hoped maybe their presence would change the old lady's mind.

It didn't. Zippy's begging fell on deaf ears.

Marshal Michael loomed large in the door. "We're out of time, people," he told the room. "Your transport leaves in fifteen minutes. We can't make a bigger production outta this."

"Hang on, man! This is my moms!" Zippy said.

"Look, I don't care if she's the queen of Spain. We gotta go. I'm breaking the rules as it is."

Curtis gave his grandma a hug. "Give 'em hell in this hot-ass apartment, Grandma. I love you."

"I love you too, sweetheart. And Curtis? Take care of your daddy. He feels bad enough."

Larissa was the last. "Good luck to you, Ms. Patrice." She wrapped her arms around the older woman, so slender and so rigid. "Please stay safe."

"Don't worry about me, honey. I'll be just fine. Imma get me a new wig. Ain't nobody gone recognize me," Patrice told her. Marshal Michael closed the door behind him and herded them to the waiting vehicles.

Three more months of limbo, of waiting in that unknown, unnamed orientation site. Three months of new paperwork, of new names, new backgrounds.

Lynette, formerly Lorna, formerly Larissa, felt like everything in her life was built on a pile of sand, was a house of cards—all the old metaphors she'd heard before now rang true and boiled her blood. Everything in her life was fragile, could disintegrate instantly. Names and memories and beliefs and relationships were all easily dispersed and broken. They'd left family and themselves behind.

Zander—once Zeke, once Zippy—was broken about leaving

his mother. "I shouldn't have left her. I should have made her come," he kept repeating.

"You know you can't make anyone do anything they don't want to," Larissa told him. "We just need to pray that she—"

"I'm just sick of all of this." He gestured around the hotel room, but Larissa knew that he meant much more than that. They all regretted his decision to talk. And all knew there was no way back.

"No way they would come after that crazy old lady anyway. You might not even recognize her with her new wig," Larissa said, thinking that Zippy would just laugh it off.

He didn't laugh.

It was horrible leaving Phoenix, where they were just starting to settle in, but they all found a silver lining—in *Dark Maestro*.

Before they left, Curtis had posted online that they were going to take a brief hiatus, but to keep watching the space for further updates.

He knew he couldn't post *Dark Maestro* at the WITSEC facility, because the Internet connection would be monitored.

But that didn't stop him from diving headlong into the *Dark Maestro* world. He had too much time on his hands as it was.

Suddenly the Dark Maestro is beset by half a dozen enemies, each more evil than the last, who have appeared as if from nowhere: the Slaymaster; the Bombardier; Sinistar; the Golem Twins; Brightleer; and Slither. Their attacks are coordinated, precise, dazzling in their intricacy—and none of them seems smart enough to be able to create such schemes on their own.

Someone else—some shadowy dark figure who knows too much about the Dark Maestro—must be the brains behind the evil cabal. But who could it be? Dark Maestro must figure it out before the next attack, which may be the last.

[Slaymaster]:
"I'm so fast when I swing this blade
They'll be no point for medical aid!

You'd a thought those slain would've got to runnin' . . .
But no one ever sees the Slaymaster coming!"

Six swings followed by a dash and a lunge—
All dodged by Maestro, as if it were for fun
Slaymaster then . . .
Infused with rage . . .
Took a swing so fast it seemed to stop the day!

Maestro played . . .
A tune so swiftly . . .
. . . It made the blade seem shifty . . .

Maestro grinned
Right before the intro of fist to chin
Lightning struck with every blow that landed
With sounds of thunder through the entire planet!

Curtis dug deep and polished cello versions of more music—including Henri Wieniaski's *Scherzo Tarantelle* and Bach's *Brandenburg No. 3*, with Curtis playing all nine parts, remixing them, tweaking, adding rap or rock or jazz vibes.

Then Zippy came up with the lyrics, and Larissa created the comic book panels. By the time they headed out, Issues nos. 17 through 19 were ready for prime time.

At last, in early spring, USMS informed them that they were moving to Greenville, South Carolina.

A week later they moved into a pair of townhouses south of town, in a new development right behind a Costco. This time Curtis requested that he live near his family. He didn't tell the USMS why: so they could collaborate more easily on *Dark Maestro.* But finding two adjacent properties proved too difficult. They'd been installed on the same block. Curtis in the end unit, and Zippy and Larissa in the middle, with two townhouses between them. It seemed like an ideal solution. The neighborhood was nice enough. Typical southern atmosphere. Humidity, flowers, generally nice people.

Greenville was too small to have jobs for sound engineers. The two or three audiovisual production studios weren't hiring. The Marshals Service found Curtis a job at a local Best Buy out on the highway, where he sold stereo equipment, chest freezers, large-screen TVs, and iPhones.

It would just be for a couple of years, Larissa told him. Just long enough to get their feet under them. Maybe figure out how to monetize *Dark Maestro*. Then Curtis could do something else. By now he was twenty-six and no longer a young prodigy, full of energy and promise and hope. Larissa's heart ached for him.

Zippy and Larissa found work easily enough. Zippy got hired as a bank teller at a large bank around the corner, and Larissa went to work at Hope Haven, which worked with teenage runaways, providing emergency shelters, counseling, and legal advocacy.

This was yet another identity shift for all of them, but this time, something was different. They all resented the fact that they had to change themselves and their lives once again—but this time it was easier. Instead of blaming each other, they blamed whoever was behind the organ transfer ring. They were at least united in that.

Several times they set up calls with the FBI. The last one was the most disheartening. Teddi Slager looked exhausted when she told them that all the trails had gone cold. They'd tried all the angles they could—trying to figure out recruitment, organ donors, and, of course, the money.

"There's got to be a money trail," Zippy said. His voice was thin with frustration.

"Of course there does," Teddi Slager told them. "We got court orders and went through every entry in every account we could. Whoever did this knew what they were doing."

More and more, they were all resigning themselves to this being their life from now on. At least South Carolina wasn't a bad place to be. They'd made a few friends in Phoenix, but now Greenville's open charm warmed them. Within a couple of months, Larissa even hosted a small dinner party for a couple of her coworkers and one of Zippy's. She invited Curtis, but he shrugged her off. He was going to the gym and then had a date. He was dating regularly; Larissa had seen the girls from a distance, but he hadn't introduced her to any, and she didn't pry.

Once every two or three weeks, depending on the complexity,

they posted another *Dark Maestro* comic. They still had only a couple hundred followers—the time away, in the WITSEC quarantine, had flattened them out.

Larissa wondered if any of them lived in South Carolina. If Curtis had sold them speakers or amplifiers or cables at Best Buy.

Life went along for a month or so as they all settled in. In Issue no. 22, the Dark Maestro traveled to Europe to battle the ever-elusive Rotator. The Rotator had vowed to torture and kill a person every day unless the Dark Maestro met him in the Roman Colosseum for a showdown of epic proportions.

As she'd done before, Larissa spent hours on the Internet searching for references to their past lives, as if, by reading social media posts, she'd hold on to some semblance of herself.

Among her many searches, she'd look for any mention of "Pamela Washington," but nothing ever appeared. The old lady had never taken to social media, and if her few friends had, and had mentioned her, she wasn't tagged. Larissa's sister Loretta seemed to be doing well, and Larissa's mom had gone to their house only last week to celebrate Loretta's daughter's birthday.

So she learned that Moni had met a guy, and Crisette had run a half marathon and had gone to an all-you-can-eat seafood buffet on the D.C. waterfront to celebrate.

Seeing all her crew's social media posts was heartrending for her. She felt like she should be able to move on—it seemed like forever since she'd "disappeared"—but she hadn't been able to fully make the leap. She kept thinking about how Patrice had stayed in touch with her best friend back in D.C., and nobody seemed to know.

And then, one cold November evening, more out of habit than anything else, she typed "Pamela Wilson" into the search engine.

She got a new hit.

She didn't hear herself, but she must have screamed as she covered her eyes, because Zippy was there in moments. She didn't have the presence of mind to click away, and so he read the words that almost seemed to shriek at them on the computer screen. Later, she remembered how he froze, standing over and behind her, but right then she was sobbing too hard to notice.

Pamela Washington, 69, of South Phoenix, passed away unexpectedly on February 27. She was a beloved mother, grandmother, and friend. She worked as a part-time hairdresser and brought joy to all who knew her. Pamela is survived by her son Zeke and his family. She will be deeply missed.

There was no mention of a memorial service, or funeral, or where she was buried.

They reached out to Marshal Thomas, their current handler, who put them in touch with Marshal Michael, who relayed few details. The Marshals Service was going to tell the family but wanted to get all its facts sorted ahead of time. Larissa's sleuthing had hit them before they were ready to discuss it.

Here's what they knew. A single-car accident. Yes, in the ravines just north of Phoenix. No, he had no idea why she was out there. Yes, it was possible her car was forced off the road. That's what they were trying to determine. Yes, it was even possible that she'd been killed first and then her car pushed off the road. The forensics weren't conclusive. The car had caught fire.

Death was the risk they ran, all of them. Patrice had known it.

But, yes, the death had been marked as "suspicious." No, USMS had no further information on who could have committed this crime—if there even was one. They would let them know as soon as they learned more.

"Why didn't she listen?" Larissa kept sobbing. "I told her to come with us! Why didn't she *listen*?"

Despite all that they'd been through, despite Mischa Rowland's death, they'd somehow felt *safe*. Intellectually they knew they weren't, but somehow it had seemed that way. Now the past reached out from the coffin, their former lives creeping out like a monster.

Once Larissa had stopped sobbing and composed herself, she stood by the window, her fingers tracing the condensation that had formed as she absorbed the nightmarishly grotesque news. She felt a crippling guilt for not doing enough to persuade Patrice to join them. For allowing Patrice to stand firm in her decision to stay in Phoenix, in the eye of danger, without them. "I knew I should've tried harder. I should've forced her to go."

"You know you can't force my mama to do anything she doesn't want to," Zippy said, almost with a laugh. And then changed to past tense. "Couldn't. Couldn't force her." He closed his eyes. "This is on me. If I hadn't—"

"It's on *me*," Curtis snarled. "I'm the reason you all had to leave. The reason she stayed."

"What if we'd all stayed?" Larissa said, turning toward the room. She hadn't thought of that before.

They all sat with that for a moment. It was brain-numbing. With her back to the window, Larissa could feel a tension in her shoulder blades. Quickly she drew the curtains, but that didn't help. Now she only imagined stealthy silhouettes slipping from car to car, creeping to the porch.

She'd been furious at Curtis for breaking the WITSEC terms and playing with the orchestra—but without knowing for sure how Patrice had been tracked down, she wondered if his pig-headedness had actually saved them.

The rawness of grief took weeks to subside, but Larissa wasn't sure any of them would ever lose the taste of their own guilt, which lurked inside them like the burn of tears behind their eyelids.

Two weeks after Patrice's death, they held an impromptu remembrance ceremony for her—in this place she'd never been to, this place she refused to come to. They drove to Reedy River in Falls Park, central Greenville, stood on the Liberty Bridge, and looked out at the cascading waterfall as it poured and poured below them. Early spring had appeared, and the leaves along the riverbank were a bright soft edible green. In a few weeks, they'd been told, cherry blossoms would explode along the walkways with delicate pink petals.

In the weak sunshine, Larissa watched Zippy fumble in his pocket for a faded deck of cards, their edges worn from years of shuffling.

Larissa laughed for the first time in days. "Where did you get those, *papi*?"

"I asked them to send them to me," he said. Patrice had hauled these with her from D.C.—she'd packed them in her suitcase, and they'd used these cards in the early safe houses. "She sure did love her games, didn't she?"

Larissa said, "She was the queen of tonk . . . and bridge . . . and spades. I swear I've never met anyone else who could shuffle cards as well as she could . . ."

"She loved her cards," Zippy said.

"Heaven help anybody who got between her and her game," Curtis said.

"I was gonna toss these in the river, but I wanna hold on to 'em," Zippy said.

"Good," Larissa told him. "Don't you be littering." She smiled at him. "Why don't you throw in a pack of Marlboro Reds, instead? Unfiltered."

Zippy's shoulders convulsed, and he put his hand to the bridge of his nose to hide his eyes. "It's all my fault. She's dead because of me. Mama," he said to the air, "I'm sorry. I'm so sorry."

She hugged him, and then hugged Curtis. She knew it was Patrice's decision to stay, but that didn't help.

Larissa couldn't shake the sensation of doom stalking them. They had to adapt, had to disappear into South Carolina. They had to get on with their new lives to stay safe.

She knew, too, that she needed to put a stop to *Dark Maestro*, but didn't know how to even begin. They all loved making the comic strips by now—it bonded them and kept them engaged with each other. Luckily they still had very few followers, so chances were good that the guys after them didn't even know that *Dark Maestro* existed—and even if they did know, they couldn't trace it back to Curtis. At least this was what Larissa kept telling herself. But it also felt like they were tap dancing on the edge of utter disaster.

More than anything else, she was afraid Curtis would do something that none of them could expect or plan for, and lead Zippy's former bosses right to them.

27

ZIPPY

PATRICE'S DEATH changed everything.

Zippy had only three people left in his life, and now one of them—his mother, as frustrating and pigheaded as she'd been—was dead. The next days and months oscillated between such extreme, powerful emotions that Zippy sometimes felt as if his head might split apart.

First was the grief. The dull saw of ache, of "never going to be able to" rubbing in his bones. Grief was a shadow that followed him everywhere, would follow him perhaps all of his life, covering him or caressing his shoulder or sliding along beneath him—he didn't know where grief was, only that he sensed it, always, from brushing his teeth to cashing checks at the bank to rapping with Curtis late at night. Grief didn't go away. But he didn't look at it, either. He didn't acknowledge its presence. He avoided getting near card games or smelling cigarette smoke.

And then there was rage, and guilt, which were inextricably bound together. He was so *angry*—angry at himself for getting into this situation to begin with; at the FBI for entrapping him and failing to fix the disaster they'd made; at Patrice, for refusing to come with them; at himself, for his inability to convince her otherwise.

Until now, he'd been a good little lieutenant—doing what his bosses wanted. Bribing the nephrologist or giving the FBI his passwords. Following all the marshals' orders.

And where had it gotten him?

Nowhere, that's where. A tiny town in South Carolina, sitting behind another Plexiglas window, handing out money that wasn't his to people he didn't know.

Zippy wanted out. Out of this life, out of this circle of grief, out of this situation.

This was his life now: always running, cowering, hiding. Patrice's death had shifted something inside him. He wanted to *protect* what was left of his family. He wanted to assure that they were all safe. He had failed, and that knowledge was devouring him.

And he wanted something better, something more, for Larissa and Curtis. He was the responsible one. He wanted to provide for them. Give them a life that they could be proud of, and that he could be proud of.

Everything was ashes now. An urn in a cheap cardboard box that the USMS had sent him from Phoenix, that Larissa had tucked on a bookshelf and that Zippy stared at dozens of times each day.

He was not going to go quietly.

The faceless bureaucracy of the U.S. marshals could only go so far. The FBI made promises, but they were busy capturing "real" criminals. Not blurry difficult-to-pin-down organ traffickers.

Zippy needed to take matters into his own hands.

Not to be a hero. To survive.

There must be a way to fight the people he used to work with. There must be some way through. However shadowy, there was a villain to battle, if he could only figure out who.

And there was one person who knew.

T Block.

The FBI had hauled him in several times for questioning. Had tapped his phones, kept him under surveillance. "Nothing," they told Zippy.

Which couldn't be true.

T Block ran drugs for a living. He sold women. He sold guns. Zippy knew this. Zippy had done this for T Block, for years.

And yet: "He's clean," Teddi Slager kept telling him. "Nothing sticks. Not even tax evasion, and we were sure we could get him on that."

Zippy brooded.

In the meantime, he'd decided, when he was still in Phoenix, to see if he could figure out another piece of the black-market organ harvesting puzzle: the organ donors. He was baffled that the FBI either hadn't done more research on them, or hadn't found more information—but then again, they didn't tell him what they knew. Updates were vague or nonexistent.

So he'd do this without them.

He hadn't worked with the organ donors—he dealt only with the recipients and the medical procedures to get the organs into the people who needed them. But where did those organs come from? Why hadn't any organ donor come forward? How did they get the donors to begin with? Were they all in international countries, China or India? Zippy didn't know. But he was going to find out.

He started dabbling in research about possible places where an unscrupulous organization might find people willing to sell a kidney or a liver—or places where fresh corpses could be mined for hearts and lungs. He searched the Internet. Spent hours on Google Maps.

And from there he did what he did best: created spreadsheets. Analyzed numbers. Looked for patterns. He tracked payments, examined advertising budgets. He started noticing what might be a pattern. But he wasn't sure.

The more he researched, the more he wondered.

Everything, he became convinced, started in D.C.

He wanted to go back to see for himself.

One night they were working together on Issue no. 28, in which Dark Maestro has captured Brightleer and used the persuasive power of his Vidawaves, featuring a hip-hop version of Tchaikovsky's *Chanson Triste*, to get Brightleer to divulge the mastermind behind the coordinated attacks against him.

Zippy was rhyming, and something Curtis did—some twist of his bow or the way he tilted his big shoulders—made Zippy stop.

For a while no one noticed, and then Larissa asked, "Something wrong? I thought this was good. The rhyme here is a little much but—"

"I got something to talk to you both about," he said. He spoke seriously, staring down at the sheet where his scribbles now seemed incomprehensible to him.

"Oh lord, here we go." Larissa said.

He just looked at her, and her grin disappeared.

"We been running for three years now," he said. "Almost four. It's only a matter of time before they catch up and do God knows what to us. I can't let that happen to you. To either of you."

"Lovely topic of conversation," Larissa said.

"I think I figured out a way to end this once and for all."

"That's great," Larissa said. "What did Teddi say?" She'd been half facing the computer screen but now turned completely around to him. Her lips were tight with worry.

"I haven't talked to them."

"You let the FBI do their jobs," she said.

"That's it, though, right? They ain't done their jobs."

"Well it sure ain't something you can do," she said.

"I have a plan. I need to go back to D.C. Please just hear me out."

Larissa and Curtis just looked at him.

"Are you out of your mind?" Curtis asked. "What makes you think you can go back to D.C. and not get smoked? Not to mention if they don't kill you we get kicked out of the program. And then it's just a matter of time."

"You're a dead man if you do. We all are," Larissa said.

Zippy said nothing.

"Okay, humor us. What's this plan?" Curtis asked.

"I've been doing a lot of research," Zippy said. "Into blood type matching." A beat. "Do you see where this is going?"

They both looked at him. "No."

"Blood banks," he said triumphantly. "And specifically two blood banks." He switched screens from the rhyming to the spreadsheets that he'd been working on for months. "Lifestream Blood Services and Vitalflow Blood Bank."

"Yeah, I heard they're really popular in Transylvania," Curtis said. "Why are you telling us about these?"

"Because they both pay more for blood. I've spent the past couple months trying to figure out where the donors come from.

Assuming they come from the U.S., that is. One thing I thought of, that Agent Slager reminded me about, is blood banks. So I started researching all the blood banks in the mid-Atlantic area, and most pay maybe twenty or thirty dollars a pop. Those two pay fifty dollars or more."

Curtis shook his head. "So?"

Larissa was nodding. "Damn. You're right."

"Why is he right?" Curtis asked.

Zippy said, "It makes sense. They need organ donors. And the question is how they're finding them. Finding the people with the right blood types. Blood banks are the obvious way. Hospital or medical records, or blood banks. And I don't think they'd go through hospitals. The recipients were all over the country—all over the world. Not limited to specific hospitals."

"What about the OPTN?" Larissa asked.

"That's just for recipients. Not donors."

"But why those two?" Curtis wanted to know. "Lifestream and—what's the other one?"

"Vitalflow," Zippy said. "And it's because they got more money. They're paying more. So that means that more potential organ donors are going there. Word on the street would be that's where you get the most money. If I were a blood bank I'd make sure I get the widest donor pool possible."

"Word on the street?" Larissa repeated. "How do you know about the street?"

Curtis was saying, "I'm sure the FBI already went there."

"Maybe," Zippy answered him, "but maybe not. And maybe they didn't know what they were looking for."

"Well, what are they supposed to be looking for, then?" Curtis asked.

"People who show up to give blood a couple of times," Zippy said. "And then they stop showing up."

"How can we possibly figure that out?" Curtis said.

"Well, one thing we could do is call the FBI," Larissa said. "You can share the databases with them. I'm sure they can track that kind of stuff."

"But you don't want to do that," Curtis finished.

Zippy didn't answer.

"You want to go undercover," Larissa said. "Get hired at those blood banks. See what you can figure out."

Zippy said, "First I'd have to get certified. But I could get a job there. See what I could find out. You know it ain't that hard to get trained for that kind of thing. How many women did you help do that?" he asked Larissa.

But she didn't answer him. She stared at him, open-mouthed. Then looked down at some space between them.

"What," Zippy asked her. "What is it?"

"There's all those women I helped get jobs," Larissa said. "That *you* helped get jobs. My crew. People at Bright Horizons. There are a bunch of medical people in the mix."

"What would you do? Reach out to them?" Zippy asked. "'Cause you know you can't."

"They loved me," Larissa said. "I saved their asses."

"They *were* loyal. But that's years ago." Zippy gripped his knees. "Any of them could just say the wrong thing, and that would be the end of us, don't you get that?"

"Some of those girls were at rock bottom when I met them."

"So?" Zippy said. "That doesn't mean—"

"It means they remember. They remember where they were. How it was. They'd want to help. They know what I've done for them. These were my *people*. And this is way less risky than you going off and trying to be a superhero," she told Zippy.

"What are you thinking?" Curtis asked. A long silence. Larissa shrugged.

Zippy stood up as well, looking down at Larissa. Her hair was long and straight, the ends tipped in gold.

"Let's save some time and ask them to apply," Larissa said. "To get new jobs."

"Where?" Zippy asked. "At—"

"At Lifestream," Larissa finished. "And Vitalflow."

Curtis said, "You must be out of your—"

Larissa rubbed her eyes. "It's just a matter of time before you"—she gestured at Curtis—"start doing something crazy with that cello. Or someone else slips up. And this is a lot less risky for all of us. The girls will just keep their eyes open and let us know if they see anything."

"I think I should go," Zippy said. "Get trained and get a job there."

"And wander around D.C. where someone could recognize you?" Larissa asked. "Great move, genius."

"What are *you* thinking?" Zippy asked her.

"I don't know, but let's let them at least apply. They can give us info on what goes on there. Names, addresses, numbers. They can get us the details. We can start looking for patterns. And then we can take it to the FBI," Larissa said. "Let's just do some legwork so they can get ahead."

"You could just tell them now. Give them the names of the blood banks and let them run with it," Curtis suggested.

All the rage and guilt and frustration boiled over in Zippy. "They haven't done shit. We have to do this. I can't effing sit here and just wait for them to finally take this seriously. Your grandma is dead because I did that. I'm not sitting around again."

Curtis nodded, took a handful of steps, pacing. "We gotta follow the trail. We need to figure out what happens to the donors. First step is to figure out who those donors are, right?"

Blood banks constantly needed qualified staff, and the two Zippy had identified were no different. Several positions were available at each—possibly the "help wanted" announcements online never disappeared, given regular employee turnover.

But they would leave nothing to chance. Curtis and Larissa agonized over the women's résumés, tailoring each one to highlight qualifications and relevant experience. Zippy formatted them, researching the most professional, industry-standard presentations. Then they all read and re-read the cover letters.

The women applied for open positions as phlebotomists and medical assistants, and within a couple of weeks two had interviews. A month later two of the women from Bright Horizons scored jobs at Lifestream and Vitalflow.

The harder thing was to get the women comfortable with the idea of breaking privacy laws, but Quanae, a phlebotomist whose husband had gotten caught jacking cars, was the easiest to convince. "Girl, I don't know and I don't even wanna know. You just tell me what you need," Quanae wrote her.

"I just want to know anything that seems a little weird to you. Something that isn't totally normal. Maybe there's nothing. But keep your eyes open. And send me whatever records you can get. Just take pics with your phone."

After a few weeks Quanae was sending Larissa screenshots of the donors' medical records. By early summer, so was Crisette, who by now had gotten a job at Vitalflow. The lists were long and boring. Names that seemed more like pseudonyms—"Mike Smith" or "David Jones" or "Carmen Ruis"—appeared multiple times but were linked to different people. One "Mike Smith" was twenty-eight; another was sixty-two. The Tuesday Carmen Ruis weighed 245 pounds; the one on Friday weighed 110. Zippy made a spreadsheet to get a sense of who was returning multiple times.

Quanae put a star next to blood donors who were getting additional metabolic panels done. These Larissa told her to watch carefully when they came in for their next blood sample.

> Quanae: I don't know if this is weird or not, but a couple of those people that have that metabolic panel? They stay in the conference room for a long time. Most people never go to the conference room at all but a couple do. And they always meet with Dr. Gershon and Candace Watkins. Normally they just get their money and get out of there.

> Larissa: What does that mean?

> Quanae: Dunno. You just told me to be on the lookout so I'm looking

> Larissa: What happens when they come back again?

> Quanae: I ain't got that far. Lemme check. I'll hit you back

A week went by, then two. Then a month.

Quanae: Okay this is definitely sus. Remember I told you about those people who met with Gershon and Watkins?

Larissa: Yeah. What happened to them?

Quanae: That's it. They dont come back. No follow ups. It dont make sense. Everybody come back here for the money. These people ain't regulars but after they meet with Gershon and Candace they just stop coming.

Larissa: Who are these people meeting with? Always those 2? Gershon and Watkins?

Larissa: Who's Watkins

Quanae: Med assistant. Candace Watkins

Larissa: You know her well?

Quanae: Nah. stuck up bitch. Always looking people up and down. Im about ready to slap her.

Larissa: She's always in the room tho?

Quanae: Yeah

Larissa: How long is it before they usually come again? The blood donors?

Quanae: Most of em, its a few weeks.

Larissa: Are there any more people with the blood panels that are meeting with the Dr.?

Quanae: Yeah. They do it maybe once a week.
Dr. Gershon is sketchy. Always extra nice with these
people. Calls them sir and ma'am. They always get
special treatment. He ain't that way with everybody
else

"I think we got something," Larissa told Zippy, and showed him the direct message exchange.

He read it. "What you think it means?"

"I'm guessing," she said, "that the blood panels are targeting potential donors. And then they sit down in that boardroom with Candace Watkins, and she offers to take their kidneys or whatever."

"So they're not coming back to draw more blood because—" Zippy started.

"Because they're having their organs harvested. I think that's when it happens. Right after the meeting."

"Did you ever hear of these people?" Larissa asked. "Gershon and Watkins? Did you ever pay them off? Any memory of them?"

Zippy shook his head. "Not that I remember. And I didn't work with blood banks at all." They looked at each other. "Go message Quanae this," Zippy said. *Can you see what happens to the people after the meeting with the doctor?*

Larissa did.

Several more weeks went by. It was now high summer, and the buzz of the cicadas kept them awake at night.

Finally, a response. It's hard to see what happens to them, Quanae wrote. Cuz they leave with Candace.

Larissa: Does Candace come back?

Quanae: Yeah but not for a while. Couple of days at least

Larissa: Nobody notices she's gone?

Quanae: Don't know. Nobody seems to mind. I know
I don't

Larissa: And the blood donors don't come back? You don't
see them again? Like ever?

Quanae: Not a one of them comes back. That's what
I'm sayin.

That night, they held a family meeting.

Zippy, Larissa, and Curtis were going to D.C. They weren't
going to tell the Marshals Service—that would be breaking the
terms of their WITSEC agreement, and they could get thrown
out of the program. They told them they were going to Virginia
Beach and would continue to check in weekly. Curtis had a couple
of coworkers who were going to Virginia Beach, and he set up
some kind of complicated relay system, which Zippy didn't bother
trying to follow, so the SIM cards in their phones went to Virginia
Beach, but the phones forwarded to the burner phones he'd purchased for them. Hopefully it would work.

They weren't telling USMS, and they weren't telling the FBI.

They were doing this alone.

It was happening.

28

CURTIS

"IT WOULD BE a lot easier if we could get into that room," Larissa told them on the drive up to D.C. She'd cut off most of her own hair, and now the green-tipped braids of her auburn-haired wig dangled past her shoulders. Both Zippy and Curtis wore aviator sunglasses and baseball caps pulled low across their foreheads.

"It'll be fine," Curtis told her yet again. "This'll be just like listening over their shoulders."

"A fly on the wall," Larissa repeated. "I know. I'm just sayin' I wish we could just be there. Behind a door."

"This is way better. Trust me," Curtis said. He watched as Larissa and Zippy exchanged glances. He imagined that they were wondering if they'd raised a criminal after all.

"This is just like Number 14, right?" Curtis said, almost giddy.

"Number 14?" Zippy asked.

"Issue number 14," Larissa said. "Where the Dark Maestro goes undercover as a criminal to infiltrate the drug smugglers. You remember you rhymed about creeping up the main hall or something like that." She shot Zippy a side-eye.

"Mussorgsky's *Night on Bald Mountain*," Curtis told him.

"Wow. You nerds are taking this seriously, ain't you," Zippy said.

In Northeast D.C., at a run-down coffee shop near Capitol Hill, Curtis and Zippy waited in the car as Larissa strolled up to a woman wearing a pink miniskirt and a white blouse. Her hair was long and flowing. The woman glanced up sharply when Larissa said something. It looked for a second like she was ready to swing on this strange lady with green-tipped hair, but then the woman hugged Larissa and they talked for a few minutes. Larissa slipped her a brown paper bag. In it, Curtis knew, was the bug—a thin sphere about the size of a quarter—and a small roll of double-sided tape, just in case. He wished they could use a camera—which would have been equally portable and unnoticeable—but he was worried about Quanae setting it up and calibrating it, and getting the angle correct. A recording device seemed safer, easier to hide, and more foolproof.

He only hoped he was right.

After a few more minutes and another long hug, Larissa returned to the car.

"Well?" Zippy said. "She good to go?"

"Yeah, I think so. She's going in for the afternoon shift at two." It was just after twelve thirty. "She'll let me know when it's set up." Larissa scratched her neck where the green braids were rubbing against her skin.

The large blue-and-silver building that housed Lifestream Blood Services, Inc., took up half a block on North Capitol Street. Across from it were a McDonald's, two pawn shops, a liquor store, and a Western Union office: THE FASTEST WAY TO SEND MONEY WORLDWIDE, read a sign on the wall. Next to Lifestream, a five-story parking garage charged $15.50 an hour to park. "Highway robbery," Zippy said as they drove in just before two p.m. Curtis figured they'd be paying several hundred dollars in parking fees. Who knew how long they'd be there.

Curtis switched on his laptop and connected with the transmitter. For a long while there was nothing, just a quiet crackle. Then, after three, the noises and rattling grew louder.

"She must be installing it," Curtis said. "You told her to put it under a chair, right?"

"I told her to put it somewhere that wouldn't be obvious," Larissa said.

Then a voice whispered, "Larissa, I stuck it under the phone.

Right in the middle of the table. That good? Can you hear me? It's gonna have to be good cause there ain't nowhere else to put it."

"Why didn't you tell her to put it under a chair, like I told you?" Curtis asked. "They're more likely to move a phone than crawl around under a chair."

"Why would they move the phone?" Larissa said. "It must be one of those speakerphones in the middle of the table."

"Sure hope so," Curtis said.

Larissa typed in a message, sent it.

"Okay, good," the woman said a moment later. "Hit me up later tonight."

Footsteps, and the sound of a door opening, then closing.

Silence for an hour. In the meantime they worked on *Dark Maestro* no. 30: "The Mastermind Revealed!," where the Dark Maestro, at last, has discovered the identity of his most deadly archnemesis.

A few minutes after four, the speakers in Curtis's laptop roared to life: the door opened, and then voices boomed so loud that it seemed like they were literally standing right next to the car. Curtis turned down the volume.

"I sure hope this isn't going to take long," said a voice—a young woman's, with an Indian accent. "If I don't get those records finished, I'll never get done."

"Fifteen minutes." This was a deeper voice, male. Sounded like he could be Black.

"Good," the woman said.

"Tanya, bring me those charts from Tuesday," the man said.

"She ain't done entering them yet," the Indian woman said.

"Well, what she been doing?" the man said.

The sound of chairs moving, people sitting down. A phone dialed, and then a voice came on over the speakerphone.

The conversation was mundane. An issue with a form not being filled out correctly. Janet and Priya were tasked with talking to the staff and making sure that Form 32-A63 was filled out in detail.

For the rest of the day, and the day after, they sat in the parking garage at $15.50 an hour, listening to the minutiae of the running of a blood bank. "If you think I'm ever gonna work in a blood bank, you lost your mind. This is punishment," Larissa told them. She'd just come back from the Fresh Greens, where she'd gotten them all salads. "None of that fast food for you," she told them. "We're eating healthy."

They sat in the car on Saturday and Sunday, since the blood bank was open then, too. Nothing unusual. Nothing unusual Monday, Tuesday, or Wednesday. Every night they drove back to their budget hotel in Virginia, exhausted from sitting around doing nothing.

After a few more days, a regular routine coalesced: two sitting in the car while the third worked out or shopped. They were all getting on each other's nerves.

And then, more than a week—one of the most boring weeks of Curtis's life—after Quanae installed the listening device, everything changed.

As before, the door opened, and people were talking. Curtis and Larissa barely paid attention. Zippy had left ten minutes ago to go to the bathroom at the 7-Eleven a block over.

"Please come in and sit down, Mr. Hernandez," came a woman's voice. They'd heard it before—it was Candace Watkins, one of the medical technicians, the one who Quanae had flagged as doing those separate meetings with a Dr. Albert Gershon.

As he'd done several dozen times thus far, Curtis hit Record on the laptop.

"This is Dr. Gershon," Candace was saying.

"Mr. Hernandez, it's a pleasure to meet you," a male voice said loudly, as if to someone who didn't speak English well.

"Hello, is something wrong?" said another voice with a heavy Latino accent.

"No, no, nothing at all," Dr. Gershon said. "As a matter of fact, you are in a unique position to help someone. And help yourself."

Silence. Then Candace said something in Spanish, and the man answered.

Curtis's Spanish was rough, but later he had time to listen and transcribe the conversation. Right then, Larissa translated as they went.

Mr. Hernandez: What do I got to do?

Candace: Just to confirm, you don't have a family here?

Mr. Hernandez: No, they're in Venezuela.

Candace: This is a perfect way for you to make money. To send to them.

Mr. Hernandez: How much money?

Candace: Twenty-five thousand dollars.

Mr. Hernandez: You serious?

Candace: Absolutely.

Mr. Hernandez: You want me to run drugs? I don't do drugs. No.

Candace: No, not at all. This is much safer.

Mr. Hernandez: (*Unintelligible.*)

Candace: You're a perfect match for someone in need of a kidney.

Mr. Hernandez: A what? A kidney?

Candace: Yes. One of your kidneys. And this person will pay you twenty-five thousand dollars for it. This person is very very sick and doesn't have long to live. So you would need to decide very soon if you want to do this. If not, we're going to be making this offer to someone else. Time is really critical right now.

Mr. Hernandez: Wait. How much time do I have? What will happen to me? I can't just lose a kidney.

Candace: People live normal lives all the time with just one kidney. The procedure is safe. Think about what this could do for you. For your family.

Mr. Hernandez: (*Unintelligible.*)

Candace: Here's how it would work. This person who needs a kidney is very rich. He's going to fly you on a private jet to the hospital. We'll perform the procedure right away. You'll then spend the next month recovering and have the option of spending another month enjoying your beautiful surroundings. We'll be paying all your expenses during that time. You'll be living in the lap of luxury.

Mr. Hernandez: Where? Where is this hospital?

(*The sound of paper rustling.*)

Candace: Here—the facility is state-of-the-art. This is the recovery suite.

Mr. Hernandez: Oh, a pool?

Candace: And the beach. After a month you'll be able to swim here. Check this out.

A long silence. Paper flipping.

Mr. Hernandez: Where is this place? California? Florida?

Candace: It's a private hospital. Five star. The food is incredible. The medical care is top notch.

Mr. Hernandez: When do I get the money?

Candace: We'll give you half the money now, and half when it's done.

Mr. Hernandez: I don't have a bank account.

Candace: We pay cash. Half now, half when we're done?

Mr. Hernandez: You have this much cash?

Candace: As I said, the person who needs the kidney is very wealthy, and time is of the essence.

Mr. Hernandez: Fifty.

Candace: Fifty thousand dollars?

Mr. Hernandez: Yes.

A long pause. Curtis and Larissa eyed each other. Zippy, who'd returned a few minutes before, hung over the back seat, listening.

Candace: Yes, we can do that.

Mr. Hernandez: Do I have to sign anything?

Candace: Yes, there's some paperwork.

Mr. Hernandez: When will we do this?

Candace: Now. Right now. This afternoon. The recipient has a private plane.

Mr. Hernandez: But—

Candace: Do you have somewhere you have to be? I thought you said you don't have a job.

Mr. Hernandez: It's so quick, that's all.

Candace: As I said, it's very urgent. You said you don't have family here. Do you have friends or people you can call to let them know where you'll be?

Mr. Hernandez: They don't got no phone. I need to know what will happen without a kidney.

Candace: Sure. Let me tell you about it. Here's some written information, too, for you to review. It's important to have good long-term medical follow-ups. You also will need to drink plenty of fluids, maintain a healthy weight and overall good health, and be careful with prescription drugs. But you indicated that none of that is a problem for you, right? So you should be fine.

Mr. Hernandez: I need to think about this.

Candace: I absolutely understand. Should we contact the next candidate? Perhaps you'd be interested in doing this in the future? But I can't promise that a donor will be wealthy enough to pay you fifty thousand dollars. It's your decision.

A pause, and then:

Mr. Hernandez: Okay. I'll do it. Right now?

Candace: If you'd like to come back later, you can, but as I said the kidney recipient is very sick. There's an additional ten thousand dollars if you want to come now.

Mr. Hernandez: Another ten thousand dollars? So, sixty thousand for one kidney?

Candace: That's right. If you want to come now.

Mr. Hernandez: Wow. Okay. I'll come now then.

Another half hour passed as the conversation continued. Paperwork to sign. No, Mr. Hernandez didn't need to bring anything with him. And yes, there was a car waiting outside.

Finally the door closed, and silence returned to the conference room.

Curtis eyed Larissa and Zippy. "Where do you think the car is?" They looked around. The most obvious spot was the parking garage where they now sat.

"There's that reserved area by the front gate," Zippy said. That was on the first floor. They were parked on the third floor, against the wall that abutted the blood bank.

"You're joking," Larissa said. "We gonna follow them?"

Curtis, who had been sitting behind the wheel, didn't answer. He started the car, and they drove down to the first floor, listening to the bug. There was no noise. They worried that Mr. Hernandez had already left. Curtis zoomed around the garage to the first floor.

They rounded the curve, climbed to the next level. On the second floor, they passed a blond woman dragging a roller bag down one of the lanes, toward the exit. Curtis spun around her, turned down the ramp, down to the main garage level, and wedged the car into a corner where they had a view of the front entrance. A late-model white Nissan Altima idled in one of the reserved spaces near the entrance. Curtis had expected a dark Buick or Lincoln town car, not this.

The woman they'd passed a few moments ago came out of the stairwell, tossed her roller bag in the trunk, and made her way outside.

"I wonder if that's her," Larissa said. "Candace. Quanae said she disappeared for a couple of days after the conversations with the blood donors. Maybe she travels with them?" They hadn't seen the woman before now. Curtis tried to memorize how she looked—he had barely caught a glimpse of her face—as Larissa took photos with her cell phone. She was in her midthirties, wearing a gray dress, with mid-shoulder blond hair. That's all he could apprehend before she turned and disappeared toward Lifestream.

They sat, waiting.

Moments later the microphone crackled.

Candace: Hi, I'm back. You still good to go?

Mr. Hernandez: [*unintelligible*]

Candace: I brought you the down payment.

Rustling. A gentle thump.

Mr. Hernandez: Thirty thousand dollars?

Candace: Yes, that's right. All cash. All yours.

Mr. Hernandez: I take it with me?

Candace: Of course. This is a specially made briefcase that only you will have the combination to. There's a lock so you can lock it to your bed and you don't have to worry. And there's the rest of the payment too, that we'll give you after the surgery.

More rustling. Clicks. Rustling.

Mr. Hernandez: This is thirty thousand dollars.

Candace (*chuckles*):   Yes, as I promised. Are we good to go?

Squeaks, clatter, shuffling. A door shutting.

"Holy shit," Curtis breathed. "They're doing it. They're coming."

In a few minutes Candace Watkins and a short Latino man appeared, got into the Nissan, and the car pulled out into traffic.

They pulled in behind. Zippy, who'd taken over the driving, let a few cars get between, and they had several minor panic-stricken moments where they thought they'd lost the Altima. But each time they found it again as it rumbled across the Fourteenth Street Bridge, into Virginia, and south to Reagan National.

But instead of the regular arrivals and departures area, the car turned into a gated lane marked PRIVATE, with a security guard manning a booth. The car pulled through and disappeared. Zippy swore.

"Damn," Curtis said. "Now what?"

29

LARISSA

"CAN WE SEE where he's going?" Larissa, in the back seat, craned around to look. But the Altima had turned a corner and was out of sight. The airfield, and planes, lay hidden behind low brick buildings and chain-link fence.

Curtis was on his phone. He sighed, defeated. "It looks like there might be eight hundred private flights a day out of D.C. I don't know, though. You need an advanced degree to read these websites."

"They must list them somewhere," Zippy said.

Curtis typed more. "They have to file a flight plan, but—" he was reading, "the FAA flight plan is not public." He looked up. "So what do we do now?"

"Teddi," Larissa said. "She can track it down."

"Yeah, and she'll ask questions," Curtis said. "Like: Where are we? What do we want it for? What are we doing?"

"We can tell her something—"

"Even if we could, how are we gonna get to her?" Zippy said. They had no direct contact with any of the FBI agents: the marshals were their only conduit for receiving or sending information. They couldn't reach out to the Marshals Service—they were supposed to be in Virginia Beach, on vacation.

They all knew this. Curtis stared at the dashboard as if willing it to turn into a computer screen, light up with the plane's destination and a plan. "I have an idea," he said slowly.

But before he could implement it, they had to return to Greenville for the monthly marshal checkup. They worried that while they were gone another potential organ donor had passed through Lifestream, so Curtis had the bug automatically record everything, just in case. They had their marshal check-ins and, the evening after Curtis's, headed back to D.C.

The next morning, AAA roadside assistance received a run-of-the-mill vehicle lockout call from a motorist stuck in a parking garage in Southeast D.C. The AAA member, one Lynette Green, waited patiently for three hours for the AAA tow truck to arrive.

"Thank you so much for coming," Ms. Green told the mechanic, slipping him an extra thirty dollars. "This is my boyfriend's car, and he'd kill me if he found out I did this. This is the third time this month." She nervously wiped her hands on her blouse.

The mechanic was busy punching data into a tablet. "We have no record of this being your car," he told her, eyeing the white Nissan Altima.

"I know." she said. "This is my boyfriend's car. I just said that. That's why I got AAA. Because I keep doing this, and he's pissed."

"Ma'am, do you have proof of ID?"

"Of course," she said, handing over her South Carolina driver's license and the AAA card.

"This isn't the car that's registered to—" he began.

Lynette Green seemed panicked now. "Oh my God, he's gonna kill me if I don't get those keys. I'm supposed to pick him up, and he's not gonna see me and oh God—" her voice went up precariously. She was really trying to keep it together. "The keys are in my suitcase. In the trunk. I lost the first set. This is the extra I had made. It's a dark-blue roller bag."

He eyed her, eyed the car. She wiped her hands repeatedly on her blouse and skirt, as if very nervous. Finally he nodded. In moments he'd unlocked the Nissan Altima. The blue roller bag was just where she'd told him it would be.

Lynette gave him an extra twenty dollars for being so nice. As he drove off, he thanked her and told her to have a nice day.

When he was gone, Lynette pulled Candace Watkins's blue

roller bag out of Candace Watkins's Nissan Altima and dragged it around the corner to where their own car waited. She got in the back. Curtis and Zippy were already there.

The roller bag was small, and held a change of clothes, a couple pairs of underwear, and a toiletry and cosmetics bag.

"Gray," Larissa said. "Light gray."

Curtis took photographs as Larissa laid out the contents carefully on the car's trunk. Zippy, meantime, had pulled out half a dozen rolls of gray electric tape and was comparing them to the bag's lining.

"It's this one," Zippy said. Curtis shone a light on the gray tape. It did seem a very close match.

Curtis held the roll of tape while Zippy clipped off a tiny square. Curtis trimmed the corners to make it even smaller, and then grabbed the tracking device with a pair of tweezers. He placed it carefully on the center of the tape. After some discussion, they decided on one of the outside pockets that held only a packet of tissues. Larissa held the flap open as Zippy inserted the tape deep on the bottom, in one of the pocket's creases. The tape was now virtually impossible to detect.

Five minutes later, the suitcase was back in Candace Watkins's car, and the waiting began again.

In the meantime, Issues no. 31 and no. 32 went live—where Dark Maestro discovers that his archnemesis, the parasitic vampire-like enemy that calls itself the "Bloodworx," has been abducting citizens, draining their blood, and burying their bodies in hidden places. The Dark Maestro is in pursuit of the Bloodworx, but he cannot find their lair or figure out how to stop them. His first encounter leaves him battered and broken, since they're able to resist his powers of suggestion and create new monsters to fight him. Are they deaf? Are they immune to his music?

Three more weeks passed, and they cranked out Issue no. 33.

Law enforcement has failed, and the Dark Maestro is the only hope for mankind. He decides to capture and study a Bloodworx soldier to learn their weaknesses. But will he be able to subdue this horrific creature and discover its secret?

"You know what I think?" Curtis told Larissa one morning. Today they were parked on the fourth floor, staring out at the other side of the building, and working on number 34. "I think we've gotten really polished. We've really learned what we're doing. This looks professional. It looks awesome."

Larissa agreed. A few nights ago she'd flipped by accident back to Issue no. 10, and ended up scanning several of the early episodes. Now they seemed comical and clumsy, the graphics stilted. Zippy's rhyming had improved, and Curtis had become much more proficient at giving his classical music a hip-hop spin. "Let's redo them," she suggested. "Same music, but you recut it. I'll revise the graphics, and Zippy can punch up the lyrics."

They'd realized months ago that many of the issues—especially the early ones—were too long. Curtis's music didn't fit neatly into a YouTube music video of three minutes max; plus he needed more time to tell the stories. Most online animated comic books were between five and twelve minutes long; his early ones were closer to twenty, because the music he'd selected—Saint-Saëns's *Allegro Appassionato*, Schubert's Ninth, Bartók's *Allegro Barbaro*, and so forth—could go on for forty minutes or more. Although Zippy had punched up the lyrics, Curtis felt that all of these early issues needed a complete overhaul. He needed to make the music absolutely unforgettable, an earworm that circled around and around and refused to get out of a listener's brain.

So first he worked on the intro and outro music. In the early issues, he'd used Schubert's Ninth, but later versions had a five-second clip of Vivaldi's G Minor Concerto. The minor key and driving rhythm fit the *Dark Maestro* theme better. He added another drum track and used a pedal and distortion to make Vivaldi G even more hard-core. The end result was a banger.

After the music was dope enough, he really drilled into the animation. Larissa spearheaded the graphics, focusing on each panel, adapting the stock images and stylizing them further. Some of the early videos were pretty rough—just eyes blinking or the Dark Maestro's bow hand sawing at the strings—so now she brought each panel to life as much as she could without turning it into a full-fledged animated short and losing the comic book vibe.

Zippy, meanwhile, dug back into the rhyming to make the lyrics stand out and feel more memorable.

Evil Beware! The People's Superhero Fights for Justice.
Where law enforcement fails, the Dark Maestro triumphs.

In the revamped Issue no. 1, a huge threat—still unnamed—looms over mankind. Out of the shadows emerges a muscled figure wearing a domino mask, broad-brimmed hat, and long duster cape. With a flick of his wrist he conjures into being a glowing weapon of scintillating beauty: his psionic cello.

He joins the battle.

The monsters that are kidnapping innocent citizens fall before him as he uses his Vidawaves to disorient and distract them; he empowers his allies, the police forces who until now have been decimated, temporarily enhancing their strength and shooting accuracy; he uses his precognitive abilities to sense eight seconds into the future to dodge incoming blows. At the end of the issue, as the finale of Schubert's Ninth Symphony rises to a crescendo, the Dark Maestro beats back his enemy.

Where they fail,
I will triumph!

To these cats,
I'm a lion!

I am Maestro!
The conqueror of quests

I'm the cold air . . .
That meets their last breath!

It's hard to not be amazed
I'll stretch them like long days,
I'm darker than hallways!

But those that I empower
Reign like sun showers

With the aim of the superpowered
Wielding a handgun

While shooting at random
But goes 30 for 30 like ESPN, son!

I am the one!
The Dark Maestro!

It's a long road,
I'm as far as their best go!

But an unknown enemy lurks in the shadows.

Then the outro music plays: Vivaldi's Concerto for Two Cellos in G Minor.

They'd just reposted the revamped Issue no. 1 when the listening device in Lifestream crackled into life and everything started up again.

30

ZIPPY

ZIPPY HAD GOTTEN used to the dead ends. By now he could recite from memory the beginning of the script with the blood donors: Candace Watkins appearing with Dr. Gershon and asking about friends or family. Unlike Gael Hernandez, most of the people who came to donate blood had a local connection waiting for them—one woman had a child at home; another was living with his brother, who had not come with them; and so forth. In each of these instances, Candace Watkins had not gotten far enough to propose the organ donation.

This time, however, the blood donor was here alone. No, he had no family here. He'd arrived three weeks ago from Venezuela.

Zippy and Larissa were sitting in the van. Curtis was out some-where. Now she texted him. He appeared in moments, panting, laptop ready. He wore a ragged T-shirt and shorts—he'd been working out, as usual. Curtis, as always, trying to control his envi-ronment.

The conversation continued in Lifestream. When Candace Watkins proposed kidney donation for $5,000, Juan Velazquez agreed immediately.

"How come Hernandez got 25K and this guy only got five?" Zippy said.

"I wonder if they have some kind of system," Larissa said.

"Maybe it's part of the urgency, people who need the kidney ASAP," Zippy speculated.

As before, there was paperwork to fill out; as before, she left him alone for a few moments; as before, silence crackled through the transmitter as Candace Watkins returned to the parking garage and came back moments later towing her dark-blue roller bag.

"We have lift-off," Curtis said, and opened a program, tapped a few buttons. A tiny blue ball appeared on a map in the middle of his screen. It traveled slowly to the right, paused, and Candace Watkins's voice came out clearly from the laptop's speakers: "Right this way, then."

Moments later, Candace reappeared at the parking garage entrance, accompanied by a tall man, well built, with glossy black hair. He looked young—perhaps twenty-five—and moved with the easy grace of an athlete. Zippy could only glimpse him for a moment, but that face would haunt him: high cheekbones, dark eyes, blank expression that Zippy would imagine was trusting, was accepting, was terrified. He never knew. But in the dark nights that followed, Zippy would imagine himself walking next to Candace Watkins, thinking about what he would do with $5,000. Did Juan Velazquez have family back in that tiny Venezuelan town? Or was he, truly, all alone?

Curtis shut off the audio transmitter hidden in the Lifestream conference room. The blue ball turned out of the parking garage and made its way to Reagan National Airport. Zippy made no attempt to follow. There was really no point, except to possibly give themselves away.

They'd endlessly debated when to bring in the FBI. By now they were all deeply frustrated and troubled by the bureau's inability to deliver the criminals. Zippy was convinced that somehow the organ traffickers had compromised someone at the bureau, that somehow data or leads were being blunted. "T Block has his mitts on everything," Zippy would tell them. "He must have figured out how to get to someone there."

So now they contacted no one: not Teddi Slager and no one at the Marshals Service. Instead they returned to the hotel, packed their belongings, and watched the blue ball on Curtis's laptop.

As expected, the flight headed south, over the Southeast. In Texas it shifted further southwest, crossed over the Gulf of Mexico, and hugged the western coast. And then it circled.

The flight landed in Costa Rica.

After four more hours, the blue ball paused and stopped on a location on the hillsides above Nosara.

Larissa wrote to Marshal Thomas:

Hi, ! I know this is last minute and I'm SUPER SORRY!!
But my boss here at Hope Haven was supposed to go to
a REALLY IMPORTANT conference in Costa Rica dealing
with at-risk youth and he can't make it and asked if I can
go? I agreed and then I realized I needed to run it by you.
I know it's international but it would mean everything and
it's already paid for, there's a grant and they have to use it.
Please??????

Lynette

Hi, Lynette, good to hear from you. Our protocols won't
allow international travel. I'm really sorry.

USMS Glen Thomas

Help! Please? It's just a few days and the speaker there
is life-changing. I'm attaching info. If I don't go it'll look
really suspicious. Plus we need this for the kids I'm working
with. I already have my passport and ticket. Begging
you!!!

L.

This is a serious breach of protocol but we'll make it work.
Check in with me once you land.

USMS Glen Thomas

They decided that Zippy and Larissa would go to Costa Rica. Curtis would stay behind and try to cover for Zippy, who would never be able to get permission to travel internationally, just in case the marshals dropped in for a surprise visit. He got them both burner phones, mimicked some of their routines so they didn't seem stuck in one place. They hoped it would work.

Then Zippy and Larissa flew to Costa Rica. As soon as they landed, Zippy texted Curtis for an update on where Candace Watkins's suitcase was. The blue ball hadn't moved from Nosara.

When Zippy went to rent a vehicle at the airport, the checkout clerk stopped him. They'd rented a small sedan, but when they said they were going to Nosara, the clerk told them that a four-wheel-drive would be much better.

Larissa translated for Zippy, who thought it was a scam to get the rich Americans to pay more for a car.

"The roads are rough," she told him. "They won't rent a regular car. Only four-wheel drives. He says we can try another rental company."

Zippy shrugged and opened his wallet. They were paying cash for everything so it wouldn't be traceable. "Let's get going."

They were both thinking about Juan Velazquez. Wondering how much time he had left before the procedure. Despite Candace's words about "urgent donors," they were convinced it would take time to set things up, to get the recipients in place. They only hoped they had enough time.

Zippy drove, feeling charged up and revitalized, heading toward the address that Curtis had sent over.

Larissa, meantime, was staring out the window at the jungle landscape. "So the only thing to do is have me go in—"

"Whoa, you go in? Absolutely not," Zippy told her. "We do this together or not at all."

"Listen, how's your Spanish? That's what I thought." Larissa said. "I can act like his sister and just see if he's there."

"You'll tip them off," Zippy pointed out. "You don't have a Venezuelan accent. As soon as someone comes sniffing around asking questions, it'll be like putting up a billboard: WE KNOW YOU'RE HERE. I'm sure they have contacts in the USA. They'd be all over us."

"*Mijo*, you want this to be over? This is how we do it."

There was a long stretch of silence. Then Zippy said, "Okay. This is what we are doing. We are going to figure out where this guy is, and we're going to call the marshals' office to get to Slager. You—we—can't just sneak in."

"Good idea," Larissa said. "Then they'll see I've broken the WITSEC protocols. I bet that'll go over well."

"Curtis can call, then."

"It's way easier to walk into the hospital and say I'm there to visit my brother Juan. Simple." Larissa said.

"Mistake number one. They'll ask for ID."

"So I'll give them my passport," Larissa said.

"Mistake number two. Then they have a record of you. Of us. As soon as you set foot in there, they track us down. Find the flights we're on. Greenville, here they come."

Larissa was silent. They should have thought this all through more than they did. But they were so focused on the logistics, on just following the trail, that they hadn't gone into the next steps.

The way forward seemed impenetrable. How could they possibly sneak into the hospital, or wherever Juan Velazquez was, as well as figure out what was going on, when only Larissa spoke the language? Surely there was a way, if Zippy could just figure it out.

The roads—mostly highways—had been broad and smooth, but as they turned off to Nosara, the asphalt disappeared and dirt spun beneath their tires. And then potholes—huge, yawning— began. The pickup juddered and bounced behind a long line of cars and semis, all heading toward Nosara. Reddish dust swathed them.

"The rental car guy wasn't lying," Larissa said.

Zippy was holding on to the steering wheel and didn't answer. The truck bumped and bottomed out on the steep road leading them toward the blue ball. Clouds of red dust hung in the air, coating the leaves. On either side of the road, high walls—once white, now pinkish-brown from the dust—guarded the privacy of whoever lived behind. Signs pointed toward the beach, toward a bird sanctuary. They passed people—some in beach gear, some more dressed up—walking or riding mopeds. Several were in golf carts.

The tracking app took them to the Pura Vida Wellness Center, perched on the edge of a bluff, with palm trees flanking the entrance. The walls—white, but stained brown—stretched sedately up and down the road. They pulled beyond the entryway.

"Keep going," Larissa said.

"What? We're here—let's—"

"There's a camera by the door. Just keep going until we're out of sight," she said.

Zippy drove another few minutes, turned down an even more disintegrating road, cut the engine. "Now what?"

A pause, as they tried to figure out what came next.

Then, from Larissa: "I gotta go in."

She was out of the car and marching back the way they came, up the rutted road, before Zippy had a chance to stop her.

31

CURTIS

CURTIS HAD RETURNED to the townhouse in Greenville, South Carolina. They'd all driven back—Zippy and Larissa had to collect their passports—and Curtis had dropped them off at the airport. He set up his laptop in the living room, cello next to him, turkey sandwich on the coffee table, and dumbbells neatly lined up at his feet.

There was no point in staying in D.C. while Candace Watkins was out of the country. She seemed to be the main point of contact for the organ donors. Although it seemed possible that someone else stepped in when she was away, they hadn't heard anyone except her and Dr. Gershon. So, until Candace Watkins got back, it didn't seem likely that they'd be targeting other organ donors. Curtis might as well work from home, pick up his normal life again.

As he waited for Larissa and Zippy to land—it was a five-hour flight—he practiced his cello, exercised, and researched the Pura Vida Wellness Center. Candace was still holed up in there. It looked like a legit upscale spa, treatment center, and vacation spot for rich Americans.

Zippy and Larissa called when they touched down. No, he told them, the blue dot hadn't moved.

All he could do was wait.

32

LARISSA

GLASS DOORS SIGHED discreetly and opened as Larissa approached.

To one side was a receptionist desk with three white-suited attendants. Beyond stretched an infinity pool, deck chairs, and more white-suited people carrying trays with drinks and food.

One of the receptionists, a young woman with huge eyes and a lot of mascara, greeted Larissa in Spanish. "Hello, can I help you?"

"Yes," Larissa answered, also in Spanish. "My boyfriend is having a procedure done today, and I wanted to see him before his surgery." She decided, spur of the moment, that "boyfriend" was safer than "brother," since they had different accents and different last names—a simpler explanation that way.

"May I have his name, please?"

"Velazquez," she said. "Juan Velazquez."

The receptionist typed something, looked at the screen, and then looked at Larissa. "I'm sorry, madam, but we don't have any record of a Velazquez. When was he admitted? What kind of procedure is he having?"

"He would have come in yesterday," Larissa said. "It's a kidney operation."

The woman behind the desk looked again at the screen, and shook her head. "I'm sorry, but we don't have any record of him. Are you certain this is the right facility?"

Larissa was convinced she was lying. "Yes," she said. "That's what he told me. His mother called me last night and told me he was already here. Velazquez." She thought about the brief glimpse of him that she'd seen in the parking garage. He'd been a little young to be her boyfriend, not much older than the kids she worked with at the shelter.

The woman typed more keys, shook her head. "I'm sorry, but we don't have any record here of him. Do you want to try texting him? Or calling? He can tell you where he is."

"His phone's off," Larissa said.

Something was wrong in this conversation. Larissa wasn't sure what it was. This girl behind the counter was perfectly pleasant, with an upper-class Costa Rican accent, but something wasn't right. Larissa wasn't going to stick around any further to find out, though, and she thanked the woman and left.

When she jumped back in the car, Zippy barraged her with questions.

"Well? Was he there? Is he alive? Did they—"

"Nothing," she told him. "They said he isn't here. They wouldn't let me in the building. Clearly something shady is going on."

As they sat in the car debating their next moves, worrying that Larissa's presence had already alerted them that someone was tracking Velazquez, Larissa noticed that several of the people passing them were wearing the same white outfits that she'd seen in the wellness center. They seemed more casual now, strolling but heading somewhere.

Larissa gestured. "Can you follow them?"

"Do I have to?" Zippy said. The road ahead had washed away, with deep ruts on both sides.

"Just a little farther," she said. "I'll get out and walk. You stay here. You stick out like a sore thumb."

They hadn't seen any Black people at all.

She got out of the truck and followed the white suits down the hill, glad that Zippy hadn't driven after all. The road had all but disintegrated. Howler monkeys screamed and threw things from the trees. After a moment the road leveled out, and Larissa caught sight of a small open-air shed, with a cluster of chairs and tables around it. Many of the white-suited people were there, smoking or eating.

"Hello," she said as she approached. "Is this a restaurant?"

One man eyed her, shook his head. "This is for locals."

"Locals?"

"Staff," he said. "People who work at the hotels and resorts. Up there." He gestured up the hill.

"Oh," she said. "That sure smells good, whatever it is."

From a stove in one corner poured the smell of cooking rice and beans. About a dozen people were sitting down, clustered around a handful of tables, while others smoked and laughed. A few glanced in her direction.

"Are you from around here?" she asked the man, who had ducked his head and was forking in a plateful of the beans.

He shook his head. "Nicaragua," he said.

"Oh. Enjoy your dinner," she said.

She made her way back up the hill, an idea slowly taking shape.

That night they found a motel that took cash, and cost significantly more than it should have, there in the depths of the jungle, miles from a paved road. They walked around, getting a sense of this place. Despite the unbelievably terrible roads, the place was very wealthy—"Seriously bougie," Larissa said. Howler monkeys trotted down electric lines while, below, wealthy gringos luxuriated in spas and yoga retreats, dining in elegant candlelit restaurants.

"I'm getting this vibe," Zippy told her as they unpacked. "It's where rich people come to play. Where they pretend they're living off the grid." Nosara was one of the famed five "blue zones," where inhabitants regularly lived longer than in other places in the world. The properties for sale—villas with views of the Pacific Ocean—sold for millions of dollars. "It's a perfect setup for black-market organ transplants. Rich people fly in, spend a hundred thousand on a kidney, and then recover in the lap of luxury, miles away from civilization."

"It's kind of perfect," Larissa said.

"This must be a new setup," Zippy said. "The FBI shut down all the ones that I paid off. I never dealt with this one. So it's only been operational for a few years."

"They never stopped," Larissa said.

"I guess not. I wonder how they got this one set up so quickly, though."

They shook their heads. Whoever was in charge of this organization really had money and brains—and balls. "I wonder how many new operations they've already started up again. Maybe they turned to private hospitals only. No more big hospitals. Just little places, off the grid. Who would know what they're up to?"

That afternoon, Larissa had taken the pickup and had driven up and down the deeply potholed roads, checking out the inhabitants. They seemed to fall into several categories—wealthy white gringos; native Costa Ricans; and a large immigrant population, many packed in backs of trucks, returning from job sites. She asked the clerk in a grocery store about them.

"Ah, *chica*, they're all from Nicaragua," she told Larissa. "They come in here, find a construction job—there's a lot of work here—and then go back home. Or send the money to their families."

Larissa nodded politely, wheels spinning. She drove back to the hotel and made dinner for her and Zippy, and they went to sleep early.

But long after Zippy had fallen asleep next to her, Larissa lay awake, thinking.

At a little after two p.m. the following day, she marched down the rutted dirt path to the local kitchen. She'd bought a pair of faded jeans and wore a loosely fitting T-shirt and a baseball cap.

She walked into the open space by the stove as if she knew she belonged. She didn't see anyone she recognized from the day before, but the Pura Vida's white uniforms were prevalent in the crowd, groups of three or more, all chatting and laughing. Rather than linger, she continued down the hill, down to the water, to tangles of downed trees and weeds. A few people perched on half-submerged logs, fishing. A howler monkey screamed right over her head, and involuntarily she ducked.

Then she trudged up the hill again, wondering how many times she could go back and forth without someone noticing how she was stalking the place. Luckily, though, this time she saw what she was after: someone in a white uniform, sitting off to the side, alone. A young woman with tired eyes and a turned-down mouth had finished eating. She sat smoking, staring off into the trees.

Without hesitation Larissa sat down in one of the vacant chairs next to her. "You mind?" she asked the young woman in Spanish. "I'm exhausted. This day has been terrible. Can I get a cigarette from you? I'll pay for it."

The other woman hesitated, and Larissa pulled out a couple of the fat wad of bills she'd gotten from Zippy. The woman handed over the cigarette.

"Thanks." Larissa took out a five-thousand-colón note—about ten dollars—and handed it over. Larissa didn't smoke but allowed the woman to light the cigarette. She put it to her lips, not inhaling.

"Where you from?" the woman asked her. "I can't place your accent."

"Puerto Rico," she said. "But I'm here looking for my boy-friend. He told me he was here, but I can't find him anywhere. Been here since Thursday."

"What's he doing here? Did he tell you?"

"He said he was coming down for some kind of operation," Larissa said. "That's why I flew down here. I had no idea he was even sick. Now I'm worried." She faked a laugh.

"Wow that's really tough. What's wrong with him?"

"I don't know. I thought he was healthy. He told me he went to this hospital in Nosara, but he's not there." She let her voice get a little ragged, as if on the edge of tears. It was not that hard to do—she was exhausted and terrified. And, in her day job, she heard women and kids talk like this every day.

"What hospital?"

"The one up the hill," Larissa said, gesturing.

"Oh," the woman said. "That's where I work. It's a wellness center. But we do have an operating theater."

"Oh my God, really?" Larissa said. "That's crazy."

"Did you talk to Carmen at the front desk? Go ask for her. She's super nice. She'll help you."

"I tried the front desk," Larissa said. "They said they didn't have any record of him."

"Was it Carmen?"

"What does Carmen look like?"

"Maybe my height? Straight hair? Long eyelashes, with lots of mascara."

"That was Carmen," Larissa said. "That's who I talked to."

"Well, if she couldn't help you he probably wasn't there," the woman said.

"But he has to be," Larissa said. "He told me that's where he was. He told me *specifically* the Pura Vida Wellness Center."

"Well, maybe her boss was around. Manuel? Big guy? She has to be all professional when he's around."

"I don't know," Larissa said. "I don't remember." She put her hands to her eyes, pressed down hard. "I don't know what to do. I'm worried he's sick. I haven't heard from him at all, and he always calls me. Or texts. He's *never* silent this long. Never."

"Oh," the woman said. "That's a shame. I'm sorry. Really sorry."

"Can you check for me? Would you be willing to look?" Larissa said.

"Me? I'm in the front restaurant. I don't have any idea about the patients unless they come in to eat. I just serve them poolside or in the dining room."

Larissa was crying for real now. She had no idea she was such an actress, and a part of herself marveled at this—but part of it didn't feel like an act. She did feel bereft, and broken. "I get it. I'm sure. It's okay," she said.

The woman didn't say anything.

"Are you sure there ain't nothing you can do?" Larissa said. "I don't want to get you in trouble but you'd really be helping me out. And look—I'll pay you. I don't have a lot, but I have something."

The woman hesitated a long while before saying, "What's his name?"

33

ZIPPY

"WHAT DO YOU MEAN?" Curtis asked from the speakerphone. His voice was tight and low. Zippy's son wasn't even trying to hide his frustration.

"She can't find him," Larissa repeated. "He wasn't there. No record of him."

"She didn't look hard enough," Curtis told her. "She's an idiot."

"She's not an idiot," Larissa said. "She said she went through the records."

They sat on the bed and the pull-out sofa in Larissa and Zippy's room in the hotel. Larissa had just returned from meeting Maria, the woman who worked at the wellness center, and whom she'd paid five hundred dollars to tell her where Juan Velazquez was.

"Maybe he's dead," Curtis said, saying aloud what Zippy was thinking. "That's the only explanation."

Zippy and Larissa stared at each other, unable to decide what to do next. With Velazquez gone, their only lead had disappeared.

Larissa repeated what she thought the best course of action should be. She wanted to stay in Costa Rica and wait for the next organ donor to arrive.

"All right, James Bond Junior," Zippy said, "we're not pros at this. You'll get caught for sure."

"What other choice do we have? We were out of options a long time ago."

"Besides," Zippy said, "who knows how long it might take? The Marshals Service would be on to you for sure. We'd all definitely get kicked out of the program."

"It's a chance we're going to have to take," she told him. "We've already been lying and breaking every protocol they've given us. What's one more?"

"We can't! It's—"

"We're so close," she said. "We've got to get this figured out. And we almost have."

"Let's call the FBI," Curtis suggested.

"That would mean contacting the marshals, and we're not going to do that," Zippy said. "No way. This is crazy. The marshals are going to catch you. We don't know how long you would have to stay here. It took a month last time. And maybe they won't even come back to this clinic—who knows how many other places they work with now?"

"And the FBI isn't international," Larissa said. "That means they have to work with local police. And that's more bureaucracy as they figure everything out. More time wasted. Let me stay here. Keep talking to Maria. Try to get a job at the Center."

"And how would that play out?" Zippy said. "She thinks you're looking for your brother. You wouldn't stay here if he's not here."

"I'll tell her this is the best lead we've got," Larissa said. "I'll tell her that I want to find out what happened to him, and nobody else is going to do it." She stood up. "I'm staying. And you," she said to Zippy, "are going home to try covering for me if the marshals' office comes sniffing around."

"This is crazy," Zippy said.

They went to bed that night not having decided anything. Zippy unwilling to leave Larissa alone, and Larissa eager to try infiltrating Pura Vida.

The next morning, though, Curtis's phone call awoke them. "The blue dot's back on the move," he told Larissa as she tried to blink awake.

"Where's it heading?" Zippy asked.

"North. Toward the Liberia airport. Candace is going home."

"Okay," Larissa said. "That does it. I'm going to figure out a way into the wellness center. Z, you're going back to the U.S. We need to keep an eye on her. And here you stick out like a raisin in potato salad."

34

CURTIS

CURTIS BURNED with boredom and impatience. He could only do so many push-ups and pull-ups a day, only run so many miles or swim so far. He wanted his life back. He wanted to move forward. Instead, he felt irrelevant. He'd returned to his Best Buy job after this extended leave of absence while he'd been in D.C.—they always needed help and were glad to have him back—but he felt like their amateur detective hour was all reliant on Larissa now. Larissa was risking her life down in Costa Rica, and Curtis was just doing push-ups. The frustration of not having any real skill infuriated him.

"You've got plenty of skills," Zippy told him.

He rolled his eyes at him. "Yeah, I can serenade them all to death with strings and bows," he said.

"You could probably crack their heads with your biceps," he said. This was also true. Zippy had told him that so many of the inmates had been bulging with muscle. They worked out at the gym for three, four, or five hours a day, as if to gain some measure of control over their lives. Curtis understood exactly what they were doing. Ever since witness protection began, he'd been doing the same. One hundred, then two hundred push-ups at a time. Fifty pull-ups. Running for miles, until his lungs and muscles gave out in agony.

Everywhere he went, he knew that a lot of people—women and men—watched him. But what did it matter? He could be as big as the Hulk but it wouldn't give him his life back. He couldn't make up for all of the time he missed out on performing. Working out gave him that tiny bit of control he needed to stay sane through this nightmare that had become his life.

Because it had become a nightmare. All he wanted to do was play the cello in concert halls—and here he was in Best Buy, selling cell phone covers to discerning teenage buyers.

Death stalked him. He thought about Patrice, about Mischa Rowland. What good were all of his cello skills? His muscles couldn't protect his loved ones.

So, in the meantime, as some type of creative outlet, he threw himself into *Dark Maestro*, revising Issue no. 2, which took a week of solid nose-to-the-grindstone. But he was happy with the results.

As he was working, an idea began to unfurl in the back of his head. It grew roots, dug deeper, until—as he worked on revamped Issue no. 2—he couldn't shake it.

He was revising the *Dark Maestro* comic the way Curtis himself had been revised. All the pieces that make up a life—what we look like, how we sound, how we move in the world, the past that ties us to what we know ourselves to be—can be scrubbed away. A computer program can give a character different eyes, different coloring, a different life.

Perhaps it was time to change his identity—Curtis's identity—once more.

One day, almost on a whim, after work, rather than rushing home to start the revisions to Issue no. 3, he spent a couple hours browsing through secondhand stores. In one Goodwill he bought a dark-brown duster with a ragged tear in the back flap. Down the road at a Salvation Army he found a wide-brimmed hat that obscured his face, and also a pair of thin black gloves.

Because no superhero costume was complete without gloves.

He knocked on Zippy's door, didn't wait for Zippy—he let himself in. Zippy, as usual, was buried in a spreadsheet, continuing to research blood banks and other potential donor locations. "Hey, man," Zippy said, glancing over, and they did the thumbtouch. "You want me to make dinner? I was just gonna stop and fix something."

"Not hungry," Curtis said. "I have an idea. We need to talk to Candace."

"You want to call her?"

"No," Curtis said, "we need to talk to her. In person."

"Did you drop one of those dumbbells on your head? You want to just give her our address and tell her bosses to stop by for dinner, too?"

"No," Curtis said. "She's our only lead. We know she has information."

"What does that have to do with talking to her? How are we going to talk to her?"

"We'd wear disguises," Curtis said. He pulled out his thrift-store finds. "These." He put on the duster, the hat, the domino mask.

"You're out of your head," Zippy kept repeating as his son dressed. "You think you're the Dark Maestro now? This is real life. Not a comic book. It's too risky. What if you get arrested for kidnapping?"

"As far as I see it," Curtis told him, "there's really only one question. Do you want to come with me or not? Because I can just have a microphone so you can hear everything. That might be safer for you."

"You're just going to walk into the blood bank and ask to see her?"

"No," Curtis said. "We're already on the run, right? So what's a little more? She'll never see my face. Our faces. We need to talk to her. Are you in?"

Zippy argued with him all night. What would Larissa say? Candace would see through the costume. Kidnapping is a federal offense. They'd spend the rest of their lives in jail.

"Are you done?" Curtis said at last. "I can do this with or without you, Dad. Are you coming or not? I literally have nothing else to lose. I'm done working at Best Buy. And I'm not going to spend the rest of my life creeping around hiding from everybody. I'm doing this."

A day later, Curtis and Zippy drove up to D.C. in Curtis's Toyota Camry. (Not the most impressive superhero vehicle, but he'd tart it up in the comic book.) It was an eight-hour drive.

They stopped only once, at the Alexandria Campus of Northern Virginia Community College. This was crucial to Curtis's plan—if it didn't work, they'd have to regroup entirely.

He'd spent many afternoons as a kid in the college's Schlesinger Hall. He'd been there so often, waiting to be picked up or dropped off, that a custodian had taken pity on him and given him the key code. He would have assumed, given that a dozen years had elapsed, that the security would have changed, been upgraded; but when he stopped by, the key code still worked. They hoped that the interior of the building would be much the same as Curtis remembered.

They pulled into the parking garage around four thirty. Curtis had obsessively checked his phone's app to see the location of Candace's blue dot. It hadn't moved, and they found the white Nissan Altima on the fourth level. The found a spot a few cars down, with a clear view of the elevator.

At six he put on his full costume. The heavy black leather boots he'd found at the Salvation Army each had four buckles that sparked in the light. The black cargo pants were just loose enough to move easily and unimpeded. The black Lycra cotton-blend shirt emphasized his muscled physique, and gave the impression of muscles on top of muscles. The worn dark-brown duster gave him a perfect V shape—his broad shoulders were what every superhero, or everyone playing at being a superhero, wanted. He used shoe polish around his eyes to fill in the holes of the Domino mask. The floppy brown hat topped off the outfit. He looked like a cross between the Lone Ranger, Batman, the Green Hornet, and G.I. Joe. When he looked in the mirror, he laughed aloud for the first time in days.

Lifestream employees, they knew from those days of waiting, got out of work around six p.m. At 6:38, Candace Watkins appeared in the elevator doors, head down as if pushing through a wind. She wore a long tan overcoat. He ducked so she wouldn't see him as she trudged over to the service elevator, took it up.

She was alone, not paying any attention to anything around her, either texting someone or scrolling through her social media. Curtis waited until she passed him, then in one lunge was behind her, trying to give his best Batman impression. Candace let out a solid "Eeep!" and reached for something in her purse. He grabbed her hand, yanked her into a bear hug, and she gasped. She struggled but was no match. Guess all the weight lifting was paying off after all, he thought grimly.

Zippy, meanwhile, with a stocking over his face, was fumbling for the chloroform-soaked cloth—and as Curtis tightened his arms around her, Zippy stuffed it in her face.

Curtis had learned about chloroform from working on one of the first *Dark Maestro* issues, where Mr. Scissors kidnapped the cellist and the other members of the string quartet. But comic books were one thing, and this was something totally different. They'd never drugged someone before. Although they watched as many videos online as they could, they worried about the dosage and the timing.

Now the blue sweet odor enveloped Curtis as well, and his head swam.

Briefly she fought him, pinched at him ineffectively, trying to rip his costume. No luck. That cotton Lycra blend didn't tear easily. No wonder superheroes used it.

She'd apparently been holding her breath, but after a few more seconds—damn, that chloroform was fast!—she went limp. He kept the cloth over her face for another couple of breaths, just to be sure she was out.

Zippy, his head in a constant swivel, looked for any observers as he opened the back seat of Curtis's car. Curtis carried her there. Just as he got her in, the elevator dinged, and more people came out. He bent over so they couldn't see him.

Once they passed, Zippy zip-tied her legs and hands together, and duct-taped her mouth, making sure not to cover her nose. He put a cotton bag loosely over her head.

Curtis, meanwhile, turned off her phone and popped out the SIM card so nobody could track it. Then he put it back in her purse.

They hoped she'd stay out until they got to Alexandria. Supposedly the chloroform would tranq her for at least an hour.

Curtis drove out to Schlesinger Hall and parked as close to the door as he could, conscious of the security cameras stationed above it. He pulled the Dark Maestro hat low over his eyes, adjusted the domino mask, pulled on his gloves. He opened the door and punched in the code, and Zippy held the door open as Curtis carried Candace's limp body through the doors.

Back behind the stage, behind old stage sets, the concert hall's second prop storage room was unlocked. He carried Candace in and zip-tied her to the dusty green vinyl chair that Zippy found in the corner. Zippy checked to make sure her hood was in place, her legs and arms tightly secured, while Curtis went out to move the car.

When he returned, she was still in the same position, but Zippy had set up the tripod with his iPhone on it, recording. Curtis glanced at the screen. Candace filled it.

Zippy didn't speak. Put a finger to his lips and nodded.

She'd wet herself—a large dark stain covered the front of her gray colored slacks. She was awake, then.

He grabbed the voice changer that Zippy used for his rapping on *Dark Maestro*. He'd practiced what he would say, and it was gratifying to finally say it.

"You have one opportunity to atone for your crimes, Candace Watkins," he told the woman. His voice sounded creepy and intimidating to him—he could only imagine what it sounded like to her. His heart was beating hard in his chest. "This is your chance. I'm going to remove the bag and tape from your mouth. You answer my questions honestly, and you get to go home tonight. You scream, or you lie, or you in any way don't answer my questions, and one of two things will happen. If I'm feeling generous, the FBI will be here to take you to jail for the rest of your life. If I'm feeling less generous, I'm going to take you to Pura Vida Wellness Center and choose which parts of you I'm going to remove and sell to someone else. I bet you have two nice healthy kidneys and that liver is still in good shape. You're not a smoker, so you have good lungs, too. Are you following me? Are we clear? Nod your head if that's clear."

She nodded frantically.

Zippy stood off to one side, away from Candace and out of sight of the phone. Curtis glanced over at him and he grinned back, beneath the stocking. The leer was terrifying.

Curtis couldn't believe this was working. He stood behind her and removed the bag and tape from her mouth. He kept one big hand on the top of her head to keep her from turning and catching sight of him.

As soon as the tape was off—he tried to loosen it gently, but some had gotten caught in her hair, and she shrieked as he tore it—she said, "Please, please don't do this—I have a family—I can pay you—I—"

"Shut up," Curtis growled through the voice changer. "Answer only the questions I ask, and you'll be home before you know it." He tried to make his voice sound like Batman. Not quite, but close enough.

She immediately shut up. He stood close enough to actually feel her trembling. He'd never felt another human being tremble before and honestly didn't think people really did it. But they did. For an instant he felt terrible—what was he doing to her?!—and then he thought about his grandmother, and Mischa Rowland, and his cello, propped in the Greenville townhouse, thought about Larissa risking her life even then. That was enough. "We're going to start at the beginning and work our way through your telling me exactly what happens to the patients after they enter the Pura Vida Wellness Center, or any other facilities. I want details."

She stiffened. "Look, I don't know what this is or who you are, but once I get out of here, I'm not calling the cops. I'm calling my boss, and you're dead."

"Okay, if that's how you want to play it," he said. He had the roll of duct tape on the table behind him and grabbed it, ripped off a piece. Crap, what would he do now? He never thought she wouldn't answer. But he pretended that everything was A-okay. "I told you that you had one chance," he said as conversationally as he could. "You just blew it."

"Wait!" she said. "Okay, okay, look, I just follow orders."

"Whose orders?" Curtis asked.

She shook her head. "I—I don't know. Really, I—" her voice rose almost to a shriek.

"Calm down," Curtis said. "You're going to follow my orders now. If you do, you'll get out of this."

She didn't say anything. It seemed, though, looking down at the part in her blond hair, that something in her shifted.

"Start from the beginning," he told her. "I want details of how this operation works. Leave nothing out. Everything from the surgeon's eye color to their brand of deodorant. Leave anything out, and the FBI will have you in handcuffs before your panties dry."

Zippy had already arranged several sheets of paper on the table he'd dragged over. Each sheet was labeled in bold all-caps: CONTACT, FINANCIALS, and so forth.

Curtis started with the first question, under BOSSES.

"Who do you work for?"

"Lifestream," she said.

"Don't be cute," Curtis told her. "You know what I mean. Who's your boss? Who's in charge of this whole little game you're playing? Is it Dr. Gershon?"

Involuntarily she gave a bark of laughter. "Work for Al?" she said. "He works for me, more like it."

"He does what you tell him, then?"

"Yeah. He just reads from the script."

"So when we . . . talk to Albert Gershon next, that's what he'll say?"

She shrugged.

"So if he's not your boss, who is? Who pays your salary? Not the Lifestream salary. The other money you're getting."

She shrugged again. "I don't know."

"How do you not know?"

"I never met anybody. I just do my job. I do what they tell me."

"And you don't know who tells you? You don't know who 'they' are?"

She shook her head.

"You've never seen them?"

She shrugged and shook her head.

He and Zippy exchanged glances. They'd hoped it would be easier but had expected as much. Curtis turned to the next sheet: DONORS.

"How do you select the people who will be organ donors?"

"Organ donors? I don't know what you're—"

"Last time I'm gonna say this," he interrupted. "I know a great deal about what you've been up to. I'm not going to give you another opportunity to answer me. If I put that duct tape over your face again, it'll be for the last time. I hear suffocation is a relatively painless way to go. I want to make absolutely sure you understand me. Do you understand? Nod if you understand."

She nodded.

"So let's try this again. How do you choose the donors for the organ transfers?"

A long pause. And then she said, "I don't. I get an email that lists the names."

"Just the names? Most of the names are fake, right?"

"The names and whatever other information we have. Blood type, height, weight, whatever."

"How else are you contacted by your bosses? Do they text? Call?"

She shook her head. "Just email."

"Never anything else?"

She shook her head again.

"How many email addresses do they use?"

"Just one."

"How many email addresses do you have?"

"Just one."

"If you have to reach them, can you text them? Call? Direct message?"

She shook her head.

"Email?"

She nodded.

"So let me get this straight. The *only* way you can reach them is by email?"

She nodded again.

"How quickly do they respond?"

"In minutes, usually. Really fast."

"Okay," Curtis said. "What happens after you get a donor match?"

"I talk to them," she said. "To the possible donor."

"Do you have a list of questions you ask them?"

She nodded.

"Where is that list of questions?"

"In my desk."

"What are they?"

She shrugged. "We basically want to know if they have any connections here. Friends, relatives, that kind of thing."

"And if they do?"

"They go home."

"And if they don't?"

She paused. "Um. We offer to buy an organ."

"What organ?"

"A kidney."

"How much do you offer for the kidney?"

"It depends."

"On what?"

"On what seems reasonable."

"How much do you think is a reasonable offer for somebody's kidney?"

"Usually five thousand dollars. Sometimes ten."

"That's all?" He remembered the $60,000 to Gael Hernandez.

"Sometimes higher."

"How much higher?"

"I'll go as high as thirty thousand dollars. Forty thousand, even."

He imagined having that much cash in the office. "How many people accept?"

"Almost all of them."

"What happens if they don't?"

She hesitated. "We up the offer."

"To how much?"

"Thirty. Fifty. Whatever it takes."

"You offer them fifty thousand dollars for a kidney," Curtis repeated.

"Yeah, if we have to."

"Do any of them ever turn you down?"

"Sometimes. Maybe once or twice since I've been doing this."

"And what happens when they turn you down?"

"They leave."

"They just leave? Do you tell your bosses about it?"

She nodded. "I write back and tell them that the person didn't accept."

"And do you know what happens to the person after that?"

"No."

"Do you ever see that person again?"

"I don't know. I don't see a lot of the patients on a day-to-day basis."

"Where do they come from? The patients?"

"From the street." She said it like it was obvious.

"Are most of the people American? Foreign-born? Black? White? Latino?"

"It's a mix," she said.

He could sense that she had more to say. "But?"

"Lately most of them are illegals. A lot from Central America and Western Africa."

"How do you know they're illegal?"

She shrugged. "They just are. They can't get jobs. They're desperate for money."

"Let's talk about money," Curtis said. "How do you get your cut? Do they pay you for every successful donation?"

"That's right."

"Every one of 'em?"

A nod.

"How much?"

"Twenty-five," she said. The word hung there, bloated. Curtis tried to not think about it right then, but he couldn't look away. Twenty-five thousand dollars.

"How many organ transfers do you do a month?"

"It depends."

"Of course it depends. Estimate."

"We used to do a lot, but the past couple years it's a lot fewer. Maybe one or two a month," she said.

Curtis tried to calculate. That meant she was pulling down half a million bucks a year, more or less. He needed to focus.

The next sheet was FINANCIALS, and it was Zippy's turn. Curtis handed the voice changer to his dad.

"How do you get paid?" Zippy growled.

Candace jumped, and Curtis realized that she hadn't known that Zippy was there. "I just told him. Twenty-five."

"Not how much. How."

"Oh." A pause. "Direct deposit in my account."

"Your regular bank account?"

"No."

"You have a special account for this?"

"Yes."

"How many accounts do you have?"

"Three."

"Three bank accounts?"

"Yes."

Zippy went on, "Once the organ donor accepts, what happens? Do you pay him immediately?"

"The deal is half on signing, half after the surgery."

"So, say it's thirty thousand. Where do you keep that kind of money?"

"I have a desk in the office. It has a special locked drawer."

"Does it have a key or a combination?"

"It's fingerprint."

"Who installed it?"

"It was already installed when I started work there."

"And you keep thirty thousand dollars in there?"

A pause.

"How much is in the drawer?"

A pause.

"How much?" he repeated.

"Fifty."

"You have fifty thousand dollars in a locked drawer in your desk," Zippy repeated. Curtis tried to imagine it.

A nod.

Zippy continued, "So let's say you give the donor thirty thousand dollars. What do they do with it?"

"It's in a special briefcase."

"What's special about it?"

"It has a passcode that they can enter. It locks around their wrist, like handcuffs."

"So you give them the money in this briefcase. What happens then?"

She shrugged. "They count it. Put it back in the briefcase."

They'd finished the FINANCIALS sheet. Zippy handed the voice changer back to Curtis, who crept up again.

They were on to DONOR TRANSPORT. "Right," Curtis said, "and then what?"

"What do you mean?"

"What happens next? They're at your office with thirty thousand dollars around their wrist. Then what?"

"We take them to a facility."

"How do you take them there?"

"What do you mean 'how'?"

"Motorcycle? Wheelbarrow? How do they get there?"

She hesitated. "In a car," she said at last.

"That's it?"

"What do you mean?"

"That's the only way you get them anywhere? You drive them?"

She paused. "There's a plane," she offered.

"Do you arrange for the plane?"

"No. It's waiting for us."

"Do you know the pilot? The crew?"

"Yeah, I've flown with them many times."

He asked for their names, descriptions, and she supplied what she could. The pilots and flight attendants only had first names—Claudia, Emily, Steve, Frank, Scott.

HOSPITAL was the next sheet, and Zippy's turn.

He asked her, "Where are these facilities located?"

"Mexico," she said. "And Costa Rica."

"That's it?"

She nodded.

"Two facilities? Were there ever more?"

She nodded. "Maybe five years ago there were a bunch. But they all got shut down." Curtis gave his dad a thumbs-up.

Zippy wasn't paying attention. "Is one place preferred?"

"Costa Rica," she said.

"How often do you go there?"

"Maybe two-thirds of the time. Maybe more."

"And you accompany the donor on the trip?"

"Yes," she said.

"How long do you stay?"

"A day, usually. Sometimes two or three, if I have some time off."

"Why usually?"

"It doesn't take that long," she said. "I fly back the next day."

Curtis's turn, and on to the next sheet. HARVESTING. "What's your contact with the organ recipient?" Curtis asked.

She shook her head. "I don't see anyone. Just a couple people at the facility."

"Who?"

"What do you mean, who?"

"Who are you dealing with in each of these facilities? Give me names and descriptions."

As she'd done with the pilots and flight attendants, she gave him descriptions of the people she generally saw in each clinic. Diego, Sofia, Alejandro, Carlos, others.

"So you have any interaction with the people getting the kidney?"

She shook her head.

"But you know who's getting it? Where they're from, age, whatever?"

She shook her head again. "I don't."

"What happens at the medical facility, the ones in Mexico or—where was the other one?"

"Costa Rica," she said.

"Right. Costa Rica."

"What happens when you get there?"

"Get where?"

"To the clinic. With the organ donor. Stop being coy. Just answer the questions. They're just sitting in the car next to you the whole time?"

She hesitated just an instant. Curtis ached to prompt her, to tell her what he knew. But he'd read enough to know that the best interrogators always stay silent. Something was going through her head. She was weighing whether or not to tell him.

At last she nodded, a slight twitch of her head. He knew she was lying. He could sense it in the way her blond hair lay across her scalp. He was a musician. His ears—and his whole body—were trained to focus on minute differences in tone, intricacies of vocal inflection. He noted, almost without realizing it, people's hesitations, fluctuations in pitch and timbre.

And right now it was like Shostakovich's Cello Concerto No. 1 in E-flat Major, when the cello erupts in the tumultuous cadenza. Curtis could *feel* it building.

"So let me get this straight," he said after a minute, slowly, trying to get ahead of her, wondering where this was going. He circled back. "You sit in an airplane for four, five, six hours, talking to the person with the briefcase around their wrist?"

"Yeah, that's right," she said. Her voice was clear. Okay, so this much was true.

"And then they get off the plane?"

"Yeah, of course."

"How do they get off the plane?"

"They walk," she said. "How else?"

But there was something. She was wary in a way that she hadn't been before. And he had to pretend that he knew all about it. That he could anticipate if she were lying. He tried to imagine the scene: they get off the plane, her and Juan Velazquez . . .

"Where do they walk to?"

"There's a car."

"And?" He wasn't going to give her any leading questions. He was going to make her do it all.

"And they get in the car."

"And then?"

"Then I get in," she said.

"And then what?"

"We drive to the clinic," she said.

And there it was: those five words. The cello crescendo was heightening, note upon note.

He waited. Counted to twenty. He could feel, sense, her breath, shallow and ragged in her lungs.

"And what happens on that drive?" he said at last, gentle. "You might as well tell me. We already know."

She drew a breath. And then: "They're put under."

There it was. The crescendo was crashing around them, silent. Curtis still wasn't quite following, so he asked, "What do you mean, 'put under'? Who puts them under?"

A long pause.

"Candace? Who puts them under?" Curtis growled.

"I don't know," she mumbled.

"How can you not know?"

Her head dropped. Curtis couldn't hear her response and made her say it again. "It's in their drink. It's there before we get there."

"What is it?"

"I don't know. It's a sedative. It's put in their water ahead of time."

"And they drink it?"

She nodded.

"And then what?"

"Then they fall asleep."

"They sleep? All the way to the clinic?"

She nodded.

"They drink something that's laced with a sedative and they fall asleep," Curtis repeated. "And then what?"

"We get to the clinic. They're waiting."

"Who's waiting?"

"I already told you."

"How do they take them in?"

"There's a gurney," she said. "They pull them out of the car and onto the stretcher."

"What about the briefcase?"

She mumbled something.

"What?" he asked.

"It stays in the car," she said.

"How does it stay in the car?"

"I unlocked it beforehand," she said.

"So they've fallen asleep, and you unlock the briefcase and they go into the clinic. And then what? What happens when the person gets inside?"

"They're put in one of the rooms."

"Sedated?"

She nodded.

"And then what?"

"I don't know," she said. "I leave them in the room."

"Do you deal with the donor again?"

She shook her head.

"You never see them again?"

She shook her head.

"So you sedate the donor, make sure they're in the wellness center, and then you leave? Go hang by the pool."

"Not always," she said. "Sometimes I just leave, right then, and come back."

Zippy asked, "What happens to the briefcase?"

There was a long silence. Then she swallowed. "I take it back with me," she said.

"You take it back?"

She shrugged.

"What about the rest of the money you were going to pay them?"

She shrugged again.

Curtis wanted to strangle her, right where she sat.

"And then what?" Zippy was saying. Curtis could hear the waver in his dad's voice.

"I go home," she said.

"And the briefcase with all the money?"

"I put it back in the drawer."

"And use it next time. For the next person."

She nodded.

"Who covers your desk while you're gone?"

"Abigail Renkins."

"Does Abigail Renkins know anything about this?"

"No," she said.

"So what happens if another potential donor comes in while you're away?"

"It happens, but not that frequently. They just have their blood drawn and come back in a couple of weeks."

"Who else works at Lifestream who's in on this?"

"It's just me. That I know of."

Curtis, from behind her, could wait no longer, and interrupted Zippy's flow. "What happens to the donor?" he said. He needed to hear her say it.

She shrugged.

"You don't know?"

She shrugged again.

"You don't know what happens to them," Curtis repeated. His heart was a fist in his throat, hammering so hard. He couldn't believe he'd been hearing this.

She shook her head, but he didn't understand the gesture.

"What do you think happens, then?" he asked.

"I don't know," she said.

"Candace," Curtis tried to inject a note of gentleness, of sympathy, in his voice. Sympathy that he was far from feeling. But somehow he thought that softness would be the way to get to her. "You're not stupid. You're a very bright person. You know what's going on. You offer to pay a crazy amount of money for somebody's organ, and then you drug the person and take the money back and use it for the next person. What do you think happens to that person, after you leave?"

She shook her head.

"Candace, what happens?"

"It's not just the one," she said, as if rationalizing everything.

Curtis wasn't following. "One what?"

"One—organ. One kidney. They don't let anything go to waste." She said it as if that would make everything all right.

"You mean they take more than just a kidney?"

"Of course. Everybody's very conscious that these are human lives we're talking about. We don't want them to go to waste."

"So you harvest all their organs," Zippy finished for her. "Lungs, eyes, bone marrow."

She nodded, as if trying to convince them that this was morally justified.

"So you know you're handing them a death sentence when you get them on that plane," Curtis said.

She must have realized how far astray she'd gone, and now she froze. Curtis was about to vomit. Nausea and disgust fought in his throat. He had to blink and shake his head a little. He and Zippy stared at each other. Zippy's eyes looked blank and hollow beneath the stocking.

Finally Zippy gestured with his chin to the sheets on the table. Time to move on to the next sheet. RECRUITMENT. "How did they find you?" he asked. "To hire you, I mean."

"I was in a car accident. Twelve years ago. And I—well, I had a lot of bills. Things were pretty tough. I lost my house. And I met— I was at a bar. One night. Feeling pretty hopeless. And I started talking to a guy."

"Describe the guy."

"Early forties, dark hair, nice smile."

"Black or white?"

"White."

"What was his name?"

"He told me his name was Ronald."

"You didn't believe him?"

She shrugged.

"And what did Ronald say to you?"

"He said that he had a job opportunity. To make a lot of cash. Under the table. There was a travel component." She shrugged. "I didn't think I had much to lose."

"Are you in charge of what Lifestream pays blood donors?" he asked her. "How do they set the price?"

"I don't know," she said. "That's above my pay grade."

Curtis couldn't stomach this. Glad his dad was interrogating.

Zippy was moving on to the next sheet. HER FINANCIALS. "Just a couple more questions, and then we're set. What's your phone's passcode?"

"What?"

"What's your phone's passcode," he repeated casually.

A long pause. Then she read out a series of numbers.

Curtis typed them into her phone. She hadn't lied. Her phone lit up.

Zippy gestured for Curtis to hand over the voice changer. "List all of your email accounts," he said.

She gave several to him—all Gmail accounts, with what seemed like a random assortment of letters and numbers. Curtis wrote them down.

"Now the password for each of them."

She read out several. A couple she wasn't sure of. Curtis wrote those down too. He was stunned that this was actually working. He should teach a course to the FBI on how to do their job.

He realized that it was all about attitude. All about appearance. It was what you projected into the world that mattered, that people picked up on. Curtis was dressed as a superhero, and he thought of himself as the good guy, as the hero. He imagined that other people would see him like that as well—or, more likely, as just nuts. Now, though, he realized that his sense of himself was fluid, was subject to other people's vision of him. To Candace Watkins, they were kidnappers, potential murderers.

"Let's talk about those bank accounts," Zippy said.

Curtis, meanwhile, found mobile apps for several banks, each with sub-accounts. Logged in. There was probably close to five million dollars, all combined. Perhaps more.

He took a deep breath. "This is really helpful, Candace," he told her. "Since you've been so helpful, I'm going to let you go."

He could feel her relax. He'd been so focused on the conversation, on the apps on her phone, that he'd almost forgotten how terrified she must be.

"You have a choice, and it's totally up to you." He tried to sound conversational, casual. "We're going to take you somewhere and let you go. Before we do that, though, we're going to let you hang here for a few minutes, and we're going to change all of your passwords for all of your banks and some of your other accounts. Just so you know. That way we can give you back your phone. It looks like a nice one. Latest model?"

She didn't answer.

"Here's what we're going to do after that. We're going to give all of this information to the police. I suspect, given what you've said, that they're gonna come after you. Hard. You're an accessory to I can't even imagine how many murders. And God knows what other crimes. The police are gonna want to talk to you. Really soon."

He paused, eyeing her. She didn't move.

"So here's the thing," he said. "I'm not going to change your email password. The one that you talk to your bosses with. Do you want to know why?"

She nodded, just a twitch.

"You probably think I'm stupid," Curtis said, "not to change the password. Because of course as soon as you get free you can tell your pals that you spilled the beans on them. And then they can go after me, right?"

She didn't move.

"Here's a little secret. They're already after us. They've been after us for years," he said. He leaned in close to her, almost whispering. "But here's another little secret. There's no way they'll keep you alive now. As soon as they hear that you've squealed, they'll come for you. And they'll find you very very quickly. Who knows? You might end up on a plane to Costa Rica."

He waited a beat. "Between the FBI and your own bosses, you're totally fucked, you know that?"

He could feel, rather than see, that she was crying now. Not gasps, but tears were leaking down her face and she was trying with tiny sniffs to hold them back.

"So here's your third option. Completely your decision. Tomorrow you can go back to work like usual. You and I will both monitor that email account. When the next potential organ donor comes in, I'll know it. You'll follow your script. If they end up in Costa Rica, you're golden. If they end up in another country, though, you're gonna have to wait till they go back to Costa Rica."

"And then what?" she asked, her voice high and tight.

"And then nothing. You do your thing like you always do. Except one difference. This time, when you get ready to go back to America, you get on a flight to somewhere else. Anywhere you want to go. I'll give you access to one of your bank accounts. That money of yours? You can buy yourself a brand-new life somewhere else. Change your name and run as far and as fast as you can—and maybe the FBI or your bosses won't be able to find you."

She didn't move for a few moments.

"What's it gonna be, Candace?" Curtis asked. "We're only giving you a choice because we're compassionate. Way more compassionate than you were to those people you murdered. But the truth is, Candace, we're not after you. We want your bosses.

"So. What'll it be?"

35

LARISSA

THE LAUNDRY FACILITY of the Pura Vida Wellness Center was reached by following the dirt path beyond the pools' chemical rooms and then going down a short flight of stairs along the cliff face. The building, of nondescript unpainted concrete, was out of sight of the teak decking, bamboo window treatments, marble countertops, and linen draperies of the guest suites, the spas, the saunas, steam rooms, yoga studios, meditation rooms, fitness center, and restaurants.

Inside the laundry facility, detergent and bleach burned Larissa's eyes and nasal passages. Industrial washing machines and dryers lined the walls, their ceaseless rumble a constant companion. The tropical heat of Costa Rica permeated even here, making the concrete walls sweat.

For ten hours a day, Larissa collected soiled laundry and fed it into the hungry machines, then folded and distributed the clean piles throughout the Center. Her hands were raw and tender from handling harsh chemicals and hot fabrics.

She didn't officially "work" for Pura Vida. But the low-paying, backbreaking jobs were constantly in flux, and she was able to slip into one of them by accessing the network of illegal Nicaraguans working there. Maria, the woman she'd befriended who worked at the restaurant, introduced her to Reyna, who had hurt her back a few weeks ago but was continuing to work despite the pain. Yes, Larissa could help, Larissa was desperate to find work, and Larissa would be grateful for the ten dollars a day.

Reyna talked to the manager, a tall sharp-eyed man named

Miguel, who studied Larissa and turned away. "I won't pay her," he told Reyna. "You pay her yourself. Or I can just find someone else."

Reyna nodded frantically. "Yes sir. I'll pay her myself."

So that was how Larissa, alongside her Nicaraguan colleague Marta, changed the bedding in the guest rooms and other parts of the wellness center. "We must ensure the highest standards of cleanliness," Reyna told her. "That means it must be spotless. Perfectly clean. If it's stained, it's recycled."

While Reyna stayed in the laundry room feeding the machines, Marta, a woman of few words, led the way around the Center. Her hands, toughened by years of work, moved with practiced efficiency as she stripped used bed linens. Her face seemed etched with lines that spoke of misery beyond anything Larissa wanted to hear.

Larissa always studied each detail of every room—each one cool, air-conditioned, sparingly luxurious. After that they trekked on to the rest of the facility: to the gym to collect used towels, to the spa to replace worn-out robes, and to the outdoor pools to gather hampers full of soggy towels.

And then to the surgical suite.

The place held an air of sterile precision and quiet intensity. Slightly removed from the main Center, it could be accessed internally or from an exterior door inconspicuously set in the high white wall that fronted the road. For the week that Larissa had been working there, she'd only entered the suite once but had done her best to memorize the layout of the seven rooms: five on one side and two on the other, near the front access door. The last two rooms had no furniture, nor a connecting bathroom. She would have thought they were storage rooms except that a gurney stretched across the center of each room, surrounded by medical equipment.

These, she assumed, were the rooms where the organs were harvested. She thought again about Gael Hernandez and Juan Velazquez.

Six days after she started work at the Center, Larissa was in the laundry facility folding towels when her phone pinged. A message from Curtis lit up the screen. Get ready. Hector Gonzalez, 32, 5'6, 162#, bearded with a tattoo on left bicep. He's leaving soon. Hope he's coming to you not sure yet.

Her stomach knotted. At last, here goes. She'd planned this out in her head but knew that it would all boil down to chance and opportunity.

She couldn't just leave her post. She had to stick to her routine, follow Marta on her rounds. So she waited, doing her regular work, stopping for lunch and heading down the hill to the open-air restaurant where she first met Maria, Pilar, and the other Nicaraguan immigrants who worked at the wealthy resorts in the area.

The Nicaraguan migrants lived in small enclaves off the main roads, in collections of one-room shacks, many without electricity or running water. The rooms were often overcrowded, with multiple families sharing the single, cramped space. Larissa had managed to find a corner to sleep in, paying almost as much rent as she'd paid to the Costa Rican hotel. The thin walls let in mosquitoes and the thrumming music, which pounded all night like a headache. Dust from the nearby road coated everything. The communal toilet was outside—a hole in the ground, inside an outhouse that was warped plywood tacked to two-by-fours. You brought your own toilet paper.

She'd befriended a young woman who worked as a Pilates and yoga instructor at the wellness center and lived in the shack next to hers. Pilar, Larissa could tell, was going to make something of herself. She already spoke fairly fluent English, and no matter what the circumstance, always seemed made up, well groomed, and put together. Like a few of the migrants, Pilar had managed to rent a small motorcycle, which she kept double-locked with thick metal chains. Everyone envied her.

As Larissa arrived at the open-air restaurant for lunch, Pilar was eating in a corner with a couple of familiar-looking men whose names Larissa didn't know. After she'd gotten her plate of rice and beans—there was a thin rind of chicken, too, today—she sat down with them, chatted and bantered and laughed as if everything was okay. She could barely force the food down, she was so nervous.

When Pilar rose to return to the Wellness Center, Larissa came with her. "Hey, *chica*, I have a big favor to ask, and you're gonna say no," Larissa said.

"No," Pilar said, marching up the path. Her white Pilates uniform was perfect, unstained. Larissa already had a smear of reddish dust on her right breast, and her short hair was sticking to her temples.

"I need to borrow your motorcycle," Larissa said. "And I'll pay you for it."

Pilar looked over at her and quoted her a figure that Larissa calculated would equal about US$4,000.

"You're kidding," Larissa said.

"Cash," Pilar said coolly. A minute ago she'd been laughing and casual, talking about how the bartender was trying to get in her pants, but now she was all business. "If you bring it back in one piece, I'll only charge you five hundred dollars. I'll give you the thirty-five hundred back."

"But that's crazy—that's as much as the motorcycle's worth!"

"Exactly. I can't afford to buy another. I bought this one on credit, so if something happens to it I still have to pay for it."

Larissa gulped. "Okay," she said, thinking. "It's going to take me a minute to get the money, but I'll get it for you tonight. Keep this between us, okay?"

"Of course," Pilar told her.

By then they were at the wellness center. Pilar turned right, into the main facility, and Larissa went left, down the hill to the laundry.

Late that afternoon, she made her rounds with the other women, and this time they stopped by the surgical suite.

Usually the place was empty, except for a nurse or two. But now the corridor was a flurry of activity. Doctors and nurses moved purposefully, many with faces hidden behind masks. Medical aides bustled about, their hands filled with trays of gleaming instruments.

Larissa blanched. It seemed for a moment that all of the rooms were occupied, but she soon realized that only one patient had arrived thus far, a frail woman in the big chamber on the left.

Larissa ducked in, pulled out the laundry bag, and replaced the shelves with several piles of fresh linen. The woman was being tested and monitored. All eyes were on her. A young woman was holding her hand. "It's gonna be okay, Mama," she kept saying in English.

"I know it. Thank the Lord for this chance," the older woman said. And then she said something more, but Larissa was already out the door, moving down the corridor, opening one door and then the next. Two other rooms were being readied. Larissa overheard talk of planes flying in, of people arriving that night or tomorrow.

There was no sign of Hector Gonzalez.

A large group of Canadians had arrived at Pura Vida, and they kept Larissa busy with extra towels and personal laundry requests. So she didn't shake free for several hours but then managed to duck into the surgery suite. Head down, as if on an errand, she headed toward the secluded rooms.

She opened the door on the end, and there she found him.

A heavyset Latino man, fully naked, was sedated on the gurney, hooked up to an IV. His tawny skin seemed pasty and white, and his penis flopped obscenely on his thigh. His eyes glittered under half-closed eyelids. The room breathed silence and cold.

She had to be quick.

"Señor Gonzalez," she whispered urgently into his ear. "Señor Gonzalez? Hector? wake up." But he remained motionless, his chest rising and falling in a steady rhythm.

She tried again, her voice barely audible over the hum of machines. "Hector," she pleaded. The sedatives held him in their grip. Could she tear out the IV? What would happen if she did? Would he have some kind of reaction? And how could she get him out of there, even if she did wake him up? She didn't know.

She'd just summoned up enough courage to yank the needle out of the man's arm when she heard shuffling from outside and backed quickly into a corner near the door. A nurse she'd seen but never spoken to came in, went immediately to the gurney, put a stethoscope on his heart.

Larissa took the opportunity to try to slip out.

"Hey," the nurse said, startled. "What are you doing here?"

"Just changing linens," Larissa said, mumbling, flushed, looking at the ground. "I'm new here, I thought we were—"

"You don't need to worry about this room. Just the north side," the woman said.

"Oh, okay. Thanks." She scurried out. She couldn't shake off her despair. She would have to try again later.

Hours passed. She made her rounds, returned to the laundry facility, stuffed wet sheets into dryers.

That evening she tried again, but although she could get in the door to the surgical suite, she couldn't reach Gonzalez's room—too many people were about, and now the nurses' station was fully manned. She carried the pile of towels and left them in a vacant room.

When she went home that night, she stopped by the bank and withdrew $4,000 cash. She'd had to text Zippy ahead of time to contact the bank, but now the cash came through without a hitch.

She handed the money to Pilar, who counted it.

"You rich, *chica*?" Pilar said. "I didn't think you'd come through."

"This is everything I have," Larissa lied. "It's really important."

"All about the boyfriend, then?" Maria had told some of the other workers about Larissa's search.

Larissa nodded. "I have a real lead."

Pilar took her outside and showed her how to work the vehicle, how to lock and unlock the chains.

"Is there a helmet?" Larissa said, realizing that she'd never seen Pilar wearing one. She wondered where she could buy one with a visor that would hide her face.

Pilar, though, was nodding. "Yeah, but I don't use it." She showed her the helmet, stashed under the seat. It had a drop-down visor. Larissa exhaled.

That night she made a practice run on the motorcycle to the wellness center. The surgical center's lights were on, and people were bustling about. She strained to catch snippets of conversation from inside, but couldn't make anything out, except the low murmur of voices, and sometimes a burst of laughter. She wanted to go in, but nerves kept her out. It seemed far too risky—none of the laundry attendants worked at night, and her presence would be too obvious. So instead she shut the door and disappeared back into the night.

In the morning, she rode with Pilar on the motorcycle to the Center, and Pilar made a show of handing her the keys. Larissa spent the morning as usual.

When it was time for their rounds, Marta and Reyna told her to take up several extra piles of sheets. "They go through a lot of them," Marta said. "Always take more than you think you need."

The surgical center remained bustling—easily fifteen or twenty people were moving in and out of rooms. The air smelled cool but vaguely unpleasant. Marta gestured for Larissa to enter the second suite on the left, where the frail woman had been. She was sleeping, accompanied by the constant beep of monitors. Two people—relatives, Larissa supposed—sat in chairs nearby. They were speaking in English but stopped when she entered. She made a show of pulling out the bag of dirty linens, replacing them with fresh.

She felt sick. She knew what had happened, could feel it in her bones. Moments later, eavesdropping, it was all confirmed. The transplants had already occurred. Three of them—a heart and both kidneys. The frail woman in the bed had gotten Hector Gonzalez's heart.

A welter of emotion tightened around Larissa's own heart—sorrow, frustration, rage, and, strangely, gratitude, that the frail woman on the bed was still breathing, still had hope. But the vision of Hector Gonzalez's short, fat penis lying on his thigh; his regular breaths; his eyes glittering under half-closed lids—all of it made her want to scream or weep or vomit.

She could stand it no longer—she was willing to be caught, if only she could figure out what was going on.

In Hector Gonzalez's room, a body-shaped bag now lay on the gurney.

She didn't need to unzip it to know what was inside. But she unzipped it anyway, snapped several photos.

She was only in the room for an instant; then she was back in the corridor, taking the towels and the dirty laundry back to the laundry building. As soon as she dropped the laundry in front of the washing machine, she turned to Reyna. "I don't feel well," she said. "I've got to leave for the day."

"You can't leave now," Reyna said. "We haven't done the gym yet—and there's all these sheets to fold."

"I think I'm coming down with something," Larissa said. "I hope it's not COVID. But I feel really terrible. You want me to stay?"

Reyna glared at her. But in moments Larissa was out on the dusty road in front of the Center. She pulled Pilar's keys from around her neck, unlocked the motorcycle, and drove past the unmarked exit door to the surgical center, to a bend in the road. She pulled the motorcycle into the dusty underbrush and waited.

The jungle air was humid and noisy. Mosquitoes droned and parrots fluttered and fought. Several families of howler monkeys, tiny babies in tow, leaped from tree to tree, munching and shrieking as they went. Larissa was tempted to take out her phone but was worried about the battery, so just sat on a stump and waited. Vehicles came and went. Employees came in for the afternoon shift. Marta and Reyna walked out together. Pilar came out a few minutes later, looked for her motorcycle, and then headed down the road on foot.

Late that afternoon, Larissa's stomach was rumbling, and she was trying to figure out if she could get a pizza delivered to the middle of the jungle when a beat-up Hyundai rumbled up. It turned around and backed over to the side entrance of the surgical suite.

Larissa unlocked the moped, put on the helmet, dropped the visor, and readied herself.

No one was on the road as two men carried the body bag out, tossed it in the trunk, and drove off.

She took several photos, and then gave them a minute's head start before following. Thank goodness she'd planned ahead to rent the moped so she could take photos—gathering evidence to send back to the FBI.

36

ZIPPY

ON THE DRIVE BACK to Greenville, Zippy logged into each of Candace Watkins's bank accounts via the VPN. Carefully, methodically, he downloaded every transaction from every account from the time the accounts were created—almost eight years ago. He was worried that the bank wouldn't have accessible records that far back, but at last they caught a break.

Once he was home, he meticulously tracked every transfer in and out of each account.

It wasn't that hard. The same account was responsible for each deposit. Then, Candace transferred the monies into different accounts, all of which she'd also given Curtis and Zippy access to. Zippy would double-check those later—but they mattered less right now.

But the funds that went into Candace's account: those were simple. Every transaction had the same payment detail. Every transaction came from one account: Zephyr Processing International, Inc.

Zippy didn't recognize the name.

And then he discovered something else.

In the very first transaction, in Candace's original bank account, she was paid by Delta Services, Ltd., another company he had never heard of.

All the accounts that Zippy had had access to—that the FBI had gotten access to—had been shut down immediately after the FBI had raided the offices. And the FBI's forensic accountants had exhaustively delved into the web of those accounts.

But Zephyr and Delta weren't part of that mess. These were active, functioning accounts.

This was a good thing. If Zippy could get access to those accounts, that might lead him to the people who controlled them.

He spent the days that followed digging into whatever he could find about Zephyr Processing International, Inc., an international corporation registered in Delaware but based in the European Union. The EU had strict privacy laws, which would make research even more challenging. He meticulously examined the corporation's public records. It had been consistently filing its annual reports and maintaining its corporate documentation, but the company listed no officers or affiliated corporations.

Since he didn't have the tax documents, he needed to "pierce the corporate veil" in order to figure out who the shareholders or officers were. But that wasn't easy. He needed court orders, and those wouldn't be something he could get.

Without the FBI, he'd hit a dead end.

37

CURTIS

PERHAPS they could have just put all the documentation into a single file and emailed it off, but Curtis was leaving nothing to chance. He had been a musician for too long—and musicians, if nothing else, pay attention to the slightest nuance of tone, repeat over and over again a single phrase to get it right. And this, he vowed, he would get right.

When it was done, he, Larissa, and Zippy had assembled over two hundred written pages delineating everything that they knew; seventy-three photos of people working at the blood banks and at the Wellness Center in Nosara; close-ups of the license plates of the cars that drove Gael Hernandez and Juan Velazquez from Lifestream to Reagan National; photos of Hector Gonzalez's corpse; and video of two men hauling the corpse into the back of the Hyundai, driving to a crematorium several miles away.

Plus over two hundred pages of SCC filings, tax filings, and online corporate documents for the corporation that paid Candace Watkins.

They delineated it all—the blood banks, the blood donors, the plane ride, the drugging, the international clinics with the wealthy recipients, the disposal of the bodies.

Curtis reached out to the Marshals Service and asked to be in touch with Agent Theodora Slager.

After the usual series of complicated back-and-forths, they all joined a secure video call: Curtis, Larissa, Zippy, and Agent Slager.

When they were all assembled, and Teddi Slager's thumbnail-sized face appeared on their screens, Larissa started off. "Hey, Teddi, are you alone?"

Slager looked ostentatiously behind herself, made a show of looking under the table. "What do you think? And nice tan, by the way."

Zippy interrupted. "We got what you need to take these people down."

She was suddenly serious. "What are you talking about?"

"We figured things out on our own," Curtis said. "We figured out where the organs come from. And we found some more bank accounts."

"What do you mean, you found more bank accounts?"

Zippy explained about the accounts that paid Candace Watkins, although he didn't mention her by name. "These aren't accounts that you've seen before. So I'm betting T Block doesn't know we have them. They're live accounts that you can hopefully trace out."

"Do you have any evidence linking T Block directly?"

"No," Zippy admitted. "But you'll be able to do that once we send you everything."

"How did you get it?"

"It doesn't really matter how," Curtis said.

" 'It doesn't really matter how'? Of course it matters. If you've obtained the information illegally—"

Larissa ignored her, explained how blood banks found donors, how the facility in Costa Rica harvested them and disposed of the bodies.

"How did you *get* this information?" Slager asked again. "And you were in Costa Rica? That's violating the terms of WITSEC, isn't it?"

"We got permission ahead of time," Larissa said quickly.

"The bottom line is that we've put it all together for you," Curtis said. "We've given you so much more info, and we think we have a way—if you're careful and don't tip them off—to get to the ringleaders. You can't share this with your colleagues."

"You don't want me to share? Now you're dictating the terms of this investigation," Slager observed, icy.

"No, no," Larissa put in. "Curtis is just worried—we're all worried—that something in the FBI hasn't been right. This investigation has been going on for years, but it keeps stalling out. It seems like they're a step ahead of you. We're worried that maybe they're monitoring your progress somehow."

"T Block's probably paying people off," Zippy said. "That's how he operates. He bribes people. Always has."

"And you think—"

"We think it's a good idea to be extra careful, is all," Larissa said.

A pause. "Okay," Slager said. "Send me everything you have. I'll go through it personally." She gave them her email address.

"What if this email address is monitored?" Curtis asked.

Slager shook her head. "Just use it, okay?"

An hour later he emailed the documentation, and then sent a hard copy, insured, to Agent Theodora Slager. In the return address he put down his own name, Curtis Wilson, and a false address.

They'd delivered so much incriminating evidence showing crimes, the dead body of Hector Gonzalez, and so much more. They'd given the FBI absolutely everything they could. Now, at long last, *something* was sure to happen.

Curtis was so excited by the prospect of getting his life back that he couldn't fall asleep. He did fifty burpees and then lost count, making plans to call his former agent. He knew the program he wanted to perform—the Kabalevsky for starters. He was so close to getting it all back. He just had to wait a little bit longer.

And then he waited.

They all waited.

A week went by.

Then another.

They waited for the phone to ring. For a text. An email. Slager showing up unexpectedly. Which wasn't possible, since only the USMS knew their location, but still Curtis kept searching for Slager's long-familiar face.

More than anything as a distraction, they continued to work on *Dark Maestro*.

It took about a week to create each issue—and that was only because he already had something to work with. Now he worked his way tenaciously, laboriously, panel by panel, through each issue—all thirty-six of them.

He pushed Zippy to be edgier and more creative with the lyrics, steering clear of the swear words and the easy rhymes with "yeah" or "uh-huh." The wordplay had to be even more creative, with metaphor and alliteration; had to break into structured rhyme; had to have sharp punch lines for a memorable, sometimes funny, impact. The lyrics had to *shine*.

> *Look at all the enemies . . .*
> *That they've thrown before me . . .*
>
> *They bore me!*
>
> *And for that . . .*
> *I am the end of the story!*
>
> *No glory comes from this . . .*
> *This is practice!*
>
> *To a gymnast . . .*
> *This is backflips!*
>
> *Be amazed when my sound waves*
> *To pave ways*
> *For better days*
>
> *The future made*
> *With every gaze*
>
> *One swing alone . . .*
> *I'll cripple hell!*

Blue or red . . .
Pick a pill!

Fight this!
Or escape this!

The Menace to the menacing!
I am what the end will bring!

No penance goes unpunished
Cross them and you gotta pay!

I am Maestro!

Forever, ready to rock and roll
When you WALK! THIS! WAY!

Same for the graphics and animation. Although money was now getting tight—the Costa Rica trip and all the time spent in a Washington, D.C., parking garage really ate into their finances—he purchased new animation software and equipment to allow him even more interesting effects. He made sure the panels had a unified and cohesive look, so each was instantly unique, instantly recognizable as *Dark Maestro*.

Between each panel, the transitions became even more dynamic, one morphing into another seamlessly; he became adept at parallax scrolling to add depth and dimension, animating different layers of the background at varying speeds to create another sense of movement; focusing on the character animation, expressions, and gestures; tweaking new camera angles; and dozens of other effects that they'd used in the past.

And always, always, he was cutting and adapting and enhancing the music—experimenting with reverb; slowing down or speeding up tempos; adding countermelodies or combining two pieces together, pushing his vibrato and himself as far as possible in a blend of real instrument and electronic augmentation.

When each issue was finished, they'd all give it a final look together—and they often couldn't believe that they'd created such an incredible video comic book. It was as if another person, far more adept and talented, had done the work and they were just standing to one side, marveling.

Despite all this, though, the number of followers on his *Dark Maestro* channel stayed low. Usually under one hundred. In the beginning Curtis would glance repeatedly at the analytics, sometimes every few hours; but when the number refused to budge, he made a decision not to look.

Over the past few weeks, *Dark Maestro* had actually lost many followers. Curtis had put a notice on the channel alerting viewers that many of the early episodes were in the process of a makeover; and the response from his loyal group was outrage and disgust that he'd change what he'd already done, or frustration that they couldn't read more, or just general trolling about what a terrible person the anonymous *Dark Maestro* creator must be. He never responded to these comments.

Curtis was doing this for himself. This was being creative: not for the applause of an audience, or for the rush of a connection with fellow musicians. As with his life as a performing cellist, all of that had fallen away, and now there was just him and the music and the art and the burning desire to express himself. To tease out, visually and auditorily, his internal longing and frustration, the boredom of those endless days in the parking garage; or the frantic rush when a note was played just right, or when he followed a town car through city streets or eavesdropped on bugged conversations.

He'd just posted Issue no. 23—"In the Clutches of Villanova!"—when he glanced down at the follower numbers. He certainly hadn't looked for the past month or so. Which was why he was sure, for several minutes, that the 193,748 follower number couldn't possibly be correct. It was probably 193 and there'd been some kind of statistical glitch. He hoped the number would've been 748 but didn't hold out much hope.

Randomly, he clicked over to Issue no. 9: 207,449 views. Issue no. 8 had 241,003.

How could *Dark Maestro* have over 200,000 followers and Curtis not be aware of it? he texted Larissa, who responded an hour later. Your dad had the idea of doing trailer videos. You should talk to him.

He called Zippy. "What are you doing?!"

"Ha, you finally noticed, huh?" his dad said. "It's giving a real punch, ain't it?"

"How are you doing it?" Curtis repeated. He'd been standing in his living room, with all the equipment around him, but now grabbed his main tablet and headed outside.

"I was checking out some of the competition a few weeks back, and they all have trailers. Ten to thirty seconds. Didn't you know that?"

"Yeah, of course I know that. But that doesn't mean—"

"So I figured, what the hell, I'd make some."

"You don't know how to use the animation software. How could you—"

"Lynette helped."

"So let me get this straight," he said. By now he was thundering up the walkway to Zippy's townhouse. "You and she have been making video trailers and putting them up all over social media?"

"Pretty much," Zippy admitted. "And if you look at the pickup rates, you can see which ones are really effective. I did an analysis, and it's the shorter ones with the punchiest music and my simplest rhymes."

Curtis knocked on the door, and Zippy let him in. In minutes he was showing him the trailers: How he'd taken Issue no. 13 with Curtis's rendition of a Mendelssohn sonata and had focused on the sonata's development section, where Villanova waits for the Dark Maestro outside the stage door, and done a smash cut with a few of the fight scenes.

How, in Issue no. 27, where Dark Maestro pushes his Vidawaves to the max as Liszt's Hungarian Rhapsody No. 2 thunders around him, Villanova casts a new dark spell that nearly destroys our hero.

There were well over twenty trailers, all based on the revised *Dark Maestro* issues. Each was beautiful, clean, and riveting.

Curtis shook his head. "I wasn't doing this for anyone else anymore," he said. "I was just doing it for myself. For us."

"Well, we've got ourselves an audience," Zippy told him. "Maybe if we survive all this we can have a career in digital comic books. You can be the next Stan Lee."

"More like Tom DeFalco," Curtis said.

Larissa had reached out to Teddi Slager when they hadn't heard back after the first couple of weeks. A few moments later she'd received the response: *Hi. Yes, got it. Thanks. Back to you ASAP.*

But what did ASAP mean, Curtis kept asking. "As soon as possible," meaning "soon" or "as soon as we possibly can, which could be a while." They didn't know.

Another month passed. They created more videos, more issues. They had more than 500,000 followers.

In the meantime Curtis had set up a Google News alert for every permutation he could imagine to deal with the organ donation. From "kidney" to "organ" to "Candace Watkins." Every day he received hundreds, sometimes thousands, of alerts, and he'd diligently click on any link that seemed promising. Always, though, it was nothing.

Finally, more than four months after they delivered the materials to the FBI, when *DM* was up to 750,000 followers, he got a real hit, in *El Diario de Nosara.*

He used a translation app to read it in English.

In a shocking turn of events, our tranquil town of Nosara was rocked by a major organ trafficking bust. The Pura Vida Wellness Center, a seemingly innocuous establishment located just outside of town, was revealed to be the hub of a nefarious black market organ transfer operation. The scheme was led by Dr. Carlos Mendoza, a respected surgeon, and his team which included Dr. Ana Maria Vargas, an anesthesiologist, and Nurse Sofia Castillo.

The local Nosara police, headed by Inspector Juan Diego Ramirez and Detective Maria Fernanda Lopez, carried out the bust after months of careful investigation. A total of 14 people were arrested in connection with the case, sending shock waves through the community. The accused are currently awaiting trial as the investigation continues. We will provide updates as they are uncovered.

Elated, Curtis texted the article to Zippy and Larissa, and that night they celebrated.

Another week passed, and then a second.

They posted *DM* revised issues nos. 33 and 34 but kept waiting to hear from the FBI. Surely this was the start. Soon the Mexican facility would fall as well. Perhaps those busts didn't make the news.

But soon, surely, the news would break about what was happening in America.

Daily, hourly, Curtis was expecting to hear that the FBI had broken open a major case, that the ringleaders had been caught. Agent Slager would text and then show up, telling them that their country owed them majorly. A parade in their honor might be too much, so maybe just a medal ceremony?

Larissa reached out again to Slager, who this time didn't reply.

"That's weird," Curtis said. "Why wouldn't she at least write you back?"

"Maybe she's busy," Larissa said, shrugging, not convincing Curtis and not convincing herself. He was sure of it.

Their life in witness protection went on.

Dark Maestro was up to Issue no. 36, where the Bloodworx have gathered all of their minions and assembled all the enemies of Dark Maestro, united them in a single goal to take down our hero. They lure him to Madison Square Garden for a showdown of epic proportions.

They had 1.5 million followers now.

Hundreds of comments speculated on the cellist's identity. Most of them believed he was a famous concert cellist in disguise— Sheku Khanneh-Mason or Pablo Ferrández. Others decided that Yo-Yo Ma wanted to mix things up a bit.

And who was the rapper? Method Man? Big Boi? Killer Mike? J.O. Blanco? The voice distortion made it impossible to tell.

Until then the *Dark Maestro* story had run on a few Internet outlets, but when the BBC spent seven minutes covering it on their evening news program, everything busted loose.

By the next day, all the major outlets in the United States and internationally had picked it up. CNN and Al Jazeera concurrently aired a segment on the anonymous cellist who'd created a global sensation. Media pages like *NowThis* and Germany's *Der Spiegel* shared the clip across their platforms. Canada's CBC News and Australia's ABC network featured in-depth segments, amplifying the buzz. French media giant *Le Monde* published a feature piece, while Russia's broadcast network RT and Japan's NHK World replicated their own versions of the story. In just under twenty-four hours, the Dark Maestro rippled across global networks.

The attention to the YouTube channel and the requests coming through Curtis's filtered emails were staggering. Books, movies, action figures, other licensed products.

"This is insane," Zippy said. "This is seriously insane." They grinned at each other around the table, over pizza and champagne.

It was their last celebration.

And it was then, just after the toast, as Curtis wondered how they'd choose which action figure company to go with, that the knock on the door came. It could have been Beethoven's Fifth— dah-dah-dah-DUM.

The knock of fate.

Because after that, everything changed again.

38

LARISSA

LARISSA OPENED THE DOOR to find three U.S. marshals standing on their doorstep. Marshal Thomas had a laptop bag casually slung over his shoulder and carried a few folders under one arm. Two other agents whom Larissa had met in passing, Agent Sterling and Agent Frye, hovered behind him.

"Hey. This our check-in?" Larissa said, trying for lightness, even if her stomach had suddenly knotted. They never showed up this late, and never with these expressions. "Is something wrong?"

"Can we come in?" Marshal Thomas said. "Looks like you're all here. Good." He peered past her, where he must have seen Curtis and Zippy hovering, but Larissa didn't turn to look.

"Of course," she said, leaning to one side so they could pass.

She closed the door behind them.

"Well, folks," Marshal Thomas said—the word *folks* seemed a strange one to use, Larissa remembered later. "I'll get right to it. This is it. It's official. Effective immediately, you're out of the program for violating the terms of your agreement."

Zippy, apparently, hadn't heard correctly. "What? It's over? They got 'em? Was it T Block?"

"Oh, it's over," Thomas said. "For you guys. We're eliminating you from the WITSEC program. Multiple violations, but this Dark Magician thing takes the cake."

Larissa wanted to correct him—it was "Dark Maestro"—but realized that would give everything away.

"What Dark Magician?" Curtis asked, as if trying for innocence.

Thomas shot him a look. "It's pretty obvious that it's you. Superhero cellist? Blood-sucking villains? Come on."

"You can't prove anything," Curtis said.

"Look, kid," Thomas said, "it's over. You've violated the protocols too many times. And this one really is over the top."

Larissa expected Curtis to argue, but he just shrugged. She knew where he was coming from: she, too, was tired of hiding, tired of the prison of these identities, tired of these people babysitting her life. Her time in Costa Rica had been a new taste of freedom.

Zippy spoke first. "So what happens to us?"

"Officially, you sign these forms, and you're on your own. The U.S. government formally withdraws its protection of you. As of"—he glanced at his watch—"five minutes from now, you will be free from the program. No more check-ins, no more monitoring. You can pursue whatever course of action you'd like."

No one spoke, and after a moment Thomas went on: "You've not only repeatedly endangered yourselves but have jeopardized the entire structure and security of the program. We can't continue providing our service or maintaining your protective identities. You can keep this identity or return to your previous ones—I don't even know your original names, but you can take those back too, if you want."

"What about T Block?" Zippy said.

"Who's T Block?"

"What about the people who are hunting us?" Zippy said.

"What about them?" Thomas said. "I don't have a clue."

"So they can come after us?" Larissa said.

Thomas shrugged. "I would imagine they can. The U.S. government isn't going to be hiding you anymore."

"But—"

"But you should have thought about this ahead of time," Agent Frye cut her off. He was a small, narrow-faced man who always looked disappointed in them. "It looks like the Dark Maestro pages have been functional for well over a year. You've had a lot of time to think this through."

Agent Thomas said, frustration palpable, "We tried so hard for you. Our jobs are to keep you all safe and we *want* to keep you safe. Don't you get that? But you just thumbed your nose up at all we were trying to do. At us."

"That's not true," Zippy put in. "We really appreciate everything—"

"Yeah, I can tell," Thomas said, cutting him off again. Agent Frye stifled a laugh. "Just so you know, we've spent the past day being raked over the coals by our higher-ups. It's gone all the way to the top. We should be put on leave and may lose our jobs over this." He sucked in a breath, clearly trying to calm himself.

Larissa was feeling sick. The whole world had just gone sideways. They were so close—maybe Teddi Slager had pinned down the bad guys?

"That's it. I hope the Dark Maestro was worth it," Marshal Sterling put in. "You were warned. Repeatedly. Your little stunt in Costa Rica. Wherever you were the past few months, when you were supposed to be here. All the unauthorized electronics." She shook her head.

"What are we supposed to do now?" Larissa asked shakily.

"Whatever you want." Thomas said, "It's out of our hands. Our protective services are hereby terminated. I need your signatures on these forms."

"Damn," Zippy said. "You guys can't just drop us."

Marshal Thomas didn't say a word. Instead, he extended a pen to Zippy.

Zippy spent the next twenty minutes reading the fine print. But it all said the same thing. That the U.S. Marshals Service was absolving itself from the responsibility of their safety. He signed, passed the pen to Larissa. She followed his lead.

When Curtis got the pen, he said, "So we're free now. This could be a good thing."

Larissa kicked him under the table.

"For your sake I sure hope so," Marshal Thomas said.

No one spoke.

And then it was done. The forms were signed. Copies for each of them. Marshal Frye gathered them up, and the three marshals filed toward the door.

"I wish you guys the best of luck," Marshal Thomas said.

And with that, their life in witness protection came to an end.

For the next half hour, everything was chaos. Larissa kept wanting to cry but wouldn't allow herself. Curtis paced from one side of the living room to the other. Zippy sat stunned, staring down at the table.

They'd been so careful—and after all, nobody except the USMS realized that they were Dark Maestro. Or at least it seemed so—until the bad guys busted down the doors and shot them dead in their beds. But they'd taken enormous precautions, and didn't even have the chance to plead their case with the Marshals Service.

More important, they were on their own. It was as if they were asleep, naked, in their beds, and WITSEC suddenly yanked its protective blanket off them. Now they blinked in the light of the unknown number of eyes staring malevolently down at them.

One thing was clear: they needed to get out. Without the USMS behind them, they didn't want to stay in this place. Curtis was more and more convinced that the reason the FBI investigation had stalled was that someone at the FBI had put roadblocks up internally—and now that same person, or people, could more easily track them down.

They all came up with different ideas of where to go, what to do; how to possibly change their names, how to hide beneath the radar. With *Dark Maestro* taking off, Curtis argued, couldn't they pay for a new identity? Maybe they could just buy an island and man it with machine guns, so when T Block tried to find them, they'd cut him down on the beach.

"I'm calling Teddi," Larissa said. "She should know about this."

"She probably already does," Zippy said.

Larissa was opening her laptop, typing in the email address that Slager had given them.

Dear Teddi,

Not sure if you heard but they've just kicked us out of WITSEC. Can you call asap?

L

Not five minutes later, Larissa's phone rang. "I can't believe you guys," Slager said.

Larissa put her on speakerphone. "So you heard."

"That you got kicked out of WITSEC? That you've created this huge channel that can identify you, that you've put yourselves and countless other people in danger? Uh, yeah. I heard."

"Yeah," Larissa said. "We messed up, but we're hoping you'll have some good news. Have you caught them yet?"

Zippy leaned over the phone. "We're trying to explore our options, and we want to know how much danger we could be in."

Silence on the other end. Then Agent Slager said slowly, "No, we haven't caught them."

"Are you close at least?" Curtis asked.

Larissa held her breath, praying.

"You all need to be extra careful. You're in a vulnerable position."

"Why?" Zippy asked.

"Since you sent me that info, there's a lot that's been going on over here."

"Like what?" Curtis asked.

"Can you prove it's T Block or not?" Zippy said.

Curtis asked, "And if you know it's him, how long before he's arrested?"

Silence.

"Teddi, please." Larissa pleaded.

A beat.

"You were right," Teddi said. "I'm concerned that this investigation has been compromised."

"What do you mean," Curtis asked.

Another beat. "I strongly suspect that there are forces that are working overtime to derail the case."

"It's T Block, I know it," Zippy said.

"I can't tell you that," Slager said. "I just need to tell you to be careful—"

"Teddi," Larissa said, "we've been kicked out of the program. You just told us to run for our lives. The least you can do is to tell us what's going on."

Slager was speaking over her. "—and if everything goes according to plan, we have a couple of suspects who should be behind bars very shortly."

"And what if everything doesn't go according to plan?" Curtis asked. "What if they make bail and are on the street? It sure doesn't seem like anything's been going the way it's supposed to."

"Then just watch your back," she said. "I can help you find new identities. I know some people."

"Teddi, you've got to be straight with us," Larissa said. "We'll do our best to hide. But please tell us what you know."

The silence this time stretched out for way too long. They all eyed each other, but none spoke. Larissa could almost feel Teddi Slager's mind weighing the consequences of divulging details of an active investigation.

"If your investigation is already compromised, they might get away," Zippy said at last.

That seemed to move the needle. Slager said, "You're right. It's T Block and his brother."

"I knew it. I fuckin' knew it!" Zippy said.

"His brother?" Curtis asked, talking over his father. "The rich one? The one out in Virginia?"

"I don't think he has any others," Slager told him.

"Why didn't you look into him before?" Zippy said. "I gave you his name."

"I spent summers out at his farm," Curtis said. "When I was little. They used to invite me out there."

"We did look into him," Teddi Slager said. "We couldn't make a connection."

"So what you're saying," Zippy said urgently, "is that we need to get out of here. Now."

"I think you should," Teddi said. "Australia's nice this time of the year. Go Down Under for a couple of months. Get out of the country. Or just lay low. I'll be in touch when we've got him."

Finally they hung up.

As soon as Slager had disconnected from the line, Curtis said, "If the FBI is compromised, who knows who else is? We've got to get out of here on our own. I don't trust anybody. We can only rely on ourselves."

Zippy said, "We don't have the money. We don't have the connections. We can't create new identities on our own. We can't whip up new driver's licenses or Social Security numbers."

"What about Teddi's contact?" Larissa said.

"If there's a mole in the FBI, do you really want to trust them?" Zippy asked her.

Curtis was standing. "We've got to get out of here."

"How?" Larissa said. "They'll know our cars."

"We'll take the bus." Zippy said.

"The bus? That's too slow and risky. They'll catch us for sure." Curtis said.

"Speed isn't a factor. We need to hide under the radar. We can't use our IDs or credit cards. We have to pay cash and stay low profile." Zippy said. They'd all prepared for this kind of eventuality: the marshals had told them to keep large chunks of cash, since bank accounts were more unwieldy and easier to track. Together they had close to $20,000 saved from the past few years.

Larissa packed some clothes and her *Dark Maestro* laptop and opened the front door. She led them out of the apartment and locked the door behind her. She'd probably never see the place again.

They ran down the stairs and out of the building. Zippy was dialing a cab company, and they waited around the corner for it to come.

In the meantime Curtis had ducked back into his townhouse, grabbed his tablet and the most powerful laptop, and wiped the others clean. He stared at the cello for a few long moments, debating on whether he could take it. But hauling around an instrument that big would make him too noticeable.

He took one last look at the cello, figuring he'd never see it again, stashed it in a closet, and headed out.

The cab dropped them twenty minutes later at the bus station. Larissa paid the driver in cash.

The bus left for Charlotte ten minutes later, and Greenville faded away. Over the next four hours, they didn't talk much. They tried to sleep in the long night that would be the first of their nights of homelessness.

In Charlotte they took a cab to South End, a charming area of the city with diners, restaurants, antique shops and secondhand stores. They sat, agonizingly, for breakfast, sipping coffee and eating toast and pancakes that none of them were hungry for, waiting for the shops to open.

As soon as ten a.m. hit, they fanned out, each into different junk stores, searching. Within moments Zippy texted the other two: he'd found it. Three dollars.

Then they flagged down another cab. Zippy had found an ad on Craigslist for a used car, a 2010 Honda Odyssey, white, in okay condition. The seller was asking for $6,500, cash only.

Fifteen minutes later they were the new owners of the vehicle. Zippy triumphantly screwed on the old North Carolina license plate he'd found in the junk shop.

Moments later, Curtis at the wheel, they headed west, into the Appalachians. They'd find a cheap motel, out of the way, that took cash.

And there they'd figure out their next moves.

One thing that they all were adamant about: they'd had enough. Had enough of sneaking around. Of the series of names that weren't theirs, of pasts that blurred into memories that other people invented for them.

They were taking back their lives.

Part 5

THE DARK MAESTRO
ATTACKS

39

ZIPPY

AT FIRST, they just drove. Took 95 north to Durham, then headed west into the Blue Ridge, that first night passing out in a motel that took cash and stank of french fries, cigarette smoke, and pungent floor cleaner.

Meanwhile, all that day, and on to the next, they argued over what to do. They could take their latest passports, drift up to Canada; or jump on a boat to the Caribbean; or charter a plane to the Pacific islands. Curtis could serenade sea anemones and dying coral reefs.

Constantly on the move, they drifted up and down the highway, often sleeping in the van, in parking lots or truck stops with an interstate blurring and roaring beside them. After the initial terror had faded to the quiet ache of boredom, they plotted one ridiculous idea after another. They tried out scenario after scenario. *What if T Block did this, and Larissa did that? What if Curtis tried to go here but this happened?* They threw out every option imaginable, no matter how harebrained or dangerous.

All through the second day and on into the third, as they spun into Tennessee and then Kentucky, they concocted fantastic ideas, one more elaborate than the next, and shot each one down. Curtis's invariably involved masks and caped crusaders. Larissa preferred stealth and bribery. Zippy calculated the odds, thought every plan had too low a success rate. They needed to do something that they could survive—otherwise what was the point?

In the meantime, they heard nothing further from Teddi Slager— and the longer the silence lasted, the more urgent their mission became. The FBI hadn't succeeded in taking down T Block or his brother. Which meant they were still out there. Which meant that Zippy, Larissa, and Curtis were exposed targets.

Meanwhile Zippy let Larissa and Curtis do most of the driving. It was taking them forever to get anywhere, because they were all driving like someone's grandmother, terrified that the cops would pull them over for a minor driving infraction.

Zippy kept his new phone plugged in and searched, endlessly, anything he could find about T Block. The mentions were surprisingly few, and all were ones that Zippy had seen long before: T Block with this senator; T Block appearing at this gallery opening; T Block's name listed at a charity event for the Building Museum.

He stumbled on a photo he'd seen many times before, this from *Middleburg Life*—what seemed like a local magazine for the horsey set out in Virginia. T Block stared out of a grainy photo, one of a dozen in a spread of self-satisfied people holding wineglasses and looking both serious and benevolent. A charity event that T Block's brother hosted every year in the summer.

T Block's brother, the very wealthy doctor.

"Hey," Zippy said aloud about an hour into Kentucky that afternoon, "what do you remember about the Lyric Virtuosity Prize?"

40

CURTIS

THE LONGER they were on the road, the more feasible—the more concrete—the crazy-ass plan became.

Daily, hourly, they tried to talk each other out of it. "You don't have to do this, you know that, right? Just drive out to Kansas and hunker down."

"And do what? Sit around waiting for somebody to come up the driveway?"

"They might never show up. Maybe they've forgotten us."

"And maybe they will. Or maybe that's all they're doing, is trying to find us. You want to wait around and find out?"

As time passed they grew more and more committed to the plan, more unified with each other.

Got your back.

All the time.

They used the Bowling Green Public Library and burner phones to search the Internet. They drove three hours east to Norfolk to try on uniforms. They paid cash for zip ties at one Lowe's and duct tape in a Home Depot four hours away. Off the Internet they bought chloroform and stun guns and tasers.

And they waited. For the last week in May.

For the annual Lyric Virtuosity Prize Awards Ceremony, to be held that year—as it was most years—at Dr. Rodney Jenkins's exclusive Middleburg estate.

To keep from going crazy, they spent hours working on *Dark Maestro*. Now they were planning the special and maybe final issue of *Dark Maestro:* no. 39, "All Shall Be Revealed!"

Their fan base just kept growing. Some issues had over ten million hits.

Zippy kept thinking that if they lived through the next few weeks, he'd have to start monetizing their success. Usually several times a day Curtis would receive merchandising offers ranging from Dark Maestro or Mr. Scissors T-shirts to limited-edition vinyl records with the *Dark Maestro* music—especially the Fauré *Pavane* and the Saint-Saëns Cello Concerto no. 1, which had developed their own minor memes. The offers for collectible action figures really revved Curtis up. Film and television production companies bombarded them.

Curtis had not responded to anyone. "Let's see if we can make it out of this alive first," he told Zippy and Larissa.

Part of what it meant to lose your identity, your name, and all that held you to society was that now it seemed easier to contemplate your own death. On some deep level that he never discussed, Curtis didn't expect to make it through what would come next.

41

LARISSA

ONE SUNDAY MORNING in early May, after six weeks wandering around the backroads of the South and the mid-Atlantic, Larissa was shopping in a Walmart Supercenter when the realization hit her.

They'd gone to Walmart because they all needed basic toiletries: deodorant, soap, detergent for the laundromat, aspirin. She needed a new toothbrush, and Zippy needed new underwear. They could shop for food, too, at this enormous store that stretched out seemingly forever, with aisle after aisle of things that other people could purchase and take back to their homes.

They'd just gone down aisle 8, past plastic hangers and stacks of storage containers, when they passed another family coming toward them. They, too, were Black, but this family was dressed as if heading to church: the young husband wearing khakis and a plaid button-down shirt, ironed and starched; the wife, in a dark green jumpsuit, searching for something in her purse; and a teenage boy, also in khakis, in a plaid shirt similar to the father's. Larissa wondered if the father and son were trying to dress like twins. They seemed to have stepped off a billboard for Happy Family.

As they passed, the father stared off down the aisle; and the wife, still looking in her purse, was saying to the son: "Maybe after, okay? We'll ask them." The eyes of the family slid away, as if pulled on a string in some other direction.

Even before they drew abreast, Larissa put her head down, stared at the shopping cart, also ignoring them. Resentment, unexpected and scalding, seethed through her. Why did these people have everything she should have had? There's no way the wife cared as much as Larissa did, no way the husband worked as hard as Zippy; no way the son was as smart or as ambitious as Curtis. They didn't have a clue what it meant to struggle.

Everything was luck—the chance collision of atoms, zooming around and bouncing randomly off each other, zipping off in another direction. Sometimes they hit one way and the board lit up: Happy Family, here we are.

Other times they spun off in different directions, and the family was on the run, was broken, damaged beyond hope.

Given all the broken and damaged people she worked with in her life, Larissa often tried to make herself think that there was a higher power at work: that there was a *reason* that her atoms dumped her into the projects, when all she'd really wanted was to have a nice life in some quiet suburb somewhere. But after Patrice's death she no longer believed in higher powers, no longer thought that some nonsensical "reason" could account for all their hurt and loss.

Because it was unfair. No one promised fairness, and Larissa felt like an idiot, thinking that after all she'd witnessed in other people's lives some grand scorecard out there would level the playing field and make things "fair." It didn't matter that Curtis was a musical genius. That Zippy acted from the best of intentions. None of it mattered. Because their atoms had zoomed off into some other direction, some place where Happy Family wasn't an option for them.

And this Happy Family in aisle 8 sailed through life, not acknowledging them. As if Zippy, Larissa, and Curtis weren't worthy of being noticed.

It was a moment that rocked her back, literally, on her heels; she had to clutch the enormous Walmart shopping cart to keep her balance.

In the eyes of this family, she didn't exist. She wasn't worthy of existing.

Larissa knew this was only in her own head; but a similar realization hit Zippy and Curtis, as well, in those weeks after they fled

Greenville. They'd lost some essential part of what tied them to the world, to society, to the regular ways that normal people—like that churchgoing family—lived.

This is what people don't tell you about grief and loss: that it detaches you from everything you've known before. That in some dark, terrible way, it's freeing. Larissa had lost her family when she left D.C., lost Patrice in Arizona, and these were difficult and heartbreaking things to wrap her head around. She mourned them, she missed them.

But, separate and apart from that grief—not lessening it, not adding to it—was the sense that the ties that once bound her were now severed and she was able to act differently, able to see differently, now that they were gone. The chains that bound the church family to their nice little community—their Dodge minivan (Larissa could envision it: silver, a couple years old, with a scratch on one panel that the wife had made when backing too close to a light pole); their neat-as-a-pin little house with the lawn that the boy, complaining, would be mowing that afternoon; the PTAs and the Rotary Clubs and the baseball teams—all of that defined them.

Larissa had no more definition. Her family had slid between all of those ties, disappeared into a bland world of Walmart parking lots and forgettable motels that took cash. Nobody spoke to them, and they spoke to nobody.

For years they'd been on the run, pretending to be someone else. For years they'd resented how powerless they felt—how they had to go along with what prison wanted, or their bosses wanted, or what WITSEC wanted. Now they no longer had to follow orders. They no longer had to pretend. They could just be themselves or invent what they wanted their new selves to be.

And in that untethered world, they formulated a plan. A plan that a few weeks ago they could never have imagined attempting.

42

———

ZIPPY

FINALLY it was the night before the Lyric Virtuosity Prize Awards Ceremony, to be hosted as usual on Dr. Rodney Jenkins's Middleburg estate.

Zippy, Larissa, and Curtis returned to a motel in Annandale, Virginia—they'd been there several times, since it took cash, didn't ask for ID, and was less grimy than a few they'd stayed at in D.C. They showered and slept in the sagging cigarette-stained-but-real bed. They worried over what they didn't know, over what Curtis, especially, had forgotten in the past ten years since he'd been to Dr. Jenkins's estate. They watched YouTube videos of the award winners, followed social media of the contestants.

They double-checked their contingency plans: made sure the uniforms fit, checked that the vases they bought in Richmond would match the vases already on the award ceremony tables.

And they worked on the next special issues of *Dark Maestro*, where they would post the names and particulars of each Bloodworx member—the leader, Dr. Rodney Jenkins; his equally diabolical brother, Anthony "T Block" Jenkins; and all of the others—murderers who were killing for money in poor neighborhoods across America, preying on the homeless, the illegal immigrants, the destitute, the hopeless. As Zippy watched, Curtis tweaked the animation and sound. Larissa leaned over his shoulder, offered advice—"Can you make the face a little bigger? What about brightening up the left-hand corner?"

In the meantime, ten million sets of eyes waited for the next issues to drop.

Only if the plan worked.

Now Zippy obsessively checked and rechecked the duffle bag that held most of their supplies, the unobtrusive packs that would hide the rest of their gear if Larissa's first piece didn't go according to plan.

They'd all tried, over and over, every day, to anticipate every eventuality, but now Zippy kept thinking—was certain—that they'd forgotten something.

No one slept well, but by ten o'clock that morning they all showered again and checked out, went out for breakfast a few miles down the road. They ducked into the Manassas Public Library, spent a few hours surfing the web for any last-minute mentions or photographs of the Lyric Virtuosity Prize.

Zippy sat and brooded and worried. He couldn't distract himself with lyrics—he couldn't rap those until after tonight. Until after they knew the truth. Tomorrow—please God, if they lived long enough—they'd harness the power of *Dark Maestro* and let the world know about the Bloodworx.

43

CURTIS

IN THE SPECIAL ISSUE *Dark Maestro*, no. 39, Dark Maestro speaks directly to the reader, explaining that the Bloodworx are real. They target the homeless, the illegals, the forgotten. Dark Maestro has employed all of his detective skills to track down a missing man to a surgical center in Costa Rica, which was killing these people and harvesting their organs in an evil black-market scheme. Despite treacherous obstacles, Dark Maestro has gathered information necessary to plan a final strike against the Bloodworx network before more innocents die.

Deviously, the Dark Maestro has managed to learn the secret identities of the Bloodworx masterminds. These masterminds exist in the real world, and they are doing horrific things.

44

LARISSA

THE DAY OF THE GALA finally arrived.

The Thursday before, Larissa had cut her hair short and had dyed it blond, and now she wished she'd done this years ago. It was easy to care for and gave her neck a new elegance. It also made her face longer and her lips fuller. When she put on thick-rimmed glasses, Zippy told her that she looked both beautiful and forbidding.

"Smile a lot," Zippy said. "You look real nice when you smile."

"I'll smile constantly," she told him.

For the past week, they'd staked out Tedesco's Catering Company, photographing the employees as they came and went, tracking them on social media, and a couple times even crashing a party to take better photographs. They stayed well out of the way of the catering staff.

Curtis was a whiz at using the search engines to identify their faces; and from there, Larissa and Zippy would spend hours trolling social media feeds to learn as much as they could about the catering employees.

They'd zeroed in on three: Jaime Hartley, a college student who worked at Tedesco's and pulled double duty as a barista at a local coffee shop; Stella Bennett, an aspiring actress and part-time caterer; and—their best shot—Sharifa McCord, a single mom with two kids.

Sharifa had a hungriness and a desperation to her. She was small and wiry, with tattoos braiding her arms and up her neck. In many photos she'd dyed her hair blue or green, but this week it was a violent, unreal yellow tinted with orange and pink. Larissa decided to forgo the pink, but tried to get the same yellows and orange. Sharifa lived with her two kids in a two-bedroom apartment in Northeast, behind a Safeway, and was often early to work. She needed this job.

"You ready?" Zippy asked Larissa now.

"Will you stop already?" Larissa said. "Of course I'm ready." But she felt in her purse one more time, when he wasn't looking. The thick wad of bills pressed back reassuringly.

As usual, Sharifa popped out of the number 6 bus half an hour before her shift started. And, also as usual, she stopped at the coffee shop on her way. *Medium latte, two sugars,* Larissa whispered.

Zippy overheard her. "You got this."

"Here we go," she said. She leaned over and gave them both quick kisses. Who knew when she'd see them again?

It wasn't worth thinking about. Focus on the present. "I got this," she repeated as she climbed out of the car, slamming the door harder than she'd intended.

She didn't look back.

Three minutes later, Larissa stood in line behind Sharifa, swallowing her nervousness. This was nothing, she told herself, thinking about Costa Rica, about the blood banks. She could do this. "Excuse me," she said aloud, "don't you work for Tedesco's?"

Sharifa turned around, suspicion brightening her face.

"I thought I recognized you," Larissa said, remembering to smile, smile, smile. "I met you at that event a couple months ago over in Northwest? The embassy? You don't remember me? We were talking over by the doors, and you were serving and I was asking you how I could get in on this gig?" Larissa was talking too much, she knew, but the chattering seemed to allay suspicion. "I'm the actress, remember? It's really great to run into you because I really need to get some experience really quick. I love the new hair color, by the way!"

"Excuse me? Do I know you?" Sharifa seemed wary, but the distrust had lessened.

"Debbie. Debbie Howard. Remember me?"

Sharifa shook her head. "I guess I meet so many people—"

"We met at the French embassy, remember? I'm taking an acting class. Method acting. I'm auditioning for this play about a caterer, and I really want it, you know? I need some real-life experience. I have been agonizing about this for weeks. I can't believe I'm running into you again."

"Yeah," Sharifa said warily. "Nice to see you too." She had gotten her coffee and was moving toward the doors.

Larissa moved to keep up. "I can't believe I found you here. I know this sounds crazy, but I got a business proposition. I need an edge at this next audition. I really want that part. Can you get me a catering gig? Just a couple of nights?"

"We're completely full at Tedesco's. We already got all the standbys for tonight. Sorry."

"How about if I take your place? Girl, I will pay you. You call in sick and say your cousin is going to cover your shift."

"You're tripping," Sharifa said.

"No," Larissa said, "Really. I need some help."

"I'm sure you can find a catering job someplace else. There's a bunch of caterers in this city."

"I know, but I've tried every place I can think of," Larissa said. "No one will take me on for just a few shifts, and this audition is coming up quick. How about if I pay you? How much do you make?"

"I ain't telling you how much I make!"

"Okay, okay, you're right. My bad. How about if I give you a thousand dollars?"

Sharifa looked at her. "You for real?"

"Yeah, for real."

"I'll do it for twenty-five hundred."

"Seriously? All right, all right, that works," Larissa said.

"You ever catered before? 'Cause I can't have you taking my place if you don't know what's going on. I'm a good employee, and I ain't never called in sick. I can't risk my job for twenty-five hundred."

"Yeah, I used to wait tables. And I'm a quick study." She tried to give this craziness a little more color, make it a little more believable, but she didn't know if she was trying too hard. "I really want to do well in this play, you know? It could be my big break."

Sharifa licked her lips. "You have the money?"

"Girl, yeah," Larissa said.

"I think I just came down with COVID," Sharifa said slowly. "You free tonight to replace me?"

45

ZIPPY

THE PLAN was working—at least it was starting to.

Larissa had gotten into Tedesco's Catering. Now there was no need to break out the contingency plan in which both Zippy and Larissa would sneak into the party wearing the catering uniforms she'd so diligently assembled: now only one of them was sneaking in—Zippy.

Zippy and Curtis left her in D.C. and drove out into the rolling hills of the Virginia Hunt Country.

Twenty years had passed since Zippy had driven down these roads, but not much had changed. Except for Zippy himself. The first time, he'd been apprehensive and proud, in the back of a town car with his pint-sized son and the enormous cello hulking in the trunk. They'd been wearing tailored suits that T Block had given them. Eventually they almost—not quite, but almost—got used to the feelings of privilege, if only for those rarefied weekends. They'd been to the estate many times afterward—probably two or three times every summer for several years. Now Zippy was a fugitive, a thief, a snitch. He wondered if he'd ever respect himself again.

The highway spooled out past shopping malls and developments until they crossed the Bull Run Mountains: dusky blue hills that separated the middle-class suburbs from the wealthy estates as neatly as a knife carving a cake.

They left the highway, slid onto asphalt roads smooth as whiskey. Zippy wished he had a whiskey right now.

Neither of them spoke. They were both in their own heads. As the countryside scrolled by, Zippy was letting go of the last of his regrets—the "I wish I had"s and "If only"s. A dull hum set up in the back of his head: nerves and adrenaline pumped a weightless giddiness through him. He couldn't believe that they were about to do this, and yet had never felt more present in his body. He felt like he could actually count each ridge of his fingerprints.

They had driven this way two weeks ago to scout out the terrain, so now Curtis took the turns smoothly and with no hesitation. To either side, beautifully manicured stone walls alternated with four-board fences. Horses grazed, coats gleaming in the late-afternoon sun.

The estates had names like Possum Hollow, Bittersweet, Puddleby, Locust Lane. Many had gatehouses. Curtis, after coming to this area for so many years, had long ago learned much about the predictable behavior of the wealthy. They were all counting on this knowledge now.

Privilege itself was the first barrier they had to overcome. Zippy had been surprised to learn that most of these estates didn't have security cameras or guards or insurmountable fences to keep out the unworthy: they didn't need to. They relied on POSTED: NO TRESPASSING signs, not private security companies, and that usually was enough. Most casual passersby would never dream of stopping along the manicured berms, of scaling the four-foot-high dry-stack stone walls. This world already felt impenetrable. Locked behind so much money and privilege that a casual thief had no hope of ever getting inside.

A handful of estates, however, took security more seriously. Cameras watched unobtrusively from freshly painted fence posts, peered out from the boughs of two-hundred-year-old oak trees. Guards rotated in and out of gatehouses.

Dr. Rodney's house was one of these.

Curtis turned left, down the dirt road that led to Dr. Rodney's farm. A quarter of a mile from the turn-in, a line of cars had queued up. Barely slowing, Curtis sailed beyond them, past two men with clipboards checking out each vehicle and then waving it through.

They cruised the driveway and forced themselves not to look at the guards or the cameras or the guests. Zippy barely glimpsed the tall wrought-iron gates, now open, and beyond them the long lane of sycamores that dipped out of sight and led to Dr. Rodney's house.

Curtis followed the lane for another quarter of a mile. Then he turned down another dirt road, and then another. They reached the break in the trees that they'd found on their last visit and turned into another grass-covered path. He parked, shut off the car. They got out and stretched.

According to Google Maps and Curtis's memory, they were directly behind Dr. Rodney's estate.

Along the main road, cameras stared down from the gate posts and along the fence line, but that was it. It was mostly for show. Meanwhile, webs of paths and bridle trails connected all the big farms in the area, and none of these were ever monitored. Most of the land was undeveloped woods or rolling pastures where you could ride your horse for hours without crossing an asphalt road: this was the Virginia Hunt Country.

Every summer Curtis would wander those paths with Trishelle, Lyndsay, Ralph, and the other kids, on the way to swimming holes or berry picking or abandoned cabins in the woods.

Zippy sure hoped that Curtis still remembered the way to Dr. Rodney's.

At a gas station along the way, Zippy and Curtis had each changed into their outfits.

They'd both grown facial hair—Zippy a sparse mustache that partially covered his mouth, and Curtis a thick bushy beard. Zippy had let his hair grow long so it curled around his forehead and eyes, while Curtis had shaved his head. Now Curtis's eyes were enormous under thick eyebrows. He didn't look like Zippy's son anymore.

Zippy was wearing Larissa's best approximation of a Tedesco's catering uniform. She had been concerned that the caterers would change their outfits for this event—what if they wore black this year? What if blue? "Stop worrying," Zippy had told her. "It's always white."

She had texted him half an hour ago from inside the Tedesco's kitchens: it was white.

So now he just had to worry about everything else. About the security, about Curtis's memory. And about the rest of the plan.

Ludicrous was the word that slid into his head then: this entire situation, their entire idea. Ludicrous.

There was no way they could pull this off.

There was no way they could survive this night.

The lush Virginia air, uncaring, encircled them. The sweetness of honeysuckle and wild rose were almost a color they could feel pressing against their cheeks. Overcautious, Zippy tried to close the van's sliding door as quietly as he could, but the sound echoed. For a moment the buzz of insects stopped, as if they were being observed, then started up again.

From the back of the van, Zippy pulled out one of two silver vases with an enormous display of ferns and flowers nodding and bobbing agreeably. They hoped these would serve as enough of a disguise to get him into the party, even though the original flower vases would have been set out long before. Still, parties always need more flowers, Larissa had argued. Zippy had hoped she was right. *What a dumb idea*, he thought now. Meanwhile, with no hesitation, Curtis slung his tuxedo jacket over his massive shoulders and headed up a trail marked by horse hooves.

Curtis, in black tie, would be a guest, rather than a caterer. They worried that his name wouldn't be on any guest list, but in reality who checked a guest list from inside the event? "You coming?" he called back to Zippy.

Zippy had no choice except to follow. "You sure this is right?" he asked him, almost jogging to keep up. Curtis cast a withering look back and continued on, massive shoulders bunching the black satin. The path disappeared into the trees.

For the next twenty minutes, Curtis paused only a few times, looking and listening. Zippy was amazed that he could remember so clearly a path he'd taken only a handful of times twenty years before; and then in the same breath, not amazed at all. For a kid from the projects, no wonder every step had been seared into his memory.

They crested a rise and almost immediately party sounds, distant, drifted up to meet them.

They'd found it. They'd taken the first tiny step forward. Zippy didn't know whether to be relieved or terrified.

In a few moments, the trees thinned and ended. Before them lay the stables and lush back lawn of Sycamore Hill. The vast stone house lay dead center in a small valley. To one side, near the pool, an enormous tent glowed, lit from within. On the other side, a warren of formal gardens surrounded a gazebo where yet more musicians played. Partygoers in long gowns and tuxedos drifted in the soft evening air, not quite real.

They cautiously poked their heads around the trees to study the layout below. They'd have to traverse a small patch of lawn before they could lose themselves behind the tent; and from the tent they could make it to the house's back doors.

Unless someone saw them leaving the trees.

Unless someone realized that Curtis wasn't a guest, or that Zippy wasn't part of the catering company.

Unless someone recognized one, or all, of them.

There were already too many "unlesses." This was a mistake. Fear clawed at Zippy now, and again the word *ludicrous*. How stupid, how ridiculous, this plan was! He wanted to grab his son, drag him back the way they'd come.

He came abreast of Curtis, still behind the trees, and leaned in to say something, but Curtis, seeing him, grinned and gave him a thumbs-up. Just as Zippy was hissing, "Hey, hold up a second, I was thinking—", he headed out, striding across the lawn, skirting the back retaining walls of the stables and disappearing around the corner of the tent. He was confident, his shoes shining in the light. Even Zippy thought he belonged. Still, Zippy waited, expecting a shout to ring up, a security guard to collar him, but the trees continued sighing in the evening light, and the music from the party danced in the breeze.

He swallowed the knot in his throat. Seeing how easy Curtis made it now gave him a measure of confidence. Paradoxically, he was eager to face the men who had destroyed his life, and his family's lives.

Zippy lifted the vase to half block his face.

In moments he'd marched down the grassy swell that led to the stables. He could smell the dusty sweetness of horses and heard them rustling inside. He'd followed the line of the barn and was just making the turn toward the tent when a big man in a dark-blue suit loomed out of the dusk, blocking his path. A coiling snake of an earpiece slithered down his hairline and into the collar of his coat. "Hey, what are you doing back here?"

Zippy froze, then tried to keep going, lifting the vase up to block his face. "What does it look like I'm doing?" he said, tension making his voice squeak. "I had to make more centerpieces. We didn't have enough. The lady told me to get more ferns."

"What lady?"

"The one having the party." Zippy wracked his brain to remember the name of T Block's sister-in-law, Dr. Rodney Jenkins's wife. Panic threatened to derail him. They'd planned for this scenario, but now his memories and all the planning had dissipated. And Zippy hadn't even gotten to the party yet. *Ludicrous.*

Then the name came, floating into his brain on a pink-shelled bubble. "Vondra. Mrs. Jenkins. She told me where to go. See?" He thrust the vase into the big man's face. "This gig don't pay enough, and they're turning me into a gardener. I bet there's poison ivy back there."

"You're not supposed to be back there in the first place," the guard said. "Didn't they tell you this?"

"Bro," Zippy told him, remembering the script, "I'm just following orders. You go tell Ms. Jenkins if you want to." He wondered where his bravado came from, but it was all part of the giddy lightness he'd been feeling for days. He wasn't playing a part because he'd lost his own identity—he *was*, for this moment, who he was playing. "I don't know where she is. Maybe she went back to the house."

He hadn't stopped moving, was around the corner and nearer the tent now, the security guard at his heels. Incongruously, having the man behind him gave Zippy confidence. As if they were a team, infiltrating this place together. He kept waiting for the guard's big paw to land on his shoulder, to spin him around, but then he ducked into the tent and used the angle to check behind him. The security guard was gone.

The opening reception was well under way. The chaos of arriving guests competed with the controlled mayhem of drinks being poured and hors d'oeuvres being passed around. As he set the vase down on one end of a long table of canapés, rearranging the other flower vases around them, Zippy looked for people he recognized—his old crew, or T Block, or Dr. Rodney's kids—but didn't immediately see anyone.

Many children, clutching their parents' hands and looking terrified, shy, or bored, stood gazing up at the adults talking to them. All the men were in tuxedos, black or white, some with bright vests—pink, yellow, emerald green—that shone in the half-light. All of the women glittered: with sequins and diamonds, with gold and rubies. The men's shoes gleamed, and the women's heels were alarmingly high. Zippy had forgotten how intimidating such wealth could be.

Caterers in white uniforms holding trays wove their way between the guests. Zippy, relieved, realized that Larissa had done her job perfectly: his uniform matched all the others.

Then the crowd parted, and Zippy caught sight of T Block, tuxedoed and bigger than Zippy remembered, as if he'd gotten bloated on all of the misery and despair that he'd created. Zippy immediately turned away and rearranged the flower-shaped butter pats, moving them all a half inch to the left.

From somewhere in front, music began to play.

The crowd shifted, and there was Curtis, standing in the middle of the tent, mouth half open, staring up at the stage, which now, too, was visible. On it sat a little girl next to an enormous instrument. Of course, a cello.

46

CURTIS

IT WAS MORE than he'd remembered: had it always been like this, the light so golden, the people's faces so smooth and so shining? And then the music began, *Invitation to the Dance*, of course.

Carl Maria von Weber had written it for his wife—they'd only been married a couple of months. The melody sounded simple even if it was extremely complex to play. A boy asks a girl to dance in the moderato opening; they whirl around the room, allegro vivace, and eventually he bows, leaves her.

Curtis could have played it in his sleep. And he probably had.

This was the world he had lost—he'd had a glimpse of it when he played with the Phoenix Symphony, but this was so much *more*. Now he was so keyed up, so terrified, and yet so comfortable— he'd been to this event for a dozen years, almost. The tables were always in the same place, the perfumes of baking meats and flowers and, well, *wealth* all tumbled together in his senses in an intoxication he could not even begin to extract himself from.

The cellist was a twelve- or thirteen-year-old girl, hair teased into a French roll, makeup disconcertingly thick on her face. Maggie Lawson, from Alexandria, Virginia, one of the runners-up. Curtis had memorized all of the performers, just in case it became helpful.

The melody modulated, and the cellist misjudged the gap between the D and A strings, playing in fourth position when she should have extended to fifth. The result was a semitone flattening of her B natural to a B flat. Curtis winced.

So did Maggie. She readjusted, reinstating the B with a smooth

slide of her finger down the cello's neck as if the note was a delib-
erate grace note intended to flow into the ongoing rhythmic
pattern. If he hadn't known better, he would have thought her
recovery was smooth enough to pass as an artistic embellishment.
But Curtis knew what had happened.

He itched to play it now, under this glowing tent. Play it as it
should be played.

Suddenly someone was at his elbow, grabbing his arm. He
looked down. Zippy, in a catering uniform, sweat standing out
on his forehead. "Hey," he whispered, "what are you doing over
here?"

Curtis came back to himself. "I was just—"

"You were just trying to get us killed, is all. Did you hear from
Larissa?"

"I—"

"You didn't check, did you? Christ. Go up to the front and
check your phone. I'm gonna move crap around like I know what
I'm doing, and I'll meet you outside in a minute."

Caterers like Zippy shouldn't be on their phones, but guests
had no such issue. Larissa was supposed to get a free moment and
text them, tell them where she was. Nonchalantly, wineglass in
hand, Curtis slipped out of the tent while Zippy busied himself
with a side table piled with hors d'oeuvres and crudités.

A bellow of laughter, laughter that Curtis recognized. His hand
clenched the wineglass stem, and he forced himself to turn away.

In a moment he was outside, on the stone path leading to the
pool, the gardens, and the main house. He checked his phone.

Larissa: In kitchn. Txt when ur clos. Ill come outside

He pretended to admire the view: the sun was just setting over
the Bull Run Mountains, hazy and gray in the distance; and the
light played over the gardens. The air was awash with music and
laughter. Virginia was possibly the most beautiful place in the
world, he thought. He wondered again if this would be the last
evening he'd ever see.

In his periphery, Zippy slipped out carrying a tray. Curtis

caught his eye, nodded, and moved off toward the house, following the exterior of the tent past a few older ladies sitting around the lily pond. He tilted his glass in greeting, and smiled. "Hello," one of the women called. "Can you get me a white wine, young man?" Curtis wasn't sure if she was talking to him or not—he was dressed in a tux, after all, not a caterer's uniform—but in any case behind him Zippy said, "Yes ma'am, of course, did you have a preference?"

"A chardonnay, if you have it."

"Be right back."

By then Curtis was a few more feet ahead. They were nearing the back door now, near the kitchen. He pulled out his phone and texted: We're outside.

47

———————

LARISSA

THE PAST FEW HOURS had been ridiculously, stupidly stressful. Even though she'd predicted it, she still couldn't believe that Sharifa had agreed to take the money, called Ms. Tedesco, and told her that she had COVID but that her cousin Debbie was coming in to fill in. She couldn't believe that Ms. Tedesco didn't ask for documentation—another thing that Larissa had been terrified of, since she had no driver's license or ID.

But, again, as she'd suspected, the caterer was frantically cooking, packing, and organizing twenty-five people to drive from D.C. out to the hinterlands; she was just grateful that Sharifa had found a replacement.

Larissa had hitched a ride with a college kid named Jason, who served and was learning bar. She made him talk about himself so he didn't ask a lot of questions about her—it was easy. Kids in their early twenties were always self-absorbed. As she knew from Curtis.

The drive out to Middleburg and actual setup weren't as rough as she'd expected. Ms. Tedesco didn't trust her to serve, so for the past three hours she'd been in the kitchen unpacking and prepping trays and food. Which was perfect: nobody noticed the catering bag she'd smuggled in with all their supplies.

When Curtis's text finally pinged on her phone, she grabbed the duffle in one hand and a tray with canapés—smoked Oriental duck—in the other and headed outside. There was so much chaos that nobody noticed.

Curtis, handsome in his tuxedo, stood texting near a back patio that led up into the house. She didn't immediately see Zippy, but then caught sight of him by the lily pond, serving white wine to a couple of blue-haired elderly ladies.

She sidled up to Curtis. He seemed even bigger and more imposing in the tux, with his shining bald head. "Oriental duck, sir?"

He grinned at her. "We prefer the term 'Asian duck.'"

She laughed.

He lifted a piece, brought it to his mouth, chewed. "Dang, this is good. You should make some when we get home."

"Is everything going all right?"

"Like clockwork. So far," he said.

"Now let's get your dad." She caught Zippy's eye, jerked her head toward the patio and French doors.

Moments later he hurried up. "Hey, babe, you okay?"

"Right as rain," she said. "You?"

He nodded. She wanted to reach out, caress his shoulder, but this wasn't the time. It made her nervous to be standing here in a catering uniform talking to a guest. They needed to get out of sight. "We can go through here, right?" she asked Curtis, gesturing toward the flagstone patio. It was flanked by urns with flowers—alternating blue and violet petunias—pouring out of them. Beyond were French doors. She remembered from studying the drawings Curtis had made that this led to the living room.

"Yeah," he said, striding up the steps. "We should be able to go through here." He pushed open a door, and immediately another security guard, wearing a dark-blue suit with a gold badge on the breast pocket, loomed. "This area's off limits. Caterers use the kitchen door."

Larissa shouldered in past Curtis. "Yeah, we know," she said. "Ms. Tedesco sent us over to take your food order. And offer you Oriental duck. You want one?"

She proffered the tray, terrified he'd look down and notice the catering bag in her other hand. The guard was focused on the tray of food, though. He popped a piece into his mouth and said, chewing, "She what?"

Larissa said, trying to sound bored, "We have Provençal roasted cornish hens, beef short rib, Chilean sea bass, or if you're a vegetarian we have ratatouille mille-feuille or a vegan butternut squash risotto."

They waited. "Uh—" the big guy said, swallowing the Oriental duck, "I didn't know I could eat."

"Yeah, of course," Zippy said from behind her, indignant. "Ms. Tedesco's good at feeding everybody. It's in the contract."

"Oh," the guy said. "The beef, I guess."

"How do you want it cooked?" Larissa asked, reciting, "It's a slow-cooked sous-vide boneless beef short rib, complemented by a ruby port reduction and paired with truffled Yukon gold potato puree and a bouquet of seasonal roasted vegetables." She held her breath.

"Uh—medium, I guess. Hold the vegetables."

"Got it," Larissa said. "Here. Take another one. Take two." Again she held out the tray, which the guard had been staring at.

He took three.

Curtis took the opportunity to slide past, saying, "Anthony said there was a restroom through here."

While the guard was chewing, they strode off into the room. She wondered when he would stop them or ask what was in the bag. She wasn't sure now which way to go. So she prayed that she remembered and marched across the living room and through the doorway on the right. She felt Zippy and Curtis on her heels but didn't dare look back.

The guard said nothing more. He had several pieces of Oriental duck to get through, after all.

Out of sight, Curtis took over the lead, hesitated an instant, and went through another door on the right, which led to an enormous dining room wallpapered in green, with a shining walnut table that could easily seat twenty and a fireplace big enough to burn a tire in. She could now hear kitchen sounds, faint.

This was always the trickiest part of the plan: to get inside and upstairs. In Curtis's time, there hadn't even been security guards; and only the family and guests—if there were any—wandered the upper levels.

"Okay, here goes," Curtis said. They locked eyes for a moment. Larissa knew what was next: the servants' hidden staircase.

Curtis ducked through a door and disappeared. Zippy and Larissa followed. A swinging door, closed now, led to the kitchen. They were in a narrow butler's pantry. Glass shelves normally stocked with crystal and serving platters rose to the ceiling; now the shelves were all empty, everything in use.

On one side, a crevice in the molding betrayed a narrow door set into the wainscoting. One of the two servants' staircases. Curtis had already pulled it open and had vaulted up several steps.

Zippy and Larissa followed, pulled the door shut.

They stood a moment, stunned that they'd made it this far. The sound of the music had fallen away, to be replaced by the buzz of conversation, the clink of silverware, the rattle of plates.

Larissa handed Zippy the bag. He rooted around inside and pulled out three sets of surgical gloves, which they put on. Larissa—the closest to the door—checked to make sure that no one was outside and then wiped both sides of the doorknob.

She closed the door behind her, and Curtis led the way up. The party sounds grew muffled.

They all took off their shoes, carried them in one hand.

The stairway ended in another door. Curtis poked his head out carefully, gestured for them to follow. They were in a back hallway. "The bedrooms are that way," Curtis muttered, pointing with his chin.

Softly he padded down the hall, hugging the wall, peeked around the corner. No one was there. Zippy and Larissa followed. "You sure you know where you are?" Zippy said.

Curtis nodded, not speaking. A few steps further he opened another door that led onto another set of stairs, again ascending. Curtis led the way, with Larissa next. Zippy went in and closed the door carefully behind him.

At the top of this staircase, they went down another hallway, with small rooms opening to each side. Most of the doors were closed. "This used to be the servants' quarters," Curtis whispered. He opened a door, and Larissa caught a glimpse of audiovisual equipment; then he opened the next one and again another staircase presented itself.

These stairs led up to the top floor of the house—once the attic, but now refitted into a home theater. Eight leather La-Z-Boy chairs waited expectantly in front of a darkened screen. They'd been worried that people would be up here—they'd worried about everything, but Curtis had assured them that the family rarely used this top floor. "They have the downstairs living room with the big TV," he'd said. "Everybody always hangs out down there. This place is too out of the way."

Larissa sure hoped he was right. Curtis had thought of this spot because it was so far removed from the rest of the house—and because of the intervening floor between this attic and the bedrooms, no one would hear them moving around.

As long as nobody came upstairs.

So many ifs. The plan's only chance of success lay in its harebrained audacity, Larissa thought yet again. "How many people died just so they can have all this stuff?" she asked, caressing the butter-soft leather. She wished she weren't wearing gloves and could feel it.

"Even one is too many," Curtis said.

Larissa offered them the rest of the Oriental duck. Curtis and Zippy soon polished it off, although Larissa was too nervous to eat.

Curtis again dug into the bag, pulling out a thin plastic painter's drop cloth. He and Zippy spread it out in a corner of the room not easily apparent from the stairs and began laying out the materials they'd brought with them, organizing as they went so it would be as easy as possible to grab what they needed. They took off their jackets and folded them in one corner.

Now Curtis pulled out a Ziploc bag and a rocks glass that Larissa had palmed earlier from the kitchen.

He handed it to her, and she polished the glass free of fingerprints. She opened the baggie and poured a powder into it, then poured in the whiskey and Coca-Cola that they'd brought with them in other small bottles. The powder dissolved instantly.

They waited. They walked around as infrequently as possible. Just in case anyone was below them.

They listened for footsteps and voices on the stairs.

Occasionally Curtis would tiptoe down and lean out a window to assess the progress of the event.

The preliminary concert went off without a hitch, he reported.

They were serving the salad.

That was Larissa's cue. She picked up the rocks glass with the Coke and the roofie dissolved in it.

"Please don't drink that," Zippy said.

"Thanks, I love you too," she told him. Then she stood up, smoothed her hair, and braced her shoulders. "Here goes," she told them. She kissed Zippy and headed back downstairs, Curtis in the lead to open doors.

She'd once spent an entire afternoon practicing carrying the glass. They were doing their best to not leave fingerprints, especially on things like a drugged glass of whiskey. Wearing gloves would call attention, though. They finally settled on the slightly complicated method of carrying the glass in a napkin and, just before serving it, cradling it in a beverage napkin.

When she and Curtis reached the final, lowest door on the other side of the butler's pantry, they paused a moment. He reached out and hugged her, one step down from where she stood, so their faces were almost aligned. She leaned over and tapped her forehead against his as he squeezed her tight for a moment, both of them careful of the drink in her hand.

"You got this," he said.

"You better believe it," she told him. And with that, she was out into the house again, turning back toward the kitchen.

Tammy, the sous-chef, caught sight of her immediately. "Hey, where have you been?"

"I got caught," Larissa said apologetically. "Somebody wanted a special drink, and they told me to get it. I've been running all over the place to try and find it."

"Who told you? What drink? You're supposed to be helping me, remember?"

"I know, I was trying—"

"Well, never mind," Tammy said. "Come back here and help me unpack these pastry shells."

"I'm not done yet," Larissa told her. "I have to get him the drink."

"There's the open bar. That's not good enough?"

Larissa shrugged. "I guess it's some kind of special shipment. Pappy Van Winkle."

"Pappy? You serious? That stuff's ridiculous expensive."

"I guess. I don't know. I just poured it."

"And he's drinking it with Coke? That's like putting ketchup on a filet mignon."

Larissa shrugged again. "All I know is that he said he wanted a Pappy's from the bar in the downstairs living room."

Tammy considered this. "Okay, well go run it out to him. But get back in here. I really need you prepping these pastry shells." She ran one hand through her frazzled red hair.

"I'll be right back," Larissa said. She followed Jason and one of the guys whose name she didn't remember out back to the tent. The musicians were playing, and all the tables were now occupied. Many guests tried to look interested, but others focused on the phones in their laps, half hidden under the tablecloths.

Larissa hugged the back wall, keeping her head down although she didn't worry that she'd be recognized. Not here and not like this.

For much of Curtis's childhood, Larissa had been to so many of these kinds of events that she could have gotten a job as an event planner.

When she arrived, three of the kids were playing, so she stood off to the side and waited. When the applause came, a few guests got up to use the restroom or head out of the tent for a smoke. Meanwhile the waitstaff surged in, filling glasses and carrying away plates. She headed along the edge of the tent toward the dais.

T Block sat on one side. She hadn't been near him in years but just in case stayed well out of his line of vision as she approached. She surreptitiously slid off the napkin, holding the glass only by the corners of the beverage nap. Her hands were slippery with nervous sweat.

A nearly untouched glass of whiskey and Coke sat by his hand. Without a pause she leaned over, replacing it with hers.

T Block said, "Hey, where you going with that?"

"Your brother told us to break out the Pappy Van Winkle for you. That's all I know," she said, going for a southern accent. Maybe she really could be an actress.

She didn't wait for a reply.

Much now would depend on how much T Block drank, and how quickly.

They had tested this too on Curtis, since he was the closest in weight to T Block. The roofie had taken about fifteen minutes to kick in. But that would depend on whether T Block was greedy and wanted to guzzle the good stuff, or if he'd had enough already.

Now he took a sip, not paying attention, and then looked down. Terror hit Larissa hard.

And then he took another sip, and then another.

She was glad they'd sprung for the expensive stuff.

She wanted to sit and wait for it to work, but Jason was yelling at her to get back to the kitchen, so casting one final glance back into the tent, she hurried out.

48

ZIPPY

THEY'D SUCCEEDED thus far, despite the ludicrous odds. But Zippy knew—was utterly convinced—that they were on the verge of disaster. He didn't know how, but the terror—closer to absolute panic—pulsed in his blood. He'd sold drugs on the street; he'd fought men in prison; but this was worse. This time, Larissa and Curtis were with him. In danger.

After Larissa and Curtis had descended the stairs, he tried to focus on the moment, to not think about them. He rearranged the supplies from the bag: taser, check. Zip ties. Check. Expandable tripod. Check. The Glock 26, so tiny and lethal. Check. And on it went. He pulled out three more lightweight drop cloths—they'd brought five—and draped them on three of the lounge chairs. At least they could wait more comfortably.

Curtis came back.

"It go okay?" Zippy asked him.

Curtis nodded. He stalked over to one of the plastic-covered lounge chairs, sat with a whoosh.

Fifteen minutes passed.

Another fifteen.

They should be well into the awards ceremony by now. Curtis couldn't remember how long that part of the evening lasted. Fifteen minutes? Half an hour? Was it all over and they'd be trapped upstairs, unable to leave?

Their nervousness only increased as Zippy went over, one by one, all the things that could—would—go wrong. The roofies hadn't worked. T Block hadn't drunk enough. Rodney had figured it out in time and taken him to a medical clinic. T Block had switched to champagne earlier that evening. The options were endless.

This was another weak point in this incredibly ridiculous plan. What if T Block didn't drink it? Zippy had remembered how T Block would down whatever liquid was shoved into his hand, but that was years ago.

"Hey," Zippy said. "You remember the first time you came here?"

"Yeah, of course. We've talked about it."

"Did I ever tell you how proud I am of you?"

"Yeah, Dad. Like every other day."

"No," Zippy said, "I mean I'm proud not because of the cello or the music. I'm proud of the man you've become. You're a better man than I could ever have hoped to be, and that's all I ever wanted for you."

"Thanks, Dad," Curtis said. "I love you too."

They thumbtouched.

Got your back.

All the time.

After another ten minutes, a commotion erupted downstairs: footsteps and voices, muffled. They could only hear because Curtis had left the doors open a crack.

Zippy closed his eyes, prayed, and waited.

Silence.

"I'm going down," Curtis said.

Zippy knew that they'd just thumbtouched minutes ago but tapped Curtis on his forehead before Curtis disappeared down the stairs again.

He loved that kid. He only hoped Curtis knew how much.

49

CURTIS

DOWN the stairs he crept.

All his life, Curtis realized, he'd been preparing for this moment.

He'd learned to perform. He'd learned to focus on details. He'd strengthened his body and toughened his spirit. He wasn't a wilting musical nerd, hiding in corners, shrinking from bullies. He'd become ruthless.

He'd become resourceful. Over the past couple of months, as they'd driven the back roads of Virginia, he'd accumulated items that might come in handy. Zip ties, duct tape, box cutters, a collapsible baton. He even bought a Kevlar vest from a military surplus shop, sewed it to his costume's upper torso. He didn't truly believe that he would need to be bulletproof, but every superhero worth their salt was always prepared. Batman wore a utility belt with gadgets for every eventuality, from rebreathers to tranquilizers. Spider-Man could use the smallest items—a paper clip, a rubber band, a piece of string—to come out on top. Dark Maestro, Curtis vowed, would be no different.

Here, downstairs, the music was louder. He strained to make out the melody, but it was too distant. He remembered all too well what it was like when he'd won. He'd been eleven the first time, and then had come every year until he'd gone off to Juilliard—at first dazzled and then a little bored by the interviews, the drinking, the dancing, the food. All the rich people patting themselves on the back and telling each other how charitable they were, talking about what a great thing they did for the underrepresented youth of the world. The usual pledges to do more for their communities followed by several glasses of wine and champagne and convenient oblivion.

Because despite all the wine and champagne and promises, the underprivileged communities remained unchanged.

This house seemed bigger than he remembered, as if it had shrunk in his imagination. Was there a wing added? He needed to focus. Voices rumbled from downstairs, but up here all was quiet. Dr. Rodney's kids were grown now. He prayed they hadn't come back for this event. They'd hated it when they were kids.

He sucked in a breath. *Here goes.*

Down the hall he slipped, past the bedroom where he'd slept as a child, turned a corner to the hall that led to the main bedrooms. A man was sitting on a chair outside one of the doors. Curtis ducked back with a gasp. They hadn't expected a security guard protecting T Block.

Now what?

LARISSA

LARISSA WAS KNEE DEEP in several dozen chocolate tartlets with white-chocolate mint ganache when Curtis's text vibrated on her phone. She looked around: Tammy, Jenna, and Marcy were piping the ganache in elegant musical-note patterns and garnishing each tartlet with another milk-chocolate musical note that they'd piped out ahead of time onto sheets of parchment paper. The two notes, black and white, intertwined prettily.

Experienced pastry chefs, Tammy and her crew got to do all the fun stuff. Larissa, meanwhile, sprinkled edible silver glitter on each of the tartlets—"not too much, it has to look elegant, not like a fucking disco ball"—and attached a mint leaf on one side. She had three hundred of these to do but was more than halfway done.

Curtis: Take a bathroom break

"Hey," Larissa called out, "I'm more than halfway done. Really cranking on these. But I need to take a pit stop. Be right back!"
She headed to the little half bath off the kitchen.

Larissa: OK, what?

Curtis: T Block has a guard in front of his room

Larissa: F#$*

Curtis: We have more roofies. Dissolve them in something

Larissa: We got to get him to drink? And drink enough?
He's on duty

Curtis: Got a better idea?

Larissa: Hold on.

She opened her phone's browser, searched.

Larissa: OK. I got it. Get the roofies. Meet me by butler
pantry ASAP

Sticking her phone back in her pocket, she flushed the toilet and washed her hands, mapping out her route. The trick was to not hesitate.

Seconds later she was out into the main kitchen again, heading back to the tartlets but angling farther toward the end of the table, where a few tartlets with broken pastry shells or badly piped ganache sat on separate plates. She snatched one and sailed on through the room, confidence in every step, and within five strides she was out of the kitchen and down the hall, turning into the butler's pantry. Nobody was there. She opened the hidden door. Her fingerprints on the doorknob.

No Curtis.

She couldn't wait for him, couldn't lurk in the stairwell. So she set the plate on a stairs and retreated back to the kitchen.

Larissa: Dessert on step. Cream filling. Roofies dissolve in
it. You gotta make it look nice. Feed to guard. He'll eat it all
lol

51

ZIPPY

THEY HADN'T THOUGHT of bringing spatulas and spoons to remove cream topping. These were the kinds of things that Zippy'd feared—the kinds of things they couldn't prepare for.

"Calm down, Dad," Curtis told him. "You'll tell him it's one of the ugly ones, but it still tastes good."

They hadn't thought about Curtis needing a catering uniform—he had the tux, so they figured he could go anywhere. So Zippy would have to venture down to the second floor and hand the guard the little chocolate pie. Curtis had lifted the cream with one hand as Zippy'd mixed the roofie powder in with the chocolate cream below it; and then Curtis stuck the cream back on top. Any resemblance to musical notes was long gone, but it still looked pretty tasty.

Now Zippy would have to go down there and hand it to the guy. "No problem," he told Curtis, even though he didn't mean it. "It's not Oriental duck, but I can handle this."

Zippy worried what could go wrong.

Curtis had changed into his Dark Maestro costume: the Kevlar, the Lycra T-shirt, the black leggings. On went the duster coat, the hat, the domino mask. He was still rocking his shiny tuxedo shoes, though. Zippy wished he could put on a disguise, but he needed to look the part of a caterer.

"I'll be right behind you, man," Curtis told him. Just in case, Curtis brought along one of the baggies, with a diaper soaked in chloroform.

He headed downstairs, Curtis in the lead. There was no point in wearing gloves; they'd have to buff the doorknobs. That seemed easier and safer, anyway. Down one flight, and then another. Curtis pushed the door open, glanced down the hall, then gestured for Zippy to slip past him.

Plate in front of him, Zippy feigned nonchalance as he sauntered down the hallway. He didn't know if he'd ever been up on this level, lined with gold-framed portraits of scrawny-looking racehorses and bowls of fruit. The corridor turned left, and the bedrooms were beyond that.

"I'm right behind you," Curtis whispered softly in his ear.

He would have thumbtouched, but his hands were full. So instead Zippy just raised his eyebrows, nodded, and forced himself to march forward.

The left wall had several doors, all closed; to the right was a railing, open to the space below, with an enormous crystal and brass chandelier illuminating it. Zippy remembered the railing overlooked the entrance foyer, and instinctively hugged the left wall more closely.

And there was the guard: Black, in a dark-blue uniform with a gold badge on the jacket pocket. He'd been playing on his phone, but stopped and straightened as Zippy approached.

"Hey man," Zippy said easily, trying to pretend this was all cool, "they sent me up to give you one of the desserts." Even as Zippy spoke, the other man was starting to look familiar. Shorter hair now, nicer threads, who could it—

Recognition crashed into him, and he stumbled, caught himself before the pie went flying.

Vernell. One of JFunk's homies, back in the day. He and Zippy had been part of the pack who ran the streets together. He'd lost his hungry, drugged-out look and seemed sharper, more deadly.

But Vernell didn't recognize him. At least not yet.

By now Zippy was almost to him, averting his face and holding out the pie.

Vernell took it. Zippy turned away, relief cascading, warm around his chest.

"What, no fork?" Vernell said.

Zippy froze. They'd forgotten the fork.

He almost welcomed the panic now—this was the kind of thing that they hadn't planned for, that they couldn't plan for. What was that old saying, *for the want of a nail, the shoe was lost* . . . and somehow that led to the loss of the kingdom. Well, here it comes.

"Oh, right," Zippy said, turning back the way he'd come, "let me get it for you. Sorry, man." He was partway down the corridor now, moving out of sight. He could get a fork, get back, and give it to Vernell. He didn't recognize him.

"It's okay, man," Vernell said. "I can just use my hands."

"I'll get you one," Zippy said. He glanced back as little as possible. Vernell had the pastry to his lips, watching Zippy retreat.

"Don't I know you?" came Vernell's voice behind him.

"I don't think so," Zippy said, not turning. "Unless you're from South Carolina? I just moved—"

"Zippy? Fuck, that's you," Vernell said.

The name echoed ominously down the corridor, bouncing off the Oriental carpeting and paneled walls.

But before the word was out, Curtis was bounding past him. In three strides he was on Vernell, who had taken an instant to put the pastry down, his mouth full, as he groped for his gun and unholstered it. But before he could raise it fully, Curtis was upon him, his solid mass of muscle tackling him, one hand extended, the chloroform-soaked diaper smashed against the man's face.

Vernell was struggling to raise the gun, bracing his legs against Curtis's assault—

And then he collapsed.

"Holy shit," Zippy was whispering. "Holy shit holy shit holy—"

"We got this," Curtis said, breathing hard. Vernell lay prone at their feet, moving weakly. "Let me take him upstairs. Go check and make sure T Block's in there." In a moment he flung Vernell over his shoulder and practically ran with him down the hall again.

Zippy waited in the corridor, unmoving, wondering if the struggle and clatter of the plate against the floor had summoned help.

But no one came.

He waited a few more moments, then opened the door a crack. Someone was lying on the bed. He slipped inside.

T Block.

Alone.

Still in his tuxedo.

Passed out.

T Block slurred something incomprehensible, eyes glittering beneath his lashes. Zippy wanted to punch him right there, smash his nose and face as long and as hard as he could. But that wouldn't help anything, he knew. He had to stick to the plan.

He wasn't big enough to carry T Block, so he'd have to wait for Curtis. He lingered near the door, not wanting to get closer, not wanting his presence to wake the big man up. He checked his phone. No messages from Larissa.

Perhaps ten minutes later, Curtis was back, shouldering his way into the room.

"There he is," Zippy said, gesturing. "You want me to help carry him?"

Curtis shook his head. "I got it. But you gotta wipe the fingerprints in here, since you took off your gloves. Did you touch anything?"

"Just the doorknob."

"Okay." He slung T Block over his shoulder with a grunt. "Christ, sure wish he'd lost a few pounds. You do the doorknobs, and I'll meet you upstairs, okay?"

Zippy used his caterer's jacket to wipe the doorknobs, went back into the corridor. There to one side lay the china plate, shattered. A smear of chocolate and cream dotted part of the wall, a painting, and the carpet. Curtis hadn't noticed it and Zippy'd forgotten, in the moment. He swore, yanked off the jacket, and piled the pieces of the plate inside, then did his best to clean up all the smears. Dark stains remained.

Would someone notice?

52

CURTIS

THE PLAN was working—it was actually, astoundingly, working. Okay, so there was the snafu with the guard, and the broken plate, and the smear of the chocolate pie on the carpet, but it was all still happening. They hadn't been caught—yet. So, granted, the chances weren't good that they'd get through this, but they'd come this far. Even that felt like an audacious triumph.

Now that they were back in the attic theater, Curtis had left Vernell passed out on the floor. Before he'd gone down to get T Block, he'd zip-tied his arms together but now did a more thorough job of it. And did his legs. Then he hauled Vernell up and put him in one of the leather chairs, against the far wall.

"What we gonna do with him?" Zippy said. "He recognized me."

"Maybe we can bribe him," Curtis said.

"Bribe him? What are you talking about?"

"I don't know. We can figure it out."

Meanwhile, in one of the other chairs closer to the stairs, T Block was out cold, a bead of drool trickling down his chin. Curtis and Zippy zip-tied his hands and feet too. His head was bent at what seemed an uncomfortable angle against his shoulder. He snored.

"No way we're listening to that for the next couple hours," Curtis said as he ripped off a good chunk of duct tape, pressing it carefully over T Block's lips, leaving the nose uncovered.

"Did you get his phone?" Zippy said.

"I didn't see it," Curtis said. "Was it next to him? On the night-stand?" They stared wide-eyed at each other.

Zippy leaned over, patted T Block's chest. Pulled out his phone.

"Okay," Zippy said. "Let me text her." Meaning Larissa.

> **Zippy**: All going good. U OK? Need to know if T Blocks wife Tracie is there. Or daughters?

A few minutes later Larissa texted back. Havent seen them but haven't been out much. Looked for them earlier tho

> **Zippy**: You ok?

> Larissa: 👍 Dessert now

"Cool," Curtis said. "So we're safe so far."

Awkwardly—it was hard to get the right angle with T Block's wrists zip-tied—Zippy pressed T Block's thumb to the screen, and the phone lit up. He maneuvered to the text message app.

They'd thought long about this part of the plan. Much depended on who was there with T Block. They hadn't seen his wife, Tracie, but that didn't mean anything. She could be there and just seated at a different table.

Vernell's presence changed things, but not as much as they'd first thought. They'd decided to send texts to Tracie and Rodney. Hey feel like shit and got Vernell to give me a ride back.

No response from either Tracie or Rodney.

Other texts pinged in. They searched for something incriminatory, found nothing. *Squeaky clean*, Teddi Slager had said. She hadn't lied.

"You should get into your costume," Curtis told Zippy.

Standing on the plastic drop cloth, Zippy changed into an all-black tight-fitting T-shirt and black cargo pants and strung the domino mask on his forehead.

They waited, talking quietly, checking periodically on their captives.

A little over an hour later, Vernell started to wake up. The chloroform was wearing off. Groggily he moaned, opened his eyes, stared blankly for a few minutes.

"Should we drug him again?" Curtis said. They'd both slid their domino masks into position.

"Yeah," Zippy said. "We better."

When he heard Zippy's voice, Vernell's head rotated as if on casters, eyes focused on Zippy. "That's a dumb-ass disguise, looking like a ghetto Batman," he said huskily. "You think I don't know who you are? You're dead, that's who you are. You're dead, Zippy." He tried to get up, realized he was tied down. "Make it easy on yourself and lemme go. Lemme go."

"Why, so you can run to T Block like a little bitch? Well, I saved you a trip." He gestured with his head toward T Block, sitting two chairs over from Vernell. Zippy took a few steps, hovered over T Block, imitated the big man. "Hey, Vernell, guess you got your dumb ass caught."

"Shit—" Vernell started, voice rising.

By then Curtis was there with the chloroform, one hand covering Vernell's nose and mouth. Vernell strained against the zip ties, face purpling, and then he lost consciousness again.

An hour passed. Vernell woke up again, but Curtis put him out almost immediately. They worried about killing him with too much chloroform, so Curtis used as little as possible.

And then T Block started twisting and rolling in the chair. He was waking up too.

Immediately Curtis was there with the chloroform.

T Block subsided back into unconsciousness.

They waited. Another hour.

Although periodically cars crunched on the gravel driveway as some of the guests departed, the exodus did not start in earnest until after one in the morning, when, finally, car after car drove off down the lane.

Then Larissa texted. Cleaning up.

The room was dark, with only a faint blue glow from under the chairs and near the screen. They sat in the theater seats, not talking, each with their own thoughts, T Block and Vernell still sagging in their chairs. Periodically Curtis or Zippy would lean over to check on them, give them a little chloroform if they seemed to be waking up.

Larissa: Finished. Coming.

Moments later her feet tapped on the stairs. She flew into Zippy's arms, and then hugged Curtis. He breathed in the smell of her hair—which didn't smell at all like her, the yellow locks still pungent with chemicals. For a few minutes they talked, caught up. They told her about Vernell; she told them how the evening had gone. How she'd told Jason that she'd be grabbing a ride in Ms. Tedesco's van; and told Ms. Tedesco that she'd be riding with Jason. She'd helped load up the vans and then crept away.

The house lay silent.

They waited.

"You two stay here," Curtis said. Again he tiptoed down the stairs, pausing on the third level. It was possible that houseguests would be staying, in bedrooms either on this level or the level below. When Curtis had stayed there, the kids often had friends in for sleepovers.

But the third floor lay dark and silent, empty.

He crept down another level, cracked open the door. From down the hall floated voices. He couldn't make out how many.

Back he went, upstairs. "It's showtime," he said.

He was eager, desperate, to become Dark Maestro. To assume a disguise. To step into someone else's life—even if that life never really existed. He understood then, as adrenaline and terror thrummed within him, why these mild-mannered reporters wore capes and Lycra: because, wearing these things, they were no longer themselves.

Curtis needed to be someone else.

Again Curtis slipped down the stairs, Zippy now behind him. Zippy handed him one of the Ziploc bags they'd prepared. Curtis squeezed it tightly, the damp fabric beneath the plastic squishing nicely. Before they'd drugged Candace Watkins, Curtis had spent a couple hours researching which type of cloth was best to use for situations like this. The consensus was a cloth diaper. These had now been soaking for days.

They crept lightly down the hallway. Zippy mimicked Curtis's every move. Curtis looked back periodically to make sure Zippy was close. *Batman and Robin, my ass! Dark Maestro and Halfnote the Wonder Dad,* Curtis thought. If the situation wasn't so dire, it would have been fun.

He led Zippy down the corridor, wondering if one of the other bedroom doors would pop open and some guest would stand there and scream. No one did.

Over to the big master suite. For a moment they stood outside the door, listening. From inside came the faint sound of movement. He opened the door a crack. He caught sight of someone moving around and then going into a farther room, turning on a light. Moments later the sound of a shower. Curtis and Zippy exchanged glances and slipped inside. The room was otherwise empty. They moved toward the bathroom, took up positions on either side of the doorway, and opened the Ziploc bags. The heady sweet scent of chloroform instantly filled Curtis's nose. His head swam, and he leaned away from the fumes.

The shower shut off. A rustle of fabric as Dr. Rodney must have pulled out a towel to dry himself.

Zippy eyed the door, motioned with his eyes that they should go in, tackle Rodney there. Curtis shook his head. They didn't know how big the bathroom was, or whether they could be seen in a vanity mirror. They would wait.

The next moments seemed endless. Curtis studied the space. A big king-sized bed took up most of one wall. On the other wall, near them, the huge TV must have been seventy-two inches or more. A long line of champagne-colored floor-length drapes framed windows looking out into the night. A thick furred rug—could it be wolf skin?—lay in front of an ornately carved fireplace. Across the room were two more doors—one half closed and the other fully open. Curtis figured those must lead to walk-in closets.

Finally they could hear the sound of someone coming closer. A moment later the half-closed bathroom door opened, nearly blocking Zippy behind it.

Curtis had milliseconds to react. He flattened himself against the wall and, as the person stepped through, he launched himself, hand outstretched, holding the chloroform-soaked cloth.

It was Vondra. Dr. Rodney's wife.

He froze.

She spun around, looking at him, a scream rising in her throat, her hands coming up to bat him away, but before she could fully yell he was on her, the chloroform-soaked rag covering her nose and mouth.

She fought him, pushing against his biceps and chest, but only for a moment. Within seconds she went limp.

"Sonofabitch," Zippy was whispering next to Curtis as he set her on the floor. "Sonofabitch. What are we going to do?"

"He's got to be here," Curtis whispered. He pulled Vondra to one side, against the wall. Her arm was bent uncomfortably beneath her, her mouth half open.

From one of the other doors that Curtis had noticed earlier—the half-closed one—a man was saying, "Honey, is everything—" and Dr. Rodney, naked, came through, toweling what remained of his hair. His gut flopped obscenely.

He stopped when he saw them. "What the—" he started, but before he could say anything further Curtis had leaped across the room, closing the distance. Dr. Rodney struggled to free himself from the towel around his arms and shoulders, and that gave Curtis enough time to clamp the chloroform-soaked diaper over the older man's nose and mouth.

He collapsed immediately, even more quickly than his wife.

For a moment nobody moved. Curtis looked incredulously back and forth, between the two prone figures. Their nakedness seemed somehow monstrous.

"What now, Maestro?" Zippy said.

"Guess we're gotta take them both upstairs," Curtis said, realizing only as he said it that it was true.

"We have enough zip ties?"

Curtis shrugged. "What do you think?" He pulled a slender pouch from the back of his belt, from underneath his duster, and yanked out more zip ties. He bound both Dr. Rodney and Vondra, hands in front of them, and their feet together. "You keep watch and I'll haul their asses upstairs," he told Zippy.

Zippy led the way, peering out of the doorway into a deserted corridor. Curtis was at his heels. He was so pumped with adrenaline that he could barely register Rodney's—and then Vondra's—weight across his shoulder.

Ten minutes later, all three—T Block, Dr. Rodney, and Vondra—were in the theater seats. On one end, farthest from the others, they tucked in Vondra. Larissa had covered her, for decency, with a couple of cashmere blankets that had been neatly folded on a shelf.

For a moment they all sat and examined their captives. In front of Dr. Rodney and T Block, Larissa had set up a tripod with her iPhone on it.

Curtis's heart rate was returning to normal. He wished he wasn't enjoying this so much. He should have been a superhero years ago.

Despite everything, despite all the crazy, impossible odds, they'd made it this far.

And now came the fun part.

53

LARISSA

"READY TO WAKE THEM UP?" Larissa said.

Zippy nodded.

Larissa had already gotten a syringe of hydrocyanic acid ready. She'd had enough exposure to drug addicts and medical personnel in her life to know how to administer an IV, so quickly she swabbed Dr. Rodney's arm, found the vein, plunged in the needle. Then she stood back and waited.

The effect was instantaneous. Within moments Dr. Rodney's eyes fluttered. He coughed and looked around him. "What the—?"

Curtis, in full Dark Maestro regalia, stood over him, legs spread and hands at his hips.

Larissa had to hand it to Curtis—she couldn't imagine what Dr. Rodney must be thinking, coming to and having an enormous muscled man in a domino mask looming over him. The Kevlar he'd added to his torso made him look even more intimidating. "Your reign of evil is officially over, Doctor. Your operation is done!"

She knew that he'd been waiting a long time to say that.

"What the hell is going on?" Rodney shook his head, then seemed better able to focus. "Whoever you are, you're dead. You hear me? Dead!"

"Keep talking like that and I'll be putting duct tape over your mouth too," Curtis said, nodding at T Block and Vernell, who were both still out cold on Dr. Rodney's left. Dr. Rodney glanced over and then focused on Curtis. Now he didn't speak.

Curtis continued, his voice a low growl, "We have a few questions for you, Doctor. Answer the questions or we'll light your ass up with this."

Zippy palmed the stun gun, showed it helpfully to the naked man in the chair.

"Try to call for help, and we'll juice it up for you," Curtis continued. "You're the doctor, right? You're still wet. I don't know how much more powerful this stun gun will be."

Dr. Rodney said nothing. He was staring beyond Curtis, at Zippy, also in the domino mask.

Larissa could almost see the gears clicking in Dr. Rodney's brain.

Just then, T Block stirred beside Dr. Rodney. They paused to watch, but he slipped back to unconsciousness.

"If you cooperate," Curtis said louder, "this will be over soon. Are we agreed?"

Rodney eyed the tripod that sat directly in front of him. Larissa peered through the camera. Zoomed in on Rodney's face.

"Who else is in the house?" Curtis asked.

"Look," Dr. Rodney said, "whoever you are, you just made the biggest mistake of your life, but I'm feeling generous. Get your low-budget Batman wannabe ass out of my house, and I won't have you killed." Despite the zip ties, despite being naked in front of three masked strangers, despite everything, he spoke with the confidence of a man who believed he was invincible.

"Who else is in the house," Curtis repeated.

Rodney didn't respond.

"Just answer the question," Zippy put in.

"Who are you," Rodney asked, looking at Zippy and then answering his own question. "Zippy Wilson. I recognize that whiny voice. I should thank you, you know that? Now I don't have to go looking for you anymore." He studied Curtis and Larissa with new eyes. "Jesus, Curtis, you really took that weight lifting seriously."

"Wrong answer," Zippy said, turning on the gun and approaching him with it. The stun gun let out a gentle hum. "Who else is in the house?"

"Okay, okay," Rodney said. He took a breath. "Just me and Vondra."

"That Vondra?" Larissa said, looking meaningfully over at the unconscious woman under the blanket.

Rodney blanched as he saw his wife, then turned to stare up at Larissa. Some of the fight had gone out of him. She felt like he wanted to say something, but he kept silent.

"Anyone else in the house?" Larissa prompted him.

"No. That's it."

"Any staff?" Curtis asked.

Rodney shook his head.

"What about security?"

"There's only the guys in the guardhouse," Rodney said. He kept staring at Zippy as if memorizing every curve of Zippy's face.

"What about T Block's people?"

"T Block has his guys like he always does."

"This guy is full of it. Just shoot him and be done with it," Larissa said. They'd decided ahead of time that she would be Bad Cop.

"There's nobody else in the house," Rodney said quickly.

"See?" Curtis said to Larissa. "He's cooperating." Then to Rodney: "Okay, Doctor. You ready?"

"Ready for what?"

Larissa leaned over the tripod. She made sure to be out of the camera's sights. So did Zippy and Curtis. Then she pressed Record.

"You will now confess on camera to all of the illegal activities you've been involved in," Curtis said, reading from the script they'd crafted for weeks. "Including organ harvesting, kidnapping, and murder."

Silence. Then Dr. Rodney let out a belly laugh. "What are you on? I don't know what you're talking about."

"Well, let's see if this jogs your memory," Curtis said, still out of the camera's eye. Larissa stood behind the tripod, watching, as he leaned over and pulled out a sheaf of papers from a manuscript box identical to the one that they'd sent to Teddi Slager. The first sheet was a blowup of the Lifestream Blood Services sign; below it, a photograph of Candace Watkins.

"Do you know her?"

"You can't use any of this stuff," Rodney spat at them. "None of this is admissible."

"Admissible?" Curtis asked.

"In a court of law," Rodney said. "This is the stupidest shit I've ever seen in my life. A confession from a kidnapping could never be used in court. You're wasting your time. Jesus, what idiots."

"Who's going to use it in court?" Curtis asked. "We're going to broadcast this all over the Internet. We're going to fucking destroy your life. The only question is whether or not we're going to kill you."

Dr. Rodney said nothing. Zippy kept flicking the stun gun, the clicks loud against the silence.

Curtis held out the page again. "Tell us what you know about Lifestream."

Suddenly, in the chair by the wall, Vondra stirred and moaned.

"She's waking up," Larissa said.

"You want to put duct tape over her mouth? We don't need her screaming," Zippy said.

Larissa went over to her, tearing off a piece of tape, and placed it gingerly on the woman's half-open mouth. "Sorry girl," she told her. "Just sit tight and hopefully this will all be done soon."

The woman squeaked and struggled. Larissa readjusted the blanket around her shoulders.

She returned to the tripod, when, as if on cue, T Block groaned and tried to stretch out his arms, which were bound in front of him. Seconds later he opened his eyes, looked dazedly around him. Gradually comprehension dawned, and then fury as he mumbled and yelled behind the duct tape.

"Guess you've woken up, sleeping beauty," Curtis told him.

The man rolled his eyes, said something incomprehensible.

"We're trying to get to the bottom of this operation you two have cooked up," Curtis said.

T Block looked at Rodney, who looked back at him.

Curtis repeated what he'd told Rodney about getting it all on tape. About a choice that was all up to them: he could cooperate or they would kill him. "This can all go faster if you want to talk," Curtis said. "Or we can just finish with your brother and move on to you. It's totally your call."

"We can be here for days," Larissa said. "I even brought sandwiches."

T Block looked up at Curtis, nodded. He appeared to be calm enough to have the tape removed from his mouth.

Larissa ripped it off, and T Block howled. "Who the hell are you? I'm gonna—"

"You know who these losers are," Rodney said, far too conversationally, as if chatting with his brother over tea and scones. "It's them."

T Block had been struggling, straining at the zip ties, his face puffy with effort, eyes still blinking woozily from the roofies. Now he stopped, stared at Zippy, and the others in turn. "Well I'll be damned," he said. "You ended up coming to me, Zip."

"This guy is a bigger loser than you ever let on," Rodney said. "I can't believe you put your trust in *this*." He jerked his head at Zippy contemptuously. And then to Larissa, "Why the fuck a smart woman like you would stay with such a limp dick I'll never know."

Zippy kept flicking the stun gun.

Curtis asked Larissa, "You ready? Let's get started."

"I knew you'd never amount to anything," Rodney told him contemptuously. "You're just a common criminal. A pathetic loser, just like your dad. You should've stuck with music, kid. Such a waste of a life."

Everything happened so quickly then.

Zippy lunged for Rodney, arm extended, stun gun on.

As he drew close, Rodney swiped up with his zip-tied arms to avoid the blow. A moment later the stun gun landed on Rodney's shoulder, and a sharp crackle rang out. Rodney grunted and fell back in the chair, gasping.

"That's just the first taste of what you're going to get," Zippy said. "Special delivery from the loser. Now start answering our questions, both of you." He looked down at his arm. "That bastard cut me with something."

He showed them his forearm, where an inch-long gash dripped blood.

"Don't let it hit the floor," Curtis said, talking about the blood.

Larissa was fumbling in the duffle bag. She'd packed gauze and bandages, just in case.

"How did he do that? His fingernails?" Curtis said. "He doesn't have anything on him."

Larissa was hunting through the bag but looked up when Curtis said, "Jesus Christ, what is that?"

He was holding Dr. Rodney's hand out. Rodney, still stunned, eyes half closed, moaned and twisted in the chair.

On his ring finger, something glittered.

Larissa wanted to pause and examine it more closely, but was more worried about Zippy's blood hitting the carpeted floor, about leaving evidence that could lead back to them. She scrambled in the bag.

"Stupid," Rodney hissed groggily. "You think that's just a cut?"

"What is that," Curtis asked.

Larissa was there now, gauze in hand, wrapping Zippy's arm. The cut wasn't deep.

Curtis, meanwhile, had lifted Rodney's arm into the light. On the ring finger gleamed a blood-red stone set in a gold band.

Larissa had noticed it earlier, even briefly wondered why he would be wearing a ring if he just got out of the shower, but didn't think much of it. Now she could see that the stone had somehow folded back to reveal a tiny half-inch blade sticking straight out. It glittered sinisterly.

"This is an eighteenth-century dagger ring," Rodney said as if he were a docent in a museum. "They're rare, and I had to have the spring mechanism rebuilt. But it works like a charm." He grinned at Curtis. "Here's a lesson for you, you loser. Always be prepared." And then he repeated himself, as if making sure Curtis remembered. "Always be prepared."

"Well, you might want to do some more preparation next time," Zippy said. "Because that tiny blade gave me just a little scratch."

"You really are stupid," Rodney said. Next to him, T Block bellowed a laugh.

"That blade was poisoned," Rodney said.

"Poison?" Larissa said. Her tongue felt thick in her mouth.

"He's officially dead in twenty minutes."

"Bullshit," Curtis said.

"He's bluffing," Zippy said, taking a step backward. "It's just a cut. There ain't no poison on that bubble-gum-machine ring."

"You'll find out soon enough when you're lying on the floor dead." He screamed as Curtis flattened his hand and carefully yanked the ring from his fingers, keeping his own fingers clear of the blade.

"What kind of poison?" Larissa said.

"He's dead unless I give him the antidote," Rodney said. "And that ain't happening until you let me and everybody else go."

"Dad? You feel okay?" Curtis asked.

Zippy nodded. "I'm fine. Where were we? Let's get started."

"It should be kicking in in another few minutes," Rodney said, gleeful. "And since you're little as fuck, it might hit you a lot sooner."

"What kind of poison?" Larissa asked again.

He looked at her. "I'm a doctor. Its chemical name wouldn't mean anything to you. Suffice it to say that I've tested it several times, and it works great. And I made sure I have an antidote on hand just in case I somehow managed to cut myself by accident sometime. As far as I can see, that's his best hope for survival."

Curtis gave a vicious twist to Dr. Rodney's arm as he let the man fall back into the theater seat. Rodney screamed, but Larissa barely noticed. She'd removed the gauze from Zippy's arm and was examining it intently. It seemed like any other wound—bleeding easily, with no red lines of infection or anything unusual.

"We can't take a chance that he's telling the truth," she said.

"What kind of poison? Where's the antidote?" Curtis said.

"Let me go, and I'll show you where it is." Rodney said.

"Screw him. Let's get back to work," Zippy said. "If he really poisoned me, I'd be dead by now. Turn the camera back on and let's finish this."

"You're a dead man walking," Rodney said.

"Yeah, and your new nickname is lefty," Zippy said. "Let's get this thing wrapped up and get on with it."

T Block had laughed, had said a few things that Larissa hadn't registered. Now she heard him say, "I can't believe you're finally using that fucking ring. Good job, bro."

"Yeah, I told you always be prepared," Rodney told him as if they were alone. "You should have worn the one I gave you."

T Block shrugged. "I like my own bling. But fuck yeah."

"Shut up," Curtis said. "Now let's get back to it."

54

ZIPPY

AT FIRST Zippy thought he was just being susceptible to Rodney's suggestion. That the blurred vision and the slight tingling in his fingertips was all in his own head. But what started out as a slight tingle soon strengthened, became a roar.

He was standing next to Larissa, on the other side of the camera, but then his legs didn't seem capable of holding him up. He collapsed, his head nearly knocking into the duffle bag.

The stun gun seemed too heavy to carry, so he laid it down.

The room spun. Nausea engulfed him. He gagged but did not vomit.

Larissa screamed. He barely heard her.

Once, when Zippy had been a child, he'd gotten a fever. Patrice had left him alone. He didn't remember where she'd gone. But he lay on the couch in the living room watching TV, and suddenly the cartoons grew distant and small. The room telescoped out. Fifteen feet became fifty or five hundred.

Far, far away, the Road Runner was chased by a coyote through red desert sands. Despite its minuscule size, everything on that screen glowed with a terrible clarity: The yellow of the Road Runner's beak. The verdant, spiking arm of a cactus. Then particles of dust, as the Road Runner's windmilling feet spun him far from the coyote's waiting grasp.

This now was how Zippy felt: everything distant, so far away, and yet so clear, and the Road Runner's spinning feet, just out of his sight.

Dr. Rodney Jenkins, leering naked at him from the chair—

Larissa, her mouth open and hands outstretched, lunging toward him—

Curtis and that idiotic shine of his costume—

T Block, still in his tuxedo shirt, stretched out as if lounging comfortably, reclining, watching with interest. How had Zippy, so long ago, so misguidedly, once thought of him almost as a father?

Vondra Jenkins, eyes wild, duct tape covering her mouth, stared, panicked, at him. He could tell beyond all knowing that she had no idea what was going on. Had no idea what her husband had been into. Much as Curtis had not known, or Larissa, what Zippy himself had done. *Collateral damage*, Zippy whispered, looking at her.

"What did you say, baby? What? Save your strength." Larissa was above him, screaming about an antidote.

But he knew it was too late for that.

Rodney hadn't lied. And now whatever it was had sunk its claws into his system and was never letting go.

The pain in his guts was beyond anything he had ever conceived of.

With extraordinary effort he turned his head, and he looked again at Curtis. Tried to speak. *I'm sorry*, he wanted to say. *I love you. Got your back.* But words were beyond him, chasing the Road Runner as he disappeared over the horizon.

He wanted to close his eyes. He wanted to let go. But this awful clarity would not leave him. It was a math problem, a spreadsheet, a set of numbers. Until now, the formulas had been blurred, the totals unbalanced.

But now everything shifted. A denominator had transformed into a numerator. A fraction rounded up into wholeness.

Now he understood. Now, at last, as a nausea too deep for vomiting shook his system, he figured it out.

He'd known, as soon as Vernell recognized him, that he was going to have to kill Vernell. But he thought he could delay it, figure it out later, push off the inevitable.

He'd thought, somehow, that the others could live.

Now he realized what he'd known, deep down, all along.

Going into this terrible evening, he'd known that if T Block and Rodney were left alive, then Zippy, Curtis, and Larissa would wind up dead. The formula was neat, clean, and absolutely clear.

Despite all their careful planning. Despite their hope that law enforcement would have to take them seriously once they saw this video of Rodney's and T Block's confessions. Despite the plans for Dark Maestro to broadcast Dr. Rodney's and T Block's terribleness across the globe.

Now he knew better. Somewhere, somehow, he had always known better. The answer had gleamed in front of him all the time. But he'd been too weak to draw the line. To add up the sums.

Here was the problem: *As long as Rodney and T Block were alive, there would be no end. They would have no freedom. Curtis would have no life. Zippy and Larissa would always be running, always hiding.* As long as—

But Zippy knew the solution. He always had known it.

It was up to him. He would have Curtis's back, and Larissa's. Always.

Finally—finally—Zippy could make a difference. He couldn't erase all that had come before, but he could make it possible for the people he loved to go on.

He didn't even have to think about making a decision: it was as if the decision were already made for him, already mapped out and plotted on the graph paper in his brain.

Now he watched with almost idle interest as his own hand reached out. Groped in the bag, through zip ties and plastic bags and sheathed knives.

His hands closed around the Glock.

It was heavier than anything he'd ever lifted.

Heavier than a newborn Curtis, the first time Zippy had picked him up. Zippy had been only seventeen. Even now he could see the ragged hem of the light-blue baby blanket that swaddled his son. Even now he could see a stray thread brushing that tiny pink cheek.

But this heaviness had a different weight to it. Had a color and a sound. Around him, faces blurred into rainbow shades.

And now he was standing, Glock in one hand, holding himself

against the wall with the other. The surface was cool and pulsing against his left palm.

And now he was staggering over to the theater seats, to where Rodney sat, and Rodney's grin disappeared and his eyes got big and he tried to say something.

Zippy was beyond words now. He had to hold himself up by leaning heavily against Rodney's shoulder. Rodney twisted away. So Zippy fumbled over to the headrest on the back of the chair and put the gun against the back of Rodney's head, forcing his head down—

As he pulled the trigger.

The gun's intense recoil flung Zippy back. He almost dropped the Glock but somehow kept hold of it. He used the momentum to totter over to T Block.

They were screaming, all of them, he was sure of it. But he was somewhere past all hearing now too. The world was compressing into grayness, the pinwheeling Road Runner's legs squeezing into a pinprick.

As he staggered to T Block, whose mouth was open, no longer self-satisfied, Zippy wanted to say something, but he did not know what—*I'm sorry*, perhaps, or *How could you have done this to me, you motherfucker*—

And Zippy shot him too, in the forehead.

Vernell was still unconscious. Curtis had drugged him again a little while before. Zippy found that he was grateful that he didn't have to look the man in the eyes as he shot him.

And then on to Vondra, in the farthest chair, her eyelids stretched inhumanly wide, her head shaking back and forth in terrible denial and realization. She must have been shrieking beneath the duct tape. But he could hear nothing.

For her, though, he summoned the strength to whisper. *I'm sorry*, he said. *Collateral damage*, he said. *Luck of the draw.* And he pulled the trigger.

Then, only then, did he let his legs buckle.

He looked for Curtis, and Larissa, and found them both, did not have time to read their expressions or try to sort out what they were saying—if they were saying anything.

With a last burst of strength, he raised one arm, felt the thumb on the end of his arm reach up through space and touch, so lightly, his forehead. He prayed he was smiling, but he'd lost all sensation in his face.

Then he reached out for Curtis's thumb.

And Curtis's thumb touched his. That, he could feel.

And then, at last, the bright pink pinprick of light that had buoyed him up faded into the loneliest gray he had ever seen.

Epilogue

THE FIRST CONCERT

THE BOX OFFICE opened at noon, Eastern time, and within an astonishing fifteen minutes, tickets were completely sold out. The rush to secure a spot in the audience became a virtual battleground, with fans on their phones or at their computers hitting the Refresh button as if conducting cyberwarfare. The sheer demand led to a virtual stampede, leaving older music lovers scrambling to navigate the complexities of online ticketing systems, determined to experience the unique harmonies of the Dark Maestro live onstage. Ticket scalpers were charging astronomical prices—some as high as $10,000. Merch sales—action figures, posters, mugs, CDs—set records, selling out before the concert even began.

When the day dawned, the fans descended on Wolf Trap Center outside Washington, D.C. Young, old; hip-hop fans; classical music lovers; comic book lovers: the fans were legion, diverse, energized. Many wore Dark Maestro costumes; others dressed up as X-Men, Avengers, Titans, Justice League. Fans arrived twenty-four hours early toting camping gear, desperately hoping for a spot in the mosh pit. From sleeping bags or folding chairs they shared stories, swapped playlist recommendations, formed bonds over the Dark Maestro's innovative sound. There were even rumblings of Heroes vs. Villains cosplayers planning a dance battle royale. Critics descended in droves, talking about the fusion of classical elegance and hip-hop beats that promised an unparalleled and visceral musical experience.

As the huge metal doors swung open, the crowd surged forward, eager to claim their spots. Within moments, the rhythmic pulse of the music began to reverberate through the stadium, and the mosh pit transformed into a sea of ecstatic concertgoers, each vying for the best view of the stage.

And then the chant began. "Maestro! Maestro!," rhythmic and endless.

Backstage, stage left, he stared out past the orchestra, into the night. The stage bristled with bows and instruments, but if he stood on tiptoe he could just glimpse the cello, shining silver on the stage. It was a state-of-the-art NS Design, specially commissioned from Ned Steinberger, to provide an even more exceptional cutting-edge design and even more advanced electronic features, like built-in humbuckers and alternate tuning pegs for the more modern music. It looked like something right out of a *Star Wars* movie.

Marsh and Lyon were warming up the crowd, playing old-school hip-hop favorites and trying a new version of the Bach Concerto in D Minor for Two Violins. They took on Method Man's hit, yelling, "M-A-E-S-T-R" and the crowd would yell, "O!"

Around him, the backstage area was chaos, feeding on the audience's energy. The two other warm-up acts were huddled together, sometimes calling over a lighting tech or a stagehand. What felt like dozens of people all rushed past, whispering into headsets and flipping through pages on clipboards. Some dragged cables for the light show that was about to dazzle the sold-out audience. No one wanted to make a mistake.

But no one spoke to him. He'd told them all beforehand that he wanted to be left alone. To focus. To prep for the performance. Others could handle the logistics.

Then she appeared out of nowhere. "We have a problem," she told him. "Gustavo Dudamel can't make it."

"What? What do you mean?" Gustavo Dudamel had been slated to conduct for months—he'd flown to D.C. two days ago to practice with the orchestra but had a last-minute engagement in L.A. that he hadn't been able to cancel. "It's just two days. I'll be a little jet-lagged, but I'll be fine," Dudamel had told him. "Back before you know it." Known for his dynamic interpretations and energetic performances, he'd been the natural choice to lead the orchestra.

"That weather system in California is stopping everything. Security is already extra tight. You know that. All your celeb pals." She tried for lightness, but he wasn't buying it. "He was trying to rent a car to get to Phoenix, but that still wouldn't have given him enough time to make it here."

He swore. "What are we going to do?"

"I've been calling around. There's a Philharmonia conductor from that church on New York Avenue. He can be here in twenty minutes," she said.

"But he hasn't practiced with the orchestra."

She shrugged. "You have any better ideas?"

He looked out again into the crowd, into the banks of chairs where the orchestra would soon be sitting. "It's okay. I can lead. It's just a performance. It doesn't really matter who leads it. People want to experience *Dark Maestro*. The conductor might be more of a distraction."

But of course it mattered. The *New York Times*, *Rolling Stone*, dozens of other press outlets, and hundreds of influencers were all out there, phones ready, ready to pounce on any flagging note or tonal inconsistency. The show would be live streamed everywhere. Everything depended on tonight's performance—kicking off the first of fifty tours worldwide. A lot of people were depending on him. Millions of dollars stood in the balance.

And yet it really didn't matter.

Seeing your father die traumatically ranked as one of the most difficult experiences in life. Some part of him never left that attic room, with those plush, blue-gray leather theater seats and the screen silvering down one wall. And the bodies, five of them, gaspingly silent.

He thought later, when Zippy had fallen, that perhaps Larissa had screamed. But perhaps it had been him. Or perhaps it had just been a scream in his head.

In comic books, the superhero waits for the authorities to show up. Right after the heavy fighting is done, the regular people appear to clean up the mess. In some comic book universes, a superpowered cleanup crew, Damage Control, specialized in making crime scenes disappear. But Superman rarely hung around and vacuumed the carpet; he was too busy jetting off to save the next citizen in need.

But the Dark Maestro wasn't Superman.

Instead, the Dark Maestro and Larissa immediately got to work. They hadn't planned on five bodies boiling there in the attic theater, but five bodies there were, and five bodies they were going to have to make disappear. They were stunned and bereft and exhausted. The stench—probably imagined—of the cooling bodies rose around them.

The next hours were the darkest and most horrible in their lives.

They wrapped each body in a plastic drop cloth.

Curtis carried them, one by one, through the house. If there were security guards, they were at the end of the driveway. The Virginia night lay silent and peaceful around them.

They worried about sounding an alarm, but there didn't seem to be one—or perhaps Rodney had never set it that night.

Forever after, the stench of honeysuckle and wild rose would flash him back to that night, stumbling along the bridle trails in the dark, terrified someone would see the flashlights of their phones, plodding in several wrong directions before Larissa's map app set them back on course.

Curtis, thank goodness, had marked the car's location on his phone; otherwise he had visions of wandering there forever, lost in the dark. But eventually they found the car, exactly how they had left it, surprisingly, and they loaded the first of the bodies in the back and returned for more.

Stumbling, using their flashlights as little as possible, they made their trips back and forth to the van. One body at a time. Rodney. T Block. Vernell. Vondra.

Daylight was coming.

On the last trip, Larissa stayed behind to clean. There was much less blood than there could have been: the painters' drop cloths caught most of it, except for Vondra's and Vernell's; and the expensive leather lounge chairs had been treated with something, so they didn't absorb the blood. They scrubbed the stains as best they could. She found a vacuum in a closet downstairs, vacuumed the entire room.

It was dawn by the time the space was as clean as they could make it.

Meanwhile Zippy's body, wrapped in one of the gray cashmere blankets, sat tucked in a corner by the stairs, head flopped on his chest as if he were sleeping, or defeated, or both.

When the Dark Maestro hoisted the body of his father over one shoulder, he had never felt less like a superhero as he navigated down the stairs, out the door.

He staggered under Zippy's weight even though he'd lifted Rodney and T Block, much heavier men, with less effort. But Zippy's weight bit into his bones, carved a place for itself in his sinews and tendons.

But they had made it. They drove and drove and drove away.

And they disposed of the bodies, far out in a remote park, in a remote lake, weighted down by cinderblocks. Curtis would never forget the splashes.

They drove all the next day, out of Virginia and through Tennessee and over to Missouri. The enormity crashed around them.

Got your back.

All the time.

They never returned to South Carolina. Another identity peeled away.

By now they'd become so adept at shedding their lives that they shook free of those final names, Carson and Lynette, that the Marshals Service had bestowed upon them. Again they chose new names, and again vowed to get on with the business of trying to make a new life. And perhaps if they reached out to one of the U.S. marshals and slipped them a few thousand dollars for a black-market contact to create yet another Social Security number, no harm was done, right?

About six months after Zippy's death they reached out a final time to Teddi Slager, encrypting their email so it couldn't be traced. They both had kept wondering why the FBI hadn't progressed further in nabbing T Block and Rodney Jenkins, so they decided to just ask.

Teddi's reply came back moments later. "Good to hear from you and I won't ask where you are or if you're okay. We actually recently discovered some discrepancies with a GS-15 Intelligence Analyst supervisor. We have evidence that she leaked confidential information and orchestrated the disappearance of some of the evidence. Heads have been rolling, let me tell you."

"Well, that explains it," he said. He thought it would add some closure, but in the end it didn't matter. In many ways, there never would be closure. The number of bodies he'd hauled through the woods made certain of that.

But always, always, there was *Dark Maestro*. They threw away the lyrics and panels of the Bloodworx episodes they'd envisioned, since they no longer needed to out Dr. Rodney and T Block.

Instead, in Issue no. 40, Dark Maestro collaborated with local heroes he'd inspired. He became an icon for the poor and silenced. The Bloodworx was vanquished, but other evil remained. Often the Dark Maestro nearly died, with staggering defeats, but he survived, mentoring burgeoning heroes and creating an army of musical fans who followed in his footsteps, paying attention to those who needed help.

He wasn't a rapper, and Zippy was gone, but they found people who could style the rhymes. The Dark Maestro went on outreach and talent searches. Rappers besieged them, desperate for the opportunity to express themselves. Desperate for the fame and a quick buck under the Dark Maestro's banner.

They were up to five million followers, then ten. Fans from Europe, South America, and Asia outnumbered domestic fans.

Meanwhile the Dark Maestro remained anonymous, which only added to the mystique. A musical Banksy.

The press and the Internet speculated over the phenomenon's identity, and the opportunities grew.

They sold film rights and merchandising rights, always controlling the product, so he could be sure that the materials weren't bastardized or diluted. They surrounded themselves with lawyers, accountants, and agents to buffer them from the public, from being identified.

Then the movie adaptation came out.

Suddenly everyone knew Dark Maestro.

And everyone clamored to hear him perform.

So, at last, six years after his father's death, he relented. This was the first concert in a year's worth of touring.

As he looked out now into the crowd, he sensed her, nervous, next to him. The stench of honeysuckle and wild rose blew in on the breeze.

The orchestra had tuned up. Violin bows lay in laps, fingers taut, ready to pluck the strings. The cello and bass lines growled the menacing diminished chord.

The show was beginning.

The crowd roared, lighters and cell phones flashing.

For an instant he tried to imagine the audience: music lovers, comic book fans, of all ages and races.

One of them was a Ms. Daniela Reyes, originally from Guatemala, who'd received an anonymous VIP ticket several weeks ago—the prize for winning a sweepstakes that she'd never entered. He'd checked with the box office; the ticket had been activated, so she was here.

In the meantime, all this time, that single spotlight had remained, gleaming, on the cello. Less a cello and more an instrument of justice. Sharp angles replaced the soft curves of the cello's ribs. The dark, warm tones of brown and orange were now replaced by shining, reflective silver.

"You okay?" the woman next to him asked. Barely a whisper.

"Yeah," he said, "I'm okay."

"You sure?"

"Yeah," he repeated as he took a step, and then another. Now, from his angle, all he could see was that cello. His gaze would be forever fixed on it, glowing. "Yeah," he repeated. "I got this."

Author's Note

As I was developing *The Dark Maestro*, real life came up and whacked me hard over the head.

It felt—feels—like the world has descended into multiple wars that continually threaten to explode beyond their borders. On the streets of America, good-hearted people with different perspectives are unable to even have a civil conversation—taunting and marching and fighting and even killing people who are different from them.

And amid all of this, for me, personally: my nephrologist informed me that I would need a kidney transplant in order to live.

So, as I've been writing this novel, as I've been reading the news and staring mystified at the vicious catfights on social media, I've been juggling doctor appointments, donor-matching issues, and the pure gut-wrenching terror that the procedure won't go well.

Yeah, you can use your imagination to go through the list of what "not go well" might mean. It's something that I've been doing on a minute-by-minute basis, sometimes. Sometimes—on the good days—it's every few hours.

The first few days after I got the news, I couldn't wrap my head around it. For a while I did my best to ignore it, distract myself with something—anything—else. (Writing a novel definitely has its merits!) But no matter how I tried, that little voice in the back of my head kept yelling at full volume, *This can't be happening. There must be a mistake.* The doctors must have mixed up my test results. Nobody in my family has had anything like this, so I couldn't either. I eat incredibly healthily—I'm a vegan. I work out daily. I don't smoke and don't drink alcohol.

After a while, the disbelief turned to being-seriously-pissed-off: at the world, at my body, at the checkout clerk in the grocery store who couldn't figure out how to change a five dollar bill. Like Curtis in *The Dark Maestro*, I wanted to punch something. A lot of things.

My situation, writ large, is what I kept feeling that the world has been going through recently. I often feel jaw-dropping incomprehensibility that the world can even continue tumbling along. Somewhere a twenty-three-year-old computer programmer is fighting and dying in a war he doesn't believe in and doesn't want to be a part of. Somewhere else, the arm of a napping kindergartner is being blown off as she's curled up in her bed, never dreaming that she isn't safe. In another country, a religious man is gunned down as he prays in the church he's gone to for sixty-odd years.

It feels like everybody, everywhere, just wants to punch a lot of things.

But punching isn't going to help.

One unexpected gift is that I didn't realize how many people cared about me. I'm blessed to have friends and family who are throwing their kidneys at me—how incredible is that?! My best friend since we were nineteen jumped at the chance to help me out. Former students have offered. My sister as well (I turned her down because she has a nine-year-old son who'll be a teenager soon—and something tells me she's going to need all of her body parts to handle a teenager). People who I've known only for a few years have offered. The level of kindness overwhelms me daily. If I ever doubted that humanity is forever lost, these people have proved the contrary.

That doesn't make my own condition go away, though. My philosophy has always been that when you're handed lemons, you make the tallest, biggest, tastiest glass of lemonade imaginable.

The Dark Maestro has been my lemonade.

I've always loved comic books. *Spider-Man, X-Men, Justice*

League, Titans, Avengers: these titles carry so many good memories for me. Not just because of the bright colors or flashy costumes, but because of the memories they evoke.

As a kid, I used to draw superheroes daily. Then I graduated to role playing, practicing my Spider-Man poses—bouncing into a squat, ready to scale a building; or spreading my fingers to shoot my web shooters. No matter how fast I ran or how high I jumped, I never could stick to the walls, though.

Then I made it to the big leagues. I formed the Spider-Man Club. I was the president. My sister and younger brother were charter members. We'd throw homemade webs—made from old sheets—at each other. My sister, aka Spider Woman, would blast her venom; my brother would muster his agility skills to escape from my headlocks and arm holds.

Those were happy times that I get to relive every time I open up a comic book—and given how it feels like the world is betraying us, and my body is betraying me, I often need those comic books. Back when I was nine, my "collection" started with six books. Forty years later, I've amassed over twelve thousand comics. Some of them are worth less than fifty cents. Some are worth several hundred dollars. To me, they're all priceless.

Curtis dons the cape and mask of the Dark Maestro in order to cope with the world around him as it's seemingly falling apart. For me, as I wrote this novel, it seemed—for only a moment—somehow possible to restore the life of that computer programmer, to defuse the bomb before it explodes over that sleeping kindergartner, to stop the bullet before it shatters the skull of the praying man.

To magic myself into full health again.

Because part of what kept me going, what keeps the world going, are those hordes of metaphorical organ donors out there. The good people who are trying, on a daily basis, to make a difference. Whether it's on the most crime-ridden corner of a destitute city, or in a high-tech hospital. I believe—I need to believe—that enough people in the world want, deep down, to help. To sacrifice their time or some money or one of their organs to help someone else have a better life.

Because we're all dealing with adversity. We're—every one of us—those computer programmers, kindergartners, priests. We're all praying in this giant temple that's rocked by bombs and misunderstanding.

But I have to believe that as long as we have comic books, as long as there are people who genuinely care about each other, we, together, will soldier through these dark times.

As for me, the hordes of doctors and technicians, and my test results, all assure me that I'll make a full recovery. This is just yet another pothole on a crazy journey. I'll keep writing; keep playing my violin; keep traveling and meeting thoughtful, caring people who share their stories with me.

Thanks for sharing this road with me. I'm unbelievably grateful.

Acknowledgments

So many people help make a book a reality—and over the past few months, in particular, I've had to lean on many supporters.

To Dr. Patricia Centron Vinales, Assistant Professor of Medicine, Division of Renal Diseases & Hypertension at the George Washington University Medical Department: Thank you for taking such good care of me. You've given me a much-appreciated second chance at life. I'll never be able to repay your kindness and caring.

To my brother Howard: Love you, dude. Thanks for being a good big brother. To my sister Robin: you're amazing. Thanks for making me laugh and supplying me with medical information.

To Michael Haley: Thank you, my friend, for your willingness to share your invaluable insight and knowledge. I genuinely appreciate your support and encouragement.

To Jordan (aka "Bully" and "J.O. Blanco") Rodriguez: Thank you for the dope-ass lyrics! Thanks for pushing me in MCOC. I'm looking forward to the day when everyone knows, as I do, how insanely talented you are.

To Glenn Fry: Thank you for your support. Thank you for making me laugh. Thank you for every critique. Thank you for helping me heal. Thank you for being there. Thank you for your understanding. Love you, dude.

To Teresa Hargis: Thank you for your unending support. Thanks for being the rock for Ian. You're a wonderful, extraordinary person, and I'm honored to call you my friend.

Thanks to all the people who provided their time and insights as I researched this book. Gary Rosen and Robert Pesce at Marcum, LLP, thank you for the research into corporate espionage and forensic accounting; Peter Lapp, thanks for your willingness to talk about law enforcement procedures; Jimmy Avalos, when I need to tranquilize someone I'm coming to you for advice; Greg Keltner, thanks for your insightful ideas, your constant willingness to brainstorm and bounce ideas, and your regular good humor (and thanks for taking those extra comics off my hands); thanks Álvaro Rodas, whose extraordinary work at the Corona Youth Music Project in Queens, New York, was an inspiration for the character of Daniela Reyes; to Sophie Brett-Chin for all the help you've provided and continue to provide; and an enormous thanks to Katherine Bellando, social media guru extraordinaire.

I also want to give a massive shout-out to my publishing team at Knopf Doubleday for believing in me and giving me yet another opportunity to write another book. To Edward Kastenmeier, executive editor, you are incredible, dude—how many drafts of this novel did you have to read? And every draft you made better than the last. Thank you, thank you, thank you. To Chris Howard-Woods, assistant editor, you and Edward are a dream editorial team—thank you for believing in this and working so hard to make it a reality. To Bill Thomas, publisher of Doubleday, thank you for reaching out, making me feel at home, and helming this incredible team. To Oliver Munday, executive director, art/design, thank you for creating such a beautiful book. To Jess Deichter, director, backlist strategy, thanks for all your hard work and hoping we can do great things with my previous books. To Vimi Santokhi, senior managing editor, thank you for keeping everything moving forward. To Kathryn Ricigliano, senior production manager, thank you for all the hard work at keeping all of the balls in the air. To Nora Reichard, executive production editor, thank you for shepherding this manuscript into a book. To Nicholas Alguire, great job on the wonderful interior design. And to Julie Ertl, assistant director of publicity, an enormous thank-you for juggling a million emails and dates and schedules, and for always being so upbeat, helpful, and encouraging.

Finally—last but absolutely not least—the greatest thanks to Jeff Kleinman for being here every step of the way. None of this would have been possible without you, and I'm very aware of that. Thank you. I deeply appreciate your kindness and generosity. You've made a huge impact in my life, and I'll always be grateful.

About the Author

Brendan Nicholaus Slocumb was raised in Fayetteville, North Carolina, and holds a degree in music education (with concentrations in violin and viola) from the University of North Carolina at Greensboro. For more than twenty years he has been a public and private school music educator and has performed with orchestras throughout Northern Virginia, Maryland, Washington, D.C., and North Carolina. He lives in Washington, D.C.